D0501806

IN DEFENSE
OF
JUDGES

ALSO BY A. W. GRAY

Bino
Size

A. W. GRAY

IN DEFENSE OF JUDGES

DUTTON NEW YORK

DUTTON
Published by the Penguin Group
Penguin Books USA Inc., 375 Hudson Street,
New York, New York 10014, U.S.A.
Penguin Books Ltd, 27 Wrights Lane,
London W8 5TZ, England
Penguin Books Australia Ltd, Ringwood,
Victoria, Australia
Penguin Books Canada Ltd, 2801 John Street,
Markham, Ontario, Canada L3R 1B4
Penguin Books (N.Z.) Ltd, 182–190 Wairau Road,
Auckland 10, New Zealand

Penguin Books Ltd, Registered Offices:
Harmondsworth, Middlesex, England

First published by Dutton, an imprint of Penguin Books USA Inc.
Published simultaneously in Canada by Fitzhenry & Whiteside, Limited.

First printing, June, 1990
1 3 5 7 9 10 8 6 4 2

Copyright © Gray Matter, 1990
All rights reserved

Library of Congress Cataloging-in-Publication Data
Gray, A. W. (Albert William)
In defense of judges / A. W. Gray. — 1st ed.
p. cm.
ISBN 0-525-24875-7
I. Title.
PS3557.R2914I5 1990
813' .54—dc20   89-25646
                                 CIP

Printed in the United States of America
Set in Trump Medieval
Designed by Earl Tidwell

Publisher's Note: This novel is a work of fiction. Names, characters, places,
and incidents either are the product of the author's imagination
or are used fictitiously, and any resemblance to actual persons, living or dead,
events, or locales is entirely coincidental.

Without limiting the rights under copyright reserved above,
no part of this publication may be reproduced, stored in or introduced
into a retrieval system, or transmitted, in any form, or
by any means (electronic, mechanical, photocopying, recording,
or otherwise), without the prior written permission of both
the copyright owner and the above publisher of this book.

For Cloyd Arrington Gray
and Dorothy Marie Brown Gray
Finally takin' it easy
Playin' some golf and bakin' some pies

IN DEFENSE
OF
JUDGES

1

Marvin Goldman, clad in black, his starched white cuffs glistening, his goatee combed into a near-perfect triangle, said, "And the evidence will show that . . ." Then he took long, purposeful strides in a line parallel to the railing that separated the jury box from the courtroom.

Bino Phillips thought, That's one . . . two . . . three . . . four of 'em, Marv. Four big ones. Now turn. That's it, not too fast. Now. Point. *Point* at the dirty fucker. You read *Presumed Innocent*, right?

Goldman pivoted, his eyes narrowed, raised his right arm, and held it straight as a ramrod. His index finger extended, his nails buffed and manicured, he said, "*This man.*" And then he paused, and during the pause a pin dropped on the carpet would have sounded like the beginning of an avalanche.

Bino thought, What man? *Weedy?* Not my Weedy, not on

your life. He reached over and clasped Weedy Clements's shoulder, at the same time favoring the jurors with his best it-ain't-so look. Seated in the front row of the jury box, a Mexican guy who was wearing a pink sport coat yawned.

"Devised a scheme," Goldman went on. "A scheme, a plan, an artifice. A scheme that . . . worked well for a while. A scheme that resulted in the importation and sale, over a period of four years, of six tons of Colombian gold marijuana. That's *six tons*, ladies and gentlemen. Enough to put all the schoolchildren in Dallas on a permanent, festering high. And that . . ." Goldman's shoulders drooped, and he shrugged. "But enough. Our case will speak for itself. And after the evidence has spoken and you prepare to do your duty as jurors, there will be only one choice for you to make. To con*vict*. Justice . . . must be served. I thank you." Goldman marched to the prosecution's table, poured himself a goblet of water from a chrome pitcher, and sat down.

Judge Hazel Burke Sanderson, her iron gray hair stiff as papier-mâché, glared in the direction of the defense table. Bino wasn't sure whether the scowl was intended for Weedy Clements or for Bino himself. Probably both. Hell, this wasn't even her courtroom, the old. . . . Bino wondered for about the tenth time since he'd come to court what had happened to Emmett Burns, the judge who had been scheduled to try the case, whom Hazel Sanderson had replaced at the last minute. Knowing old Hazel, she'd probably read on the docket that Bino Phillips was the lawyer for the defense, gotten together with Goldman, and muscled Judge Burns out of the way. "Does the defense wish to make an opening statement?" Judge Sanderson said. "Mr. Phillips?"

Weedy raised his arm and beckoned. Bino bent his head and leaned closer. In a hoarse stage whisper, Weedy said, "What the fuck's a *festering high*?" Weedy was short and blocky, with long, thinning brown hair combed straight back on a head that was shaped like an anvil and was attached to his body by a thick neck that looked to be about an inch long.

He was wearing a blue suit. Bino thought that Weedy looked about as at home in a suit as Charles Bronson in a ballerina costume. Visible behind Weedy, the two U.S. marshals who had escorted him over from the county lockup lounged in chairs that were backed up to the rail.

"I don't know myself, Weed," Bino said. "*Festering* has something to do with a sore. Sometimes Goldman gets all wound up and gets stumped for words; maybe he just made it up as he went along." He smiled and nodded in the direction of the bench, although showing Hazel Sanderson a genuine-looking smile took some doing. "If the court please, Your Honor. We do have a brief statement."

Bino stood to his full six foot six and glanced out at the twenty or thirty spectators in the courtroom. Dodie was in the front row with a spiral notebook in her lap and a ballpoint pen in her hand. She was wearing a blue business dress that stopped a couple of inches above shapely knees. Her blond hair flowed softly to her shoulders. Seated beside her, Half-a-Point Harrison was thin as a skeleton and looking worried. Usually nothing worried Half except point spreads that didn't create enough action on both teams, and every other Tuesday when the grand jury met. Dodie flashed Bino an encouraging smile as Half clutched his windpipe and gagged silently.

Bino adjusted the knot on his red-and-silver-striped tie, then went around to the jury-box side of the defense table and sat on its corner. He left his charcoal gray coat unbuttoned and spread his palms out on the table behind him in his best folksy posture. At the prosecution's table, Marvin Goldman rolled his eyes. The clean-shaven FBI agent sitting next to Goldman leaned over and said something. Both men snickered.

"You-all are going to hear some bad things about my client, Mr. Clements, here," Bino said. "Some real bad things. Because it's the government's job to make Mr. Clements look bad, just like it's my job to make him look as good as possible." Twelve heads moved as one as the jurors gazed at Weedy. Bino tried to read something in their expressions. He couldn't. One girl—a General Services Administration secretary who Bino recalled from the juror list—was chewing gum, and the Mexican guy in the pink sport coat didn't look as though he could stay awake through the opening statements. If Goldman were to kick him right now, the Mexican would probably snap wide awake and holler, "Guilty!"

Bino swept a lock of snow white hair away from his forehead and sat up a little straighter on the table. His hands now resting on his knees, his expression more intense, he said, "But it really doesn't matter if what I say about Mr. Clements is true, or if what the U.S. Prosecutor Mr. Goldman over there"—here he looked at Goldman, who stared straight ahead in the direction of the bench—"says about him is true. What matters is guilty or not guilty. Now, I didn't say guilty or *innocent*, and there's a big difference. After the prosecution says what it's going to, and after I say what I'm going to, Judge Burns . . . excuse me, Judge *Sanderson*. This is Judge Burns's courtroom, but he couldn't be here today so Judge Sanderson is sitting for him. Anyway, when we're all through blowing our trumpets, the judge is going to give you an instruction about how the prosecution has to prove its case beyond a reasonable doubt. You've all heard about reasonable doubt on lawyer TV shows, I know that, and the bottom line is that I don't have to prove Mr. Clements is innocent. I'm not even going to *say* that Mr. Clements is innocent. Heck fire, look at him. His nickname is *Weedy*, for goodness' sake."

He glanced in Weedy's direction. Bino'd have to say this much for Weedy, the guy was keeping a poker face even though his toes were probably knotting. Goldman's upper lip was beginning to curl, which meant that he didn't like Bino telling about Weedy's nickname before Goldman himself could get the moniker in front of the jury. Score one for Bino. Now even the jurors were looking interested, shifting around and scooting forward in their chairs. The girl from the General Services Administration had stopped chewing her cud. The Mexican's eyes were wide and round. Score two for Bino. He raised one finger in a teaching attitude and went on.

"But the government hasn't charged Weedy Clements with smuggling a little marijuana, or even with *selling* a little marijuana. If they had you'd all be at home and Weedy would've already pled guilty and be at Bastrop or El Reno or Big Spring or one of those other nice places the government has. But no. No sirree. They've charged Weedy with *conspiracy*. They've got to prove—beyond a reasonable doubt, mind you—that Weedy got together with some other folks and plotted. That he said to one guy, Okay, you buy the marijuana, and to another guy, Okay, you bring it over the border, and so forth. But that isn't all the government has to prove, not by a long shot. If Weedy just gets together with some friends of his and plots, that isn't against the law. There's got to be an overt act, somebody he's plotting with has got to go out and do something shady to further the deal. That's what we're talking about here. Conspiracy. Ladies and gents, I don't care if Mr. Goldman shows you a full-color picture of Weedy Clements in between two bathtubs, one filled with marijuana and the other with hundred-dollar bills, if there's nobody else in the photo with him they ain't proved a thing."

Here Bino paused long enough to throw the jury a broad wink, and for an instant he thought the girl from the General Services Administration was going to wink back at him. Then he heard Judge Hazel utter a disapproving gasp. That was okay with Bino; if the judge was getting pissed off it meant that he was putting across to the jury just what he wanted to. Fired up now, Bino said, "Remember it, folks. Above everything else you're going to hear in this courtroom, remember. Conspiracy. We'll do our best to make it interesting for you-all." He got up quickly, circled the table, and went back to his seat, conscious of Dodie beaming at him from beyond the rail and feeling pretty proud of himself. Clarence Darrow, Melvin Belli, Racehorse Haynes, bring 'em on. When Bino Phillips was on a roll, he didn't take a backseat to anybody.

Judge Hazel leaned forward and clasped her hands, then bent her head to regard them for a moment. She raised her gaze slowly, her thin lips pursed, her wire-frame Martha Washington glasses perched on the slight hump in her nose. "Theatrical, Mr. Phillips." Then, to the jurors, "Ladies and gentlemen, I fear that jury selection and opening statements have wasted the morning. We'll break for lunch now. You're to return promptly at one. And remember. You're not to discuss this case with anyone, including yourselves." She banged her gavel, tossed a curt nod in Goldman's direction, and made her haughty exit by the judge's private door. She didn't so much as glance in Bino's direction.

Weedy made a fist, protruded his middle knuckle, and thumped Bino on the upper arm. Showing a craggy grin, Weedy said, "What a lawyer. Main man, huh?" The two marshals had come forward and now stood behind Weedy's chair, one on each side. They both wore tan Stetsons and brown cowboy boots, western-style suits and black string ties.

Bino rubbed his arm where Weedy had frogged him. "You don't need a main man, Weed. You need Houdini, but I doubt if *he* could get you out of this. Jesus Christ, your own *brother* is going to finger you. You want a trial, we'll give 'em one, but you ought to think over what I said about copping a plea. With the regular judge in the courtroom we might've stood a chance, but wait'll you see *this* woman in action once the testimony starts. Goldman's a lazy bastard at heart; he might still make a deal." The marshals were fidgeting, shifting their weights from side to side.

Weedy's features twisted, and Bino thought, just as he had for years, that Weedy Clements was the only guy in the world who could actually, physically, get his nose bent out of shape. "My mama didn't raise no cop-out artist," Weedy said. "Fuck 'em. Tell 'em to crank it up."

Bino expelled a long breath. Jesus, what was it with these guys? Weedy Clements was a two-time loser; you'd think he'd been dragged through enough courtrooms to know the score.

Bino guessed it was the hope that springs eternal, or whatever they called it. He said, "Whatever goes, buddy. Like you say, fuck 'em." He raised his gaze to the two marshals and said to Weedy, "Here's your keepers. I'm going to grab a burger. See you at one." He brightened. "Hey, I saw them bringing the food over. Ham and cheese. You'll probably eat better in the holding tank than I'm going to." The marshals took Weedy away, each of them taking one step to his two as he hustled along between them.

Bino looked toward the exit as he approached the railing gate. Dodie waited by the courtroom's rear door with one spike-heeled foot slightly in front of the other. Half was back there, too, reading—Jesus, was it? That was what it was, okay. Half-a-Point Harrison was standing near the exit from the federal district court reading a racing form. Bino shook his head and started to go through the gate. As he did, Marvin Goldman brushed in front of him, stood aside like a theater usher, and swung the gate open. He made a sweeping bow.

"Great opening statement, buddy," Goldman said. "I don't know what you're going to do for an encore, but your opening had them on the edges of their seats. I can't match you in bullshit, Bino. No way can I. Only in hard facts and evidence."

Bino cleared his throat, more as a stall than anything else. Applauding Bino's opening statement was something that the U.S. prosecutor would rank right along with carrying out the garbage. But Goldman had put just enough barb in his congratulations that Bino was now supposed to yodel, beat on his chest, and start laying out to Goldman what evidence the defense was holding to rebut the government's passel of witnesses. Bino wasn't falling for that one. Not old cagey. Besides, in Weedy Clements's case, Bino didn't know that he *had* any evidence.

He showed Goldman a bland smile and said merely, "Thanks, Marv." Then he went past Goldman and through the gate, turning his head to hide a grin. He'd gone a couple of steps up the aisle when he turned back to Goldman, snapped his fingers, and said earnestly, "Hey. What happened to Judge Burns? He sick or something?"

Well, Goldman had taken *his* shot, now Bino was trying one of his own. If the U.S. prosecutor came back with something wiseass and off the wall, Bino was going to know that the last-minute change in judges was in fact a federal shenanigan. Which would tell him that maybe, just maybe, the government's case against Weedy Clements wasn't all they were building it up to be. Bino cocked his head and waited for an answer.

Goldman's reaction was a surprise. His gaze averted, not looking directly at Bino, he said, "I've got nothing to do with it, buddy. Nothing at all. Judge Burns . . . well, you'll find out soon enough. I can't talk about it."

Bino knew Goldman well enough to know when the prosecutor was lying—which was pretty damn often—but this time Goldman wasn't. In fact Goldman was just a little bit shook. Bino was bursting at the seams to ask more, but he knew better. He moved on up the aisle toward Dodie. His white eyebrows were knit in puzzlement.

Bek's Hamburgers was a cafeteria-style, order-'em-and-rassle-to-grab-'em hamburger joint in the tunnel that connected One Main Place to InterFirst Tower, First Fidelity Plaza, and points beyond. Bino stood in the entryway and craned his neck in search of a table while leggy secretaries in spike heels and businessmen in Brooks Brothers or Hart Schaffner & Marx suits—all of the suits navy or gray, one solid color or the other—strolled up and down the corridor, peered in shop windows, and pretended not to notice one another. Inside the restaurant Hispanic teenagers in red and yellow uniforms, each one wearing a paper chef's hat with the Bek's logo on its crown, fried greasy burgers, cooked sizzling baskets of fries, and spooned mounds of chili onto open-faced sandwiches. One older black man, wearing a uniform identical to those of the teenagers, yelled out orders and shot frigid glances in the direction of whichever Mexican wasn't spooning chili or turning patties fast enough to suit him. Bino recognized one lawyer, who was seated at a table for two in the far corner, in a little raised area that was wide enough for a row of two-seater booths in addition to the tables. It was Frank Bleeder, a classmate from South Texas College of Law. Old Bleed 'Em and Plead 'Em was ignoring his cheeseburger and fries and talking a mile a minute to a tall redhead seated with him. Bino gave the redhead a quick once-over (not being too obvious about it, mainly because Dodie was standing at his elbow and he could feel her breath on his neck) and got an overall view of skin the color of milk, a trim figure that was likely to cause a few collisions in the hallways, and wide, blue, let's-party eyes. Bleeder, a big guy who'd grown one helluva potbelly since Bino had last seen him, whose hair was graying, and who had a good ten years on the redhead, zoomed in on Bino and gave him the thumbs-up sign. Bino lifted a hand to shoulder level and waggled his fingers.

Dodie shook Bino's elbow. "There's one over there," she said. "Right there in the center. Wow, it's been vacant ever since we've been standing here. When you get through looking up everybody's skirt, let's eat. God, I'm famished."

And there *was* an empty table. There it stood, its top made of slatted blond, polished wood, standing out like a sore thumb and looking lonely among all the other identical tables, which had two, three, and four people crowded around them. "Damn. Don't know how I missed it, Dode," Bino said. He stepped aside and extended his arm. Dodie sniffed a little sniff and led the way. Half-a-Point, who had been off to one side studying his racing form, folded the form under his arm and strolled along behind her. Bino brought up the rear, shooting another glance at the redhead and thinking that she was a little out of Frank Bleeder's class. By a couple of miles or so.

Finally seated, Bino studied the menu. It was encased in laminated plastic and featured a cartoon character, a chubby little guy wearing the Bek's uniform and chef's hat, in several poses: frying a burger, cleaning off a table, and running like hell to deliver a take-out order. There was a pad of order blanks on the table, held inside a wooden slot with a pen attached to it on a chain. Bino took one blank and wrote down a Number Four—hickory sauce, relish, and mustard—for himself, then hesitated. Finally he decided to cut the onions. He wouldn't mind breathing a little onion breath in Goldman's face, but he never knew when he'd have to get close to the jury box in order to make a point. Dodie checked out the supply of Certs breath mints by the cash register, then told Bino she'd have a chili and cheese. Bino wrote that down, then said to Half, "How 'bout you? I'm buying; suit yourself."

Half had taken a paper napkin from the holder and was wiping down the table with little circular strokes. "Onions. I love 'em. I been dreaming about 'em. But I already got enough heartburn fooling with these ponies. Saladburger. Well done. *Super* well done. Bino, you tell those cooks that if I see a spot of pink in the center I'll have the law down here raiding the joint. Bet half the help around here is wetbacks. I can smell 'em a mile away."

"Wait a minute," Bino said. "What's this *me* tell 'em stuff? What's wrong with you telling 'em yourself? How come it's always me that's waiting in line?"

"I wait sometimes," Half said. "When it's my turn."

"Hold on. When *is* it your turn? Once, I can remember once. We were in high school. You waited in line for hotdogs at the Mesquite Rodeo, only later I come to find out that the hotdog guy owed you and Pop money from betting on football. You waited in line so you could dun the guy when he gave you the hotdogs. Maybe one other time in our whole lives. I tell you, Half, I'm sick of always waiting in line."

"And you're both making *me* sick," Dodie said. Her eyes were probably bluer than those belonging to Frank Bleeder's redhead, though not quite as wide. "Please, no more back-to-Mesquite stuff. Here. *I'll* go. I need some bucks, boss. Come on, fork over." She stood and held out a tiny hand, palm up. She was making Bino feel a little guilty, but what the hell? He'd be damned if he'd stand in line. Half could starve to death before Bino'd stand in line again. He handed Dodie twenty dollars. Hips swaying, she folded the twenty along with the order blank, went over, and stood hesitantly beside the serving line. The line extended almost into the corridor outside, men in suits and women in business dresses, holding money, waving credit cards. A young guy, thirty or so, clean shaven, and with an I'm-a-banker look about him, took a plastic tray from the stack and slid it along the counter, then got a load of Dodie and did a double take. He stopped and said something to her. She showed him a grateful bat with her eyelashes, took two trays for herself, and cut in line ahead of the guy.

"She's getting one helluva lot better service than you could," Half said. "From now on she's elected. Who's the guy?"

Bino was keeping a close eye on the eager beaver who had let Dodie in line, not really blaming the guy but watching him anyway. "How'm I supposed to know?" Bino said. "He's a guy that wants to hit on Dodie."

"Not *that* guy. I'm talking about the dude with the redhead, the one you waved at. Lawyer, ain't he? I've seen him down at the courthouse. He acts like a real asshole, from what I've seen."

Bino glanced over to where Bleeder sat. The redhead was now bent forward and apparently reading old Frank the riot act, her hands balled into fists on her full, round hips. The fun look was gone from her eyes. Bino said, "It's not a good idea to go around talking about other lawyers, Half. It just doesn't look good."

"Okay, so I won't talk about him. *You* talk about him. Who's the guy?"

"Frank Bleeder."

"Jesus Christ. *That's* Bleeder? Yeah, I've heard about him.

From some guys wish they *hadn't* heard of the guy. He's a jail jockey. Hangs around down at the county and buddies up to the prisoners' wives and mothers. He gets 'em to up him a little front money, then that's the last they ever see of him."

Bino felt a strange sadness. "Too bad. Too bad there's a whole lot more like that. Yeah, that's old Frank. Wasn't always. But is now. King of the court appointments."

"King of the what?" Half said.

"Court appointments. You know, bugs this judge and that judge to death. To get rid of him the judge appoints him on indigent cases; hell, Frank has more of those than anybody in town. Bim, bam, thank-you, ma'am, the guy goes off to the pen and Frank gets a check from the county. There's some funny stories going around about how he gets all those court appointments, but don't ask me to repeat any of 'em. I'm taking enough of a chance talking about another lawyer, but I'm sure as hell not saying anything about how a *judge* takes care of his business."

"I read you," Half said. "There's things you don't *want* to know. Jesus, Bino, how's a guy like that ever get to be a lawyer in the first place? If he was a bookmaker and got a reputation like that, somebody'd tar and feather him."

Across the restaurant, Bleeder was now leaning back in his chair with his palms facing the redhead. He was defending himself about something, his jaw working nonstop. The look on the girl's face said that Bleeder wasn't doing a very good job of talking his way out of whatever it was he was trying to talk his way out of. Bino pictured a much younger Frank Bleeder, flat bellied and with hair the color of licorice, pleading, tears in his eyes, turning a jury to mush and saving a black boy from the electric chair. The black kid had done okay. He'd gone to school in prison, earned early parole, and now ran a youth center on the south side of town, saving a lot of ghetto youngsters from jail and much, much worse.

Bino cleared his throat. "With that particular guy it was a lot of work to be a lawyer. He didn't have it easy, and I'll tell you something, Half. Fifteen years ago I've seen Frank Bleeder stand toe to toe with some of the ballsiest prosecutors in the state and make 'em holler uncle. Late sixties he took on some cases I didn't think anybody could've won. But Frank did. And he wasn't just in it for the money. Back then if Bleeder didn't see something in a guy he was going to represent, he'd tell him to take a hike."

Half fished a packet of Rolaids from his inside coat pocket and popped one of the white tablets into his mouth. His pencil mustache was beginning to show some gray. "We talking about the same guy? Bleeder? What in hell happened to him?"

Bino shrugged. "Who knows? He had a nasty divorce once, but that was three marriages ago, and the others don't seem to have bothered him any. Might be liquor, but I don't remember ever seeing Frank when he was drunk. At least not any drunker than I was at the time. Maybe he just quit caring. A lot of 'em do, you know. Being a lawyer is a lot like being a cop. You see this turd and that turd, every day another turd, and not all of the turds are the guys charged with the crime. After a few years of finding out that the whole fucking justice system is a game, and that both the good guys and the bad guys are playing it . . . well, some people take the easy way out. Tell you what, I bet old Frank makes a lot more money today than he did when he was practicing law for real. If money's any way to keep score. I've heard around that he takes a lot of Vegas trips. Gambling high as a kite, from what I understand."

"Damn, maybe he likes to bet on football," Half said. "What's the guy's phone number?"

"You'd be wasting your time. Betting football's too slow for a guy like that. Bet on a team and then wait for a week, three or four days at least, to find out how you came out? No fucking way. Not when he can make the same bet on the pass line, let 'em roll, and then bet some more. A guy like Frank is looking for fast action."

Bino sensed, rather than saw, Dodie's hip on a level with

his shoulder. She was standing beside the table balancing two trays, one in each hand. "Did I hear somebody say 'fast action'? I swear if you make me stand here any longer I'm asking for a tip." One tray was stacked with wrapped sandwiches, the chili on Dodie's burger soaking the treated paper. On the other tray were three white plastic cups with interlocking lids, straws poking through holes in the lids like upright candy canes. Condensed moisture clung to the sides of the cups, a few large drops rolling down and making rivulets.

Bino hustled to his feet, balanced the tray of burgers on the box-shaped, metal napkin holder, then set one drink in front of Half, one at his own place, and one before Dodie's empty seat. "Quick trip, babe. How'd you get through the line so quick?"

She sat down and crossed her legs. "I've got ways. Cost me a phone number. Wow, I wonder whose number it was."

They ate. Dodie took itty-bitty bites, laying her sandwich down and chewing slowly between each one. Half opened his sandwich, inspected the meat like a USDA sleuth, then shrugged and ate the burger in four big gulps. Bino took his own time, drinking icy Coke through a straw after each bite. Dodie's dimpled knee was just inches from his thigh. He didn't think she was doing it on purpose, but it bothered him. The first time with Dodie had been two years earlier and had been something of a lark. The second occasion had been only weeks ago, and that time he'd needed her badly. Neither of them had talked about it since, but. . . . She caught his eye fleetingly, shifted in her chair so that her knee pointed away from him. Her cheeks flushed slightly.

Half spoke a little faster than normal. "What's the story on Weedy? You going to be in trial the rest of the year or what?"

Bino hesitated. Half had forced it, like somebody who was changing the subject even though nobody was talking about anything. Could it be that he knew about Bino and Dodie? Probably not, at least not for sure, but the three of them had spent too much time together for Half not to snap that there was something going on. Finally Bino said, "I hope to hell not. I got to say I thought Weedy Clements was smarter than this. It isn't like he's never been around. I've seen Goldman's witness list, and I don't guess there's anybody that knows Weedy that isn't going to testify. But the silly bastard won't make a deal, no way. What can I do about it? Hell, I can't *make* the guy plead guilty. I don't know what Weedy thinks is going to happen, but trying this case? Shit, he's going to be lucky if he gets out of jail before the turn of the century."

"Well, talk to the guy," Half said. "Jesus, I got a lot to do without sitting around court watching Weedy Clements go down the tube."

"I've *already* talked till I was blue in the face. You think I *want* to be in trial? Hell, nobody's covering the office. Which reminds me, Dode, you checked the answering service? We get any calls?"

Dodie laid down her burger and rolled her eyes. She swallowed. "Smokes, can't I finish eating first?"

"That's the trouble," Bino said. "Everybody's sitting around eating and stuff, nobody's taking care of business." The look on her face made him feel like biting his tongue off. "Hey, I'm uptight, okay?" he said. "Take your time, Dode."

She made a sour little face. It was a *cute* sour little face, but anybody who didn't know Dodie was pissed just didn't know her very well. "Never mind, boss, I've lost my appetite." She stood. "On my way, massa. Want me to check the cotton crop too?" She went off in the direction of the pay telephone, her backside twitching.

Half watched her go, then said matter-of-factly, "You been giving that little girl a lot of shit lately, Bino, and I don't see that she's done anything that calls for it."

This lunch wasn't going too well. It wasn't going worth a shit, matter of fact, now *Half* was getting on Bino's case. A lot of cracks went back and forth between the two of them, cracks that didn't amount to a hill of beans. But the number of times in their lives that Half had let him have it for real? Bino could probably count them on one hand. He drank some Coke. "Well, maybe I have. Maybe I been fucking up from here to El Paso. Look, maybe I better go on back to the courthouse by myself, okay? Take Dodie back down to the office, give her a few hours to cool off. Hell, I don't need the two of you, I got Goldman and Hazel Sanderson to fight. Jesus, not to mention my own client. Old Hazel, the last time I tried a case in her court she wound up turning me in to the bar association. This time she'll probably throw my ass in jail for contempt. Hell, I . . . Never mind. I'm taking off. Maybe I can talk sense to Weedy, I'm not doing too good with my own people." He got up and tossed his wadded paper napkin on the table.

"Well, suit yourself," Half said. "You ain't going to bother me none. I been bitched at by guys which are a helluva lot tougher than you. But while you're fucking around town you better think a few things over, Bino. I mean, this ain't you, the way you're acting. Dodie Petersons come along about once in a decade, and I don't mean just broads which *look* as good as her. You better think about what I'm telling you." He turned away and directed his gaze to the far wall.

Bino took a half step forward, drew in his breath to say something, then slowly let it out. Half was right on the money, of course. But what good was it going to do to . . . ? What the hell? Bino spun on his heel and made for the exit, feeling like ten kinds of an asshole but not being able to do anything about it. Maybe later. He hoped so.

He'd made it about three-quarters of the way across the restaurant, squinting to read the clock in the Zale's jewelry store window across the corridor from Bek's, when there was a loud crash on his right. Glass shattered and tinkled. A hush fell over the crowd. Bino stopped in his tracks. He turned and stared.

The redhead stood looking down at Bleeder, hands on hips and eyes blazing. Old Frank didn't look too happy himself.

The gal had dumped his lunch on him. Greasy meat coated with melted cheese and French fries slipped and slid in his lap over a bed of droopy lettuce and squishy tomato. Bleeder was watching the redhead with fear in his eyes, like a guy up for sentencing. Bino was conscious of the piped-in music outside in the corridor. "Jingle Bells." Happy Holidays.

The girl said something to Bleeder, then made tracks, heels clicking. The flesh around her eyes was red, puffy, swollen. Her mascara was streaked. Bino stood there with his mouth open like a flytrap as she headed straight for him. She didn't even see him. Jesus, this girl was going to walk straight through him as though he was Topper's ghost. Only he *wasn't* a ghost. If he didn't get the hell out of the way, she was going to run over him. He closed his mouth and started to step aside.

He wasn't fast enough, and she plowed right into him. As she uttered a soft, startled "Oops," her red hair tickled his chin and the fragrance of face powder drifted into his nostrils. He fell back a step, then caught himself. Her blue eyes widened. Her red lips parted. Her chest rose and fell in rapid succession. Bino got another, this time much closer view of milk white skin, a full mouth that ought to be smiling but wasn't, and long, long legs that were meant to be shown.

He said lamely, "My fault."

She looked for a second like she was going to start bawling again, then said, "Oh, I'm so . . . *sorry*." With a small sob from somewhere deep in her throat, she brushed past him. Her pale calves flashing, she left the restaurant and disappeared down the corridor in the direction of the Elm Street elevators. Bino thought about going after her; nobody should be wandering around alone in her mental condition. Just as he started to move, a heavy hand dropped onto his shoulder from behind. He turned.

He hadn't had a close-up look at Frank Bleeder in a while, and Bleeder's appearance hadn't taken a turn for the better. His cheeks and jowls were beginning to sag, and his entire face was an unhealthy red. In the old days Frank's hair had

□ 17 □

been a real attention-getter; it had been coal black with a sheen about it. Bleeder was graying now, and his hair was dull and limp. There was a scabbed-over nick on his chin where he'd cut himself shaving. "Hey, Bino, no big deal," Bleeder said. His voice was hoarse, maybe from too many cigarettes, maybe from yelling for too many sevens and elevens that never seemed to come. "Just a little boy-girl hassle is all, nothing to it. She'll be okay."

Bino glanced down at Bleeder's clothes. There was a greasy stain on his pants leg, and a slice of tomato still clung to the hem of his coat. Mentally, Bino had an instant replay of Dodie, her butt twitching as she stalked away to use the telephone. "No sweat, Frank," Bino said. "Happens all the time. Hell, I nearly got a plateful of lettuce in my lap a while ago myself. Would've served me right, come to think about it."

Bino was beginning to think that Weedy Clements's brother favored Marvin Goldman a whole lot more than he looked like Weedy. Bino wasn't sure *why* he thought the brother favored Goldman, so he looked them both over again. Well, the brother had a goatee and mustache like Goldman did, but the brother's hair was sandy red where the U.S. prosecutor's was coal black with little touches of silver mixed in. And where Goldman was slim, trim, and fit, did a lot of jogging and worked out with the weights, the brother was built like a fireplug. Yeah, the brother was *shaped* like Weedy, so what was it? Bino snapped his fingers. Sure, that was it. It was the way that the brother was *pointing* that reminded Bino of Goldman. Weedy's brother was pointing at Weedy in exactly the same manner in which the prosecutor had pointed. As though Goldman had rehearsed the guy or something.

"And are you positive?" Goldman said.

"Yep. I guess I know my own brother," Weedy's brother said.

There was a stirring in the jury box as an elderly woman in a print dress leaned forward and squinted in Weedy's direction, then did the same in the direction of Weedy's brother. She settled back in her chair, her gaze now on Goldman. Bino felt a faint spark of hope. Maybe the juror felt the same way Bino did, like maybe Goldman had slipped his own brother in as a witness in place of Weedy's brother.

"Please let the record reflect," Goldman said, "that the witness has identified Andrew Clements, the defend-ant." He leaned against the witness-box railing and folded his arms. "And what, if anything, did the defend-ant say? If you recall."

"Well, he told me to stack the weed in the back end of the pickup. Tell you the truth I didn' want to. I mean, the stuff had been out in that field for a week and it had been raining like hell. It stunk. You ever smelled wet marijuana?"

"I confess I haven't," Goldman said. Bino suspected that Goldman had smelled plenty of weed, though, when it was rolled into a joint and burning at one end.

"Well you ought to sometime," Weedy's brother said. "Anyhow, I told Weedy I didn' want to load it, but he said for me to get to piling the bales or it was gonna be my ass."

"*He* told you that?" Now it was Goldman's turn to point. Counting two points by Goldman, plus one apiece by the other two witnesses who had already testified, Bino figured that this made six points at Weedy so far. And they were just getting started.

"Yes, sir," Weedy's brother said.

"The defend-ant."

"Nobody else."

Weedy leaned over close to Bino and whispered, "I didn't have no idea he was gonna say *this* shit. Call King's-X. I think I wanta make a deal."

"That's what I been telling you all along," Bino said. "But it might be too late; this trial might be too far out of hand. I'll give it a shot, Weed, it's all I can do." Bino caught movement in the corner of his eye. A pink-cheeked man wearing a dark green suit had come into the courtroom. He paused, came through the railing gate, and laid a thick folder on the prosecution's table. Then he stepped back and nodded at Goldman. Goldman returned the nod. The new guy wasn't a prosecutor; his suit was the wrong color. Probably an FBI who was new on the job and hadn't learned how to dress yet.

"Well do *something*," Weedy said. "Hell, they're barbecuing me. Stick a fork in me, I'm done." He glared at his brother and curled his upper lip.

Bino stood. "Your Honor . . ."

Judge Hazel took her glasses off and blinked. "Are you objecting, Mr. Phillips? We have a witness here."

"No, Your Honor. I want to have a word with Mr. Goldman. In . . . private."

"Irregular, sir," the judge said.

Bino grinned, feeling slightly foolish. "How 'bout it, Marv?"

Goldman shrugged and spread his hands, palms up. "I've got the time, Your Honor. If the court does."

"Well be quick about it, Mr. Phillips. I'm warning you." Judge Hazel replaced her glasses on her nose and produced a small gold watch from the pocket of her robe. Weedy's brother adjusted his position in the witness chair. Goldman strolled over beside the prosecution's table and waited expectantly.

Bino came over to Goldman and tapped his index finger on the file folder that the man in the green suit had brought in. "What's this stuff?" Bino said to Goldman. "We already had discovery, you know; you can't run in a bunch of crap out of left field."

"Extraneous and irrelevant, my boy," Goldman said. "Doesn't even have anything to do with this case. What is this, anyway? You're calling time out in the middle of direct examination to ask me about this file? The proper procedure is for you to make a motion—"

"I know the fucking procedure, Marv. My client wants to make a deal. One count, he'll cop to it. Five-year max."

Goldman scratched his cheek with his index finger. "Okay," he said.

"Or two counts at the most. He can't . . . *huh?* What'd you say?"

Goldman sat on the corner of the table. He was grinning. "I said, 'Okay.' One count, five-year cap. You want to try for two?"

Bino couldn't have been more surprised if the U.S. prosecutor had unzipped his fly and started pissing on the table. Bino said lamely, "What's the deal, Marv?"

"Well if you *got* to know, the deal is that file there. The one you were asking about. Something's come up, and to tell you the truth I got no more time to fuck with Weedy Clements. Bigger fish to fry, or whatever you want to call it."

While Goldman's herd of civil-service-pool typists were upstairs fixing up Weedy's plea-bargain agreement, Bino used the pay phone in the hall. He punched in his own office number, then stood and listened to the clicks and rings as he gazed down the corridor past the courtroom entrance—ceiling-high door, stained and carved, with a glassed-in vestibule on the left for government witnesses and FBI agents to lounge around in and shoot the shit—to the end of the hallway. There was a plain vanilla entryway down there, identified by gold lettering over the door as the U.S. Attorney's trial headquarters. Bino wondered briefly how much it would cost for a defense attorney to have, in addition to his main office, headquarters outside every courtroom in town. Naw. Never be able to afford it. He'd already counted six rings, and just as he'd decided he'd called the wrong number and was ready to disconnect and try again, Dodie picked up the phone on the other end and said, "Lawyer's office."

"What took you so long?" Bino said. "I was getting worried."

"I was on the other line. Worried about what, massa? We-uns is heah."

He shoved his free hand into his pocket and closed his eyes. "Say, Dode, I've been meaning to tell you. You don't know how much I appreciate the . . . job you're doing."

"No, you don't," she said.

"Hey, not true. You're number one, I've said it all along. Let's call a truce, huh?"

There was crackling static on the line, accompanied by the sudden clatter of Dodie's typewriter keys. "What's to call? You're the boss, I'm the secretary. No big deal. You want your phone messages? And by the way, how come you're not in court? What'd you do, throw poor Weedy to the wolves?"

A plump woman in her forties, wearing a pink slack suit, came down the corridor lugging a stack of papers, did a column right, and went into the courtroom. Probably Weedy's cop-out deal. "I don't get it," Bino said. "I'm *in* court. Where do you think I am?"

"Well *I'd* of probably started looking for you at Joe Miller's Bar. But I didn't tell the judge that. He called for you."

"*He!* The judge is a woman, Dodie. Judge Sanderson."

"Wow, you're right. Score one for you, I'd forgotten. The judge that called was Emmett Burns. That's why I thought you weren't in court."

Bino thought, Jesus Christ. Now his head was going around in circles. Judges just didn't call lawyers out of the blue, not lawyers who had cases pending in the judges' courts. Not *defense* lawyers, anyway. And Emmett Burns wouldn't be calling *either* side; the guy was too straight arrow. Besides, Emmett Burns wasn't Weedy Clements's judge anymore, was he? Bino said, "What'd he say?"

"Well, after he said, 'Is Mr. Phillips in?' and I told him you weren't, he left a number. It's right here. Gee, I should have noticed before, but this exchange isn't a downtown number. He must be at home. You want it?"

Bino fished a pad and pen from his inside breast pocket and cradled the receiver between his jaw and shoulder. "Okay. Shoot."

The number was an Oak Cliff exchange, and Bino had a fleeting image of nice old homes nestled among the elms and sycamores and winding, mossy creeks near Stevens Park Golf

Course. Bino thought about trying again for a truce with Do-die, then decided he'd better let the water settle some more. He thanked her, disconnected, and tried the Oak Cliff number. Marvin Goldman was now standing in the courtroom entry-way motioning to him. Bino held up one finger in Goldman's direction as, over the phone, Judge Emmett Burns's calm and cultured tenor voice said hello.

"Bino Phillips, Judge."

Emmett Burns would be all business, at least that was the way he had always come across. Bino figured Burns to be around sixty, but the voice over the phone belonged to a man twenty years younger. The judge said, "I've already mailed you a retainer, Mr. Phillips, which is going to be sufficient for me to start calling you Bino. I live at four seven eight Crystal Hills. The street intersects Hampton Road just south of I-30 and winds around to Colorado Boulevard. Can you come by around seven?"

Burns wasn't really asking, he was telling, and there was enough authority in his voice to make Bino snap to. "Yes, Your Honor. I'll be there."

"Emmett will do, if you're going to be my lawyer. And the retainer puts us in an attorney-client relationship. Which means you're not to tell anybody about this."

Goldman was now waving like a third-base coach sending the runner home. Bino said, "Absolutely. I'll see you then."

Judge Burns disconnected with an abrupt, businesslike click.

As Bino approached the courtroom entrance, Goldman said, "Jesus Christ, hurry up. The judge has already got her panties in a knot over all this plea-bargain shit. You're the only guy I know with enough nerve to keep a judge waiting."

2

The way that Daryl Siminian had it figured out, there was nothing in Texas but steers and queers. And he didn't see any horns on any of the phony dipshits who were strutting around inside the lounge at Houlihan's Old Place in Northpark East Shopping Center. They sure looked like a bunch of queers to Daryl, guys wearing fancy suits or some kind of hey-mama-ain't-I-pretty tailored outfits from Lands' End or some other fancy shops that sold strictly cockhound clothes; guys who came in from the parking lot in London Fog or Habersham overcoats, hands jammed deep into their pockets and hunching their shoulders against the frigid north wind, then paused in the entryway long enough to watch themselves in the gold-framed mirror while they combed their hair, finally sidling up to the bar and ordering something that looked to Daryl like a pink cherry fizz. The way they leaned on the bar and shot goofy-looking grins around at all the broads just about gave Daryl indigestion. What a bunch of assholes. Give Daryl Siminian the Loop or Rush Street any old time, hunk of real pizza—not any of this phony frozen shit these Texas fuckers called pizza—and a hot-blooded Italian broad with a faint mustache on her upper lip.

And from the hot-pants looks that the women were giving the phony assholes, Daryl supposed that these dipshits were about the best that Texas had to offer. Like the broads didn't know any better. If any of these turdkicker lovelies wanted a load of something that would make them damp between the thighs, all they had to do was move up to the bar and have themselves a look-see at old Daryl Siminian. The same. The same matinee idol who was reflected right there in the mirror that ran the length of the wall behind the bar, full head of dark, curly, finger-running-through hair, dark eyes under full, soulful brows, corded, olive-complexioned neck that contrasted perfectly with a snow white turtleneck sweater. Scrumptious, broad shoulders that filled out a tan corduroy, knee-length Harbor Lights jacket from Marshall Field's. *Come on ovah, Mary Lou, get yoself a gander at this sweet thaing asittin' heah.*

Daryl held one finger over the top end of the stir straw that floated in his drink—Johnnie Walker Red and H_2O, none of that pink, foamy crap that the Texas assholes were drinking—then lifted the straw and put the open end in his mouth. He removed his fingertip and let a stream of cold Scotch run onto his tongue as he spun his barstool around and looked out the picture window directly behind him across the lounge. Past the dangling baskets of green, leafy ferns and fuzzy cactus it was bitter outside. Under a cold, gray sky, rows of Caddys and Mercedeses—plus some Chevys and little foreign makes that doubtless belonged to the leggy secretaries, and probably a few hookers, who were wiggling around inside Houlihan's and hoping one of the phony dipshits would buy them a drink—rocked slightly in the wind. Visible beyond the parking lot, traffic on the North Central Expressway was at a five-o'clock crawl, cars creeping off the freeway to mingle into a choking mass of confusion in the parking lot surrounding Northpark Mall across the way. Rows of green and red lights that formed the outline of a Christmas tree twinkled on the white rock wall at the entrance to the shopping center. Daryl thought that Christmas in Texas was a phony bunch of shit just like Christmas in Chicago; okay time for buying a broad a watch or necklace and then spending the next twelve months hitting on her for an extra blow job or two, but not much else to it.

A husky female voice on Daryl's left said, "It's like a zoo, isn't it? I've always heard, but in real life it's unbelievable."

He'd noticed the broad when she'd sat down—peach-colored slack suit, cheap wool overcoat, short, curly, dish-water-blond hair, thirty-five or so, chubby thighs that pressed against the fabric of her pants—and he'd wondered how long it would be until she tried to get chummy. Part of the price of being a hunk with a Tony Curtis face and a Sly Stallone body, Daryl supposed. He let her have another second or two of strong profile angle, then quickly spun his stool toward her and gave her the full frontal view. "Oh, it's okay. Something to do, but don't it get *boring*?" he said. Then the knockout punch, a slow-spreading, glad-to-know-ya smile, showing his sparkling white teeth. Zocko. The bridges installed at the federal joint in Springfield, Missouri, were about the only thing that the prison fucks had done right. The Thorazine shots, also administered at Springfield, which had turned Daryl into a walking zombie for two years, had been an unnecessary bunch of shit just like everything else in the system.

The broad wriggled like a puppy and showed her upper gums in a smile. "Oh, I do get bored sometimes. But I try to keep busy. I don't come here often enough so that it's old hat. So I'm Sue, who are you?" She giggled, and Daryl thought she sounded more like a horse with an oat bag over its mouth than she did a horny broad on the make. "Whee, I made a little rhyme," she said. Visible beyond Sue, occupying the barstool on her other side, were a shapely, milk white calf in nylon, a spike-heeled shoe on a petite foot, a long, slender thigh underneath a navy skirt.

"Sue?" Daryl said. "Well, I'm Bud. They call me Bud, okay? I've been noticing you. You know?"

"Oh?" She'd been drinking a lime daiquiri and now slid her empty stemmed glass slightly in his direction. "Well just whatever did you notice?"

"Well first of all I noticed that you were sitting there on that stool next to me. Be kind of hard *not* to notice that, wouldn't it?" By bending to his left and leaning against the bar, Daryl could see the small waist and swell of boob that belonged to the shapely, milk white calf.

"Oh, I suppose," the dishwater blond said. "I suppose you couldn't help but notice. I'm a supervisor at J. C. Penney's, across the freeway in the mall. So what do you do, Bud?"

"I don't do much. Say, I'm not through telling you what I noticed. Don't you want to know?"

She leaned her elbow on the bar and rested her cheek on her fist. "I'm fascinated. Sure I want to know."

"Well let me put it this way, Sue. I been noticing that you don't have no makeup on."

She touched her faintly pink upper lip and tilted her head slightly to one side.

"And something else I been noticing is that your legs are too fucking fat. You know? Jesus, you ought to do some bicycling or something. Hard for a guy not to notice things like that when he's hanging around looking for a little pussy. You know?"

She choked back a sob and turned to face the mirror behind the bar. Her purse, a big, brown-leather job with shoulder straps, sat beside her empty glass. She touched it with trembling hands.

"And the last thing I've noticed," Daryl said, raising his voice, "is that as long as your fat ass is sitting there on that stool I can't concentrate. So why don't you get the fuck gone? You know?"

Her face turned a deep shade of crimson, and tears rolled down her cheeks. She clutched her purse in both hands, uttered a soft, almost inaudible "Excuse me," then hurried off down the length of the bar and disappeared around the corner in the direction of the ladies' room.

The elegant milk white legs and tiny waist and swell of boob belonged to a redheaded dish seated one stool over, and she hadn't seemed to notice what had been going on beside her. She held her drink—brown liquid and ice, either a Scotch or a bourbon and water, Daryl couldn't tell—in both hands, sipping slowly and thoughtfully and watching the mirror.

Daryl picked up his own drink and slid over beside her. The taped music jumping from the speakers was "Young Blood" by Elton John and Neil Sedaka. Daryl said, "Say, I like red hair. You know why?"

She bit her lower lip and turned wide, blue eyes in his direction. "Today you're going to have to like somebody else's red hair. Hey, I'm really sorry, but I didn't come here to meet anybody. I've just got some thinking to do." She talked like a broad who'd been to college. Probably had.

Daryl put his finger over the end of his straw, this time dribbling a small pool of liquor on the bar in between them. "What a coincidence, Red. See, I didn't come here looking to meet anybody, either. Tell you the truth I'm in the market for a car."

She uncrossed her legs and recrossed them again. In addition to the spike-heeled pumps and navy skirt, she wore a blue-and-green checkered blouse with the sleeves rolled up a couple of turns. There were fine, light-colored hairs on her forearms. A dark fur jacket was draped over the back of her stool. There was a plain gold friendship ring on her right hand. "I confess that's a novel approach," she said. "Any other time it would be cute. I'm just not in the mood for . . . Well, I've had some problems, not your fault."

Daryl swirled his drink around and listened to the ice tinkle. "Don't everybody? Like I said, I'm looking for a car. Pontiac Tempest. Yellow, seven, eight years old."

Her right eyebrow arched. There were tiny dark smudges under her eyes, as though she'd been crying. Her nails were painted to match her scarlet lip gloss and flaming red hair. "What's this about a Tempest? Do you know me?"

He ducked her question. "Zippy little Tempest, really gets up and goes in the traffic. Say, I'm not from around here. What's that big stone building downtown? One Main Place, that's it, between Elm and Main. I bet a car like what I'm talking about could make it from there to here in, say, fifteen minutes. What do you think?"

"Look, I . . . don't really know what you're getting at, but if you've been following me or something you can get yourself in serious trouble." Her tone was harsh and even angry, but the look in her eyes told a different story. Uncertainty, nervousness, and the beginnings of fear. It was just the look that Daryl wanted to put there. Not that she had shit to be afraid of now. The real fear would come later.

Daryl showed her his sparkling pearly whites in a grin and lifted his hand. "Red. Red, Red. Just cool it. I understand what's bugging you, fight with the boyfriend and all. It happens to everybody. Man oh man, a guy wouldn't want to get on your bad side. He might get himself a lapful of lettuce. You know?"

"*Boyfriend?* Is that what . . . ? Look, what are you trying to get from me? Are you a friend of Frank's?" Her voice had softened and now had a crackly, almost sleepy sound. Daryl imagined that Red would be okay to shack up with. For a couple of days anyhow.

"Why, I don't know no Frank," Daryl said. "Frank's his name? Like I told you, Red, I'm strictly a car man. And a leg man, too, you know? Bet you hear a lot of compliments on them legs of yours." He let his gaze flick downward, then slowly raised his eyes.

She began to slide her arms into her jacket. At first Daryl had thought the coat was rabbit, but he'd been wrong. The rippling soft fur was real ranch mink. She said, "Listen, I've already told you that I want to be alone. I don't care who you are or what you want from me. But I'm leaving now, and you'd better quit following me. You'll regret it if you do."

"No, you got— Hey, slow down. What's your hurry, Red? I think we need to visit. Kick around a few things, you know?"

She tossed her head, her red mane waving, then settling back down. "No. No, we don't. I don't have anything to say to you. The only reason I'm not calling the police right now is that I'm running late. You keep away from me. I mean it." She was scared to death, trying to cover it up.

Daryl decided to let it go for now, sat with his straw between his lips and watched her leave. As she went outside, she buttoned her jacket and jammed her hands deep into her pockets. He thought, Jesus, what a parade, tight ass wiggling below the hem of the waist-length mink jacket, milk white calves moving in rhythm with the click click of her heels on the pavement, the bend and curve of her thighs as she climbed into the yellow Tempest.

Daryl made a make-believe pistol out of his hand, cocking his thumb and firing a couple of imaginary rounds at the Tempest as it wheeled out of the parking lot. Its brake lights flashed and its nose dipped as it slowed in thick traffic. "I'll be seeing you, Red," he said to himself. "Oh yeah, I will. I'm not shitting you one fucking ounce. Count on it, Mama Longlegs." Then he got up and went to use the pay phone, shouldering aside a couple of phony Texas dipshits who were getting in his way.

3

Bino thought that his white Lincoln Town Car probably needed a tune-up. Every time he gave the Linc a little extra gas to climb one of the hills on the winding road that ran through Stevens Park, he heard a metallic clatter under the hood. Might be nothing but the bitter cold, and it *was* a damn-sight chillier than it was supposed to be this time of year. This frigid stuff wasn't supposed to hit Dallas until early January, and maybe the Linc was just reacting to the weather change. But Jesus, these new high-powered buggies were supposed to be tested all the way down to thirty below or some such thing. Might be something wrong with the air-pollution crap, converter or whatever.

On the clipped brown fairway to his right—Stevens Park Muny, where the earliest ball in the rack was the first one off the tee, and where a five-dollar Nassau was the locals' idea of a high-stakes game—two lunatics were actually playing golf. There they were, a couple of guys in their fifties or sixties pulling handcarts along behind them, wearing scarves that flapped from around their necks in the breeze, both of them bent forward to fight the wind as they trudged down the sixteenth fairway between stately trees whose branches were stripped naked like skeleton arms. It takes all kinds, Bino thought. Two older men with a love for the game, their noses red and dripping from the cold. Come to think about it, though, there were worse things to do on a day like this. Like sit in a bar and drink whiskey and look out at the miserable weather, feeling sorry for yourself while the world passed you by.

He left the golf course behind and steered the Linc among modest brick homes, most of them built before the war—the Big War, not the Korean or 'Nam skirmishes—most of them well kept with pruned trees and knee-high evergreen hedges in front. Bino liked this section of Oak Cliff. The snooty, nose-in-the-air money lived in Highland Park for the most part; the fast-buck, here-today-gone-tomorrow crowd out in Las Colinas or Bent Tree. The people who'd kept their homes in Oak Cliff through recession after recession—and the decline of some of the surrounding neighborhoods into ghettos—were a sturdier, more down-to-earth, more dependable lot. Guys who had always been there and who were always going to be there, and who were damn proud of what they'd built for themselves. In a quiet, elegant sort of way, of course. Judge Emmett Burns was a guy like that.

It was getting dark in a hurry, and Bino wondered briefly how the two golfers he'd just seen were going to fare as they struggled up the eighteenth fairway, stopping every fifteen feet or so to squint in the growing blackness in search of their golf balls. It might be a while before they finished their round. As Bino slowed to read a street sign, then turned right onto Crystal Hills Drive, the automatic sentinel turned the Linc's headlights on.

Bino wasn't sure exactly how he felt about going to Judge Burns's house. Curious, sure. Why would a guy like Emmett Burns need a lawyer to begin with? Or even more to the point, why would he need a Bino Phillips? Coke & Hamilton, maybe, or Winstead, McGuire, Sechrest & Minick, some big firm like that to draw up a codicil or search a title on a piece of real estate. That would figure. But Bino couldn't remember ever having drawn up a will—most of his clients didn't have anything to leave anybody, and the ones who did have something kept it all in cash and buried somewhere in a tomato can—and the only time he'd been to the section of the courthouse where they kept the deed records had been years ago, when he and Annabelle had thought about buying a home. The divorce had ended the house hunting long before they'd gotten serious about it. Besides, Emmett Burns shouldn't ever need a lawyer in the first place; the judge had forgotten more law than most attorneys had ever learned.

Bino had tried four cases in front of Emmett Burns through the years. He'd won one and lost three, but that wasn't a bad record at all in federal court. Bino couldn't remember exactly how much of a sentence Judge Burns had handed down in each case, but he did recall that they'd all been fair. And he didn't have any bones to pick with the judge about any motion ruling or decision over an objection. Emmett Burns called 'em the way he saw 'em regardless of *which* side his decision hurt, and in this day and time that was about all a defense lawyer could hope for.

Emmett Burns had his critics, of course. Hell, didn't everybody? The old boy ran a tight ship, no two ways about it, and there were times—one incident in particular, Bino recalled, when he himself had gotten his wires crossed and had shown up about twenty minutes late one day when he'd been in trial—when Burns could turn the courtroom air a nasty shade of blue. He could make lawyers tremble and defendants cower, and clerks and bailiffs move like rodents when the cat was on the prowl. In the old days, Bino'd heard, back when Burns himself had been a practicing lawyer, the judge had never been much of a showman, a gag man, or an idea man. Burns had been sort of a plodder, in fact, but there was one thing that nobody could take away from the guy. Never once, according to the old-timers—not one single, solitary time that anybody could recall—had Emmett Burns ever come into the courtroom unprepared. He'd spent hours boning up on every single case of his, and his stickling for detail had carried over into his days as a judge. If Emmett Burns knew everything there was to know about the case at hand, then every lawyer in his court had by God better know it, too; and woe be to the guy who had to call time-out in Emmett Burns's court to go over notes or try to stall.

Sure, Emmett Burns had his critics. But what Bino liked about the judge was that the bellyaches came from both sides of the fence. With Hazel Burke Sanderson, Bino thought with a little shudder, the whines and moans around the lawyers' watering holes were all from the defense guys, with Bino himself as one of the chief table thumpers. Not so where Emmett Burns was concerned. And anyone who could cause somebody like Marvin Goldman to order a double and down it in a hurry was okay in Bino Phillips's book. Make that double okay.

The house at 478 Crystal Hills was a surprise, and Bino sat behind the wheel and looked the place over for a moment before he cut the Linc's engine. Not that it wasn't a nice house; hell, it was a *neat* little house, a dark red–brick one-story with friendly white trim. A Christmas tree decorated with red, green, and blue lights that flashed on and off in sequence stood in the front window, and a life-size sleigh—complete with a jolly Santa and eight reindeer trailing Rudolph with the lit-up nose—sat with its runners tilted upward on the high-peaked roof. On the lawn, two pruned and shaped fir trees bent slightly in the wind. There was a bricked mailbox at the curb, and the lettering around the circumference of the wreath on the front door of the house read "Welcome to the Home of the Burnses." Nope, it wasn't that the house looked like a great place to live that was a surprise. It just didn't look very *judgy* was all. Bino struggled into his tan Sam Spade overcoat, grabbed his briefcase, climbed awkwardly out of the Linc, and shivered his way up to the front door.

The doorbell played the first five notes of "Home Sweet Home" in xylophone chimes. Bino hugged himself, turned his back to the wind, and hopped up and down to keep halfway warm. In a couple of minutes, Judge Burns opened the door in person and said, "Good. You're early. You can help me move a table."

Emmett Burns was tall and rangy with almost no fat around his middle and was wearing jeans and a navy velour pullover. He had a full head of auburn hair with just the barest trace of gray, and his cheeks were smooth and unlined. He moved like an athlete—in fact Bino had heard that Burns had been a fair country basketball player himself, once upon a time, at tiny McMurry College out in Abilene—and had a big friendly nose. His eyes were blue under clipped auburn brows. Bino thanked the judge, went inside the house, and was at once conscious of a crackly blaze in the fireplace and the fragrance of cedarwood.

"We need to hurry," Burns said. "Ann will be along pretty soon; she's shopping. Here. Throw your coat over the hall tree and set your luggage down in the living room." Burns turned and began to move with a fast, all-business stride. Orders given. Now let's get on with it.

As Bino shrugged out of his trench coat and hefted it onto the hook, he said, "Sure thing, Judge. I'll—"

"Emmett." Burns paused and glanced over his shoulder, an index finger upraised. "Remember that. I'm Emmett, you're Bino. When I'm ready for that to change I'll let you know."

Bino swallowed hard, then said sort of meekly, "Oh. Sure, Emmett, but it'll take some getting used to. Where's the table? We'll rassle 'er wherever you want."

With Bino scrambling along behind, Burns marched into the living room. It was comfy and sweet smelling, with padded beige carpet and deep-cushioned Early American sofa and chairs. The Christmas tree that Bino had seen earlier from outside—a real pine, with sweet-scented, dark green needles—sat before the window with its red and blue and green lights twinkling. In the fireplace, orange and yellow flames danced and crackled and hissed. A log burned in two, sagging to the brick and sending out a shower of sparks. Burns pointed to a place on the floor beside the sofa. Bino set his briefcase down and followed the judge into the kitchen.

The kitchen had been redone, and not too long ago. The custom cabinets were newly stained dark wood and the floor sparkling green-and-white terrazzo. The breakfast table was going to weigh a ton. It was solid dark oak, oblong with a leaf in the middle, and Bino had a quick mental image of the judge seated there while ordering dishes to jump into the dishwasher and eggs to crack open and fry themselves. Burns planted his feet and grasped one end of the table from underneath. "Right over there," he said, jerking his head in the direction of six chairs in a cluster across the room. The chairs were a matching set, hand carved in foliage designs, the same dark oak as the table. "I've decided to start eating over there. There are some things going on that've been giving me a shitty perspective on the world. A different slant on breakfast might change that." He gave Bino an impatient look, a look that said, What the hell are you waiting for?

Almost without thinking, as though the judge had taken control of his mind and body, Bino stepped up to the opposite end and grabbed ahold. He lifted. The table didn't budge. He took a deep breath, regrouped, and lifted again. This time he grunted as the table came about two inches off the floor. He was conscious of Emmett Burns, an odd look about him as though he thought the sight of Bino busting a gut was funny or something, carrying the other side of the table as Bino struggled and sweated under his load. Jesus Christ, no way on God's green earth could Bino carry this heavy sonofabitch. Not no, but *hell* no. He had to set it down. *Had* to. He. . . .

Emmett Burns was staring at him. Their gazes locked. The judge seemed cool as a cucumber, as though the table—this solid oak, thick, godforsaken, heavy-as-lead motherfucker of a table—was light as a feather. Jesus, thought Bino. The guy's faking it. Sure he is. Hell, he's fifteen or twenty years older than I am. Trying to show me up, huh? Well I'll show *you*. Bino forced himself to grin. Step by faltering step, his shoulder sockets feeling as though they might give way any second, he lugged his end of the table over to where the chairs were and set it down. Dropped it, really, the legs thudding on the tile while Burns, who was continuing to tote *his* end of the load as though there was nothing to it, went on giving Bino a funny little aren't-*you*-a-pansy smile. Bino kept right on grinning himself, though what he really felt like doing was groaning, clutching his windpipe, and collapsing on the floor.

Burns dusted his hands lightly together. "Another little chore out of the way. One thing at a time, that's the way I do everything. You want something to drink?" He waited expectantly.

Bino wanted something to drink, okay, a tall, cold something with a foamy head and little slivers of ice floating around on top, and he opened his mouth to ask for it. But somewhere inside his head a little warning bell went off. Something told him that a beer right now was the wrong thing to ask for. He swallowed, the inside of his mouth like dust. "I'll have a Coke. If you've got something like that."

"That's good," Burns said without hesitation. "I don't want anybody working for me who drinks liquor when there's business to talk." He walked to the overhead cabinet, got down two stubby tumblers, and set them on the counter beside the refrigerator. Then he opened the freezer and filled the glasses with ice. Finally he produced a red can of Coke Classic, filled one tumbler with the fizzy stuff, and handed it to Bino. Then he reached underneath the sink, brought out a square fifth of Jack Daniel's Black Label, and poured himself three fingers. The ice cubes in his glass shrank as if by magic and floated to the top. He gulped and made a face. "Smooth. Now you're wondering why I'm drinking after what I just said. Well, I'll tell you. It's because I'm the client. I don't want a drinking lawyer, but as far as I'm concerned a drinking client is okay. Particularly when I'm the client. Come on into the living room, I'll fill you in."

As Bino followed the judge through the swinging kitchen door, the warmth from the fireplace touched his cheeks and neck. Wrapped packages were piled beneath the Christmas tree, the twinkling lights on the tree reflecting from shiny red and green paper and silver twine. Bino was beginning to be just a little bit sorry that he'd come. He still didn't have the slightest idea what Burns had on his mind, and he was thinking that maybe he didn't want to know. Bino was used to calling the shots, used to telling his clients what to do and when to do it. There would be none of that with Emmett Burns. Bino was about to make up some excuse for why he couldn't take on any clients right at the moment, but before he could the judge was standing beside the tree, peering anxiously out the window, shifting his weight from one foot to the other.

"I don't know where the hell she is," Burns said, his gaze still out the window. "But it's just as well. I haven't told her anything as yet, and I'm not even sure if I'm going to. Depends on what happens in the next couple of days." He crossed the room and sat in an easy chair beside a wooden smoking stand—a real old-timer, probably an antique—set his drink on a coaster, and began to fill a pipe with tobacco from a pouch. "You smoke?" He grinned slightly. "Lawyers that smoke are all right. It's just the drinkers you have to keep an eye on."

Bino wanted a cigarette, maybe even more than he'd wanted a beer a few moments ago. The problem was that he was now sitting on the couch across from the judge, his hands were busy with the Coke, and holding an ashtray in his lap was going to require more of a balancing act than he was up to. He shook his head.

Burns smoothed the surface of the tobacco in the pipe's bowl, produced a wooden kitchen match from his pocket, and struck it on the bottom of his shoe. He lit, his cheeks puffing furiously. Smoke billowed around his head and drifted toward the ceiling. "I'll tell you something, Bino. This is a first. There's never been a lawyer in this house in my whole twenty-two years on the bench. No judges, either. That throw you?"

Bino wasn't sure whether that one was supposed to throw him or not, so he opted to say, rather meekly, "Well, I'm honored."

"Don't be. You wouldn't be sitting there, either, if it wasn't for this shitstorm that's going on. I've never allowed any lawyers over here because they all want something. They're assholes. They think just because you pour a little whiskey down their gullets you're supposed to do something for them the next time they show up in court representing some dope peddler or the other. You know what I mean?"

Bino felt his butt sink a little deeper into the cushion. "Well I guess I do. There are some lawyers that might, well, try to take advantage of a situation."

Burns's eyes glowed like pale blue lights. "Not some. All. Every stinking one, including you. So once this little fiasco I'm going to tell you about is over, don't you get any ideas about buddying up to me. It'll get your tit in a wringer you won't pull it out of. That clear?"

Now this is getting to be a little too much, Bino thought. Jesus Christ, you'd think I was the one who'd called *him*. He caught himself just in time to keep from telling the judge where to get off, then said merely, "It's clear, Emmett."

"See that it stays that way," Burns said, settling back, laying his pipe aside, taking a pull from his Jack Daniel's. "And as for other judges, well, they just don't have anything interesting to say. So I don't hobnob with them either; I'd rather stay at home and read a book. Hell's bells, I'm with lawyers and judges all day, why would I want one of the bastards in my home?"

Bino didn't know why Burns would want to have any lawyers or judges over for dinner, and he was beginning not to give a damn anyway. Bino himself didn't pal around with lawyers either, but he sort of doubted that Emmett Burns ran with any guys like Barney Dalton and Half-a-Point Harrison. He tried to steer Burns in a different direction, saying, "I guess you spend a lot of time with your wife."

There was just the barest flicker, a chink in the tough old bird's armor, a sudden sadness at the corners of Burns's mouth and eyes. Then it was gone. He said, "My wife's dead. Old girl kicked the bucket, let's see, June a year ago."

"I'm sorry," Bino said.

Burns waved his hand in a brushing-off motion. "One of those things."

Jesus, what a tough nut, Bino thought. "You talked about somebody named Ann a while ago. Ann is your . . . ?"

"Daughter." On Burns's left, the fire was dying out. There was a glowing pile of ashes, and tiny blue flames licked the underside of the lone remaining log. "Daughter," he said again, almost vacantly. Then the steely front returned. "But enough about that. You've been here fifteen minutes already, by that clock over the mantel, and you've yet to ask a question about why I wanted to talk to you. Don't you want to know?"

The judge was beginning to remind Bino of an American lit professor he'd had at SMU, a guy who had been really caught up in his subject and who had figured Bino and Barney Dalton (who'd taken American lit because he'd needed the three hours to stay eligible for basketball, and because all of the PE classes had been full that semester) for a couple of fuck offs. It had taken some real humping on Bino's part to finally make a B in the course, and he'd always had the feeling that the old prof had taken a closer look at Bino's essay questions than those turned in by the other students. Bino cleared his throat and looked Emmett Burns straight in the eye. "Sure I want to know," Bino said. "I was sort of, you know, letting you pace yourself. Here, let me take a few notes." He set his Coke aside on an end table, fished in his briefcase for a spiral notepad, crossed his legs, and held the pad in his lap, stenographer style. He reached for the pen in his inside breast pocket. It wasn't there. He tried his shirt pocket. The sonofabitch wasn't there either. His face reddening slightly, he laid the notepad on the couch and stood. "Hold on a sec, Emmett. My pen. It's . . . in my overcoat." He went quickly into the entry hall. The bastard of a pen had damn sure better be there. Otherwise Emmett Burns was going to have more ammunition, and Bino already felt like enough of a jackass.

The pen was there, nestled innocently in the trench coat's inside pocket, a black U.S. government ballpoint with a silver-colored button on its end for exposing and retracting the point. Goldman had swiped Bino's pen that afternoon while the two of them had been going over Weedy's plea-bargain agreement; Bino'd retaliated by heisting the government job while the clerk of the court hadn't been looking. Now, standing in Emmett Burns's entry hall, Bino held the black pen lightly between his thumb and forefinger and looked outside through the leaded-glass window in the front door. It had begun to snow. Tiny flakes drifted rapidly down, fluttering in the wind and reflecting in the porch light like white confetti. Bino went back into the living room, sat down, and picked up his notepad. "Now. Where were we?"

Burns looked amused, like a man watching a TV sitcom that wasn't quite hilarious but was about halfway funny. "We were where you were going to ask me about why I'm having you over here," he said, brushing a thick wave of auburn hair off his forehead. "Weren't we?"

"Yeah. Yeah, right," Bino said. "Okay, Emmett, what seems to be the problem?" He got ready to write and cocked his head in an attentive attitude.

Burns took a deep breath and expelled it. Then he picked up his pipe and relit it. "Well," he said, puffing, the flame from his match fluttering over the pipe's bowl, "the bastards are going to indict me."

Bino's jaw slacked. "*Indict* you? What bastards?"

"What bastards do you think? The bastards I've been

working my ass off for all of these years. The Feds, son. They're going to do it."

Bino pictured Goldman that day in court, his hands lightly on the big file on the defense table, a blissful look on his face like that of a man in the middle of ejaculation, a slight tremor in his voice as he'd said, "I got no more time to fuck with Weedy Clements. Bigger fish to fry."

"What'd you do, Emmett?" Bino said.

"What kind of a question is that? I'm hiring you because you're somebody who knows his way around the courthouse. You're *supposed* to be, anyway. Jesus Christ, I don't *have* to do anything. When the U.S. Attorney's office gets ready to hammer somebody, they just do it. That's what I want *you* for, to find out in advance what kind of nonsense they've come up with as charges and head them off at the pass."

Bino paused to gather his thoughts. Sure, he knew how the game was played. Rule 1: A prosecutor never brings indictments against anybody whom the prosecutor knows really didn't commit the crime. Rule 2: If the target of the investigation is a big-time dope dealer, a Mafia figure, or anybody whose case is going to generate a lot of publicity for the U.S. Attorney's office, Rule 1 does not apply. Basic federal practice rules. But hearing it straight from a federal judge sort of took Bino's breath away. Bino said, "Are you sure about this? I mean, we're not being paranoid, are we?"

Burns sat up a little straighter in his chair. "Being paranoid isn't one of my faults. No, it's for real. That case you were trying today in my court? Well, the chief judge called yesterday and asked me—hell, he *told* me, that's more accurate—to excuse myself. That, coupled with some shithouse talk from some of the other judges. They're like old women, you know, all of them. I'm not going off my rocker. Sometime in the next couple of weeks I'm going to be the seventh federal judge in U.S. history to get his ass indicted." Burns held his glass at eye level, moved it in a circular motion, watched the ice and liquor swirl around. "How's that grab you?"

Bino looked the judge over closely. There he was, a slim, handsome man a good twenty years older than he appeared, looking calm and collected, right at home in jeans and a velour pullover, sitting there in front of his fireplace smoking a pipe, discussing his own pending indictment as calmly as if he were talking about the college basketball scores. Bino said, "Well, how's it grab *you*, Emmett? That's what's important. You haven't given me a whole bunch to go on yet."

"It's just, just another boulder in the road," Burns said.

"Yeah, but— Don't you have at least some kind of feel for what they're talking about? I mean, for real or not, they've got to have something to hang their hats on."

"I've thought about that. It'll be some kind of bullshit."

"Sure," Bino said. "Some kind of bribe, more'n likely. What about that? Has anybody, you know, offered you something under the table maybe?"

"Don't be ridiculous," Burns said.

"Not just money. Favors, anything."

"Anybody that knows me has more sense. They'd be looking at some time in the crossbar hotel if they even hinted." Burns got up, walked halfway to the window, and peered outside around the Christmas tree. "Christ, it's snowing. What in hell's keeping her?" He went back over to his chair and sat down.

Bino was beginning to feel a tiny surge of adrenaline. Goldman was going to have his work cut out for him trying to build a case against *this* guy. "Think hard, Emmett," Bino said. "If they're really coming after you, they'll have to have witnesses. I mean just anybody, maybe even somebody you ran into at a cocktail party, acting like it was a joke."

"I don't go to cocktail parties," Burns said, scratching his chin. "But there was one deal."

"Now we're getting somewhere." Bino clicked the button on the end of the government ballpoint, twice. The point disappeared, then shot back into view.

Burns exhaled a plume of bluish smoke. "Probably not. I

don't think you're going to make anything out of an offer by the prosecution. I'll bet you'd like to, though." He smiled.

Bino's head tilted to one side. "Prosecution? Who?"

"It didn't really amount to a hill of beans. At least I didn't think so at the time. I wrote it off as a young guy trying to bull his way to the front."

"What young guy?" Bino said.

"I was about to try a case. The defendant was a guy named Thorndon. Interstate stolen cars, a pretty good-size lot of 'em. You know Buford Jernigan?"

Bino nodded. Yeah, he knew Jernigan, a fresh-faced youngster straight from UT Law School. Followed Goldman around like a valet.

"Well, Jernigan called me one day. I don't guess the government had shit for evidence, because Jernigan wanted me to have a private meeting with him to go over some things they were going to bring up at trial. I had some short words for him. I said, 'Look, sonny, I don't have meetings with either side in a criminal case, not without the other side sitting there. You'd better remember that when you're in my court, else you're liable to wind up touring the county jail from an angle you hadn't considered.' I hung up on the guy. Then I forgot about it. A lot of these prosecutors think just because we're drawing our paychecks from the same outfit they can get real chummy with the judge. They learn different in a hurry if they fool with me." Burns's jaw thrust slightly forward for emphasis.

Bino made a note that said simply: Buford Jernigan—Thorndon—*Goldman!!!* Then he laid the pen aside. "I've written that one down, Emmett, but you're right. I doubt that's going to have anything to do with what we're talking about. Hell, the government's not going to indict anybody for playing footsie with the prosecution. Now if the *defendant* had called you up . . ."

"It'd be a horse of a different color."

"Right. Let's try a different angle. What about income taxes, they like to fool around with that a lot."

"Up to snuff," Burns said. "Look, I see all of this every day. My taxes are paid; hell, they probably owe me a refund. I'm not even into any land deals, though I can't say the same for some of the other guys on the bench. Hey, I won't even fill out a financial statement for a bank, that's another place where people are vulnerable to prosecution. If somebody gets a hard-on for 'em." He flashed another brief smile. "I may be a horse's ass when I'm on the bench, like some folks say. But I'm not a fool."

No, he wasn't. One look at those piercing blue eyes would tell you that. Bino was getting nowhere fast. He laid the notepad aside. What the hell *were* they after this guy for? "I guess my work's cut out," Bino said.

"*Our* work's cut out," Burns said. He nodded toward the Christmas tree and the frost-covered window beyond. "We're going to have to cut this short. Ann's home."

Bino turned. A swath of light bathed the window, then disappeared. Bino stood just in time to see twin headlights wink off in the driveway.

Burns assumed the same I'm-telling-you posture that Bino'd seen in the courtroom. "Put those notes away," the judge said. "And not a word about this. I'll handle my family. You're here doing a survey. No, that's not any good; you're trying to raise some money for the bar association." He snapped his fingers. "Not worth a shit, either, she knows better. I . . . invited you over to do a will for me. Something like that. What time can I meet you in your office tomorrow?"

Bino thought that one over. He wanted to do some snooping before he talked to Emmett Burns again. "Let's make it ten," he said.

"That'll do," Burns said. "Now you're going to meet my daughter. Remember, there's nothing wrong. I'll let her know, whatever, when I'm ready for her to know. Not before. She's . . . got enough of her own problems."

Bino's eyebrows lifted. "Anything I should know about?"

Burns said, "Nothing for you to know about. Nothing that's any of your business. I don't worry about anybody's family when I'm on the bench, and nobody's going to worry about mine. Not one word to her, you understand?" There was a sudden sagging to the judge's features, like those in a face of wax too near a flame.

Bino was having a hard time keeping up with Emmett Burns's moods. One minute like a dictator, the next, just mentioning his daughter, on the defensive. Almost *fearfully* on the defensive. Bino said, "Well that's—"

Burns held up a stern, silencing finger, his brows knitting. There was a sudden icy draft on Bino's cheek as, out in the hallway, the front door creaked open. High heels click-clicked on the hallway tiles. Then the same redhead Bino had seen earlier, the same girl who'd dumped Frank Bleeder's cheeseburger all over half of Bek's Restaurant, pranced gaily into the living room and said, "Hi, Daddy. Were you worried about me?"

The judge stood. The girl smiled at him, went over, and gave him a daughterly peck on the cheek.

Bino got respectfully off his butt, stood, and folded his hands before him. He was thinking, Jesus Christ.

Burns hugged his daughter. She was wearing a waist-length mink jacket, one that looked like more of a high-dollar item than a guy like Emmett Burns would likely buy. For himself, anyway. Bino was getting the idea that Burns's daughter would be a different proposition altogether when it came to the judge shelling out a few bucks. "Ann," Burns said, "this is Bino Phillips. He's a lawyer I've got drawing up a will for me." He was talking just a little too fast; his expression was a little too taut. If Ann Burns didn't snap that her father was lying, she was a whole lot dumber than she looked.

The slight, quick tilt to her pointed chin and the almost unnoticeable narrowing of her eyes told Bino that she wasn't dumb at all. Her eyes were something else. Damn near as pretty as Dodie's. Maybe not quite, but close to a dead heat. She said simply, "Well hello."

Bino glanced at the judge. Burns's expression said that he

knew he wasn't fooling anybody, but he was going on with it anyway. Bino licked his lips. He said to Ann Burns, "Hi."

There was a short silence that weighed a ton. Burns nervously cleared his throat. Finally Ann shrugged her shoulders and said, "Well it's nice that you've come, Mr. Phillips. But a will isn't something that Daddy's going to need for a while. He'll outlive me, five'll get you ten." So she'd decided to play along. Two Class-A bullshitters and one girl who was pretending to believe what they were telling her continued to look back and forth at one another.

"A will," Bino said. "That's something everybody should have."

"Do tell," Ann said. She was studying him closely, and Bino wondered nervously whether she remembered him from Bek's. Hell, it shouldn't bother *him*; he wasn't the one who'd dumped old Frank's food on him. But it bothered Bino anyway, and he had the sudden spooky feeling that he needed to know exactly what was going on between this girl and Bleeder.

Burns stepped forward. "We're just finishing up, hon. If you can give us a couple of minutes." He was dismissing her, or trying to, but what he'd seen so far told Bino that Emmett Burns didn't run over his daughter the same way he did the folks in his courtroom.

This time, though, she apparently decided to let Burns get away with it. She said, "Sure. I've got some things to do." Then, her lashes lowered, "Nice to meet you, Mr. Phillips." She went out into the kitchen, shooting a final glance over her shoulder that told Bino it really wasn't so nice to meet him, and if he and the judge thought they were putting one over on her they had another think coming.

Bino told Burns as much as he stood on the porch while the judge held the front door slightly ajar from within. "It's your business, Emmett. But your daughter knows you're putting her on."

Burns said, matter-of-factly, "She might. She might not. Ten o'clock?"

Okay, Bino thought, I'll keep my nose where it belongs. "Sure, ten will be fine."

"I'm a prompt man, Bino," Burns said. "And I expect everybody else to be just as prompt. See that you are." With a final nod, he closed the door and left Bino standing alone in the cold.

Bino sat behind the Linc's steering wheel for a while and listened to a Barbra Streisand tape as the heater warmed the car's interior. Big, wet flakes of snow were melting and running down the windshield as he pulled away from the curb.

Emmett Burns used his handkerchief to wipe frost from the windowpane, then watched the big white Lincoln pull smoothly away through pelting snowflakes. His shoulder brushed the Christmas tree. Ornaments clicked together, and tiny silver bells rustled and tinkled. Burns drank more Jack Daniel's, the liquid cold on his tongue and then burning its way down his gullet. He felt a sudden, hard knot in the pit of his stomach. His shoulders sagged momentarily, then straightened again. As he went back to his chair beside the smoking stand, he mentally gritted his teeth and willed the scary feeling to go away. *Forced* it out of his system. Mental toughness. That's what had gotten Emmett Burns through it when Margaret had died—cancer, Christ, just when they'd had everything to live together for—and that's what was going to see him through the fight with *these* dirty bastards as well.

He smiled grimly to himself as he wondered whether Bino Phillips had any idea how deeply afraid his new client was. Burns doubted it. *You aren't going to see Emmett Burns taking the gas, Mr. Phillips. You might think you're tough, Mr. Bino Phillips (and you* are *pretty tough, I've had my eye on you since you played basketball, though you don't know it), but you haven't seen tough until you see somebody try to put Emmett Burns down for the count.*

Then, just as Burns had gotten himself in the right tough-as-nails frame of mind, he had another sinking spell. Christ, it had been like this ever since he'd gotten his first inkling of trouble. Ever since Ezra Martin (the presiding judge from the courtroom across the hall, just another milquetoast puppet for the U.S. Attorney's office as far as Emmett Burns was concerned) had buddy-buddied up to him and filled him in on what was going on, Burns's emotions had been going up and down like a yo-yo.

If they want you, they get you. Burns had heard that for years, heard it from defense lawyers, even from a few stand-up defendants at sentencing. Well they'd better by God bring their lunches and their suppers too if they were going after Emmett Burns. With a final mental bracing (he couldn't, just couldn't, give Ann more problems, what with everything else she was going through, Jesus Christ, wasn't she coming through like a champ, though?), he got up and went into the kitchen.

Ann sat at the breakfast table, the same table that Bino (bet you didn't know the old judge was straining just as much as you were, Mr. Phillips) had helped move a little while ago. She was eating a dish of ice cream. Rocky road, the same forbidden, wonderful stuff in which Burns had indulged her when she'd been a little girl and her mother hadn't been watching. Hadn't hurt her figure one bit, Burns thought with a tiny surge of pride.

He sat down and placed his drink on the table. "Having a snack?"

She gently licked the spoon, her gaze dull. Something was wrong here. Something was wrong when his daughter didn't look at him. She bent her head as she took another spoonful. "It's good," she said.

His own problems seemed suddenly far away. "What is it, Princess?"

"What is what?"

"What is what? What is it that makes you not look at me? Why do I have the same feeling that I used to when you didn't want to show me your report card?"

She shrugged, continued to stare vacantly at the cabinets across the kitchen. "It's nothing, Daddy."

"Nothing, huh? You come home to find a lawyer in my living room for the first time in your life and you don't even want to know what he's doing here? And you're telling me it's nothing? You can't fool your old man, kid. 'Fess up, what is it?"

She seemed to grow smaller, her shoulders hunching closer together. "Did it have anything to do with me?"

"What, precious? Did what have anything to do with you?"

"The lawyer being here."

"No," he said with a smile. "Why, do you need a lawyer?"

"I hope not," she said.

He studied her. He was worried about her, but at the same time almost relieved to have something—anything—to take his mind off what was going on in his own life. "Maybe I can help," he said.

She carried her bowl over to the sink. The ice cream was half eaten. She turned on the faucet and watched the watery chocolate flow down the drain. "Let me try being a big girl for a change," she said. "If I find out I'm still a little girl, I'll look you up." She looked over her shoulder at him. "I promise, Daddy, okay?"

On his way home, Bino took a little detour. He left Dallas North Tollway at Lemmon Avenue, tooled along for a few blocks on Lemmon, and stopped off at Joe Miller's Bar. The lighted sign at the curb, and the headlights passing one another in opposite directions on Lemmon, made upside-down reflections in the standing water on Joe Miller's asphalt parking lot. Bino hunched his shoulders against the cold and tightened the belt on his trench coat. Snowflakes pelted his cheeks and neck and made icy rivulets that ran down under his collar. On his way to the foam-padded front door, his feet splashed through a couple of shallow puddles.

The inside of Joe Miller's was about half full of chattering, sipping night people, seated in clusters at tables and scattered the length of the bar. The stereo jukebox was playing an old Brook Benton tune, "Snap Your Fingers, I'll Come Runnin'." Barney Dalton was holding forth on a barstool, entertaining two brunettes. His broad shoulders filled a tan alpaca sweater, and his rust-colored mustache jiggled up and down as he spoke. Bino located a place beside Barney and slid in. The bartender, a chunky but pretty girl named Melinda, took the cue from Bino's upraised index finger and delivered a tap Michelob.

Barney's back was turned, his elbow propped on the foam padding. He was saying, "—and I don't mind telling you, I had a helluva choice to make. If I hit the three-wood and come off of it any at all, my poor little *pilota*'s going swimming, and then it's Katy, bar the door. I can lay up, o' course, maybe a soft seven or a hard eight, and have the berries on a five. But remember I'm one down, I'm trying to make four on the hole."

The closest of the two brunettes wiggled on her barstool. She had a cute pixie face, and she reminded Bino of an old art school ad that used to run in *True Detective* magazine. The ad was a shaded profile sketch with a caption underneath reading, "Draw me." The brunette batted her eyes vacantly in Barney's direction. "What's a soft seven?" she said.

"A soft . . . ," Barney said. "Well, it's how you're going to hit the club. You know, half swing or full swing."

"Oh," she said, still looking as though she didn't know what the hell he was talking about.

Bino took a pull from his beer and swallowed. "You forgot the third way you might hit it. Cold-shank the bastard, if they were betting you enough money."

Barney swiveled his head. "Hell, I'm no choker. Bino. Where you been, I got . . . Hey, this is Dolly and Betty. This is my buddy, girls, the one I was telling you."

The pixie face wrinkled her nose, and Bino decided that she had to be Dolly. The other brunette, the one who looked like a Betty, was long and on the lanky side with black hair falling straight to below her shoulder blades, like Cher's. She said, "Hiya." She was wearing jeans and a fuzzy blue sweater.

"Glad you came along," Barney said. "Betty's needing some company." His back was now to the two girls, and he flashed Bino a guarded circle with his thumb and forefinger.

Bino watched bubbles rise in his glass, watched them disappear as they blended with the foam at the top. He was conscious of the lanky brunette as she leaned forward expectantly; then he had a sudden mental picture of Emmett Burns, wagging his finger and cussing drinking lawyers.

"Not tonight, Barn," Bino said. "Tell you what, I'm going to finish this one and call it a day. I got a lot to do tomorrow."

4

Since the weather had turned to shit, and since he couldn't put his plans for Red into motion until tomorrow anyway—and maybe not even then, it depended on a couple of things—Daryl Siminian decided that he might as well pick up a few extra dollars shooting pool. So he cruised around on Lower Greenville Avenue—stopping for a beer in a number of joints, looking around at hardwood, sawdust-sprinkled floors, at six-pocket tables covered in faded and scarred green felt with double-quarter slot plungers in the side that ran four bits a game, talking it over with fat, old barmaids who sat on stools beside the registers and looked pissed off when anybody wanted a beer or change for the juke or pool table—until he ran across two cowpokes who looked like they might have a little money in their pockets and who looked too dumb to know what they were getting into. The cowpokes were shooting pool in a place called Dee's, a hole-in-the-wall with just enough room for two pool tables and a juke besides a short bar that would seat around a dozen. Dee's was on Ross Avenue a couple of blocks off Greenville, and the barstools inside had cotton stuffing poking out in places. A girl was watching the cowboys play. Couple of Butch and Sundance drugstore motherfuckers.

One of the cowhands was skinny, six-two or so. He stood with his pelvis forward and his narrow shoulders back, chalking up a rack cue as he said, "You spotting me the seven, Rib. You spotting me the seven, 'less we ain't playing for no more'n a beer." He was wearing a big gold belt buckle with the words "Golden Nugget—Las Vegas" in red, raised letters around its perimeter. A shaded light hung over the pool table, spotlighting the cowboy's blond, curly hair. Daryl had found himself a real ramblin', gamblin' man.

Daryl sipped from a lukewarm Bud longneck—Jesus, he was glad he hadn't had to settle for Lone Star or Pearl or another one of those turdkicker brands—as he sized up the one called Rib. Full, dark beard, western shirt, pretty big gut hanging out over his belt, Stetson pulled low over dark, shaggy brows, sitting on a barstool with his cue lying across his lap and his western boots propped up on the rung that encircled the legs of the adjacent stool, the one occupied by the girl. "Spot died," Rib said. "Dead an' buried. Shit, a beer a game's okay with me, I ain't looking to get rich offen you." Real bright hustler. Fast Eddie of the turdkicker set. Daryl leaned on the bar and turned his face away to hide a grin.

"Aw, come on," Skinny said. "We got to make it innerstin. Five. Five a game, you spot me the seven."

The girl ambled over to the jukebox and spun four quarters into the slot. She was pretty young—in the dimness it was hard for Daryl to tell just *how* young—with long hair in a ponytail to her shoulders and a gap between her blue-jeaned thighs about three fingers wide. She stood with one hip higher than the other and pressed the buttons. Willie or Waylon,

Daryl thought. One or the other, it's got to be. Willie Nelson's mellow, singing-through-his-nose voice vibrated through the speakers. "Blue Eyes Cryin' in the Rain." The girl held her round chin between a thumb and forefinger as she read over the other selections.

"Well I'm a fool for it," Rib said. "But shoot 'em, you got the seven. I can't stand to see a grown man cry." Daryl thought, Now if the dumb, skinny shithead knows anything he'll ask for the seven *and* the eight, right here.

The skinny cowhand giggled like Festus and racked the balls, nine in the center with eight other balls surrounding it in a diamond pattern. Daryl couldn't believe the two guys. On Clark Street they'd spank the both of them and send them home to they mama. Daryl pulled a wadded five-dollar bill out of his pocket and motioned to the barmaid. She farted around about it, moving slowly, but finally brought him three singles and eight quarters. Daryl got up, moved over, and laid two of the quarters on the edge of the pool table, then retreated to his barstool. "Can anybody play?" He smiled. "Or is this a private game?"

Judy Roo watched the newcomer's reflection in the plastic jukebox cover, shifting her position until the image flattened out some and the guy didn't look so much like something you'd see in the fun-house mirror, out at the fair. Pretty good-looking dude, but boy was he ever out of place. White turtle-neck sweater, tight slacks that molded around his thighs, tan corduroy coat with the collar turned up. Looked Spanish, but might be Sicilian (Judy wasn't sure just where a Sicilian came from, but she'd seen a lot of Sicilians on "Wiseguy," the TV show, and she thought that Sicilians were pretty cool). The guy sure wasn't no Tex-Mex, his skin was too light colored. Groovy build, too; his coat was unbuttoned, and she could see the sharp indentation of his narrow waist and the bulges where the front of his sweater molded around his chest muscles. He had a thick, corded neck. The dude must have some bread, too; those clothes of his looked pretty expensive. George and Rib would've spotted the clothes, too, and right now would be figuring that this was just the dude they'd been looking for, either to take his money on the pool table or, if that didn't work, beat the ever-loving shit out of him and leave him propped up in an alley someplace with his pockets empty.

It sort of pissed Judy Roo off to think about George and Rib doing that to a guy as good looking as this one was, but there wasn't any way that she could stop it. If she were to give Rib any lip about it, he'd just loosen a few of her own teeth. And Judy Roo had had plenty of experience in getting the shit beat out of her by guys and didn't want any more of it. So she selected "Twinkle, Twinkle, Lucky Star" by Merle Haggard and kept her gaze riveted on the panel.

She watched the stranger's reflection as he climbed down from his barstool and walked smoothly—dude had a little strut about him, his shoulders rotating slightly—over to the pool table and laid his money on its edge, listened to the dude asking Rib and George if he could play (and caught the quick look that passed between George and Rib, saw Rib adjust his position on the barstool so that one of his cheeks was hanging off the side of the seat), watched the stranger sidle back over to the bar and sit down. The guy had a funny little smile on his face, a quirky grin that probably meant he thought that George and Rib were a couple of assholes (you don't know what *big* assholes they are, Judy thought) but that he'd put up with them long enough to shoot a couple of pool games. Judy resisted the urge to turn, walk straight over to the good-looking guy, and say, "Hey, mister, don't you know what the fuck this is? Don't you know that George McCaffey's brother Bob is the baddest cat in the Texas Department of Corrections; only when Bob gets out on the street every few years, he's scared to death of his brother George on account of George is so crazy you never know what the fuck he'd going to do? And that Rib Breland, the prospector-looking dude sitting there on that stool, is George McCaffey's cousin, and that the two of them held up the Kentucky Fried Chicken on Mockingbird Lane last Tuesday night and in the process pistol-whipped a nigger cook half to death and jammed his hand into a basket of sizzling grease just because they didn't believe him when he told them he couldn't open the safe? Jesus, mister, you better get yourself gone from here if you know what's good for you." But Judy couldn't just go up and say that to the guy; she'd wind up either getting hurt bad herself or getting toted back down to the halfway house. And from the halfway house the county deputies would handcuff her and give her a ride back to the Women's Prison Unit, down to Gatesville. Judy checked the clock behind the bar. Nine-thirty. In two and a half hours she'd have been gone from the halfway house for three days, and in the morning they'd be putting out a warrant for her. Judy pressed one more selection—"I'm Not Lisa," by Jessi Colter, soft and sad, one that Judy used to listen to in her cell at Gatesville—and went over and hopped up on the barstool between Rib and the stranger who was probably fixing to get himself robbed. She crossed her legs and liked it when the stranger glanced at her long, firm thigh.

"You're the background-music lady, hey?" the stranger said. "Can't shoot good pool without good music. You know?" He was watching Judy in a way that she liked, a sort of friendly smile on his lips as though he wouldn't mind getting in her pants at all, but he wouldn't give her much shit if she didn't want him to. From the pool table came a soft thump and then a series of clicks and rumbles as George broke and the balls rolled and collided and bounced off the rails.

"I *luuve* music," Judy Roo said. "It puts me in the mood for fun." She could have said "in the mood to fuck" or "in the mood to blow some dope" and would have if she'd been talking to George or Rib or somebody she sort of knew. But she didn't know this new guy—and probably wasn't going to *get* to know him once George and Rib got through with him—and if she were to talk just a little bit dirty he might take it wrong and come over and try to feel her up or something. Just because Judy Roo liked to talk a little bit dirty didn't mean that she didn't like to get to know a guy some first.

"Music?" The guy had an up-north accent, sort of like a rich insurance man from Cleveland, Ohio, a guy that Judy had lived with for a while. The same guy who had turned Judy in for burglarizing his farmhouse, which was what she'd been doing down in Gatesville to begin with. "I dig music, too," the new guy said. "Some kinds. Not any honking shit, just good beats. You know?"

Judy lifted her leg three or four inches and clasped her hands around her shin, looking at the stranger sort of over her shoulder and giving him a little cheesecake pose. "Is *that* right?" she said. "Well whatcha call honkin' shit? This is progressive country, what we're playin' in here. No Ernest Tubbs or Hank Snow or anything like that. *Everybody* digs on progressive country, case you don't know it."

Over beneath the shaded light, George sank the five-ball with a click and thump, then threw his head back and yelled, "Awwl *rootie.*" The barmaid, a woman in her forties with a bony figure and dyed black hair, who was wringing a wet towel out over the sink, said, "Come on, hold it down. We got enough trouble letting you shoot for money in here without the law bustin' in on account of you makin' so much racket." George cradled his pool cue as though it was a dancing partner and did a few shuffle steps to "Blue Eyes Cryin' in the Rain."

"Progressive . . . ?" the stranger said. "Yeah, I guess it's progressive enough. But I meant like, you know, on Rush Street, up in Chicago. Maybe a little jazz, some blues, Al Hirt kind of stuff. So I'm Daryl." He was talking to Judy but watching the pool table, his eyes excited, as though watching George and Rib shoot pool was a better show than watching Judy Roo strike a little cheesecake pose. Judy thought, The sonofabitch.

George missed the eight ball—O' course, Judy thought, just the idea of playing Rib in pool makes George choke up —leaving it right in the center of the pocket, then walking around the table muttering under his breath. Really making a show out of it, making like he was really pissed, all to show this Daryl guy how much it was hurting George to lose. On Judy's other side, Rib's breathing was a little too loud as he slid from his barstool and approached the green felt table.

"Hiya, Daryl," Rib said from the side of his mouth. There was a bulge of snuff in his lower lip that Judy hadn't noticed when Rib had been sitting down. "Hey, Daryl, you ready to play? Looks like Georgie-boy has shot his load. You'll be playing me, Daryl, this cowboy's finished. I'll make all the rest of 'em, bet your ass."

Judy arched her back, deciding to give this Daryl guy a little boob shot to remember along with the earlier cheesecake pose, deciding to give Daryl a little extraspecial to keep on his mind right up to the moment when Rib and George went to work on him. It was the least she could do for the guy. She said, "Up where you come from Daryl, you play a lot of pool? These two guys play all the time, they're pretty good."

Daryl rotated on his stool like a boxer in between rounds, watching Rib make the straight-in cripple eight ball, watching while Rib blinked in satisfaction as the cue ball drew away from the rail for perfect side-pocket shape on the nine. Rib Breland moved around the table in a coordinated, shuffling gait, like a stalking grizzly. Daryl said to Judy, " 'Scuse? What'd you say?"

Now Judy was really getting pissed, almost hoping that Rib or George would kick this guy in the balls one extra time for her. The fucking bastard was *ignoring* her. She said, "I ast you if you played a lot of pool. I'm *whispering* or something? You spaced fucking out, Daryl?"

"Oh, yeah, I . . . hey, good shot. Real professional." Daryl grinned, his teeth stark white against his olive skin in the dimness. "Well, yeah. Down around South Chicago, Cicero. You know? I mean, I'm not good enough to where somebody'd want to try to break my thumbs. But yeah, I play some."

Rib Breland cupped a hand underneath the faucet and splashed water on his face. He raised his head slowly, met his own slightly bloodshot gaze in the mirror. There was a crack in the glass, bisecting his reflection, and one side of his face appeared slightly higher than the other. Beads of water stood out on his beard like cake frosting. He yanked three coarse paper towels from the rack and mopped his whiskers.

About two feet to Rib's left stood George McCaffey, straddle legged, his fly open, his dong exposed, and a yellow stream of his urine splattering on filthy porcelain. George's eyes were closed. "Ahh, the pause that refreshes. Hey, Rib, the pause that refreshes. That's a good one, ain't it?"

Rib thought, Jesus, how'd I get mixed up with *this* silly bastard? My own cousin, dumb as a post. He said, "It's a good one, George. Funny as shit."

George finished pissing and began to shake his dong. A drop of moisture splattered against Rib's forehead. George said, "Hey, Rib. When you going to turn on your A game? We're two hundred loser, ain't it time for you to start letting him have it up the butt?"

"A game. *A* game? Don't you know I'm wide fucking open? A game my ass, this Yankee cat can play. You see that eight-ball shot, the one where the nine had him snookered? Bent that fucker from here to Grand Prairie and back is what he did. I tell you I can't beat the man. Not on the square, anyway." Rib stepped aside and leaned against the wall, feeling the sharp edges against his upper arm where the paint was chipped. He hooked his thumbs through his belt loops and waited for George to use the sink. On the wall above the pisser was a lettered sign reading "Please do not throw cigarette butts in urinal." Underneath the sign somebody'd written, in smeary ink, "It makes them soggy and hard to light" and drawn a picture of the finger.

"That mean we're going to have to party with the guy?" George asked.

"Could be. Depends on if you want to go home broke or not." Rib felt his upper lip curl as George closed one nostril and blew a wad of snot into the sink.

"Rib, you don't reckon . . . goddamn, what a *monster*. You don't reckon he's a cop?"

"Naw, he . . . what's a monster? Man, you talking about that *dick*? That picture somebody drawed?"

"Well, yeah," George said. "If you was hung with that one the whores'd all back down. How you know he ain't?"

"Jesus Christ, you're looking at a picture of a dick on the wall. Vice squad can't bet you nothing; it's a bad bust if they do. And ain't no fucking cop shoots that kind of pool; most of 'em miscue all the time. They got to— The fuck you looking at now?"

George was now bent over the sink, reading squint eyed some writing on the wall beside the mirror, his skinny butt poking out. "Hey, Rib, it says, 'Mary Ann—Tight Pussy.' There's a phone number, you want to write it down?"

Rib's jaw slacked. The air smelled of urine mixed with smoke mixed with stale beer. "Naw. Naw, I don't want to write it fucking down. I want to talk about the dude out there, the guy who is separating us from our money. Money which we worked our asses off for, down to the Kentucky Fried Chicken, remember?"

"That ain't much for us to talk about. Tell him this pool table don't roll true, that we want to move this game further on out Greenville Avenue. Then when we get him outside we Rambo the motherfucker. Rambo him, hey? That's a good one, ain't it, Rib?"

Rib stood away from the wall and unhooked his thumbs. "Yeah, okay. For a cousin I got me a stand-up comic. Say, George. I ain't got no pencil. You want the number remember it in your head. Just keep on sayin' it over and over, you'll remember it. Okay?"

Just before George and Rib came out of the bathroom, Judy Roo came within an inch of telling Daryl what they had in mind for him. She didn't like picturing this handsome dude with his nose broken and bleeding—or even worse, with a buck knife shoved between his ribs or a bullet drilled through his skull and into his brain—lying cold and alone in the gutter while George and Rib argued over which one of them was going to keep that bitching corduroy jacket Daryl was wearing. Besides, Judy Roo was beginning to have something in mind for Daryl herself, and it didn't have anything to do with him getting the shit beat out of him on any cold, dark street.

She was seated on the stool beside Daryl, her elbow propped up on the bar, and doing her best to act as though his blow-by-blow description of each shot he'd used against Rib in the last eight-ball game was the most interesting fucking thing she'd ever heard, and she'd just parted her lips to interrupt him and tell him what was going on when the door to the men's room creaked and banged open. Judy closed her mouth, then managed to whisper, "I'd sure watch myself if I was you."

In the semilight, Daryl grinned. "You don't have nothing to worry about, background-music lady. Watching out for myself is what I do best. You know?"

Floorboards groaned as Rib and George approached. Light from behind the bar glinted on George's big, round belt buckle as they stood side by side in front of Daryl and Judy, and Judy knew just what they were thinking and saw the look about them. Rib's thick lips moved silently between his beard and mustache.

George said, "Rib says he can't figure out the roll on this here pool table. So we were thinking, maybe we need a different table. Rib says he'll play you for so much money it'll choke you up, if we can call the place."

Daryl brushed against Judy's upper arm as he shifted his weight. She was getting the feeling that he hadn't needed for her to fill him in, that this pretty guy Daryl knew just what was coming and wasn't even worried about it. Shit, that maybe he even liked the idea. Daryl said, "So show me a new table. Show me four. Tell you the truth, you two broncbuster assholes kill me. Isn't a table anywhere you can beat me on, you know?"

Rib's eyes narrowed, and he started to say something.

George stopped him with an elbow to the side and said, "You got a big fucking mouth, mister. So how much we going to shoot for, if we name the table? Hunnerd a game?"

"Hundred a game, shit, five hundred. I'm not going to be losing it, so it's all the same to me."

Rib now said to George, "I think this fella's cocky, cousin. How 'bout we ride him down to Loretta's?"

George looked thoughtful, using one index finger to tilt his hat away from his forehead. "Yeah, Cousin Rib. Loretta's is okay. How 'bout it, big mouth? You follow us down to Loretta's? Down there they got a nice, smooth pool table, maybe down to Loretta's we can close your big mouth some, huh?"

Daryl climbed slowly to his feet. He threw Judy a sideways wink, then extended his hand toward the exit, palm up. "After you, Festus. Jesus Christ, I can get to shoot pool with you two turdkickers I'll follow you anywhere."

There was just an instant when Judy thought that George and Rib were going to jump Daryl right there, not even wait until they could get him outside. Both of them tensed. A mean-looking scowl appeared on Rib's face, the same look he'd had the night of the Kentucky Fried Chicken robbery, the look Judy'd seen on Rib just before they went inside and left her at the wheel with the motor running. But then, as if on cue, they relaxed as one. George put on his phony good-ole-boy expression and said, "Fine with us, mister. You follow us; we'll drive real slow. Now don't lose sight. We don't want to have to hunt for you."

Rib and George shuffled side by side for the exit. Daryl fell into half-swaggering step behind them. Judy hesitated. Shit, she hated to see the good-looking dude take a beating. But then she had a mental picture of bone crushing bone and a shivering thrill ran up her spine. She hopped up and threw her cheap wool overcoat—a prison-issue number they'd given her when she checked out of Gatesville—around her shoulders. As she followed the men outside, she was vaguely conscious of the barmaid, who was putting bottles away and wiping down the counter.

Cold air tingled Judy's cheeks. It had stopped snowing; shallow drifts not yet muddied by traffic lay piled against the curbs in the moonlight. Her breath caught in anticipation as she watched Daryl follow George and Rib between a supercab pickup—George's truck, Judy remembered—and some kind of a dark-colored Ford or Chevy that must be Daryl's. Her inner thighs tingled as George turned abruptly sideways and braced himself, swinging his right arm up from behind his back, moonlight reflecting from the foot-long piece of metal pipe in his hand. Judy thought, Holy shit, this is where pretty Daryl's going to get it all right. She thought about Daryl's blood reddening the snow, and her nipples were suddenly taut and hard.

Daryl took one step forward, turned to his right, and brought his knee up between George's legs. George grunted and doubled over. The pipe clattered to the pavement, rebounded, and crunched softly into a snowbank. Suddenly, from somewhere, a pistol was in Daryl's grip. Holy shit, Judy thought. She wasn't no gun freak, but the big mother of a gun in Daryl's hand looked to her like something out of a Dirty Harry movie. Daryl stepped quickly over George and put the pistol's barrel on the point of Rib's chin. Rib froze, his fist cocked.

"Man, you two corn pones would never make it through the night on Rush Street," Daryl said. He patted Rib down, found his little derringer, and tucked it into his own waistband. "Okay, now, turdkickers. Put your hands over there on the fender of that truck. Move. You, too, skinny, unless you want me to shoot your nuts off so they don't hurt no more."

Rib went to the front of the supercab and assumed the under-arrest position, legs spread, hands out flat on the fender. Limping, moaning softly, George did the same. Daryl went through both men's pockets, straightened with a wad of bills in his fist, put the money away. Judy watched from the curb, her eyes wide, her mouth agape, her fast breath turning into wispy fog.

"Hey, Jesus, thanks," Daryl said. "Hey, you saved me some time. Now I don't have to play no more pool with you two boring assholes. Easy as pie, you know? Now I'm going to give you Choice A and Choice B. Choice A is, you can get in your fucking truck and leave. Choice B, you can stand right where you're at. 'Course, if you stand there more than thirty seconds I'm going to shoot your kneecaps off, but don't say I never gave you no choices, you know?"

Wordlessly, the two left. Rib climbed into the truck's driver's seat while George, still groaning, got in on the passenger side. The truck's engine fired; its tires spun on slick pavement. A block away, it careened onto Greenville Avenue. Its cab was bouncing up and down as it disappeared behind the Sears Department Store sign at the corner.

Daryl turned to Judy, putting his gun away, grinning at her. "I hope they're not friends of yours, background-music lady. Hey, I wouldn't be rude to no friends of yours on purpose. I want to be on your good side, you know?" He shrugged. "So, well, the pool game's over. Where can I take you?"

Judy jammed her hands into her pockets and shivered. "Holy shit, Daryl. I s'pose it's up to you. I got to tell you, though, I got my period. Don't matter none to me, if it don't matter none to you."

5

The next morning was Wednesday the ninth of December, and Bino woke up refreshed and with a clear head. He hadn't been waking up feeling this way too often of late; the closer it got to Christmas the more the crowd down at Joe Miller's Bar liked to party, and the more they liked to party the guiltier Bino felt if he didn't hang around and tip a few along with them. Hell, there'd been an instant last night when he'd been afraid that Barney Dalton might haul off and punch him in the nose, just because he'd wanted to go home.

He took a little bit longer than usual over his coffee and sweet roll, enjoying the undisturbed whiteness of the new-fallen snow through his breakfast-nook window. A trail of prints, made by tiny high-heeled shoes, led from the apartment entry across the courtyard. The trail ran through the courtyard, made a detour to leave some trampled snow in front of the newspaper rack in the breezeway, then wound its way down the sidewalk in the direction of the parking lot. A brunette Delta flight attendant had moved into the apartment last month. Little lady must have had an early flight this morning.

Even Cecil the oscar fish was in a better mood this morning. Lately he'd been regarding Bino with a fishy leer, but today he only stared vacantly into space as he hovered motionless between waving fins near the surface of the water in his aquarium. " 'Bout time you brightened up," Bino said. "You don't know how close you've been to a trade-in on a school of guppies, pardner." He dropped two live minnows into Cecil's tank instead of the usual one. Cecil flicked his tail, ran the darting little buggers down one at a time, and swallowed them whole.

Bino dressed in a charcoal gray suit, added a red tie for a splash of color, and checked the time. Only a couple of minutes after eight. He punched his office number into the phone, muttered under his breath while the answering service let the line ring seven times before they picked it up, then told the service to give Dodie the message, when she came in, not to look for him at the office for a couple of hours. He put on his trench coat, wound a blue wool muffler around his neck, and trudged through wet snow out to where the Linc was parked. On the way, icy water seeped through his shoes and wet his socks. As he climbed into the Linc's soft velour front seat, he sneezed a couple of times. He cranked up the Linc, plugged a David Allan Coe cassette into the stereo, and headed downtown for Marvin Goldman's office.

Bino wasn't sure whether Goldman would tell him anything about the government's case against Emmett Burns at this stage of the game. Since no indictment had come down yet, Goldman didn't *have* to say a word. But Bino was counting on Goldman's ego. If the U.S. prosecutor had any case at all, he would be busting a gut to tell somebody about it. And when he found out that the guy representing the judge was going to be none other than Bino Phillips . . . well, then Goldman would *really* lay it on thick. So the only reason that Goldman would refuse to say anything would be if the government's case was pretty weak. Bino hoped.

As he steered out of the parking lot onto Dallas Park way, Bino held his breath and put a choke hold on the steering wheel, halfway expecting the Linc to slide across three traffic lanes and bang into the median. But the pavement wasn't even slippery; the Linc's radials gripped the parkway surface like insect legs. The concrete was wet, okay, and muddy sprays of water shot out on both sides of him, but the ice was all gone from the road. He breathed a sigh of relief and whipped onto the tollway, headed south. The temperature was rising. By noon the whiteness would be turned to dirty mush; by mid-afternoon it would be only a memory.

Downtown, Bino parked in a lot across Commerce Street from the Federal Building, got a ticket from the attendant—a wizened old guy in a gray uniform with "Park 'n' Lock" stitched over the breast pocket—and hustled across the street just as the traffic signal switched from green to amber and the pedestrian light switched from "Walk" to "Don't Walk." A traffic cop, one arm straight and the other windmilling a line of cars along, tooted his whistle. Bino kept his gaze straight ahead and pretended not to notice the cop as he dodged around two women carrying shopping bags and ducked quickly inside the Federal Building.

He shared the elevator with a cute blond who exited on four—IRS—and a grumpy-looking gray-haired woman who glowered at him suspiciously during the ride and threw a final sniff in his direction as she got off on eight. The eighth floor housed the U.S. Parole Commission. Jesus, Bino thought, how'd you like to be coming up for parole and throw yourself on *her* mercy?

The United States Attorney for the Northern District of Texas, along with his gang of assistants, took up most of the eleventh floor. About half the U.S. Attorney's offices were for lawyers—tile-floored cubbyholes for Grades 12 and 13 mid-dlemen; pretty classy layouts including posh couches and private toilets for GS-14 and grades above—with the rest of the space taken up by pool typists, computer rooms, law and payroll clerks, and a legal library that contained every research book known to man. With a setup like this, Bino thought, it'd be even money to spring Manson.

If he could get away with it, Bino wanted to walk in on Goldman unannounced, didn't want to give old Marv a chance to dream up a line of bullshit while Bino sat cooling his heels in a waiting room. With that in mind, he kept his gaze on the floor and went by the receptionist without looking in her direction, watching from the corner of his eye as she barely glanced up from the paperback edition of *Hollywood Husbands* by Jackie Collins that she was reading. Well, he'd cleared *that* hurdle. In his gray suit, and with nothing in his hands that looked as though he'd taken any work home with him, she'd probably figured him for one of the U.S. Attorney's boys. He went to the end of the hallway and turned the corner.

About thirty feet ahead on his right was a dark wood secretarial desk that sat in front of a closed door. A young, square-jawed guy with a government haircut—two inches long at its fullest and completely minus sideburns—who was wearing a navy suit and starched white shirt, and who was drinking coffee from a Styrofoam cup, was perched on one corner of the desk. The cute trick who was sitting behind the desk was giggling into her cupped hand at something the guy was saying. Your tax dollars at work. Bino breezed up to them and stood at attention. "What happened?" he said. "Old Marv move his office?"

Nazi-hair looked irritated. Bino checked out the swell of bosom underneath the fuzzy pink sweater the secretary was wearing and really couldn't blame the guy for not wanting any interruptions. The guy said, "Marv?"

"Marv. You know, old Marv Goldman. Golly, he told me to meet him at nine, and to tell you the truth I might've taken a wrong turn. You folks have got a lot of halls around here." Bino grinned and tried to look dumb.

The girl started to say something, but Nazi-hair put a hand on her arm. He said, "You got an appointment with Mr. Goldman? What are you, a lawyer or a witness?" He was doing a lot better job of looking dumb than Bino was.

Bino thought the question over, then said, "Well I might be a little of both. You might say."

"A little of both? You can't be both. Listen, are you representing somebody or—"

"Stop *grilling* him, Tommy." The girl frowned at Nazi-hair, then flashed Bino a smile that would've melted butter. "You're in the wrong wing, sir. Turn around and follow this hall until it ends. Turn right, it's the only way you can go. Then another right, and Mr. Goldman's suite will be the second door on your left." She reached for her phone. "If you'll give me your name I'll just—"

"No . . . thanks," Bino said. "Thanks, but I'll find it. You know old Marv. Never gives the right directions." As he retreated he felt Nazi-hair's gaze boring a hole between his shoulder blades.

He found Goldman's door. Nothing marked it but a room number on a white paper sign. Bino hesitated, took a firm grip on the knob, turned it, and went inside. Goldman had a small reception area with a secretarial desk that right now didn't have a secretary sitting behind it, two stuffed chairs, and a couch. Goldman had been around as a federal prosecutor for long enough that Bino figured that the closed door to his right led to Goldman's private toilet. A man who had a puffy, red-complexioned face was seated on the couch, and it took a couple of seconds for it to register on Bino that the guy was Frank Bleeder.

Bleeder looked up from an issue of *Sports Illustrated* and sucked in his breath. "What are *you* doing here?"

Goldman stepped quickly into the reception area from his office and stopped in his tracks, gaping at Bino. "What are *you* doing here?"

Bino shrugged. "Visiting. What are *you* doing here?"

Goldman cocked his head to one side. "Me?"

"I know what *you're* doing here, Marv. And I don't care what *he's* doing here. I just thought if everybody was going to ask *me*, I'd . . . hell, skip it. Hi, Frank. You got some federal clients these days? I thought your hangout was the county jail."

Bleeder's gaze dropped. He cleared his throat. He didn't say anything.

Goldman said quickly, "Yeah, Frank and I have a few things to kick around. But what brings *you* over? I thought the Weedy Clements case was put to bed. If it's about Weedy I'm going to have to refer you down the hall to another guy. Like I told you in court, I'm all caught up in a new deal."

Bino got the same uneasy feeling that he had when Barney Dalton cussed at his hole cards and then checked. If Barney cussed and checked, he was almost sure to raise if anybody bet into him. There wasn't anything out of line about finding a lawyer visiting the U.S. Attorney's office; hell, thousands of lawyers came up here every day. So what were Goldman and Bleeder acting so strange about? Bino said carefully, "Oh, this doesn't have anything to do with Weedy. Weedy's tickled pink with the plea-bargain agreement. I'm here about another case. Look, if you and Frank need some privacy I can wait till you're through. I'm not in any hurry."

"Well I'd reserved my whole morning for Frank." Goldman selected a peppermint wafer from the bowl on the secretarial desk and untwisted the ends of the cellophane wrapping. "But I guess I could give you ten minutes or so. If it's important. What do you want to talk about?"

Bino took just an instant to make up his mind what to say. His business with Goldman was as touchy as nitroglycerin, and he really shouldn't bring it up with anybody in the room besides the federal prosecutor. But he was picturing Bleeder with a lapful of lettuce and squishy tomato. And Ann Burns close to hysterics as she left Bek's restaurant. Bino glanced at Bleeder seated on the couch, then directed his gaze back to Goldman. Here goes, Bino thought. He folded his arms, leaned against the doorjamb, and crossed his ankles. "Oh," Bino said casually, "it's about a new client I got. Judge Emmett Burns."

Goldman froze with the peppermint inches from his mouth. His eyes widened. No big deal; Bino *expected* Goldman to be shook. It was Bleeder's reaction that Bino was looking for.

And did Bleeder ever react. The color drained from his face. His jowls sagged like deflating air bags. The magazine slid from his lap onto the floor. On the *Sports Illustrated* cover, Moses Malone leaped high for a two-handed stuff.

The silence in the room was as loud as city traffic.

Finally Goldman poked the wafer between his lips and crunched on it. He said, "Come on in, buddy. You can wait, can't you, Frank?"

Goldman's tone said that Bleeder had damn well *better* wait, and Bleeder nodded woodenly. Goldman stalked into his private office with his back stiff as a ramrod. Bino glanced at Bleeder—old Frank hadn't even bothered to pick up the magazine—then went in after Goldman. Goldman closed the door and sat down behind his desk. Bino waited for the prosecutor to offer him a seat. Goldman didn't. Bino stood.

"You've got Judge Burns for a client?" Goldman said. "What'd he hire you to do?" Goldman's desk was blond wood with a pane of glass covering its top. On the wall to Bino's left was a framed print, two white horses charging across a clearing underneath a skyful of thunderheads. To Bino's right was another print, a mean-looking eagle in flight, talons extended.

Bino spread his fingers and looked at his nails. "You tell me," he said.

Goldman grabbed a hard red rubber ball from his top drawer and began to squeeze it in rhythm. "You should try this. Strengthens the grip." Underneath the glass on his desktop was a color photo of a small Caribbean island in deep, clear blue water. His framed state and federal law licenses were on the wall directly behind him. There was one window in the office, and through it the parking lot where Bino had left the Linc was visible along with the Holiday Inn over on Elm Street.

Bino decided that he was by God going to sit whether Goldman liked it or not. He grabbed a straight-backed chair from against the wall, positioned it in front of Goldman's desk, sat down, and crossed his legs. "We can sit and grin and fill one another full of bullshit, Marv. That's one way to do it, but it's a helluva waste of time. Another way to do it is for you to let me know up-front that you're not going to tell me anything about your case, at which point I'll leave. The third choice is for us to lay a few ground rules and maybe open up a little bit, probably save one another a lot of silly discovery motions once the bell rings. How do you want to handle it?"

Goldman bounced the ball lightly off his desktop, switched hands, and kept on squeezing. His expression said that he was having a pretty good time. "I'll probably opt for Number Two," he said. "The one where I don't tell you anything and you leave. I don't think you can tell me anything I don't already know, and I'm too busy to sit here playing a lot of mind games with you."

Goldman would have kicked himself if he'd realized it, but he'd just said a mouthful. "I'm not telling you anything," translating into "We don't have much of a case, but we're going ahead with the indictment and making the details up as we go along." Vintage Goldman. Now Bino needed to find out everything he could about where Frank Bleeder—and Ann Burns—fit into the picture.

"Well then," Bino said, "I don't guess I'm going to get what I came after, but it's good that you're telling me without a lot of beating around the bush. Any chance of you letting me know before the indictment comes down? So I can get my client ready for the worst? I think the U.S. Attorney's office owes Judge Burns that much. Don't you?"

Goldman scratched his goateed chin with his free hand while continuing to squeeze the ball with the other. Bino wouldn't swear to it, but he didn't think Goldman's hair had as many silver threads in it as it had had the other day. Maybe a touch of Grecian Formula. Goldman said, "Nobody said there's going to *be* any indictment. Like I told you, buddy, I'm opting for choice Number Two."

One thing sure, Goldman wasn't kidding. He wasn't going to give the time of day. Bino said, "Well thanks for your time, Marv." He got up, took one step toward the door, then halted and snapped his fingers. "Oh, by the way. Is Buford Jernigan helping you out on this one? My client says he hasn't seen Buford since the . . . the Thorndon case, I think he said."

Goldman gripped the rubber ball as though he was trying to rip it in half. Then he put the ball away and closed his drawer with a bang. "You're not going to get any mileage out of that one, Bino. Who's going to testify that Jernigan did one damned thing on the Thorndon case? Your client? It's his word against ours."

Goldman calling the judge "your client," as though Emmett Burns was some two-bit dope pusher the cat had dragged in, was getting under Bino's skin. Not a month ago Goldman would have said that Burns was a number-one jurist and the salt of the earth. The Feds would turn on their own in a heart-beat. Bino said, "Somebody's going to have to testify? That means there *is* going to be an indictment, doesn't it?"

For a second, Bino thought the prosecutor might bite his tongue. Goldman touched his fingertips together. "Fuck you, Bino," he said.

Bino plunged ahead. "And what witnesses are you going to use? Shit, Marv, Bleeder's a weak link. You think a jury's going to believe him over a federal judge?"

"Bleeder's not the only one who's going to . . ." Goldman trailed off as it dawned on him that he'd taken the bait. "I think you'd better go now," Goldman snapped. "I don't want to talk to you anymore."

Bino grinned as he opened the door. "Anything you say, Marv. Man, but you're a tough nut to crack. You won't tell anybody anything, will you?"

Bino decided to walk to his office. It was only seven or eight blocks, besides which, he'd paid a full day's parking for the Linc in the lot across from the Federal Building, and besides which he wanted to walk because he loved being downtown. Was crazy about it. They'd taken the boy out of the country a long time ago, when Bino had left the dusty streets of Mesquite for Dallas to play a little basketball at SMU, but taking the country out of the boy was something else again. No matter how many times he walked the city streets, Bino'd never been able to shake the feeling he'd had as a kid when he'd peered at Big D from the backseat window of his mother's station wagon with his nose pressed to the glass.

Horns honked. Exhaust fumes drifted in the moderate wind. Skyscrapers with mirrors as walls reflected neighboring buildings and the blue sky above. Skirts flapped around pretty calves and thighs. Girls smiled as their breaths turned to fog. Hustling businessmen scowled. Bino took it all in, striding easily along with his hands in the pockets of his trench coat, whistling over and over again softly the opening bars to "Fly Me to the Moon." He was across the street from his office in the Davis Building, just about to cross the street with the light, when a gloom came over him and he paused.

He looked up at the Davis Building, at her old tan-brick sides, at the sculptured stone lions that had stood guard over her entryway for more than half a century. The spot of gloom in his mind enlarged to a full-blown thunderhead as for maybe the hundredth time he read the sign that stood on the curb in front of the building.

The sign—at least six feet high by eight feet wide, red and blue letters against a white background—told one and all that this was the future home of Martin Tower, which was to be a fifty-story shrine complete with moats and fountains in its lobby. Underneath that announcement was a row of seven-figure numbers, a column that bragged loudly how much money Citibank, MBank, and TexasBanc were each putting up to bankroll the deal, and underneath the row of figures was the statement that Henry C. Beck Company would begin construction on the new tower around the first of March. Big plans. Big bucks. Big deal.

Progress, thought Bino. Piss on it.

What the sign really meant was that in less than two months a special crew was going inside the Davis Building to drill some holes at strategic locations and then insert a few little sticks of dynamite. Then, a couple of days later, with crowds held back by ropes and TV cameras whirring, a guy who was standing a block or so away was going to press a plunger—or push a button, or wave a wand, or whatever it was they did these days—and blow the old girl to kingdom come.

Demolish her. Raze her. Kill the old queen dead.

Sure, it had to come sooner or later. There were only so many coats of paint and new carpets and retiled floors and dropped ceilings that the management could install. The foundations and unstressed steel superstructure and slowly rotting wood interior beams were the same ones that had been there when FDR had been in office and a whole passel of Texas boys had dodged bullets—or some, not so lucky, had failed to dodge bullets—and nearly frozen to death in places with names like Barronne and Wiesbaden and Normandy. And elevators that still needed operators to run them were a thing of the past, and the cost of installing automatic cars was prohibitive in relation to the rent that the old building's offices would bring, and blah-de-blah-de-blah. Bino'd heard all of that a thousand times and couldn't argue with a single word of it. That didn't make him like it any better, though.

With a final, wistful glance upward at the lions, Bino crossed the street and entered the building. He paused in the entryway, reached out to the Davis Building's brick exterior wall, and patted it gently.

Dodie stopped clickety-clacking her typewriter keys long enough to say, "Mr. Bainbridge called. His number's on your desk." She was being maddeningly polite and was wearing a robin's-egg blue long-sleeve blouse and some bluish mascara. Bino liked her looks a lot more when she wasn't wearing eye makeup. Dodie knew that, of course.

He went over to the visitors' couch and looked down at the end table beside it. The shaded lamp on the table was off. He switched it on. Just as he'd thought. The same issue of *Sports Illustrated* that Frank Bleeder had been reading, the one with Moses Malone in action on the cover, lay on top of a pile of magazines. He picked up the stack, rummaged through it, and replaced the *Sports Illustrated* with a six-month-old edition of *Field & Stream*. He shoved the *SI* into the center of the pile. "Mr. Who?" he said.

"Bainbridge. He's with the management company. Wants to know if you're going to sign the lease that's been in your top drawer for six weeks. He says that the new building is filling up in a hurry."

Bino dropped the stack of magazines back onto the table. "If it's filling up so fast, why's he bugging *me*? We're only talking about one itty-bitty suite, just enough room for you and me and Half. I want to think it over some more."

Dodie picked up a yellow pencil and tapped the eraser end on her desk blotter. "Golly, you need to make a decision. You can't call up somebody and say, 'I believe I'll take an office,' and then move in the next day. It takes some planning."

Bino licked his lips. She was right, of course, and putting off signing the lease as though his holding out was going to somehow prolong the Davis Building's life was really pretty silly. But that was exactly what he was doing. "You call him for me, Dode. Tell him I'll let him know something within a week. Any other messages?"

"Weedy Clements. He wants you to do something about the food down at the jail. He says they gave him a rotten orange."

"He's lucky to have an orange at all. He's lucky he's not doing thirty years. In a few weeks he'll be in the federal joint, and they'll feed him roast duck or something. Oh, hell, I'll call the jail captain, maybe he'll do something. Anybody else?"

She brushed her blond hair back from her ear and arched an eyebrow. "Umm-hmm. Somebody *big* else. Judge Burns. He's coming in at ten. Also, an envelope came from him today with a check in it. A *big* check. What's the deal?" She batted round blue eyes and looked expectant.

The diamond-shaped clock on the wall behind Dodie was showing a quarter to. And Emmett Burns would be prompt, you could bet on that. "I'm doing some work for him, Dode. Oh, and mum's the word on that, at least for now. I'll fill you in later. Half in?"

She looked pouty and said that he was. Bino went over, opened the door without knocking, and entered Half's cubbyhole. The odor of old wood under new paint hit his nostrils, Half's war-surplus desk, which Dodie had painted by hand.

Half-a-Point was bent over a copy of *Football News*, making changes in the line with an accountant's mechanical pencil. "You should holler or knock or something," he said. "How do I know you ain't the law? Jesus, you'll have me swallowing a bunch of betting slips for nothing." He stroked his pencil mustache. He was wearing a pin-striped vest with a pale blue shirt, and his collar was open. A narrow tie hung on the rack behind him along with a plaid sport coat.

Bino struggled out of his trench coat, folded it over his arm, then sat down across from Half and crossed his legs. "I got to interrupt your life's work for a while. You got time to do some investigating?"

"Yeah, I guess. Business is pretty slow. Nothing left on the football sheets but the college bowls and the pro play-offs. Be a lot of action come Christmas week, but for now I ain't got much to do. Whatcha think about SMU, Bino? They're playing Notre Dame in the Hula Bowl, out in Hawaii. Gimme the inside poop." Half's thinning brown hair was combed straight back from his forehead. It didn't seem to matter how many cheeseburgers and sundaes he ate, the guy stayed skinny as a rail.

"Hard to say," Bino said. "The NCAA investigation on SMU makes them tough to figure. Hell, they don't even know if they're going to have a team next year. It might make 'em not give a shit, but then it might make 'em so they really want to pop it to somebody. But don't ask me. The last time I got you some inside poop on SMU, it cost me five hundred bucks. Remember?"

"Don't remind me." Visible through Half's window were tall, mirrored towers that dwarfed the Davis Building and the narrow ribbon of concrete that was I-45, stretching far in the distance to the south. Half put away the *Football News*, then hauled up a yellow legal pad and got ready to write. "So I'm all ears."

Bino put his feet on the floor and his elbows on the arm-rests of his chair and leaned forward. His trench coat was now folded across his lap. "I've taken on a pretty touchy case, Half. The Feds are about to indict Judge Emmett Burns."

Half laid his pencil crosswise on top of the pad. "You're shitting me."

"Nope. I'm serious as cancer. I wouldn't have believed it either; in fact when the judge had me over last night to fill me in I thought he was just being paranoid. But this morning I've been over to see Goldman. Believe me, the bastards are going to do it."

"And Goldman's going to be doing the prosecuting?"

"Yep."

"Jesus Christ." Half picked up his pencil and cocked his head.

Bino smoothed a wrinkle in his trench coat. "For starters, I want to know everything Frank Bleeder's done in the past three years."

"Bleeder? The guy in the hamburger joint?"

"None other. I want to know how many times he's been to Vegas and how high he's gambling. I don't think Frank's got a drinking problem, but if he does I want to know about it. Check the court records. I want to know every swinging dick or female he's represented for the past three years, and if their case happened to be federal and in Emmett Burns's court, then I want to know everything about the client from the time he or she was in three-cornered pants."

"Hold on," Half said. "You're giving me finger cramps. This ain't like taking the line down over the phone."

"We don't have time for me to slow down. Emmett Burns is going to be here in a few minutes, and by the time he gets here I want you should be gone. Bleeder is the Feds' star witness; I've been able to find out that much. I don't know what it is that Goldman's got on Bleeder, but I need to know. How big Goldman's hammer is is going to tell us how much they're going to get Bleeder to say. And when you get through with Bleeder, there's somebody else I want you to check out. This one's pretty delicate, Half."

"How can you get any touchier than Emmett Burns? A federal judge."

"By talking about his daughter. Ann. That's who I want to know about. She's the girl that dumped Bleeder's lunch on him yesterday."

"The redhead?" Half said.

"Yep."

Half gave a long, low whistle.

Bino rested his chin on his clenched fist. "Judge Burns puts on a tough act, but it's not that hard to see through. And one thing sure, he thinks his daughter hung the moon. That's what's so touchy; if I'm going to do any kind of job representing the guy I got to know what's what. I'll tell you, if the judge gets any idea at all that we're nosing into his little girl's business . . . shit, I don't even like to think about it."

Bino paused long enough to allow Half to finish the line he was scribbling on the tablet, then went on. "I met her last night. That was before I knew that Bleeder had anything to do with all this, so I wasn't watching her too close. But come to think about it, she acted a little funny. Said hello, a couple of other things, then beat it the hell out of there. She didn't like finding a lawyer in her daddy's house, I'll tell you that."

"*Any* lawyer, or just you?" Half said. "You sure you wasn't staring at her tits or something? She might've wanted you to leave before you started drooling on her. I saw the broad yesterday, you know, she don't exactly look like no old maid."

"I don't have time for funny jokes," Bino said. "I can, you know I can be professional when the time comes. Jesus Christ, you think I'd be hitting on her with her father standing there?"

"You might if you thought he wasn't watching."

"Fuck you. Come on, Half, I'm in a hurry. I want everything there is to know about Ann Burns from the cradle up. In particular I want to know what her connection with Bleeder is. I could be wrong, but I don't think the tie-in is that Bleeder's fucking her."

"You hope. That way you might get a shot at her yourself."

"Ha, ha. Look, if I want a funny guy for an investigator I'll hire Steve Martin."

"Yeah, go ahead. Bet he can't get you the point spread every day."

"Well, you got a point," Bino said. "But, no shit, I can't afford to screw around with this. You got everything?"

Half made a couple of more notes and tore the sheet from the pad. "So far I do. What else? This is a lot to do."

"I know it's a lot to do," Bino said. "It's a *ton* to do. But I'll tell you. If this case involves even a third of what I think— and from the way Goldman acted this morning it does—then what you got to do there is just for starters."

Bino came out of Half's office and softly closed the door. Dodie bent over her desk and placed a silencing finger to her lips. Then she tucked her chin in a stern attitude and made two jerky motions with a clenched hand as though she were banging on her desk with an invisible hammer. Finally she pointed a red-nailed thumb, hitchhiker fashion, at Bino's office door.

He didn't get it. Did she want to take him in his own office and beat the shit out of him with a hammer? Sure, they'd had their differences lately, but . . .

He shook his head in confusion.

She wrote something down on a tablet, frowning in concentration as she did, then held the tablet in both hands and faced it in his direction. He stepped closer.

She'd written: The JUDGE is in there, dummy.

Oh. He nodded and went into his office.

Emmett Burns was wearing a three-piece brown suit with tiny blue pinstripes. His hands were clasped behind his back, and he was looking at the old basketball picture that hung on the wall behind Bino's brown imitation-leather couch. The judge's slightly graying auburn hair was center parted, and Bino didn't think that Burns looked near so much like a judge as he did an aging movie star.

"Morning, Emmett," Bino said. He'd almost called Burns "Your Honor." Being on a first-name basis with *this* guy was going to take some getting used to.

Burns's handshake was just right, something the judge probably practiced a lot. Emmett Burns wasn't going to get into a knuckle-crushing contest with anybody, but the firmness of his grip let you know that you were dealing with somebody who was used to being in charge. "Morning," Burns said, then, gazing at the picture on the wall, his voice softening slightly, he said, "That's your championship team, isn't it? The Final Four year?"

Bino gazed at the photo, at the much younger image of himself, complete with flattop haircut, as he'd held the giant conference trophy aloft; at Barney Dalton, minus rust mustache and wearing a flattop also, grinning like a possum as he reached upward to get his arm around Bino's shoulders. "Hell's bells, Emmett, I didn't know you were a fan," Bino said. He was surprised at himself, standing here talking to a federal judge as though the guy was an old drinking buddy, but then it dawned on him that Emmett Burns had the knack for making people deal with him in whatever manner the judge wanted them to. Bino said, "Yeah. Yeah, that was the year, okay. We had breaks out the ying-yang, I guess."

"Hell you say," Burns said. "You *made* a lot of breaks for yourselves. Nobody just *gets* breaks. You're what, six-six? That's short for a post man, even back when you were playing. Today you'd be a guard or forward. But I'll tell you something. You guys might've taken it all that year if you hadn't gotten hurt out in California. Against UCLA, wasn't it?"

Bino went around to sit behind his desk, trying not to get the big head over what Burns was saying but not being able to help it. Emmett Burns might be a dead-on-the-level guy, but he hadn't snared an appointment to the federal bench without knowing how to play a little politics. Hell, nobody did. "You've got one helluva memory, Emmett," Bino said. "Sure, UCLA. We'd never been up against anything down here in the Southwest Conference like that Alcindor, and to tell you the truth my ankle still hurts me sometimes. Here, sit down. Take a load off."

Burns did, crossing his legs and taking his pipe from his breast pocket. He produced a folded tobacco pouch from another pocket and began to fill the pipe. "You mind?"

Actually, Bino *did* mind. He smoked three, sometimes four filtered Camels a day himself, but never in his office because he didn't like the smell. It gave him the best of both worlds; he could join right in with the no-smoking freaks in pointing the finger, but when he was alone he could light one up and puff away. But anybody who thought Bino was going to tell Emmett Burns not to smoke had one too many holes in their head. With a smile that felt a whole lot weaker than he hoped it looked, Bino found a square glass ashtray and slid it across the desk in front of the judge. "Help yourself," he said.

Burns lit up and exhaled blue smoke. "Did you get my check?"

The smoke burned Bino's nostrils and caused his eyeballs to sting, but he kept on smiling. "It came in this morning's mail," he said. Dodie had called it "a *big* check." *Big* in Bino Phillips's operation was probably peanuts to a lot of guys, but Emmett Burns would have known the going rate and would have been pretty generous. And would damn sure expect his money's worth. "I appreciate it," Bino said.

"You won't for long," Burns said. "We're going to work our butts off."

A little warning bell tinkled in Bino's subconscious. Something about the way Emmett Burns had used the word *we*. Bino said, "I *expect* to work. I've already been over to the federal prosecutor's office this morning. Laying some groundwork."

"You've already . . . ?" Burns's forehead creased in a frown. "I don't know if I like that or not."

Uh, oh, Bino thought. So far he'd felt pretty intimidated representing a judge, but he was beginning to realize that somewhere he was going to have to draw the line. Yeah, Emmett Burns was a judge and a lawyer—lawyer, hell, he was one of the premier legal minds in the state—and as such was going to be a lot more hep to the system than the run-of-the-mill criminal client. But that was just what he was, a client, and a client who went around trying to call the shots and be his own lawyer was acting a fool. That might not be exactly the way they worded it in law school, but the gist was the same. Bino said merely, "Why not?"

"Because we need to talk things over first," Burns said. "You running around over there stirring them up might *get* me indicted, where if we let well enough alone they might just go away."

"Well, I don't do anything without putting a lot of thought into it," Bino said. "I had a pretty good idea who your prosecutor was going to be, if they were going to do anything. Marvin Goldman. So I went over and checked his water."

"Christ," Burns said. He reached out and emptied the bowl of his pipe into the ashtray, then put the pipe, stem first, into his pocket and stood. "Get your gear."

You're not thinking, Emmett, Bino thought. Underneath all the bluster and hard-nosed front, Emmett Burns was just another guy who knew he was under criminal investigation. Scared to death, almost on the verge of panic. Bino leaned back in his chair and touched his fingertips together. "Why? Where we going?"

"Why, over there to the Federal Building. To see Marvin. Hell, they're never going to seek any kind of indictment after they hear what I've got to say."

It was time. Time to take over. Or time to lose the client, Bino thought, he wasn't sure which. He had a quick mental image of the fee Burns had sent over, wings attached, fluttering away. "Well, okay, if that's what you want. Go on over, but you'll be going without me."

Burns pointed a finger. "Careful, now. You're working for me." He's forgetting himself, Bino thought, trying to throw his weight around. Which was a normal reaction under the circumstances.

Bino took a deep breath and plunged ahead. "No. No, I'm not. I'm *representing* you. If you want somebody to work for you, hire a butler. Sit back down."

Bino thought that it was a toss-up as to whether Burns would stalk out of the office or jump across the desk and punch him in the mouth. But the judge's reaction threw him. Burns's features sagged. So did his shoulders. He sank slowly down in the chair and in an instant seemed to age ten years. The stonewall front was beginning to crumble. Bino felt a twinge of guilt, but he wasn't about to let up now. He leaned forward over his desk.

"Of all people I shouldn't have to go over this with *you*," Bino said. "But I'm going to anyhow. You're a target, Emmett. You're somebody, and we're not sure exactly why as yet, but you're somebody they've decided to go after. There's not a guy walking around out there that the Feds can't charge with *something* if they've a mind to, and you know that as well as I do. So what happens if you go dancing over to the prosecutor's office? Well, Goldman's going to give you the red-carpet treatment. He's going to lock you in a closet with him and one of his flunky FBI's, they're going to give you all this pals-forever bullshit, and then the three of you are going to have a buddy-buddy session. Only when they finally get around to *indicting* you"—Bino felt his own tone of voice growing more tense, he was getting pretty excited himself—"and you go to trial, the FBI agent's going to take the stand and, guess what? Any similarity between what you and Marv and the FBI talked over and what that guy's going to *testify* that you said over there is going to be a pure coincidence. Anybody under investigation who gives those bastards the time of day has got rocks in his head. And you know I'm right, Emmett. So why you want to go over there and make an ass of yourself?"

Burns removed his pipe from his pocket and toyed with it. Something to keep his hands busy. Bino recalled the tough-guy act from last night, the show of strength in moving the table, the almost flippant attitude the judge had shown when he'd told about the pending charges. All a cover-up. Burns's eyes were now dead as marbles, his gaze vacantly on the edge of Bino's desk. "It's . . . ," Burns said. "I've got a problem with all this that maybe the average guy doesn't have. The trouble is that I know the system. I know what they can do, and it scares me."

"Sure it does," Bino said. "And it ought to. I'd probably be drunk somewhere, if I was you. All this shit is choreographed. All these hints—the chief judge taking you off the case, the guy across the hall telling you about it and acting like he's letting you in on something. Every one of 'em is in on it; hell, the U.S. Attorney and all those other judges have probably held a meeting. There isn't any reason for them to do all that, all they need to do is, boom, go over to the grand jury and get an indictment. Hell, the grand jury is a bunch of stooges; those people don't know anything about evidence. They indict whoever the prosecutor tells them to. So why all the hints? They're trying to panic you. And going over there and talking to Goldman would be jumping just the way they want you to jump."

"Yeah," Burns said. "Right through the old hoop. Christ, how can I be so dumb?"

"Dumb doesn't have anything to do with it. That bunch over there could shake up Job."

Burns cleared his throat. He held the pipe a little tighter in his fist, his features firming, his eyes taking on a little spark. "So what are you going to do? Play 'em close to the vest?"

"Now you're talking," Bino said. "Look, I got enough of a gist of what's going on to know that Goldman doesn't have much of a case. Now he's going on with the indictment, you can count on that. Somebody's told him to; old Marv isn't doing all this on his own. And you can expect a bunch of press coverage; Goldman would have Joan Lunden doing "Good Morning, America" from the courthouse lobby if he could figure out a way to get her to. But whatever we do, we're not going to go hollering around and make their case for 'em. Let 'em dig their own dirt."

Inwardly, Bino was breathing a sigh of relief. Instead of flying off the handle as he had halfway expected, Burns was simmering down. He was no longer talking "we." Taking on the Feds was enough of a hassle without fighting the client as well. Instead of blustering, Emmett Burns was now thinking. You could see the wheels turning. Bino was now wondering whether he should fill the judge in on seeing Bleeder over at Goldman's and had just about decided to do so when the intercom buzzed. Bino pressed the button, picked up the receiver, and said, "Yeah, Dodie?"

Her voice was almost a whisper. "I don't think the judge should hear this. A reporter's on the phone. Skip Turner, *Dallas Morning News*."

Bino hadn't noticed the blinking light that indicated a line on hold, but now he steadied his gaze on it as he said, "What makes you think so?"

"Think what?"

Jesus, how to say it. He glanced fleetingly at Burns, who was studying his folded hands. Bino said, "That . . . that *Half* shouldn't know about it."

"Half?"

"Dodie. Think hard, now."

"Oh, wow. I get it. The *judge*. Well, that's the first thing this Mr. Turner wanted to know, if you were representing Emmett Burns."

A prickly sensation rippled across Bino's scalp. "I'll take it out there, at your desk." He hung up, then said to Burns, "This is personal, Emmett. Won't take a minute."

Bino went briskly into the reception area, closing his office door behind him. Dodie punched the flashing button on her phone and handed him the receiver.

Bino put his free hand in his pocket. "Bino Phillips, Mr. Turner. I'm sort of tied up. What can I do for you?"

Bino'd met Turner briefly one other time, in the parking lot of Bino's apartment complex. Bino had been naked except for a towel around his middle and had just been doing his damnedest to shoot a guy named Buster Longley through the rear window of a pickup truck. It hadn't been a real neat meeting. Now Turner said, "I hope I haven't caught you after your shower again."

"I said I'm *tied up*, Mr. Turner."

"No sense of humor. Okay, one question. A source of mine says Judge Emmett Burns is going to be indicted in an hour or so. Any comment?"

Already. Bino's shoulders drooped. "When did Goldman call you?" he asked.

"I didn't say who called me. Any comment?"

"None for you. I've got a comment for Goldman, when I see him."

Turner's chuckle was slightly metallic. "I'll put you down in my story for a 'declined comment.' That may be a new nickname for you someday. 'Declined Comment' Phillips. How about that?"

"Suits me," Bino said.

Turner hung up without saying good-bye.

Bino gently recradled the receiver and looked helplessly at Dodie for a moment. Then he headed back into the office to tell Burns about the call. He'd as soon have taken a beating.

6

Judy Roo told Daryl Siminian that when she had been fifteen, she'd let her uncle finger-fuck her so he'd take her from Corsicana to Dallas. It wasn't like he was her *real* uncle or anything; he was just this guy who'd married her Aunt Mavis, her mother's sister, and he'd been wanting to get away from Mavis just as badly as Judy Roo had been wanting to run away from home. It happened during the fall, Judy remembered, during about the fourth occasion on which Judy's mom was down in the county jail for writing hot checks around the supermarkets. Things weren't looking so good. The same misdemeanor prosecutor who'd handled Judy's mom's other hot-check cases was the assistant DA assigned to the current matter, and this time he'd enhanced Judy's mom's charges into a felony based on the past record. The prosecutor was being pretty hardheaded about the whole thing, not offering any reasonable plea-bargain deal, and it was beginning to look as though Judy's mom was headed for some penitentiary time. With none of her immediate family left at home, Judy decided that she'd go up to Big D and try to make her own way in the world.

So she went right up to this guy, her stepuncle (James was the guy's name, around thirty-five and not too bad looking except that his two front teeth were missing and a pretty good bricklayer when he felt like working), one afternoon when he was sitting on the porch. James was drinking beer while he listened to an AM country station on his portable radio, one of the old-timey white plastic models that used big round glass tubes instead of transistors and worked on size D flashlight batteries. Judy stood barelegged on the porch and asked James to take her up to Dallas and drop her off someplace downtown.

"Shee-it," James said. "That's thirty miles. Ain't no gas in my truck, who's gonna pay for it?"

That's when Judy made her proposition about letting James finger-fuck her in exchange for the lift. She wasn't exactly sure where she'd gotten the idea; Judy had always had a pretty good imagination, and the thought had popped into her head the previous evening while she'd been cooking French fries and noticed James looking at her bottom with his mouth set sort of funny. Letting James stick his finger in her wouldn't really be anything new to Judy. She'd already allowed four or five boys down at the junior high (Judy had been in the eighth grade at the time, even though she was already fifteen; she wasn't really *dumb*, but she had been sort of a slow learner) try to make her come using their middle digits, but she had made up her mind that she was going to stay a virgin for a couple more years.

On hearing the proposition, James took his feet down from the porch railing and let his wrought-iron chair come to rest on all four legs. "How I know you won't tell nobody? You're unnerage."

Judy had assured James, she told Daryl now, that she wouldn't tell anyone and that she'd do *anything* (except let him put his *business* in her, of course) in order to get to Dallas, that's how badly she wanted to go. James had gotten off his ass in a hurry, found a few dollars for gas in Mavis's purse (Aunt Mavis had been the only family member with a job at the time, and she'd been away at work down to the Dairy Queen), and away they'd gone.

When Judy had told James he could finger-fuck her along the way, she hadn't really meant the *whole* way, but that was how James had taken it. He forced her to sit close to him in the rattly Ford pickup's cab with her feet on the dash and her knees spread apart while he steered with one hand and fooled with her twat with the other. There were a couple of times when Judy was afraid that the pickup was going to jump the median and have a head-on collision, because it looked to her like James was paying more attention to his finger-fucking than he was to his driving. Anyway, by the time they got to Dallas, Judy was pretty sore.

At this point in Judy's story, Daryl Siminian said, "Why are you telling me all this?" He was on his naked belly, propped up with his elbows digging into the mattress through the sheet.

"Well you *ast* me," Judy said.

"No, I didn't."

"You did, too. You ast me how long I been in Dallas. Just a minute ago you did." Judy was sitting upright against the headboard with her ankles crossed Indian style. She was wearing beige bikini panties; the elastic band that encircled her waist and held her sanitary napkin in place was visible through the thin material. Jesus Christ, Daryl thought, the broad didn't even bother to take off her white athletic socks last night.

"Well, yeah, I did ask you *that*," Daryl said. "But that question only takes a short answer like 'one year' or 'six months.' You know? Not all of that other shit." He turned his head, rested his cheek on his folded hands, and looked out the window. The drapes were open a slit, just enough to let some light in. Outside, most of the snow had melted; only aprons of white remained around the edges of the motel lawn. Airport Freeway had small piles of dirty slush on its surface, and the passing cars made swishing noises. Beyond the freeway, on the stretch of lawn that marked the entrance to Texas Stadium, someone had built a snowman with a carrot for a nose. The snowman stood dripping and melting like a stack of soaked cotton balls.

"I can't tell what you want, Daryl," Judy said. "You ain't being fair. I thought you wanted to get to know me, and the only way to get to know somebody is to know somethin' about their background."

Background? Jesus, Daryl thought, this broad doesn't have any background. He rolled onto his back and clasped his hands behind his head. "Look. Yeah, okay, knowing something about you might be kind of interesting. But every time I ask you something you got to give an answer that's half-assed kinky. Last night I asked if you wanted to go somewhere with me you started telling me about your period. Then we come out here to this motel and started getting it on, and, don't get me wrong, that was okay. But then just as you were going down on me you asked me if I wanted you to swallow it or spit it out. Jesus Christ, don't ask me, I'm not doing the swallowing *or* the spitting. Now then, I just want to know how long you been living around here, you start talking about somebody finger-fucking you. *Finger-fucking*, that's what you call it. Can't you think of another word even? Somebody that's got to say something dirty all the time . . . well, it's pretty disgusting, tell you the truth. You know?"

She brought one knee up and hugged her shin. "Am I makin' you mad?"

"I didn't say mad. I said disgusting."

"Well I say what I mean. What's disgustin' about that? Some people don't say what they think. Some people keep stuff hid."

Daryl's chin moved slightly to one side. He sat up and faced her. "What do you mean by that?"

Judy's gaze shifted, just the barest flicker, but enough. "I don't mean nothin'."

Daryl swiveled his head. The top bureau drawer was open a crack. Not taking his gaze away from the dresser, he said, "What do you fucking mean by that?"

She sniffled. She didn't answer.

Daryl leaped to his feet. He came around the bed and grabbed Judy's arm. Jesus, nothing pissed Daryl off like a foulmouthed broad, unless it was a *nosy* foulmouthed broad. He hauled her to her feet and twisted his fingers in her hair. "You looked at them, didn't you?" he said.

"Daryl . . . God fuckin' *damn*, Daryl, you let—"

Still twisting her hair, hearing her gasps, her little breathy sobs, he herded her step by step over to the dresser. He opened the drawer wide and flopped a stack of eight-by-ten color photos on the top of the bureau. "Well let's *both* look at the fuckers again," he said.

She pulled away from him. He could have held her easily, but he let her go. She stood a few feet away, her chest rising and falling, her small pink nipples erect. "I didn' mean nothin'. You was asleep. But you carryin' *those* around and then givin' me a ration of shit about the way I talk . . . well it just ain't fair."

He put his hands on his hips and looked down past his flat, muscled belly, past his hairy crotch and semierection, at his bare toes on the carpet. "What's wrong with them?" he said.

"What's *wrong* with 'em?" Braver now, she stepped forward and thumbed through the photos, slapping them down one at a time. "Ain't nothin' wrong, I guess. This one he's eatin' her pussy . . . here she's givin' him a blow job, Jesus, you can see her asshole . . . now this one here's a real beauty, right up the ol' dirt road, huh? Ain't nothin' *wrong* with 'em, Daryl, it's just that you're runnin' around with *those* and puttin' me down for the way I talk. That's all."

He sat down on the bed and spread his hands out flat behind him. "Well, somebody might have those pictures for another reason. Not just because they're a *pervert*. You know?"

"Sure. *Sure*, Daryl."

"I mean it. Look at her."

"Look at who?" Judy sniffed and folded her arms across her bare breasts.

"The girl in the pictures. Come to think about it, I want you to look at her good. What do you notice about her?"

She bent forward over the bureau, still hugging herself. "She's got a little bitty mouth. Shit, she can't get but half of it in."

"What else?"

"Daryl, this is . . . holy shit, silly. She's got red hair on her pussy, iffen it ain't dyed. That what you're talkin' about?"

"And on her head, too. Right?" He sat forward, hands on his knees, watching her.

"Well, yeah," she said. "I think redheads look sort of funny neckid, myself. Skin too white."

"Maybe they do. But look at her *face*, Judy. You're giving me an idea. Remember what she looks like, 'cause pretty soon you're going to see her in person. I think you can help me out. You know?"

Judy picked up the pictures and studied them more closely. "I ain't posin' for no porno pictures, Daryl." She dropped the photos and looked at him. "Leastways not any where I'm gettin' it up the ass. I got a little pride, Daryl, I ain't no whore or nothin'."

7

One look at the herd of reporters and photographers gathered around outside the Grand Jury Room at the Federal Building told Bino that he and Emmett Burns shouldn't have come within a city block of the place. Emmett Burns wasn't the only one who wasn't thinking straight; Bino could lay the blame for *this* fuckup right on his own shoulders.

Actually, Bino's thinking hadn't been that bad. His gut reaction to Skip Turner's phone call—once he'd filled Burns in on what the reporter had had to say, and then had spent a few minutes calming the judge down—had been to charge over to the grand jury and put Burns on the witness stand. *Force* Goldman to let the judge testify; hell, it was Burns's right. And anybody would have to admit that hearing his side of the story told in Emmett Burns's straightforward manner, backed up by the judge's steady, level gaze, would make a grand juror think twice before voting to indict the guy. No, Bino's thinking had been pretty good under the circumstances. It was just that he hadn't counted on what Marvin Goldman was going to do.

As Bino and the judge stepped quickly off the elevator and rounded the corner in the direction of the Grand Jury Room, Goldman was finishing off a lecture. He was standing amid a cluster of newspeople—Bino recognized a few of the newshounds: short-haired, Ivy League Skip Turner, of course; at Turner's elbow one older, grizzled reporter who in the old days had covered SMU basketball for the *Herald* but since Watergate had turned into an investigative journalist along with a million others; and Susie Sin (which *had* to be an assumed name), the dark-haired, dancing-eyed Oriental anchorperson from Channel 5, whom Bino'd always thought was quite a dish—with one arm upraised like George Bush on tour. On Goldman's right stood the same red-faced guy who'd delivered the file to Goldman during Weedy Clements's trial. The guy's dark green suit was gone; in its place he wore a severely cut navy ensemble, matching Goldman's suit in color. When Goldman saw Bino, the prosecutor stopped in midsentence and stared. One by one, the newspeople's heads began to turn.

Bino said, out of the side of his mouth, "Uh-oh. Maybe we'd better retreat."

Too late. Susie Sin said, "It's the judge himself. And Mr. . . . the lawyer." Then, to a man in shirtsleeves who had a portable video camera, "Angle in on them, Freddy."

The man raised his camera and pointed it. Bino considered *really* giving the guy a scoop by going over and punching Goldman, then thought better of it. Instead he raised his voice and said, "My client's here to testify, Marv. When can you put him on?"

Goldman did his best to look regretful, but he wasn't fooling Bino. Goldman was tickled to death. "Testify?" he said. "I'm sorry, but you're too late, buddy. The foreman's already returned a true bill. They're typing up the final copy of the indictment right now." His gaze darted fleetingly at Emmett Burns; then the prosecutor lowered his eyes.

At Bino's side, the judge said, "Now *hold on*, here. You can't just—"

Bino squeezed Burns's elbow. The guy beside Goldman— the guy *had* to be an FBI agent, Bino decided, and probably Goldman's grand jury witness as well—was whispering something in the prosecutor's ear. Goldman's brows were furrowed in thought.

Bino stepped forward. "Now come on, Marv. Jesus Christ, the guy isn't going anywhere."

Goldman waved the agent away. "Yeah, okay, forget it. There's going to be an arraignment, of course." Bino had been right. Goldman had actually been thinking about having Burns arrested, right there. Had probably decided that it wouldn't look good on TV. The sonofabitch, Bino thought.

From within the cluster of reporters, Skip Turner said loudly, "Any comment, Judge?" He was wearing a green-and-gray checkered sport coat, pale yellow shirt, and green tie. His pen was ready over his notepad.

The former sportswriter—Grimes, Bino remembered, formerly known as Grimy around the locker room but now going under the byline "Torrance"—chimed in. "What plea will you enter, sir?"

Emmett Burns cleared his throat. "I—"

A clear, strong female voice interrupted. "Judge, do you think that undercover payments to jurists are common throughout the system?"

The question had come from Susie Sin. She was wearing a dark beige dress that showed her knees to good advantage and brown high-heeled shoes. Her almond-shaped eyes were narrowed. *Terry and the Pirates*, Bino thought. The Dragon Lady, moving in for the kill.

Burns squared his shoulders and stood erect. "I don't know of any. None have come to me, you can bet on that."

"Did anybody say that you *have* received illegal payments?" Susie Sin now looked suspiciously back and forth from Bino to Burns.

Bino decided that he was going to have to do something to pull Burns's chestnuts out of the fire. For the time being, anyway. In the judge's current state of mind, somebody like Susie Sin would eat him for lunch. Bino stepped between Burns and the reporters. "My client has no comment at this time."

If this were happening in the movies, Bino thought, right now about half the newspeople would come running up to him, firing questions and poking microphones in his face, while the rest would go barging down the hall and get into a free-for-all over use of the pay phone. But it wasn't the movies. Susie Sin folded her arms and regarded Bino as though he were a blind date and she'd just realized when he showed up at her door that he had terminal halitosis.

"And what's *your* name, sir?" she asked coolly. "For the viewing audience."

"I know him, Susie," Skip Turner said. " 'Declined Comment' Phillips. Jockstrap, ran into a phone booth one day and came out as a lawyer." One corner of Turner's mouth lifted in a crooked grin.

Now Susie Sin turned her gaze on Turner and to Bino's satisfaction gave the Ivy League reporter a look that the teacher's pet generally reserved for the prime dunce-cap candidate. Even Turner cringed. Man, this gal was in *charge*. Was she ever. To Bino, Susie Sin said, "I've heard of you, Mr. Phillips. First name Bino, isn't it? To go with your . . . hair. How about it, Mr. Phillips? Any comment?"

Bino hesitated. He was pretty sure that they were going to barbecue Emmett Burns in the paper and on TV no matter *what* Bino had to say (any media person who'd been sympathetic to the defense in the past was automatically left off the list when Goldman called the press together), but he also thought that if he handled things up to snuff here, they might keep the fire down to a simmer. Bino put on his best I'm-with-you-guys smile and said, "Hey, look. We want to cooperate with the press all we can. But to tell you the truth I haven't even seen the indictment as yet. Hell's bells, I don't even know what my client is charged with. Tell you what. Give us a day or so to go over things and we might call a press conference. Okay?"

The Dragon Lady checked a tiny, expensive-looking gold watch. "When?" One spike-heeled foot did a toe tap. Beyond her, Goldman and the FBI agent looked as though they were enjoying themselves. Bino wondered briefly how often Goldman sent bonbons over to Susie Sin.

Burns said, in a loud whisper, "I don't like the way this is going. I'm going to talk to them."

Bino glanced over his shoulder. Burns was holding up pretty well, but a few signs of strain were beginning to peep through the mask. No wonder. Bino thought that if all this was happening to *him*, just about now they'd be fitting him for a straitjacket. He winked at Burns and said evenly, "Right now it'd be suicide. They don't really want to listen to what you have to say. They just want you to utter some words so they can twist them around to make them mean whatever they want. Let me handle it."

Burns licked his lips, started to say something, then closed his mouth. Then he said grimly, "You're calling the shots."

Before Burns could change his mind, Bino turned to Goldman. "What about the arraignment? When?" Bino said.

"It'll have to be soon," Goldman said. "We need to get the matter of bail worked out. Tomorrow, say one o'clock? I think I can dig up a magistrate by then."

"Good," Bino said. "Tell you what, Miss Sin. Have your crew down here tomorrow. By then we'll know what we're looking at and we'll give you a statement."

That seemed to satisfy the Dragon Lady for the time being. At least she had Freddy put his camera away and began to stow her own things in an enormous beige purse. Bino decided to get the hell out of there before she changed her mind and started firing questions again. As he steered Burns in the direction of the elevators, a hand firmly grasped Bino's forearm. He turned.

It was Grimes, the old sportswriter. There were deep creases that ran from his nose diagonally to the corners of his mouth. "Long time, Bino," Grimes said. "Hey, let's have lunch. Maybe kick around old times." He looked furtively around him, then leaned closer and whispered, "Come on. I need a break."

Bino eyed Grimes. "You're too late, Grimy. Eighteen years too late. I can't even touch the rim anymore."

On the elevator ride to the ground floor, Bino said casually, "By the way, Emmett. Do you know Frank Bleeder?" He tried to make the question sound like an afterthought.

The judge seemed distant, almost as though Bino wasn't even standing there. He said, "Bleeder? Yes . . . attorney, isn't he?" No shock. No tremor in his voice. No furtive shifting of his gaze.

Emmett Burns was either dead on the level or the best fucking actor that Bino had ever run across. As the elevator doors rumbled open to reveal the lobby, Bino hoped it wasn't the latter. Burns was in for a lot of grief if Goldman could find a crack in the armor.

After lunch—which consisted of Polish sausage and steamy sauerkraut at the Blue Front Restaurant, and during which Emmett Burns toyed with his food and stared off into space quite a bit—Bino sent the judge home. He had a lot to do, and at this point Burns would only be in the way. "Tomorrow's tomorrow, who knows?" Bino said. "What you need to do is think about what to say to the newspaper guys." Burns had lost a lot of his get-up-and-go; he nodded docilely and wandered off as if in a daze. Bino made a mental note to have a talk with Ann Burns, to tell her to keep an eye on her dad. In addition to some other things he might want to talk to her about. As he hustled down Main Street, folding his trench coat over his arm—the temperature had soared into the fifties and the sun was beaming down—Bino wondered fleetingly how Half was making out.

At the office, Dodie's attitude wavered between frigid and lukewarm. Oh, she was being a crackerjack secretary as usual, handling files and taking calls and never missing a beat, but every once in a while there was a sharpness to her tone of voice accompanied by a defiant tilt to her chin. Bino decided that it was going to be a while before she cooled off completely.

Around one-thirty she buzzed him on the intercom. When he answered she said, "Phone for you," and clicked abruptly off the line.

Bino gazed at the blinking light for a second, then called Dodie back. He had to buzz her twice before she picked up her receiver and said, "What is it?"

"You forgot to tell me who's calling, Dode."

"No, I didn't," she said.

"Yes, you did. I don't have the slightest idea who it is."

"I didn't say I told you who it was. I said I didn't *forget* to tell you."

Life without Dodie would be tough, but she was doing her damnedest to make it imaginable. He said, "Cute. *Cute*, Dodie. Who's calling?"

"Mr. Bainbridge, the—"

"*Who?*"

"—management company guy."

"Oh. *That* Bainbridge. I thought I told you to talk to him for me," Bino said.

"You did," Dodie said.

"Then why's he calling *me*?"

" 'Cause I didn't." She hung up.

His neck reddening, Bino reached into a side drawer and took out a stack of legal-size papers that were the prospective lease on offices in the new building. The one they were going to build after they blew the Davis Building to smithereens. He pressed the flashing button and said, "Bino Phillips."

Bainbridge sounded over the phone like a game-show host.

Bino'd never seen the guy, but he pictured a wide, smiling mouth with big white teeth suspended in midair over a polka-dot bow tie with tiny red lights blinking on either side of the knot. Bainbridge said, "Well, busy man. You're a hard one to catch."

"Yes, sir, well, I've been . . . running around, you know how it is. Look, I've gone over the lease. It looks okay, but I don't see any provision for where we're going to stay while the new building's going up."

"Not to worr-eee, Mr. Phillips. It's all arranged. We're providing suitable interim space for you in one of our other buildings. At the same rent you're paying now, of course."

Bino pictured unpainted, rotting wood floors, a rusty fan creaking in the window, rats scrambling and squeaking in the ceiling, and a sign at the front door of the building that read "Dallas—40 miles," with an arrow pointing to the north. "Oh, I'm sure it'll be a nice stopgap office," Bino said. "One more thing. How does this new lease affect my present arrangement? In case the plans should fall through and they leave the Davis Building standing as is." He tried not to sound hopeful but didn't quite put it over.

"Leave it standing?" Bainbridge gave a dry laugh. "That couldn't happen. The ducks are all in a row, and I don't think the Davis Building would stay even if Martin Tower doesn't go through. I think the city would condemn the junky old rattletrap, if you'll pardon my French."

Junky old . . . ? Bino felt an edge creeping into his tone as he said, "Well let me think it over for a few days."

"A *few days*? Act *now*, Mr. Phillips. We're letting you in on the ground floor. Tell you what, I'll have my man drop the original of the lease over and you can sign it. Have a nice day, Mr. Phillips."

"A nice . . . ? Look here, Bainbridge, I haven't made up my—"

The line was dead. Bino held the receiver in a death grip for a moment, then buzzed Dodie.

She said, "Are you through with your call?"

"Yeah, I'm going to—"

"Good. There's a man out here with some papers for you."

Jesus Christ. Bainbridge must've gotten his start as a door-to-door encyclopedia salesman. Bino slammed the phone into its cradle and strode purposefully toward the outer office. No high-pressure sonofabitch was going to run over old Hard-nose Phillips.

He burst into the reception area and said, "Now listen, you can tell Bainbridge to—"

Dodie's blue eyes were wide in a question. Goldman's sidekick, the red-faced FBI agent, was standing across the desk from her. He was holding a sheaf of letter-size, typewritten pages that were stapled together in the upper-left-hand corner.

The agent said, "Who the hell is Bainbridge?"

Bino expelled air from his lungs. "Nobody. A . . . client. What can I do for you?"

The agent held the papers out. "Mr. Goldman sent me over. It's the indictment in the Burns case. You know, the judge? He's your client, too, at least he was this morning." He showed Bino a shit-eating grin. "You really ought to take it easy, Mr. Phillips. You got too many irons in the fire, it looks like to me."

Bino finished reading the indictment over for the third time, then stacked the papers in an uneven pile on his desktop, put four fingers of each hand over his eyelids, and rubbed them. Hell, he *still* didn't know what the charges were. He had Dodie bring him a fresh cup of coffee—she carried the steaming black liquid in a Styrofoam cup and showed him a final haughty twitch with her backside as she left—then looked down from his window for a moment at the tiny cars streaming back and forth on Main Street. As he watched a pickup truck, a blue one with a white top, sideswiped a little red foreign make that was turning left onto Main. The drivers got out and faced each other with hands on hips. Finally Bino returned to his desk, leaned back, raised his legs and crossed his ankles on the desk's corner, picked up the indictment, and looked it over again.

He wondered if the damn thing would make more sense if he read it aloud. He tried it.

"Count Two. On or about January 12, 1987, in the Northern District of Texas, Emmett Randall Burns, in furtherance of the aforementioned scheme"—Jesus Christ, thought Bino, why does it always have to be a *scheme*? A *plan*, maybe? Hell, they mean the same thing—"with intent to defraud and to obtain money, and intending to do so, did knowingly and willingly cause an envelope to be placed in a depository for United States Mail, said envelope addressed to the United States District Clerk, Earle Cabell Federal Building, Dallas, Texas 75202, a violation of the United States Code, Title 18, Section 1341."

So *that's* what he did, Bino thought. All the time that Bino had figured Judge Emmett Burns for a pretty good old boy, the conniving schemer had been going around putting envelopes in mailboxes! Marv Goldman sure had the judge by the balls, okay. Good ole Marv, protector of the citizens. Can't have these scheming bastards going around mailing letters, no sirree. Hell, even worse, Emmett Burns was *causing* letters to be mailed. Didn't even have the guts to do it yourself, huh, Emmett? Ought to get twice as much time in the joint for going around *causing* people to mail letters.

But what was the fucking *scheme*? Bino thumbed through the pages and went back to the introduction. Basically, after wading through five pages of gobbledygook that used the words *scheme, artifice*, and *defraud* a total of forty-two times, Bino had deciphered this: The government was claiming that Emmett Burns had schemed to use his position as U.S. district judge to obtain money, and that he had met with Frank Bleeder and had conspired to run around causing a bunch of letters to be mailed in furtherance of the scheme. Conspiracy, one count. Mail fraud, five counts. Total of thirty years' penitentiary time if they convicted Burns of everything and got him the maximum sentence on each count. Boy, were those scheming, conspiring letter mailers ever in for it!

Wait a minute, thought Bino. Bleeder was over there conspiring with Marvin Goldman just this morning. How about *that* for a fucking scheme, huh? Maybe Bino should blow the whistle on Goldman. Nope, it would never work. Then he'd have to talk Goldman into indicting himself. Never get off the ground.

The long and the short of it was that Goldman had slipped the indictment through without revealing exactly what crime he was claiming that Emmett Burns had committed. And you could bet that Goldman wouldn't tell just what the charges were without some encouragement, say in the form of a court order. No, Goldman would like for the defense to wander around in the dark until the trial, and then it would be too late. Bino made a note that his first order of business, right after the arraignment tomorrow, was going to be a clarifying motion, something to force Goldman to tell him exactly what the defendant had done. Taken bribes? From who? For doing what? Jesus, if the government could get away with putting out this kind of garbage, why didn't they just do away with written indictments altogether?

He buzzed Dodie and told her to call Emmett Burns for him.

She said, "Did you break your dialing finger?"

"It's strategy, Dode. Look, I want the judge to know I've got his indictments, but I don't want to have to go over them over the phone. Hell, I don't even know what the charges are all about yet. If *I* talk to Emmett, he's going to give me the third degree. But you can play dumb. Just tell him . . . the arraignment tomorrow is at one; tell him to come down to the office at eleven-thirty. Maybe I'll have something to tell him by then. Okay?"

"I guess I can handle that," she said. She wasn't really being *testy* about it, but there was a slight edge to her tone.

"Good girl. Now then, whatever I'm doing, if Half calls I want you to interrupt me. I need to talk to him." Bino watched a fly circle lazily, then light on the rim of his Styrofoam coffee cup. There weren't supposed to *be* any flies in December.

Slowly, carefully, holding the receiver between his shoulder and jaw and remaining perfectly still except for his hands and arms, Bino picked up a copy of *Football News* that lay on his desk and rolled it into a cylinder.

"Half's *already* called," Dodie said.

"Dodie . . ." Bino clapped one hand to his forehead. The fly hightailed it, buzzing across the office to the window and lighting on the sill. It directed its huge eyes in Bino's direction and rubbed its forelegs together. Bino wondered fleetingly whether this was a fly's version of the finger.

On the line, Dodie sniffed. "I guess I can't do anything right. Wow, you've shut yourself up in there like you were plotting a prison break . . . if I'd have put Half through you would have yelled at me for *that*."

Bino felt a quick rush of guilt. "I apologize, Dode, I'm just . . . What did Half say?" He eyeballed the distance from where he was sitting to the windowsill. The fly was safe for now.

"Well," Dodie said. "First he had me go into his office and use the black phone, to call Pop and get some current point spreads. Then I came back to my desk and read them to Half."

Bino took a shallow breath. "What else?"

"Then he left a number for you. Where you can reach him."

He picked up a ballpoint and tore a corner from one of the pages in Emmett Burns's indictment. "Well now we're getting somewhere."

She gave Bino the number, then said, "You had another call, besides Half. *Ann* Burns. Who's she?"

"She's the . . ." Bino paused to let that one sink in. Why would Ann Burns be calling him? Unless she knew about the indictment. Hell, it had probably been all over the radio by now. Hopefully Emmett Burns had had a chance to break the news to her before she'd found out elsewhere. "The judge's daughter," Bino said. "Let's put her on hold for now, Dode. I don't want to talk to her until I can find out what Half's been doing. Call the judge for me, okay?"

He disconnected, then watched the button on the phone relight, probably Dodie calling Burns. Bino got on an unoccupied line and called the number that Half had left. It was a North Dallas exchange, a number Bino didn't recognize. After two rings a gruff male voice answered, saying, "Yeah."

"Horace Harrison, please," Bino said.

"*Horace?*"

"Half-a-Point."

The guy went away. In a few seconds, Half said on the line, "Make it quick. I'm dealing."

"*Dealing?* I thought you were investigating."

"Bino. I already did." There was a pause, followed by Half's muffled voice—probably he was holding his hand over the mouthpiece—saying, "Pass me. This'll take a minute." Then, clearly, "Bleeder represented one guy in Burns's court, guy name of Thorndon. I got that from Billy, down at the clerk's office. Billy still owes me a little from football, you know how it is. He remembered the deal with Thorndon and Bleeder real good."

The Thorndon case again. The same one about which Emmett Burns had gotten a call from Buford Jernigan in the U.S. prosecutor's office. The same case that had gotten a rise out of Marvin Goldman when Bino had mentioned it that morning. Bino wondered fleetingly how he'd ever passed a college math course. Hell, he couldn't even put two and two together. He said, "What did Billy remember? And who the hell *is* Billy, anyway? I thought we made a deal about you taking bets from anybody who works for the county or the Feds. Talk about shitting in your mess kit."

"Now hold on. I didn't make no deal about guys that were already betting me. Just *new* guys. And Billy don't count. Jesus, the guy calls me three or four times a day, what do you want me to do?"

"How many others are there? Guys that don't count." Bino spotted the fly again. It had taken up residence on his team photo and was just crossing the bridge of Barney Dalton's nose.

"Oh, one or two. Look, Bino, you want to talk about Emmett Burns or you want to talk about my customers? I don't say nothing about your clients. Hey, you got some real fuckheads for clients, how'd you like it if I went around saying that all the time?"

"It isn't the same . . . Oh, shit. You were telling me about Billy. What was it made the Thorndon deal stick out in his . . . mind?"

"Well this— Naw, hey. Deal around me again, I'll catch up on the ante. Okay. Bino? Anyway, this Thorndon was big in the hot-car business. They tell me he still is. Cars *and* parts, got them coming in from up north, Chicago, shit, all over. And get this, when the case comes up in Burns's court, Thorndon had been to the joint three times already. Figured to be the nuts to get twenty or thirty years. Billy says this Bleeder's the last guy he would've figured to be Thorndon's lawyer. This fucking Thorndon got connects, the kind of guy you'd figure to waltz into the courtroom with Phil Burleson or somebody. Shit, Fred Bruner, Charlie Tessmer, some big-shot lawyer like that. Even Bino Phillips, Billy said, only don't you start getting no big head over it."

"Get to the point, Half. Hell, I've got a bar association roster right here in my desk drawer." Bino took a sip of coffee. It had cooled, almost to room temperature. He thought about asking Dodie to bring him another cup, then decided to leave well enough alone.

"I'm getting to it," Half said. "So anyway, Thorndon hires Bleeder, and the next thing, guess what? The fucking guy is *walking*. Zappo, right out in the street. One day the Feds drop the charges, the next day Thorndon is over in state court copping a plea. For *probation*, yet. Shit, Thorndon figured about as much a candidate for probation as Lee Harvey Oswald. But he damn sure got it."

Probation. Bino wondered whether Emmett Burns had known what Thorndon's state sentence had been. Probably not; judges didn't keep up with what happened to dismissed cases. Burns had told Bino about dismissing Thorndon's federal case, but not . . . Distantly, Bino said, "What did you come up with on Bleeder? How much he's gambling, all that shit. And what about Ann Burns?"

"I ain't sure about the girl," Half said. "I'm hearing one thing and then another. There's this guy Stanley, works at the county records office. You know, Stanley the Stiff."

"Jesus Christ, Half, not another bettor."

"Stanley the Stiff? Naw, a bettor's a guy tries to pick winners. Stanley the Stiff couldn't pick a winner if there was only one team playing. You want to know what I found out from Stanley?"

Bino watched the fly mosey across his own flattop haircut, over on the wall in the photo. "Look, Half, and I'm really not putting your customers down. But does it ever occur to you that we might need to use some of these guys as *witnesses*? In front of a jury? Stanley the Stiff, Jesus. I go, 'Please state your name for the record,' Goldman hollers, 'Don't forget the Stiff part.' "

"Good thinking, Bino," Half said. "Only the fucking *mayor* don't happen to know anything which I'm trying to find out. Anyhow, Stanley says that Ann Burns had her name changed back from Satterwhite. Did it legal, papers and all. She brought along a Cook County, Illinois, divorce decree. From a guy name of Eddie Satterwhite. I don't know anything about him right now, but I'm working on it."

"Working through who? Richard the Rat?"

"I don't know no Richard the Rat. He another stiff?" Half said.

"Skip it. I'm being funny," Bino said.

"No you ain't. Look, this Bleeder ain't got no gambling *habit*, exactly. It's more like a monkey on his back. I mean, this guy really takes off. You and me and Barney are gonna see it tonight, firsthand. I got to take Barney along. Shit, he might win something; then he can pay me what he owes me."

"We're going to see it firsthand where?" Bino asked.

"The old Spring Valley Tennis Club. You know, the joint

that went bankrupt. They're setting up a floater out there tonight, you know, some stand-up craps, sit-down twenty-one. I don't guess I have to tell you who's running the game.''

No, Half didn't. Bino already knew. The same guy who had his finger in all the rest of the gambling in town. Dante Tirelli, who also happened to be married to Annabelle, Bino's ex. Oh, there'd be some different faces dealing the cards and handling the sticks on the galloping dominoes. But Tirelli would be behind it all, you could bet on that. Bino'd heard that Tirelli's games had taken on an eastern flavor. Seemed Tirelli had some new partners, out of New York. Bino said, ''I think I know. Italian guy, huh?''

''Bingo. It's a private deal, invitation only. Bleeder's going to be there with bells on. I . . . well, wrangled us a pass. Between you and me, Bino, that's why I'm taking Barney along. Shit, the two of *us* can't get invited, we ain't big enough suckers. So meet me at eight, Joe Miller's Bar. Me and Barney.''

The fly was suddenly airborne, swooping over and lighting on Bino's desk. He said, ''I'll be there,'' reached for the *Football News*, and began to roll it up.

''Oh, and one more thing,'' Half said.

''What's that?''

''Back to the Thorndon deal, and Emmett Burns. Now this is strictly rumor, Bino. From some guys around I sort of know. But word is that just before he cut his deal with the Feds and state, Thorndon was waving some money around. Wanting to pay somebody off.''

''Interesting,'' Bino said. ''Evidently he didn't get around to offering it to my client. At least Judge Burns didn't say anything about it, and I think he would.''

''Yeah, maybe,'' Half said. ''But that ain't the word. Word is that Burns *did* take the money. That's what they're saying around anyway.''

Bino tossed the *Football News* into the air. It flopped onto the desk. The fly buzzed away.

8

Bino showed up at Joe Miller's fifteen minutes late, and it was a big mistake. The extra quarter hour gave Barney Dalton enough time to down a couple of extra Scotch and waters. Then Barney insisted on lugging a roadie along, a double mixed in a large Styrofoam cup with "7-Eleven" stamped on its side in red and green letters. To make matters even worse, Barney also insisted on driving. Bino left the Linc parked at Joe Miller's and rode between Barney and Half. He spent most of the twenty-minute trip either closing his eyes and jamming an imaginary brake pedal to the floor or mopping his pants leg with a handkerchief whenever some of Barney's drink sloshed out over the cup's edge.

At the clubhouse entrance to the Spring Valley Tennis Club, Barney said to the doorman, "So I'm Dalton. Where's the action?"

The doorman, an athletic-looking guy of around thirty who had a slim nose and a full head of dark, wavy hair and who was wearing a black tux, white shirt, and black bow tie, folded his hands at the hem of his coat and said offhandedly in a strong New York accent, "Oh? What action is that, sir?"

Bino stood behind Barney and off to one side on the cement porch. He'd worn a houndstooth sport coat over a navy velour shirt and tan slacks. The parking lot was loaded with fifty or so Caddys, Mercedeses, and even one Bentley in addition to Barney's midnight-blue, five-year-old Monte Carlo. The grounds of the club were bathed in bright moonlight. Beyond the parking lot were the green wire fences that surrounded the sixteen tennis courts. A few minutes ago Bino had noticed a jagged hole in one of the fences and some high brown weeds around the perimeter of one of the courts. The temperature was below freezing; Bino shivered. On his left, Half stabbed the air with a forefinger in the direction of Barney's back and rolled his eyes.

"*What* action?" Barney stroked his rust mustache and grinned crookedly in turn at Bino, then at Half, then said to the doorman, "*The* action. You know, pal, the spot where you step up and lay your money down. Where they separate the men from the boys."

The doorman's healthy frame was silhouetted in light from the carpeted entry hall. Beyond him was a coat-check counter behind which lounged a blond in a sequined, high-necked gown. In the coat closet were racks of hangers loaded down with mink, fox, and sable evening jackets and Habersham and London Fog overcoats. The doorman said, "This is a private party, sir. I haven't seen anyone laying any money down here."

"Hey, buddy, don't you think we know what's going on? What are we, a bunch of lightweights or something?" Barney lifted the flap of his cloth overcoat, fished in his pocket, and waved a money clip. The clip was stuffed with bills, a hundred showing. If Bino knew Barney, there'd be a couple of hundreds covering a stack of five- and one-dollar bills. Barney said, "Cash talks and bullshit walks where we come from, pal." Underneath his overcoat he wore a beige alpaca sweater-jacket and a striped knit shirt.

The doorman raised his hand to stifle a yawn.

Half stepped forward. "Jesus Christ, Barney, you're going to get us run off from here." Then, to the doorman, "We got invited. Mr. Blanchard sent us, from Fort Worth."

"Well why didn't you say so?" The doorman straightened and took a step backward.

"I wanted to," Half said, "but I was havin' a hard time getting a word in edgewise. So I'm Harrison. Bino Phillips here. And this gent"—he clapped Barney on the shoulder—"is Mr. Dalton. The high roller, the one I told Blanchard about."

The doorman arched an eyebrow. "Him?"

Barney shot the doorman a huffy glare and swept on into the hallway. The coat-check girl wrinkled her nose in a grin as Barney tossed her his overcoat. "Here, luscious," Barney said. Half shook his head slowly from side to side as he followed two paces to Barney's rear. Bino started to go after them, then stopped and faced the doorman.

"Don't let appearances fool you," Bino said. "He *is* pretty . . . loaded, you know."

Bino decided that the rumors he'd been hearing about Dante Tirelli taking on partners were true. These sure weren't any Texas boys who were popping cards expertly from dealing shoes at the ten blackjack tables, herding groups of clear red dice across the surfaces of the two jam-packed crap tables, shuffling foot-high stacks of chips one handed, or simply watching the action with folded arms through sleepy-lidded eyes. They were strictly green-felt-jungle types.

The noise in the room wasn't quite like a Vegas casino, and Bino had to think for a moment before he figured out what was missing. Then he got it. The slots. No *clink*, no *whirr*, no *ching-ching-ching* when somebody hit a jackpot. Otherwise the sounds were the same, the click of asbestos chips, the monotonous drone of the stickmen ("Dice comin' out, folks, place your bets, take *se*-ven, e-*lev*-en, any *cray*-ups, a new roller a new bowler, they're comin' out now") backed up by the squealing and clapping every time the dice rattled off the padded sideboards. There were a hundred or more players at the crap and blackjack tables, mostly men in suits or groomed women in slacks and sweaters or winter party dresses. Bino recognized a banker he knew, a guy in his fifties with receding gray hair and thick bifocals. Bino waved. The banker met his gaze for an instant, then looked quickly away. The snub bugged Bino until a girl in her twenties with enormous boobs and springy permed and frosted hair hugged the banker's arm to her breast and kissed his ear. Bino made a mental note not to recognize the guy again.

The casino had once served as the tennis club's dining room—Bino recalled having lunch out here once upon a time, with a girl whose name he couldn't remember nearly so well as he remembered the sight of her fanny jiggling around in a tennis dress—and full-length action photos of Rocket Rod Laver, Billie Jean King, Pancho Gonzales, plus a ten-year-old shot of Chris and Jimmy with their arms about each other's waists still hung on the walls. The deep red carpet had seen better days; a few dark stains were visible, and the gray backing showed through in spots. Bino tried to remember when Spring Valley Tennis Club had given up the ghost and closed for good. Seemed like around three years ago, but it could have been longer.

Seated at one of the blackjack tables, Barney whipped out a hundred-dollar bill and waved it expansively at the dealer. Bino took a position behind Barney and watched. The dealer, a sharp-featured woman with no lines in her face who could have been twenty-five or forty-five and who had straight, coal black, shoulder-length hair, smoothed the bill out picture up on the green felt. Then she placed the edge of a small wooden slat on the center of Benjamin Franklin's nose and poked the bill through a slot in the table. Her fingers hovered over the rack of chips in front of her. "Nickels or quarters, sir?" she said. She tapped a red-nailed middle finger, first on the red chips, then lightly on the green. She had a New York accent, like the doorman. Hell, thought Bino, everybody around here's some kind of Bronx Indian.

"Gimme the big ones," Barney said. "Hell, I come to *play*."

To Barney's left sat a guy with razored silver hair wearing a diamond pinkie ring that looked to be around a carat. He shot Barney a glance that would wilt roses and impatiently clicked his black chips together. The dealer showed the guy an apologetic smile as she dropped four green chips into the painted rectangle in front of Barney. On Bino's right, Half slid quietly into the end seat and bought fifty dollars in red. Bino expelled a small sigh of relief. Half wouldn't be betting much, but he'd watch Barney like a hawk.

Bino caught Half's eye and pointed first at his own chest, then in the direction of the nearest bustling crap table. Half nodded. As Bino moved on, Barney said loudly, "Gotcha a four-deck shoe, hey? What, you're trying to take the edge away from us *counters*? Hey, where's a guy get a drink around here?"

At first Bino didn't see any sign of Frank Bleeder, not among the crap-table crowd that was straining at its leashes, not among the quieter group hunched over their twenty-one hands. It took him two full turns around the casino to finally spot Bleeder, and when he did see old Frank he thought that it was no wonder he'd had a hard time finding the guy. There was too big a crowd around Bleeder for anybody to see him.

Old Frank was the center attraction, okay, standing as though he owned one end of a crap table with chattering, clapping men and women four deep at the rail on both sides of him. He was wearing a purple velvet sport coat and match-ing tie with navy slacks and a navy silk breast-pocket hankie. (Jesus, thought Bino, I wonder if old Frank would wear that getup when Goldman put him on the stand. Naw—be too much to hope for.) Bino had to admit that Bleeder looked a whole lot healthier in this environment than he had in the daylight. His graying sideburns were neatly clipped, and his cheeks—almost crimson that morning in Goldman's office—appeared ruddy in the soft light from the hidden fluorescents. And old Frank was giving them some action, too. Boy, was he ever.

His lips pulled back in a desperate-looking grin, Bleeder dipped into a rack loaded with black chips and came up with twenty or more, then distributed the chips in four-high stacks on the come line, behind the four, five, six, eight, nine, and ten across the board. Bino gulped. The guy had just made a couple of thousand dollars' worth of bets, and the move had barely dented the rows of black chips on the rail before him. Then, just as a woman with blued silver hair, who had deep lines in her face and who stood at the opposite end of the table from Bleeder, was shaking the dice, ready to roll 'em, Bleeder motioned to the stickman. The stickman nodded, then quickly held up the shooter long enough for Bleeder to put hundred-dollar bets on the seven, eleven, and all the hard-way numbers. Bleeder, looking at the stickman, moved a flattened hand in the air from left to right. The stickman let the shooter roll. The number-one player had made his move; now the game could go on.

Bino circled the crowd, looking for an opening, then turned sideways and wedged himself in between a brunette who was wearing a gray pantsuit and a guy in a tweed coat (the brunette, slightly tipsy, said, "Oops," and giggled in Bino's ear), finally creating a space for himself two places to Bleeder's right. The woman with the blued gray hair now tossed the dice. They rattled, danced, and came up five-deuce. Bleeder collected on his come bet, his don't pass action, and five for one on his hundred-dollar seven. The house man stacked Bleeder's winnings before him with a flourish, then quietly sacked away the bets that Bleeder had made behind the line, on the eleven, and on the hard-way numbers. Bleeder didn't seem to notice.

Bino found a hundred-dollar bill in his pocket, bought

twenty red chips, and made single five-dollar bets on the pass line and the field. Here I am, fans, he thought. Bino the Greek.

Bleeder hadn't spotted him as yet, and that suited Bino just fine. Come to think about it, Bleeder wouldn't have noticed his own mother at the moment, not if she'd been standing right beside him. His nostrils were flared like those of a horse after a gallop, and his gaze shifted wildly from the chips on the board to the stickman to the group of dice as the stickman herded them over the green felt and back to his stack of chips again. It was the same longing expression that Bino had seen on Deep Elm winos when they saw someone wagging a fifth of Cutty down the street. Nope, Frank Bleeder didn't have a drinking problem. But what he did have was much, much worse in a lot of ways.

Quickly, almost as though he was scared to death that someone was going to stop him, Bleeder placed his bets for the next roll. A red-nailed and manicured female hand snaked out of the crowd and tugged at his arm. He shook it off. The hand tugged again. An irritated look crossed Bleeder's face as he bent to listen. Red lips moved close to Bleeder's ear, and Bino was so caught up in watching Bleeder that it took a few seconds for it to dawn on him that the girl talking to old Frank was Ann Burns.

Bino had been dropping his own chips, one at a time, from one hand to the other, and now he damn near let the whole stack fall to the carpet.

Ann Burns was wearing a dark green velour slipover and puffy light green slacks. Her hair was tied back with a green silk scarf, showing her delicate ears. She wore plain gold earrings. The last time that Bino had seen her talking to Bleeder— in Bek's Hamburgers—she'd been mad as a hornet. But she wasn't mad at Bleeder now. There was a soft pleading in her eyes, and her lips quivered slightly as she spoke. Bleeder finally nodded and, barely glancing at her, handed her some black chips out of his pile. The chips numbered a dozen, give or take, Bino wasn't sure exactly how many. Ann edged close to the railing and reached out to place a hundred-dollar bet on the come line. Her blue-eyed gaze met Bino's. She froze with her chip still in her hand. Her lips parted.

So *now* what did Bino do? Grin? Snap his fingers? Yell "Seven come eleven"?

He raised his empty hand to shoulder level and waggled his fingers. She smiled, left the rail, disappeared for an instant behind Bleeder—who was oblivious, wildly stacking chips on the pass line—then reappeared as she squirmed her way through the mob in Bino's direction. She came around the curve in the rail with her eyes raised in surprised greeting. As she drew near, Bino was suddenly conscious that Bleeder was staring at him.

Old Frank looked like a man who was trying to swallow a whole grapefruit. His eyes bugged, and his cheeks puffed. As Ann Burns reached Bino's side, Bleeder's jaw dropped. Ann leaned over close to Bino and said softly, "Hello. I missed you today."

The voice was the same, but the tone was different. When Bino had talked to her at her father's house she'd been Delightful, Protective Daughter. Not now. The voice was now husky, a little on the sultry side. And the tone was guarded. He didn't have any idea as yet what she had to hide, but something told him that whatever it was had a whole lot to do with the trouble that was brewing for Emmett Burns. For the time being he took it that she was just bluffing her way through. Bino was the last person she'd expected to see here— or had *wanted* to see, for that matter—but now that he'd spotted her she was going to do her damnedest to act as though running into him in a speakeasy gambling joint was no more out of line than bumping into him at the supermarket. He decided to play dumb.

"Missed me?" he said. "Why, we just met, Ann, I'm flattered."

She touched the soft red hair at the nape of her neck. "No, didn't . . . ? I called, didn't your secretary give you the mes-

sage?" Her accent was back-East Vassar with just a hint of a
Texas twang.

He snapped his fingers. "Doggone that Dodie, I'm going
to have to have a talk with her." Across the crap table the
lady with the blued hair was ready to roll 'em again. Bino said,
"They're coming out, Ann. You going to bet, or what?"

Absently, she dropped a black chip on the don't pass bar.
A hundred-dollar chip, as though it was nothing. This might
be Emmett Burns's little girl, but she'd learned her gambling
from somebody else. "Hundred plays," she said to the stickman, then to Bino, "I wanted to talk to you about my dad."

He started to tell her that he'd been wanting to talk to
her about the same thing, then caught himself. Hell, he wasn't
even sure if she knew about the indictment. Odds were that
she did—it had been on the radio even if Emmett Burns hadn't
filled her in—but he could be letting the cat out of the bag.
Even though this particular cat was going to get out sooner
or later no matter *what* Bino did. He said casually, "Oh? Well,
I'm sorry I missed your call. Look, Ann, I don't know if this
is the right time to be bringing up anything heavy. Maybe we
should wait till we can talk in private." He gave her an earnest
grin and hoped it didn't look too much like a leer. Friend or
foe, this lady's looks were something else.

Determination lines bunched at the corners of her mouth.
"I don't *want* to wait. It's too important. You are defending
him, aren't you?"

Well that answered the question as to whether she knew
about the indictment. The dice shooter had rolled another
natural, an eleven. Amid whoops and hollers, the houseman
paid off the winners and scooped Ann's chip off the don't pass
bar. She dropped another black to replace the one she'd just
lost as though she couldn't have cared less.

Bino cleared his throat. "Well I might be defending him.
Why don't you ask your gambling partner?" He glanced fleetingly in Bleeder's direction, then looked back to Ann.

Her lovely head tilted to one side. "Gambling . . . ? *Frank?*
He's not really my . . . Do you know him?"

"Yeah, I do. Since law school."

"He never told me that. Look, Frank and I didn't come here together, if that's what you mean."

Bino's eyes narrowed. So they hadn't come together, but she hadn't minded hitting Bleeder up for gambling money. Funny thing, too, she hadn't registered any surprise when Bino had told her to ask Bleeder about Emmett Burns's criminal charges. No surprise at all. Jesus, speaking of Bleeder, what was the guy doing? Piling his chips into carrying trays, motioning to a houseman. Leaving, that was what Bleeder was doing. Hightailing it, trying hard not to glance in Bino's direction. As though he was avoiding somebody or something.

Bino touched Ann's shoulder and said, "It'll have to be later, Ann. I've got to talk to your buddy, or whatever you call him." He dodged around her, smelling her face powder and hearing her sharp intake of breath, then elbowed his way through the crowd in the same direction Bleeder was going.

Bleeder was headed for two long, linen-covered tables near the back of the room. Behind one of the tables sat a couple of hard-eyed gents, one fiftyish and balding and the other in his thirties with shoulders the width of a forty-foot trailer rig, both wearing tuxes and black bow ties. These would be the payoff men, and Bino would've bet that one or both of them would be wearing a shoulder holster. He caught Bleeder about halfway there. He put a hand on Bleeder's forearm and, none too gently, spun Bleeder around. "Hiya, Frank," Bino said.

Bleeder was carrying two chip racks under the arm Bino had grabbed, and he nearly dropped the whole mess on the floor. Both racks were full, all black chips, rows of twenty, five across, a hundred chips to the rack. Bleeder shifted his load from one arm to the other and said, "Oh. Fancy meeting you here."

"Yeah." Bino let his gaze fall on Bleeder's shoes, then brought it slowly back up until the two of them were eye to eye. "Fancy," Bino said. "Fancy clothes, fancy meeting. That's a pile of chips, Frank; you must have hit the big time. It's a lot easier than representing people for real, isn't it?"

"Representing . . . ?" Bleeder was trying hard but couldn't meet Bino's gaze. Seen up close, Bleeder's cheeks lost their healthy ruddy color and returned to their ugly crimson shade. His jowls sagged. "Well, my practice is doing okay, I guess. Say, this is the third time we've run into one another in the past couple of days. Why if I hadn't had to visit with Marvin Goldman this morning about this case I'm handling—"

"Stow it, Frank," Bino said. "Case your ass. I've seen the Emmett Burns indictment." Visible behind Bleeder, the older of the two guys at the payoff table jerked his head in Bino's direction and said something to the younger guy.

"What indictment?" Bleeder's expression said that he knew damn well what indictment, and his voice quavered like that of a man running on a treadmill.

Bino squared his shoulders. Bleeder's forehead was on a level with the tip of Bino's nose. "Well the Feds call you an unindicted conspirator," Bino said. "The boys in the pen up at El Reno have got another name for it. Look, Frank, I guess however low you want to sink is your business. I just wanted to tell you, hombre to hombre, that there was a time when I had as much respect for you as I did any lawyer in town. That time's far past. Not that you're particularly going to give a shit what I think." Bino caught movement in the corner of his eye. Athletic, coordinated movement. The younger of the two payoff men was moving, almost casually, in Bino and Bleeder's direction.

Bleeder said weakly, "Well under the circumstances, then, I don't guess I ought to talk to you."

Bino hesitated for an instant. Sure, he knew he should shut his mouth, right now, but he'd gotten himself too worked up to stop. Only his lips moving, Bino said through clenched teeth, "No, I don't guess you should. Come to think about it I don't know anybody you *could* talk to, not on the same level. I—"

A voice near Bino's ear said, "Something wrong, Mr. Bleeder?" It was the bouncer, or payoff man, or whatever they called the guy, shouldering his way firmly in between Bleeder and Bino. The bouncer's tenor voice was mild and business-like, and naturally he had a New York accent. His nose had been broken, more than once. Bino would hate to run into the guy who'd broken *this* citizen's nose.

Bleeder opened his mouth to speak, but Bino interrupted. "Nope. No sir, nothing wrong. Just a couple of old buddies having a little chat." He grinned at the bouncer. Bino was only pissed off at Bleeder; he hadn't *completely* lost his marbles.

"Let's get Mr. Bleeder's side of it, Whitey." The bouncer raised an eyebrow.

Bino held his breath, mentally kicking himself for causing this dumbass scene to begin with, while Bleeder carefully took his twin chip racks from under his arm and held them in both hands. The bouncer (Jesus, Bino thought, he looks like Dick Butkus or somebody) looked expectant. Finally, Bleeder said, "No trouble, Dirk. Just a chat. Listen, are you fellas ready to settle up with me?"

The guy Dirk let a flash of disappointment cross his face, then set his features in stone. His dark hair was crew-cut length on top, long and swept back on the sides. His jaw moved slowly as though he was chewing gum. "Have it your way, Mr. Bleeder," Dirk said. "But I got to tell you that didn't look like no friendly chat to me. Tell you what, Whitey." Now he faced Bino and held out a hand the size of a T-bone in the direction of the crap table, palm up. "Why don't you just go have yourself a good time and quit bugging the customers. I'll be watching you, pal." He said it in a mild and friendly tone, but his eyes meant plenty of business. Directly behind him in a color print on the wall, John McEnroe grunted through an overhand serve.

"Well, sure, I'll . . . good time, that's what I'll have." Bino breathed a sigh of relief and retreated—trying to move casually, resisting the impulse to make a dash for it—to the near fringe of the crowd around the crap table. He'd forgotten all about his small hoard of five-dollar chips. Evidently he'd slipped them into his side coat pocket while he'd been hassling Bleeder, and he now located the chips rattling around in there and took them out to rub like pacifiers as he stood behind a couple—a thin man who was only a couple of inches shorter than Bino himself and a stocky dishwater blond with short, frizzy hair—and pretended to be interested as hell in the crap game. From the corner of his eye he kept on watching Bleeder.

Swaggering, his shoulders rotating slightly as he moved, Dirk led Bleeder over to the linen-draped cash-in table. The older, balding guy seated there, who had a take-charge air about him and who had to be Dirk's *capo di tutti* or whatever they called them, took the chips from Bleeder and stacked them across the table in equal ten-high cylinders. He counted the stacks, rapidly tapping each one in turn with the end of a black ballpoint, then took a small notepad from the breast pocket of his tux and wrote something down on the top sheet, tore off that sheet, and wrote something on the second page. Then he raised his eyebrows in a question as he held the single page and the notepad side by side and showed them to Bleeder. Bleeder nodded. The houseman handed the single page to Bleeder and put the notepad back into his pocket.

Bino pursed his lips in a silent whistle.

So Bleeder was playing with these boys on credit. And some line of credit, too, judging from the mountain of black chips that he'd been toting around. Where did Bleeder come off getting that kind of tab? This was something else for Bino to check out, if he could find a way to do it. Maybe he should ask Dirk. Yeah, ask old Dirk and then run for cover. Maybe Half could . . .

Movement on the far side of the crap table—a flash of soft red hair and a glint of light from gold earrings—caught Bino's eye. Over there the stickman was offering the dice to Ann Burns, and she was turning him down with a shake of her head. Then she changed one of her black chips into twenty reds and hesitantly, almost fearfully, began to place five-dollar bets across the board. Bino expelled air from his lungs and, Bleeder and Dirk forgotten for a moment, studied Ann's face.

She seemed in a trance, her movements wooden, small lines—of fear? panic?—at the corners of her eyes. A few moments ago she'd seemed casual about her gambling, as though she plain didn't give a damn whether she won or lost. But that wasn't true, was it? Nope, that was far, far from true.

Ann was placing her five-dollar bets with her right hand; in her delicate left she clutched three black chips. *Three?* How many blacks had Bleeder given her? At least a dozen, maybe even more. Assuming that the number *had* been twelve, that meant that in the time (two minutes? not over five) it had taken for Bino to make an ass out of himself over Frank Bleeder, Ann had run through around eight hundred bucks.

Bino watched her plucked red eyebrows knit in concentration as she bent from the waist to place a bet on the field, and he pictured a slightly different scene. Vegas. Vegas had them in droves, downtown at the Golden Nugget, the Horseshoe, the Four Queens; in smaller but just as desolate bunches at the posher joints along the Strip. Women who started the evening out with their purses chock-full of money and who, as their bankrolls dwindled, lessened their bets in order to string their habits out. Half called them the nurses. You'd see them in the wee hours of the morning, finally reduced to pumping quarters—and even dimes when they got broke enough—into the slot machines. And each and every one of the Vegas nurses wore her own personal version of the same miserable, puzzled expression that was spreading over Ann's face right now. Sickos, one and all.

In ways Ann Burns's gambling problem was even worse than Frank Bleeder's. A guy like Bleeder was a plunger, hell bent for leather. He'd make a big bet, lose it, double up, and keep coming back for more, and Bleeder was subject to lose more in one night than a lot of folks could earn in a year or two. But Bleeder was also going to win some of the time. Boy, was he *ever* going to win some of the time. The way that old Frank covered the numbers, hard ways, front line, and proposition bets, all it took was for the dice to stay hot a couple of times around the table and . . . well, Bino had seen a man who gambled Bleeder fashion one night in action out at Caesars Palace. He'd been a short, thin guy, nervous as a cat, who'd lit one Pall Mall right after another and waved the burning cigarettes around in the air while he placed his bets, at the same time keeping a running line of chatter up with the pit boss. This guy had gotten hot, about as hot as Bino had ever seen anybody, and housemen had come running in droves as Caesars Palace switched dice, stickmen, and finally even crap tables in a frantic effort to cool the little twerp off. Finally even Caesars Palace had hollered uncle, taken its beating, and closed down the game for the night. Bino didn't have any idea how much the guy had won, but it had taken four uniformed security guards to haul the loot over to the cashier's cage. Yeah, guys like Frank Bleeder were subject to break the bank at times.

But a gambler like Ann Burns simply couldn't win, no time, no way. The more she lost the less she'd bet, and once she got behind there wasn't any way for her to catch up. Never in a million years. Sure, Ann would die a slower death at the tables than a bettor like Frank Bleeder, but a much, much surer one.

And the fact that she'd taken money from Bleeder to gamble on was just more proof of her problem. Anybody could see with one eye closed that Bleeder wasn't one of Ann's favorite people. Hell, she loathed the guy; the scene at Bek's Hamburgers had shown that much. If she'd take money from Bleeder to gamble . . . well, just how low *would* she stoop to stay in action? And on the other hand, what was Bleeder's incentive to give her the money? Sex? Possible, but Bino doubted it. For a degenerate gambler like Bleeder—and Ann Burns even more so—betting was a substitute for fucking. Sex just didn't play any part in their lives, though a lot of them would go through a little humping to keep up appearances. Bino wished sex *was* the answer; it would make things a lot easier.

He decided that if he was going to tie all this in to defending Emmett Burns, he was going to have to have some fast answers. And he knew only one place to start getting them. He swallowed hard, then left the crap table behind and took long, determined strides over to the cash-in table where Dirk and his keeper sat.

The older houseman was counting a small pile of red chips with a couple of blacks mixed in while two women—a couple of stylish gals, one a brunette and the other a blond, both in sequined winter dresses and both clutching small, rectangular evening purses—waited expectantly. The houseman chewed thoughtfully on a toothpick, rubbed his shiny scalp, then pulled an enormous roll of bills out of his pocket. He peeled off two hundreds, several twenties, and a few fives, then put the bankroll away. He counted the girls' winnings and handed over the money with a smile. "Pleasure doin' business with you ladies. Tell 'em where you got it, huh?"

The women divided the money. The blond giggled. "Neiman-Mah-cus, heah we come," she said. The women left. The houseman lifted his eyebrows and regarded Bino. Also seated at the table, Dirk cracked his knuckles and adjusted his bow tie. His jaw was working slowly from side to side.

"Say, listen," Bino said. "Is old Dante around?"

The bald guy shifted his toothpick from one side of his mouth to the other. "Dante who?"

"You know," Bino said. "Old Dante. I haven't seen him in a while, and I thought I'd drop by."

"And who's askin'?" the houseman said. "Goin' around talkin' about old Dante."

Dirk butted in. "Watch this character, Ralph. He's the same guy's hasslin' Mr. Bleeder. I ain't seen him place no bets on the table, but he's sure innersted in everbody's business. Ain't you, Whitey?"

Dirk looked strangely familiar, and it suddenly dawned on Bino why. He'd watched a late movie a few nights ago, *The Killers*, starring Lee Marvin and John Cassavetes, and there'd been a character actor playing one of the heavies whose name

Bino couldn't quite place. Gulager? That was it, Clu Gulager had helped Lee Marvin lock a guy into a steam bath and turn the juice on high, then later in the movie had held one dainty ankle while Lee Marvin held the other and the two of them dangled Angie Dickinson out the window of a high-rise building. Hell, even down to the way he cracked his knuckles and rolled his head around on his neck, Dirk was the spitting image of the guy. Bino said, "Interested in . . . ? Hey, not me, I'm not a nosy guy. I just want to chew the fat with old Dante."

"Ralph asked you what your name is, Whitey," Dirk said.

"Bino. Bino Phillips. Me and Dante have got a lot in common." Mentally, Bino winced. They had Annabelle in common, but not much else.

"*Bino?*" Dirk said. "What the hell kind of a name is that? I like Whitey better." He rose to his feet, his shoulders square, his arms limply at his sides, slightly akimbo, in perfect position to bring his fists up in a hurry. "Look, Whitey, I think you better—"

Ralph lifted a hand. "Siddown, Dirk. Jesus, this ain't no . . ." Dirk hesitated, not liking it, but sat down. Ralph showed Bino a crooked grin. "You might be okay, friend. But then you might not, you can't never tell. Tell you what. You fill me in on your business, then I'll make a phone call. Whatcha say?" This guy was a pro, being offhanded about it but at the same time letting Bino know that his business with Dante Tirelli had better not be a lot of bullshit.

Bino decided that he'd better level. "I'm a lawyer, working on a case. I want to know some things that might help my client. If the information I'm asking for won't help me, then it won't go any further. You want to check me out, I'll give you references. I'm not looking to give anybody any shit; it doesn't make me any difference if you set up a gambling joint underneath the Federal Building." He grinned. "Come to think about it that might get you a lot of action. Some prosecutors I know, well, they're pretty big suckers."

Ralph played with his diamond pinkie ring. "Phillips. You that judge's lawyer? Burns?"

"Well, yeah. How'd you know that?"

"You're in the evenin' paper. '*Bye*-no'? Shit, I been reading it 'Beano.' You ought to change the way you spell it."

"Well how would *you* spell it?" Bino said.

"I dunno, I ain't no English teacher," Ralph said. "Say, you sure you're Phillips? I'd look for some pink-eyed albino guy; shit, your eyes're blue."

"I . . . hell, I was born this way," Bino said. "So I'm a cotton top; they gave me the nickname when I was a kid, playing basketball. I might rather be called Stony or Iron Man or something, but I'm stuck with it."

Ralph scratched his front tooth, then stood and backed away from the table. "Well I'll make the call, it's all I can do. Tell the truth, pal, I don't think you're gonna find out shit. I mean, we ain't too worried about judges which gets indicted. They can lock all the bastards up for all we care. But stick around, I'll let you know." He started to walk away, then paused. "And don't let Dirk worry you none. He ain't going to hurt you, long as you're on the square." He walked to the rear of the room and disappeared through a door that, Bino remembered, had once led to the men's locker room at the tennis club.

Bino located a metal folding chair against one wall and sat down across the table from Dirk. Dirk stared glumly at him. Bino drummed his fingers on the linen-covered table. "You got a deck of cards?" Bino said. "Maybe a little gin to pass the time."

Dirk folded his hands and looked as though he didn't think Bino was very funny.

Bino glanced around at the tennis pictures on the wall. "Quite a change, huh?" he said. "From tennis joint to gambling joint. From racquet to racket, you might say." He grinned.

Dirk didn't look as though he thought that was very funny either. Visible behind him, Ralph came back in through the locker-room door and started toward them. He was still chewing on a toothpick, and he looked as though *he* thought something was funny. Bino wondered briefly if he should try the "racquet to racket" line out on Ralph. Might make a better straight man.

"You must have some stroke, pal," Ralph said.

"How's that?" Bino wasn't sure, but he thought Dirk looked sort of disappointed.

"Well, you got an audience," Ralph said. "You wait five minutes and then you go out the front door into the parking lot. Somebody's gonna pick you up."

"Good old Dante," Bino said. "Man, I haven't seen him in a coon's age."

Ralph's eyes narrowed. "Didn't nobody say nothing about no Dante. You keep talking that name around here, they'll be picking you up at the *back* door." His craggy features softened, and he flashed what Bino assumed to be Ralph's version of a reassuring wink. "Just some friendly advice, pal. You have yourself a nice ride, Mr. Phillips. Come back and see us sometime, huh?"

Bino gave the crap table a wide berth—he didn't want to run into Ann Burns again, not just yet—on his way back over to the blackjack game. Barney hadn't moved from his seat. He was drinking a tall highball—it'd be Scotch and water, Chivas if the house was picking up the tab—and talking a mile a minute to the silver-haired guy seated beside him. Bino approached from the rear. He stopped. He blinked.

Barney was winning. Instead of the four lonesome twenty-five-dollar green chips he'd started with, a double six-inch stack of hundred-dollar blacks now sat at his elbow. Barney was waving his drink around. Some of the liquor dribbled over the edge of his glass to wet the silver-haired guy's sleeve. The guy dabbed at his sleeve with a handkerchief and looked sort of resigned.

Barney was saying to the guy, "Just watch this one, buddy. The old doubleroo." He threw his arm around the guy's shoulder, palsy fashion. The guy shrugged him off.

Barney was holding his cards so that Bino, or anybody else who happened to be standing around, could read them. They were an ace and a nine, soft twenty. The dealer—a new one, a skinny guy with thinning hair and a bored expression—had the king of diamonds showing. Barney turned his ace-nine faceup on the table and doubled his two-hundred-dollar bet. The dealer's eyes widened. He glanced at Barney and started to say something. Then, with a what-the-hell shrug, the dealer slid one card facedown under Barney's stack of chips and moved on to the next player.

Bino winced. Jesus Christ, you don't double down on soft twenty with a *face card* showing on the dealer's side of the table.

After the other players had stood pat or taken a hit, the dealer turned up his own hole card—a five—and dealt himself a queen. "*O*-ver," he said, deadpan, and paid off around the board.

Barney elbowed the silver-haired guy, who had hit twelve with a ten and busted his hand. "Jus' stick with ole Barn," Barney said, "an' I'll show you a thing or two about this game. Come to papa." He raked his winnings into a jumbled pile.

"Great play, Barney," Bino said.

Barney looked around. "Bino. Where you been?" Then, to the dealer, "Hey, how 'bout a drink over here for my buddy?"

"Nope," Bino said. "Nothing for me. Just keep on truckin', Barn." He circled the table to where Half was sitting. Half was playing with his own small pile of red chips and eyeing Barney with a long, sad look, like that of a basset hound.

"Boy, ain't *he* some kind of player?" Half said. "Between you and me, Bino, I like the sonofabitch better when he's losing."

"You got a point," Bino said. "Look, I'm leaving. Don't ask me any questions, okay? Call my apartment at seven in the morning. If I'm not there send out the bloodhounds."

Half shrugged and nodded. He might not like it, but he'd go along. Bino gave Half's elbow a squeeze, then went out through the lobby into the parking lot. He grinned at the doorman as he left. The doorman stifled a yawn.

Outside, the wind had picked up. The faded cloth awning

that hung over the sidewalk whipped and rustled. Bino hunched his shoulders and thrust his hands deep into his pockets, then went to the curb and stepped down into the parking lot. Two wads of paper skittered over the asphalt like Ping-Pong balls. Bino's ears stung momentarily, then went frigidly numb. Muttering under his breath, cussing himself for leaving his trench coat in the Linc's backseat in Joe Miller's parking lot, he zigzagged his way between rows of cars to stand by the fence surrounding the nearest tennis court.

Fifteen minutes, which seemed like hours, passed. He'd stand facing the wind until his nose and cheeks were numb, then turn his back until his ears felt as though they might break off. He cupped his hands and blew into them. He hopped up and down. Nothing worked. Hell, his *toes* had lost all feeling. Just as he decided that *anything*—including, even, having Dirk beat the crap out of him—was better than freezing his ass off and took a couple of long strides back in the direction of the building, twinkling headlights came down the road and turned into the parking lot. Probing beams of light illuminated the chain-link fence and sent gridlike shadows moving over the surface of the tennis court. The headlamps passed, and Bino squinted to make out the low-slung outline of a Caddy Eldorado. The Caddy flowed its way to the awning-covered sidewalk and shined its lights on the tan brick wall of the tennis club, then made a sweeping U-turn and came back in Bino's direction. The headlights brightened, then dimmed. The Eldo stopped beside where Bino stood. Its passenger-side window hummed and slid down.

Bino bent from the waist, his hands still deep in his pockets, and peered in through the open window. It didn't matter *how* cold he was—Jesus, even his teeth were numb—or how warm it was inside that car, he wasn't taking any chances. Not with the folks he was dealing with. He was tense, ready to run for the tennis club.

First there was a throaty female chuckle, then Annabelle said, "You look cold, buster. Don't you know that only lunatics stand around outside on a night like this?" The dashboard lights illuminated her firm lower jaw, highlighted the frosted ringlets of her hair, and glinted fleetingly from her slightly crooked front tooth.

He hadn't laid eyes on her since the nasty goings-on of a few weeks ago, involving Winnie Anspacher. Before then it had been ten or eleven years. She didn't affect him nearly as strongly as she had when they'd been married, but she still affected him some. First love died hard, and all that.

Finally he said, "I guess Tirelli sent you. Wanted to rub it in or something."

"Never in a million would he," she said. "I'm on my own. If you should ever run into Ralph again I wouldn't let him know it was me who showed up to meet you. I sort of . . . well, fielded Ralph's call and he sort of got the idea I was relaying messages back and forth between him and Dante. Dante's . . . out of town. I guess I'm really wicked."

One corner of Bino's mouth tugged downward. "So what else is new, you being wicked. Too wicked for me, babe." He turned and started to walk back toward the tennis club.

She put the Eldo in reverse and idled along beside him. "But I haven't come empty-handed. I'm bearing gifts. Ralph said you want to know some things."

"Yeah, I want to know some things. But not what *you're* teaching." He lowered his head and trudged on.

"I don't guess you do," she said. "Unless you'd like to find out about Frank Bleeder."

He stopped. "How'd you know that?"

One of Annabelle's shapely legs was visible in the dash light, bent at the knee and raised slightly on the other side of the steering wheel. She was wearing jeans and some sort of dark fur jacket. She was smiling. Her arm rested on the seatback. "What do you say, little boy?" she said. "Want to ride with the dirty old lady?" She unlatched the passenger door and opened it.

He stood in the cold and watched her. Finally he shrugged. "Sure," he said. "Why not?"

9

As Ann Burns hesitantly changed her last black chip for five-dollar reds, the old, familiar panic set in. It was a physical thing, a dull ache that began somewhere in her belly, spread throughout her system, and lodged a heavy, painful lump solidly in her throat. It was panic mixed with dreadful certainty, the terrible knowing that she'd done it again. The knowledge that no matter how many vows she seemed to make ("Hello. I'm Ann Burns and I'm a compulsive gambler. We're all friends here, aren't we?"), or to whom she made them, even God, all her promises flew out the window once she came anywhere near a dice game, a racetrack, a slot machine. For just an instant she thought she was going to vomit, right there on the carpet. She shut her eyes tight, fought off the nausea, and made five-dollar bets on the pass line and on the seven. The shooter rolled ace-deuce craps, and the houseman swept her money away. She watched in a stupor.

She took a breath and stepped back to look around the room, at the laughing, good-time crowd across the casino hunched over their blackjack hands, at the tennis photos on the walls. A short, graying man at the opposite rail on the crap table was ogling her, as were several other men. She never had gotten used to that, the smirks and winks from men, the flashing of rolls of money. God, she hated it. Absolutely despised . . .

Frank Bleeder had gone. Good, good, *good* riddance. The sorry bastard had finally called it quits for the night. No more of his . . . No more *loans*, if that's what you want to call them, dearie, a hollow voice inside her said. And once you foof off your last hundred bucks, you'll be going, too. Unless you can find some more money, hon. Hey, that old gray-haired goat over there doesn't look so bad, does he? The well's running dry, little girl. Drier and drier and . . .

The older woman with the blued gray hair was ready to roll again as the thinning crowd whooped it up. This time Ann tried a don't pass bet. The woman rolled seven, clapped her hands, and danced a little jig. Ann uttered a choking sob as her money disappeared. Not much longer, little girl, the voice said. Not to worry, not to hurry, it'll all be over before you know it.

But wait. Bino Phillips was around here somewhere. After all, he *was* Daddy's lawyer; surely he wouldn't mind if she just asked him for . . . God, Ann, what are you *thinking* about?

Why, you're thinking about a *stake*, little girl, the hollow voice told her. From *anybody*, it doesn't matter who, as long as the money keeps you in action. Doesn't matter what you have to do for the money either. Earn it on your fucking back if you have to. You've tried that a few times, haven't you, doll? The hollow voice laughed, and a tear ran down Ann's cheek. She found a napkin on the counter beneath the rail, wiped the tear away, and blew her nose.

She looked up toward the linen-covered table where Ralph and Dirk sat, both expressionless, both with folded hands. It was their fault. It was all their fault. No credit for Ann? Just who in the ever-loving hell did they think they were? She was good for the money, those men knew that. Wasn't her father a *judge*? The hollow voice laughed again, practically in hysterics now. *Used* to be good for it, little girl, it told her. Not anymore. Not since Daddy's got his own troubles. You want to blame Daddy, too? Of course, you can get more credit. All you have to do is . . .

Frantically, losing control (God, if she'd ever had any control to begin with), Ann covered the board, five dollars each on the pass line, seven, eleven, big six, big eight, and the field. The blue-haired woman (God, was she looking at Ann? It seemed to Ann that she was) shook the dice and tossed them. They skittered over the table, bounced off the rail, came up double-six. Another craps. Thirty dollars (God, it may as well have been thirty thousand, the amount of money never seemed to matter) of Ann's money vanished in one fell swoop, the houseman's hands moving as if by magic. The nausea returned. Ann stood back and coughed into a cupped hand.

A man's voice beside her said, "We're having a bad night of it, aren't we? Maybe we should pool our resources; it might change our luck."

She turned. It was the gray-haried man from across the table, now standing a foot or so away. He had a bulbous nose with a lot of blackheads. A single hair protruded from one of his nostrils. His gray suit coat was unbuttoned; he wore his pants high, almost to his armpits, his round belly pushing against the gray cloth. His expression was hopeful, almost in awe of her.

"What do you think?" he said. "Could we . . . get together, maybe?" He held some hundred-dollar bills in his chubby fingers. His breath smelled of garlic.

Ann eyed the money and listened to the hollow voice. Just another man, honey, it told her. Just one more, and what the hell? He's got money. Money. Another stack of chips, more action, more seven come eleven. What's he want? A quickie, maybe, just a little hump in his backseat, with him sweating and humping and breathing his old garlic in your face while he . . . ? Nothing to it, babe. Just like falling off a . . .

She gagged. A clammy sheen broke out on her forehead and on her upper lip. Nausea flooded over her, and for just the barest instant she blacked out. Then, her head swimming, she tried to focus her gaze. She couldn't. The man, standing just feet from her with his money in his hand and a hopeful look on his face, seemed miles away. She managed to say, "No, it's really time for me to—" Then she left the table, left her hopeful suitor standing there with his mouth open like a flytrap, and staggered drunkenly for the exit. She made it into the hallway—almost colliding with a woman in a silver pantsuit and a man in a brown tweed coat—and went to the parking-lot door. The doorman flashed her a strange look, started to say something, then closed his mouth and stepped aside. Ann went out into the cold night air.

The frigid wind whipped her hair and stung her cheeks. She barely noticed. She stopped, swaying, stood just off the curb on the asphalt and looked for her yellow Tempest. She panicked for a moment; the car wasn't there. The godforsaken car wasn't there, that little yellow Tempest, the one that Daddy'd given her when she was in college, the only link remaining with what used to be, it just . . . wasn't . . . *there.*

Yes it is, little girl, the hollow voice said. Right over there between that Porsche and that Mercedes. What the hell's the matter with you? Your fucking car's here, all right; don't get your panties in a knot. Now you've found your car, go on back inside and give that guy a roll for his money. You give him a roll in the hay, he'll give you a roll for the galloping dominoes, now ain't that fair?

"You go to hell," she said aloud. Her head clearing, she went over to the Tempest, fumbled with the key in the lock, opened the door, and climbed into the front seat. She sat for a moment with her forehead resting against the steering wheel and watched a dark Caddy Eldorado, its headlamps illuminating the pavement, leave the parking lot and disappear down the road in the direction of the North Central Expressway.

She started the Tempest and raced the engine; the car's radio popped to life with Stevie Wonder singing "I Just Called to Say I Love You." She'd just dropped the shift lever into Drive and was ready to leave when a realization struck her. She threw the lever back into the Park position, sat for a moment, and chewed on a cuticle.

Her coat. Her lovely waist-length mink jacket—God, the proud look on Daddy's face when he'd given it to her as a homecoming present, on the day she'd flown in from Chicago and that other worthless life she'd been leading—was back there hanging in the tennis club's coatroom. She had to go back. Had to get the coat. That wouldn't be any problem, but it was a relief that she'd remembered it. What would she say to Daddy if she were to come home without it? With a nervous laugh she reached for the door handle. She froze.

The coat's *worth* something, you dumb broad, the hollow voice said. Worth a pretty penny, matter of fact, now you think you can't get back in action with that *mink* as collateral. Get your ass back inside and talk to good old Ralph; he'll have you a fresh stake in a heartbeat if he's holding on to that coat. Now get your butt in gear and quit screwing around.

I won't, I won't, I *won't*, she told the voice. Not my *coat*. She began to cry. The tears flooded down her cheeks and wet her velour slipover. She was still clutching ten red chips. Ten filthy five-dollar chips, ten screaming reminders of the depths to which she'd sunk. Sobbing, her chest heaving, she rolled the car window halfway down and flung the chips into the parking lot. They bounced and rolled across the asphalt.

A soft, twangy female voice said from the backseat, "You crazy, lady? Whatcha crying about? You look pretty fucking rich to me."

For an instant, just a heartbeat, Ann thought she was

□   138   □

hearing the hollow voice from within her. But she wasn't. This voice was real, somebody sitting scant feet behind her in the backseat. But it couldn't be. Had to be her imagination; that was it. Had to . . .

Ann turned. Someone was there, all right, some *shape*, some unclear presence back there in the shadows. Someone who was wearing dark clothes (jeans and a sweater, Ann thought, but she couldn't tell for sure) and whose face was hidden behind a dark knit ski mask. A girl. A *young* girl, from the tone of the voice, whose smooth cheeks and long-lashed eyes were visible through the hole in the mask. The edges of the hole were outlined in white. The eyes were dark, maybe brown, maybe black. But it *was* only a girl.

Ann had heard a lecture once upon a time, from a police captain who'd been telling a group of women what to do in case of an assault. "Act *tough*," the cop had said. "Ninety-nine percent of these crazies are pure chicken. If *you* don't get scared, they will. They'll panic and run."

What the cop had said had sounded good at the time, and now Ann tried it. She raised her voice and said, "What are you doing here? You get the hell out of my car."

The girl in the ski mask straightened. She raised her arms and held the biggest pistol that Ann had ever seen just inches from Ann's face. "I ain't going to ast you but once, lady," the girl said. "You turn around an' quit fucking looking at me."

Her heart pounding and tearing at her breastbone, Ann faced the front. Beyond the nose of the Tempest was the chain-link fence surrounding the tennis court. The car rocked slightly in the wind.

There was sound behind her, movement, flesh sliding under cloth, even breathing now just inches behind her ear. "You drive this car the fuck out of here," the girl said. "And you fucking go where I tell you. If you look at me again I'll shoot you. Don't think I won't, I ain't a bit scared to."

Ann clutched the wheel and dropped the shift lever into Drive. Woodenly, she pressed her foot on the accelerator. The

Tempest jerked, its engine cold at first, then smoothed out. The car moved to the exit and turned onto the road. Its radials bumped over cracks in the pavement. Somewhere a woman was crying pitiful, wracking sobs. It was a few seconds before Ann realized that the cries were her own.

"Ain't nothing to *cry* about, lady," the girl said. "I'm just going to show you some *pikchers*. Ain't nobody going to hurt you, 'less you try some fucking around."

10

Annabelle held the toothpick carefully. She looked over the thingamajig that was impaled on its tip from all angles. The thingamajig was dried beef rolled into a cylinder with a gob of cream cheese in the center, Bino's special party hors d'oeuvre that he'd never come up with a name for over the years. Finally Annabelle popped the meaty cylinder into her mouth and chewed thoughtfully. "Mmmm. I haven't had one of these tasties since we lived together. Has it changed much?" She laid the toothpick carefully on a saucer. The saucer sat atop rumpled sheets on the king-size bed.

"Has *what* changed much?" Bino said. The drapes moved slightly in the draft from the heat vent. From the living room down the hall, Al Hibler crooned "The Twelfth of Never" over the stereo speakers.

She smirked at him, then reached over and set the saucer

on the nightstand. A diagonal crease appeared briefly in the flesh of her back, running from her shoulder blade to her slim, bare waist as her body twisted. She rolled to face him and rested her cheek on her fist. "You know," she said.

"Know what?"

"What has or hasn't changed."

"The dried beef and cream cheese?" Bino said.

She nudged his bare calf with her foot and wiggled her toes against his skin. "The sex, dodo."

Matter of fact, Bino thought, it has changed quite a bit. They'd been really young when they'd gotten married, and somewhere between then and now Annabelle had learned every bedroom trick there was. He glanced at the nightstand where, in addition to the saucer holding the toothpicks, the glass of hot water sat. Annabelle had taken a mouthful of the hot water just before she'd gone down on him. The sex was kinkier and earthier, okay, but something was missing. The sweetness? That was it. Sort of like the difference between making it with your high-school prom queen and spending some money on a high-class hooker. Bino might be old-fashioned, but he'd take the prom queen any old time. "It's been a long time, Annabelle. What do you think?"

"It's hard to compare," she said, running a fingernail lightly over his chest. "And probably not fair, like apples and oranges. Most of the time before, you had that cast on your ankle. God, that thing must have weighed fifty pounds. Back then I had to do all of the work. You're holding your end up pretty well these days, I'll say that for you." Gravity pulled her fine breasts downward. Her left nipple brushed the sheet. Her springy permed hair was tousled.

Visible beyond Annabelle and down the hallway, soft light from the living room highlighted spots on the carpet. Cecil's tank stuck out beyond the end of the hall. Cecil floated motionless between waving fins, about half of him in sight. From this angle he looked like the stuffed bust of an oscar fish that was mounted on the wall.

"You, too," Bino said. "Your end is . . . really held up. And I got to admit it's a little scarier now."

Her graceful eyebrow arched. "You mean because of Dante?"

He drew his leg up and rested a forearm on his knee. "Well, yeah, now that you mention it. What *would* old Dante have to say about this?"

She squirmed onto her back and looked at the ceiling, stretching her legs out and crossing her ankles. "He'd kill you," she said.

"That's a comfort."

"Italians are like that. They can screw around all they want to, but nobody messes with their women. He might have your penis cut off and stuffed in your mouth, but that's an old-timey way of doing things."

"Jesus Christ."

"Oh, don't worry," she said. "He wouldn't do it himself. He'd send somebody like Dirk and Ralph."

"Would they do it so it wouldn't hurt as much?"

"You've got a two-tone ceiling," she said. "What happened?"

In the semilight, the unpainted circle of plaster showed up even more than it did in the daytime. "Damn that Tilly," Bino said.

"You're changing the subject."

"No, I'm not," he said. "Tilly Madden. She's the manager of this apartment house. Her husband and her son, well, they fixed a hole in my ceiling. Or they were supposed to; for what they charged I should get a new carpet and a fur-lined toilet seat. That was a month ago and they've never been back to paint the damn thing."

She bent one leg and rested her ankle on its knee. "What made the hole?"

"A shotgun."

"Oh. Was that when you were shacked up with the girl FBI agent and the shooting started?"

"Annabelle. I wasn't *shacked up*. Not exactly."

"Well whatever you want to call it. I'm married, Bino, I don't care who you're screwing. But I thought that the FBI agent shot the guy with a pistol."

"She did. The shotgun was the other guy's. One of 'em. How'd you know about that? Nobody's supposed to. Hell, the FBI busted their ass covering it up."

"How do I know about anything?" she said.

There was a matching nightstand on his left. He opened its drawer, fumbled, found a pack of filtered Camels, lit one. "I thought Dante kept you in the dark about the rough stuff that went on."

"*Used* to keep me in the dark," she said. "That was before. Before the thing with Winnie Anspacher. I told him I'd leave him if I caught him hiding anything else from me. I still don't have a peaches-and-cream marriage, but at least I'm up on current events from the netherworld. Which makes me a conspirator, I guess. That's how I know about Frank Bleeder."

"So we're finally going to talk about old Frank," Bino said. "And here I was thinking you just used his name as bait, so you could jump on my bones."

"I don't need any bait," she said.

He had a lungful of smoke. He blew it upward and watched the wispy stream flatten out, ghostlike, on the ceiling. "I didn't, and it was on purpose that I didn't, I didn't say anything to the dynamic duo at the tennis club about Frank. How'd you know I wanted to talk about him?"

"Oh, two and two. You're representing Judge Emmett Burns. Hey, ex-hubby, you look okay on the tube. Like an actor or something. Real stage presence. You're the judge's lawyer and Frank's going to testify against him. Two and two."

"And Tirelli's got a file on Bleeder?" Bino said. "What for?"

"There aren't any files, dopey."

"Well, yeah, I know. No records. It was just a figure of speech. But, hell, Tirelli must do business with a thousand people. Why would you have the lowdown on Frank in particular?"

She raised herself on her elbow and wrinkled her nose at him. "Because I introduced him to Frank. It's all your fault."

"*My* fault? *I* told you to get Frank and Tirelli together?" The ash on Bino's cigarette was about an inch long. There was a glass ashtray on his nightstand, and he tried to flick the ash into it. He didn't make it; the gray cylinder dropped off the cigarette and broke up on the sheet. He brushed the ashes onto the floor.

"I swear you've got the memory of a retard," Annabelle said. "Where did you go to law school?"

"South Texas C of L," he said. "Harvard of the ghetto."

"In Houston, right?"

"Well . . . yeah," Bino said. "Downtown, you got to carry a shiv in your notebook if you got any night classes."

"Total recall. And do you happen to remember who you were married to in those days?"

He pointed his finger at her. "You, right?"

"What an impression I've made on your life. Since we've called *that* up on the screen, do you happen to remember where I met Frank Bleeder?" she said.

"Sure. He's another South Texas C of L guy. Tough cookie."

"So he is," Annabelle said. "About a year ago Dante took me to a basketball game. He had heavy action on it or something, the Mavericks and the Utah Jazz. So I'm sitting there, Dante's gone for popcorn or to take some layoff or something, and who sits down right beside me but Frank Bleeder and this girl. First time I'd seen him since . . . you and I, you know. He sees me and gives me this big phony hug, you know how he is, and then he goes, 'Well where's the big albino?' Needless to say there was a pregnant pause."

"You mean he thought—?" Bino scratched his head. Sure, it had been years since he'd been married to Annabelle, but Bleeder wouldn't have any reason to know that. In the college years and shortly thereafter a lot of folks had gotten married. Hell, half of them were divorced by now; who could keep up?

"I guess he did," she said. "So when Dante got back I introduced them, Susie Social Director, and they sort of hit it off. I tell you, Dante hits it off with everybody."

"Or hits everybody he doesn't hit it off with," Bino said.

"I wasn't paying much attention to them, but I remember that Frank told Dante he had a bet on the game, and that shot my hubby's antennae straight up. There isn't anything more to tell about that night—oh, Frank did goose me a couple of times and acted like it was an accident. But then last month when I set my foot down and told Dante I was leaving him if he didn't start leveling with me? Well among other things Hubby told me was who was the biggest gambler in town. Not moneywise—God, some of these oilmen lose more in one night than you'd ever believe—but the most consistent. You know, shows up every single time there's a game set up. Can you guess who it is?"

Bino shrugged. "Bleeder, I guess. That's who we're talking about."

She shook her head, her frosted curls bouncing around. "It's a close race, but Frank's probably second. According to Dante, the most consistent gambler in town is the girl who was with Frank at the basketball game. And lo and behold, she's that judge's daughter. The one you're representing. You look sort of confused, bucko."

"Ann Burns? She's got the fever, okay. But Jesus, where's she get that kind of . . . a federal judge makes pretty good, but you can bet she isn't getting the money from Emmett Burns. Not if he knew she was going to use it to gamble. Where the hell's she get her money?"

"Now that I can't tell you, but I do know her credit's been cut off. I know where Frank Bleeder gets *his* money, though."

"Where?" Bino said.

"Legal fees. He's representing a lot of Dante's friends. You know, you scratch my back, I'll scratch yours. Frank's not much of a lawyer, at least that's what they say, but he's convenient. They let him gamble on credit, it gives them a free lawyer in the long run. And Dante's crowd doesn't *need* much of a lawyer, not to run back and forth between them and the DA saying, 'My client will take three years,' then telling the client, 'He says he'll give you five if you'll cop out.' "

Bino's white eyebrows knit. "Jesus Christ, I knew Tirelli was big. But not *that* big, where no matter what spot Frank lays his money down Tirelli's got a finger in the pie."

Annabelle put both elbows on the mattress behind her and arched her back. Bino pictured her in a similar pose, one night by the lake up on Flagpole Hill around twenty years ago; her body hadn't looked much different then than it did now. Real showstopper. "I could tell you some things," Annabelle said, "that I could get in real trouble for." She spoke suddenly from the side of her mouth in a Texas version of a Brooklyn accent. "I mean, bein' da head moll don't give a girl no license to go shootin' her mout' off." She was being funny—and the accent *was* pretty cute—but Bino caught just a hint of bitterness in her tone as well.

"I'm a stand-up guy, Annabelle. I'm paid to be one."

"So I remember," she said. "So awright awreddy, I'll snitch. There's been a lot of changes lately. Gambling around here is a lot more organized. There are even precinct chairmen."

"There's *what?*"

"Precinct chairmen. That's what *I* call them; it's a throwback to my Junior League days. There's a game like that one at the tennis club every single night now, but never two nights in a row in the same place. Each precinct chairman has his own night to operate, and woe be to the guy who has a game on a night he's not supposed to. That's what Ralph is, cute thing, a precinct chairman. Dirk is sort of his assistant. The hired help, stickmen and dealers and whatnot, they sort of shift around from place to place."

"And town to town," Bino said. "Jesus, I haven't seen so

many New York Indians in one place since Half and I went to Miami Beach one time. I guess those guys know their business, but in Dallas they stick out like a sore thumb. They'll bring heat on those games, federal *and* state.''

"That's Dante's problem," Annabelle said. "Him and his partners, I'm not really sure who they are. But anyway, that's how he keeps up with who's playing where and who's losing what. And that's how I keep up with people like Frank. And Ann Burns. Your little girlfriend." She scratched her ankle. Annabelle was wearing pink toenail polish that appeared iridescent when struck by rays of light from the hallway. "Oh and by the way, lover. In case you were thinking about it, the word on little Ann is that she has the equipment but doesn't use it very well. So I'm told." She batted her eyes.

"Come *on*. Her father's my client."

"That wouldn't stop any lawyer *I* ever saw," she said.

"Go on, abuse me." His cigarette was suddenly red hot between his fingers; he dropped it into the ashtray and shook his hand. There'd probably be a blister on his index finger in the morning. "Shit, I got to quit smoking." He sucked on his index finger and studied her. He tried a shot in the dark. "Annabelle. You ever heard of a guy named Thorndon?"

She reached over and intertwined her fingers with his, schoolgirl fashion. "*Lou* Thorndon?"

"Lou, I guess it could be. He's a guy Bleeder represented in Judge Burns's court. What does the guy do for a living?"

"He's some kind of Yankee, from up north. He sells cars, for one thing. Dante bought my Eldo from him, and I've heard some other folks talking about buying theirs . . . Pretty interesting guy, really. Damon Runyon gone uptown. I think you'd like him. Funny your asking about Lou, under the circumstances."

"Why's it funny?" Bino said.

"Well, you know Dante's sort of into politics sometimes. He sponsored a fund-raiser last— Oh, I forgot. It was Art Stammer's fund-raiser where I ran into you, at Winnie Anspacher's.

Well, not at the same party, but another get-together around the same time at the Adolphus Hotel. Another fund-raiser for Art Stammer. The mayor was there, and a bunch of city councilmen. Lou Thorndon came, and I remember I thought that was sort of strange because Lou was under indictment at the time. You know how these political types are careful who they rub elbows with. In public, anyway. Lou brought a date with him. Everybody at the party was talking about her, and I've got to confess she looked absolutely stunning. And that's a compliment coming from me, love. Old Super-Stunner herself. She had the ladies of the club all atwitter."

"Hell, Annabelle," Bino said. "All those kind of guys have pretty women around. It goes with the size of their bankroll." It occurred to him that what he'd just said was sort of a slam to Annabelle, but it was too late. He'd already said it.

She didn't seem to notice. "Maybe. But don't you want to know who she was?"

His jaw slacked. "Don't tell me," he said.

"Right. The judge's daughter again. Little Miss Roll Them Bones."

11

Daryl Siminian, deadpan, said, "Now please don't give me any double-talk. I can't *stand* that kind of shit. No stories, I don't want to know anybody's life history. I'll ask what I want to know, and you give me plain, simple answers. Like a pop quiz, you know?"

"Daryl, why you want to do me like that?" Judy Roo said. "Hell, I ain't a *bay*-bee." She was standing beside the bureau, having just dropped the car keys on top, having laid the black knit ski mask alongside the keys, and now unzipping her navy nylon windbreaker. She was wearing new, unwashed jeans.

"I just don't need any more finger-fucking stories," Daryl said. He pointed the hand-held remote control and pressed a button; the TV set went instantly mute and David Letterman and Madonna continued to grin at each other, their lips moving like mimes' lips. Daryl had the sheet bunched around his waist. His chest and shoulders were bare. "Did you show her the pictures?" he said.

"Sure did."

"And?"

She folded the windbreaker and dropped it on the dresser to cover the keys and the ski mask. "She quit actin' so scared and looked like she was tryin' to shit a watermelon. I don't like doing this; I ain't never held a gun on nobody before." Daryl's pistol, a big Browning P-35 9 mm, lay on the foot of the bed where Judy had placed it moments ago.

"You're doing fine," Daryl said. "Did you remember to tell her what I said?"

"Sure did."

"Word for word?"

" 'Course."

"Repeat it to me," he said.

She was wearing the pink sleeveless sweater that Daryl had bought her that afternoon in Foley's Irving Mall, at the same time he'd bought the jeans and the windbreaker. She put her hands at her waist and cocked her hips. "Daryl, I ain't *stupid*. I ain't a baby and I ain't stupid."

He showed a slow-spreading smile, lips pulling back from even white teeth. He patted the mattress beside him. "I'm making you mad. Come sit by me."

Looking dubious, cringing slightly, she went over and sat. She rested her hands on her thighs and peered at him over her shoulder. "You ain't making me *mad* exactly. Just hurting my feelings."

"You see this, Judy?" Daryl was pointing at the mass of scar tissue on his left shoulder. A surgical scar, sutures outlined, led away from the lumpy mass, upward and over his collarbone.

Her gaze stayed on his shoulder. Her lips parted.

He said, "It fucks up the whole looks of my body, doesn't it? Now being a polite girl and all, I know you wouldn't say anything about it. But I seen you looking. It hurts like a bastard sometimes. What I'm trying to say is, somebody not telling something the way I said for them to, that's what cost me this."

"What, in a holdup or something?" she asked.

"In prison, Judy, in the federal joint. Oxford, Wisconsin. What happened was that this guy was making some brew. Wine, with oranges from the chow hall and a little yeast and sugar. I was working in the kitchen, and it was up to me to bring the oranges. Teamwork, you know? Like what we're doing here, you and me."

"You ain't making me feel like I'm on your team," she said. "Bossing me the fuck around."

"Any team's got to have a captain, Judy. That was the trouble with the orange wine, not anybody in charge and a bunch of guys running around with their fingers up their asses. I swiped this whole sack of oranges and hid it outside, four or five dozen juicy navels, and I told this guy Jerry to tell the hack that's running the kitchen that I was going up to the commissary after an ice cream. That would have been okay, see, we could leave the chow hall if it was our time for the commissary. They treated us like a bunch of drips with all that shit, but you got to expect it in the joint. It's the way of life.

"So I've covered my ass with the hack, him thinking I'm at the commissary; at least that's what I thought. So off I go. I hauled the oranges over to the dorm, that's what they call a cellblock in the federal joint, and gave them to the guy making the wine.

"But this stupid fucking guy Jerry, you know what he told the hack? Not that I'm going to the commissary like I said, but he goes up to the hack and tells him I left. Just, old Daryl's left, like I'm not a convict and I can go wherever I want, and also the message is like I'm telling the hack to go fuck himself. Pisses the hack off, you know? So the hack gets a hard-on a foot long and goes tearing over to the dorm looking for me. He doesn't find me, no way; I've got the good sense to make a detour over by the commissary and for real *get* me an ice cream to, you know, cover my tracks. But he does find this guy that's making the wine. The hack comes up, and there's the guy, standing there cutting up the oranges with a butcher knife, which is dangerous contraband in the joint and a case in itself, just having the knife if the U.S. Attorney wants to be a horse's ass about it. Besides the stolen oranges the guy's got the sugar and yeast and shit all spread out. Off goes the winemaker to the hole, thirty days in solitary they give the fucking guy plus taking thirty days of good time away from him, and all because this guy Jerry didn't say what I told him to, word for word.

"So there sits this guy, the winemaker, down there in the hole with no air-conditioning and a bunch of flies and shit buzzing around and thinking I've snitched him off to the hack. *Me*, I'm supposed to be the snitch, not this Jerry that fucked up the deal in the first place. So not only is the whole joint cut off from its wine supply, now old Daryl is going around wearing a snitch jacket. I don't mind telling you I was not having such a good time.

"Along about the third night the winemaker's in the hole, couple of his friends look me up. One guy holds a pencil in my ear—Jesus, one push and the point goes right into my brain—while the other guy goes to work on me with this sharpened screwdriver he copped out of the cable factory. I got to stand there and take it and can't yell or anything 'cause it would bring the hacks running and then I'd be a snitch again. When they finally got finished carving up my shoulder—Jesus, you could see the tendons hanging out—I went and found this Jerry guy that fucked up the story with the chow hall hack to begin with. I was hurting like a bastard, okay, but I did find this guy Jerry. I couldn't even lift my arm, but I could kick. I give this guy Jerry a size-nine hard-toed shoe right in the balls, two times in a row.

"Now this Jerry asshole, he doesn't seem to care if he gets a snitch jacket or not, 'cause he goes to screaming his ass off and the hacks come running. Four of the motherfuckers, but by then I'm so much in pain with my shoulder and up to here with all the bullshit that I don't care. So I haul off and kick the first hack through the door right in the balls too.

"So the hacks, they get me all chained up and handcuffed besides beating the shit out of me some more, and then they shoot me up with Thorazine. Thorazine, that's for crazy motherfuckers, which you can see I obviously am not. That stuff will make a walking stiff out of you but fast, which it did out of me for two years after that. One little rumble, the silly bastards give me two years on Thorazine. They took me down to the prison system medical center at Springfield, Illinois, wrote me up that I was dangerous, and threw me in there with the spookiest bastards you ever saw. And all of that because this Jerry guy didn't tell the chow hall hack word for word what I told him to. But I did learn a lesson, Judy. You want to know what it is?"

She said, uncertainly, "What?"

"That the next time somebody gets me all fucked up by not doing what I told them to do, that somebody is going to get dead. You know? So now, Judy, are you ready for this little pop quiz that we are going to have?"

Her lower lip quivered. "How you spect anybody to do anything right with you going around scaring the shit out of them?"

"Oh, I expect them to," he said. "But, I'll tell you something, I can be nice. I mean I can be. Nice. If somebody's trying to get along. So show me how you're trying to get along. What did you say to this broad?"

"What you told me."

"Which is what?"

"Daryl, I done just like you said. I had her drive me to where I hid the car, out in the trees, you know, and then I showed her the pikchers and told her to keep cool, we'd be calling her. Then I dropped her off."

"You told her we'd be what?" Daryl said.

Judy sat up straighter, raising her arm, protecting her face. "Calling her. Whatcha think I said?"

For just an instant Daryl didn't move, just sat there grinning at her. Then, his neck muscles bunching, sneering, he picked up a pillow, raised it two-handed over his head like Moses with the Ten Commandments, and slung the pillow against the wall. It slammed into the painted Sheetrock, hung suspended like a stop-action photo, then slid down onto the carpet.

"Goddamnit to fucking *hell*," he said. "That's what I'm *talking* about. I didn't say anything about *calling* her."

"Well maybe I didn't say exactly them words," Judy said.

"Oh, yeah, you did. I can tell by that dumb fucking look on your face."

"Daryl, you . . . holy shit, calling her, sending her a letter, what's it matter?"

"Because word for word, you dumb little hick, I said for you to show her those pictures and then tell her she'd be *hearing* from you. Not by phone. Not by letter, not by fucking carrier pigeon. That's all, *hearing*. That way you haven't done anything. You haven't threatened her and you haven't asked her for anything."

"I ain't *done* nothing? I pulled a fucking gun on her," Judy said.

"Yeah, you have. And made her do what? Did you rob her? Hell no, and you didn't rape her and you didn't hold her for ransom. Nothing. But now you've gone and told her you were going to call her on the fucking phone."

She blinked. "Daryl, you're the weirdest dude I ever saw."

"Shit, I— Yeah, maybe I am. Maybe I'm weird and dumb as all get-out for not doing this all by myself. Conspiracy. You know what the fuck that is? I doubt you can spell it."

"Well . . . don't it have something to do with a gang? Somebody planning something," she said.

He expelled a long sigh. "Jesus Christ, what do I expect from somebody rides down the highway getting finger-fucked?

□ 155 □

Conspiracy has to do with two people, which is us, planning something, which we did. But it isn't a federal crime until one of us does what you call an overt act. The overt act has to do with helping the plan, and the plan has to be to do something against federal law. I learned all of this shit the hard way, believe me. Now get this; planning to use the fucking phone to tell somebody how they're going to keep you from flashing a bunch of pictures of them around is a federal beef. Until you told this broad you were planning to use the phone to get in touch with her, the only law you broke was a *state* law. Fuck these state of Texas shitheads; they can try to make a case till the cows come home."

"You're bein' awful *picky*, Daryl," she said.

"Well I've been through— To hell with it. If you did it, you did it. What else happened? What did you say and what did she say?"

"You got me so fucked up with all your yelling I can't remember," she said.

He smiled. He put a thumb on one side of her deltoid muscle and a forefinger on the other side and squeezed. "Well *try*, Judy. Try hard."

"Daryl, she— Ouch! Don't do that." He released her. She rubbed her shoulder, tears rolling down her cheeks as she said, "She ast about some guy."

"Great. Who?"

"She wanted to know if them pikchers come from some guy. Eddie Somebody-the-Fuck."

He looked thoughtful. "So she thinks old Eddie gave them to me. Good, let her."

"Who's Eddie?" she said. "She said Eddie South, I think."

"South? Say, Judy, that's pretty good for a dumb fucking hick. You know? Try Eddie Satterwhite. That more like it?"

"That's it," she said. "Who's he?"

"He used to be her— A guy I know. Did she say anything about a guy named Lou? Lou Thorndon?"

"I reckon not," Judy said.

"Well that's good." He smiled at her, a relaxed smile this time, and put his arm around her. "Come here. Listen, I want to apologize. Really. I've been pretty rough on you, but then this is a pretty rough game we're playing. You know?"

She scooted over on the mattress and leaned against him. "It's okay, I ain't hurt none. But listen, don't call me a dumb hick no more. I might *be* a hick, but I ain't dumb."

"Yeah? Yeah, I apologize for that too. There wasn't any call for that, I got carried away. You know?" He stroked her thigh. "We're going to be just fine."

She wriggled like a puppy. "Hey, Daryl. Listen, you want to turn off the light? Leave it on if you want to; it don't matter none to me."

12

Bino had a tough time concentrating at Emmett Burns's arraignment and bond hearing the following afternoon. There were several reasons why he couldn't keep his mind on the courtroom goings-on. First of all, the proceedings were pretty cut and dried. William Sanderson, the U.S. magistrate who'd been scheduled to preside, had taken the afternoon off, so Goldman had to go barging around through the Federal Building at the last minute to find John Tolle, the other local magistrate, in order to hold the hearing at all. Everybody and his dog knew that personal recognizance was automatic for a guy like Emmett Burns, and even Goldman didn't kick up much of a fuss when Judge Tolle released Judge Burns without any security (though Marv did manage to make a couple of We-the-People speeches and throw some icy glares around at everybody).

Another thing that got in the way of Bino's concentration was the vision of Annabelle that kept floating through his mind. The feel of her flesh against him, her firm tongue touching his neck and licking around the perimeter of his ear, her warm, frenzied breath on his cheek as he had pounded into her . . . Well, all of that was pretty strong stuff, but even stronger was the feeling of something not right about it. Jesus Christ, she *was* married to somebody else now. And not just any somebody else. No *way* did Bino want Tirelli on his trail. No fucking way. Just the thought of Tirelli and his band of merry men made Bino want to sit down and cross his legs.

Near the close of the arraignment, Judge Tolle's deep bass voice cut through the fog. "What are the defense's views on that subject, Mr. Phillips?"

Emmett Burns stood at Bino's side. Burns was wearing a navy suit. His hands were clasped in front of him, and his head was bowed. Bino thought that a few silver threads were visible in Burns's auburn hair, but he wasn't sure; it could have been the light in the courtroom. On Burns's other side, Goldman and the red-faced FBI agent—who was really getting into the act now, wearing a black suit like Goldman's and marching around like a drill instructor—stood at attention. The court reporter, a plump woman in her thirties, sat with her fingers poised over the shorthand machine. Seated at the bench, Judge Tolle adjusted the collar on his black robe and blinked, pleasantly but expectantly.

Bino cleared his throat. "Well I'd have to think about that, Your Honor. There are . . . a number of options to consider." He was conscious of Emmett Burns as Burns threw him a sideways glance.

"Oh?" Tolle said. "What options are those?"

There was pin-drop silence. Bino was racking his brain, not having the slightest idea what Tolle was talking about and trying to think of something clever to say, when Judge Tolle saved his bacon by going on.

"I mean," Tolle said, "either we do it or we don't. On the record and up-front, there isn't a judge in the Northern District who hasn't sat at one time or another on some sort of committee with the defendant. So we can either call in a visiting judge from another district or we can put one of our own judges in the position of having to state his neutrality when there's an obvious conflict of interest. Now you're saying there are other options, and I can't see what they are. Enlighten the court."

"What I meant was that there are a lot of other . . . districts, and . . . a lot of other judges, Your Honor. A lot of other jurists to consider." Bino's collar was suddenly a couple of sizes too small for him.

"I think we're capable of finding a judge, Mr. Phillips," Tolle said. "I'm giving both sides thirty days to file whatever briefs and legal authorities they may wish on the subject of a change of venue. Pretrial motions on"—he checked his calendar—"January 27, unless the judge who is selected to try this matter wants to change that. Any problem with that, Mr. Goldman?"

Goldman's heels clicked like a Nazi corporal's. "Fine, Your Honor. The government will be ready."

"How about the defense, Mr. Phillips?" Tolle grinned. "Or do you have other options to consider?"

Bino felt as though he'd shrunk about six inches. He checked on his right to make certain he was still taller than Emmett Burns, then said, "No, sir. Not me, Judge. I'll have some pretrial motions whipped up by then all right." Like a motion to force Goldman to 'fess up as to what the government's case was all about.

Tolle looked as though he were about to burst out laughing as he said, "Very well," then banged his gavel and said, "Court is adjourned."

Bino turned. Burns fell into step beside him. They took one long, synchronized stride in the direction of the exit, then halted as one. Susie Sin and her gang of reporters and cameramen stood waiting in the spectators' section like Chinese bandits.

The press conference had completely slipped Bino's mind, what with everything else that had happened, and fielding a barrage of questions was something he didn't want to put Emmett Burns through. Burns had done a one-eighty today. Where yesterday he'd been in a fighting mood, a feisty glint in his eye, today the judge was having a sinking spell. He'd visibly aged overnight, and instead of offering his two cents' worth on every subject from Goldman to the way the case should be tried, Burns was now acting like a whipped dog. An *old* whipped dog. Earlier this morning in Bino's office, Burns had sat with his head bowed and responded to Bino's questions with mumbled yeses and noes and imperceptible nods and shakes of his head. The shock of the indictment was beginning to sink in hard, and, worried, Bino didn't like what he was seeing.

Plus there were the rumors floating around, coming through Half, that Burns *had* in fact taken some kind of bribe. Bino didn't like to think about that. They were just rumors, of course, but . . . well, eighteen years in the trenches had taught Bino that street rumors were about as reliable as anything else. For now the best thing that Bino could do was keep his client the hell away from all those newspeople.

As Bino grasped Burns's elbow and steered the judge— who was moving woodenly, ready to be guided in just about any direction—toward the side exit, two things happened. First, at the rear of the spectators' section, Susie Sin loudly cleared her throat. At the same instant, Bino caught a glimpse of royal blue and a flash of shapely, milk white calf in the corner of his eye.

Ann Burns was sitting in the front row, just beyond the railing. Bino had wondered about her, whether or not she'd show up for the arraignment, and had even glanced around in search of her as they'd entered the courtroom. He'd resisted the impulse to ask Emmett Burns where his daughter was—

Lord knew the judge had enough to worry about—and seeing her seated there gave Bino a little relief. Here was the perfect opportunity to send his client on his chaperoned way while Bino took his own chances with Susie Sin.

Bino stepped toward the rail and said, "Hi, Ann. It's lucky you came." Then he got a straight-on look at her and wondered whether it was lucky or not.

In her own way, this girl looked every bit as whipped as her father. Beneath her luxuriant mane of red hair—in spite of what he was finding out about her, Ann's physical appearance still practically took Bino's breath away—her lips were rigid and drawn. At first glance Bino wrote it off as just the aftershock of a big losing night at the tennis club. But that wasn't it at all. Nope. People with Ann's problem had remorseful gambling hangovers, all right, but the expression on her face was something entirely different. She was scared to death of something. Or somebody.

She showed a smile that was obviously forced and said, "Well it's about time that something lucky happened."

Bino came within an eyelash of pulling a boner by mentioning the night before and the tennis club, then remembered Emmett Burns at his side and closed his mouth. When he opened it again he said, "Look, Ann, I'm going to have to talk to these newspeople. Could you give your dad a lift back to my office?"

She uncrossed her legs and stood, wearing a modestly cut, blue, knee-length dress and a blue silk scarf in her hair. She squared her shoulders. "Anything to help out. Let's go, Daddy." She waited hesitantly behind the rail. Bino indicated first the reporters, then the side exit. She nodded, came through the gate, and took Emmett Burns's arm. She took a small step forward and, with her father positioned behind her where he couldn't see her lips, mouthed silently, "I need to talk to you."

Bino nodded, then glanced at Emmett Burns. Burns hadn't noticed. Ann stepped back, smiled up at her dad, and led him out through the side exit.

Bino swallowed some air and strode purposefully through the gate to face Susie Sin. He briefly wondered whether Barney Dalton would like to sub for him. Hell, Barney was the only winner Bino could think of right now.

It made Emmett Burns hot under the collar to be going around acting like a whimpering fool, but there wasn't anything he could do about it. Try as he might, he couldn't brighten up. He felt like the protagonist in "Buried Alive," by Edgar Allan Poe, alert and fully aware of what was going on but unable to speak or move a muscle while shovelful after shovelful of damp earth plunked onto the lid of his coffin. But what Burns's own lawyer didn't even know—Bino Phillips had been treating Burns as though he was a retarded child, and Burns had *really* had a bellyful of that—was that the criminal case wasn't what had the judge so down in the dumps. It would take more than a bunch of lawyers from the U.S. Attorney's office to make Emmett Burns cower and simper. What had Burns off his feed was the way Ann had been acting.

He'd been awake when she'd come home the night before, though she hadn't known it. It had been after three in the morning, and he'd been staring wide-eyed at the ceiling, tossing and turning, when she'd finally pulled her car into the drive. Then he'd crept barefoot to the kitchen door and peered in at her, sitting at the breakfast table, her head bowed, her shoulders heaving with pitiful sobs. He couldn't deny it any longer; her problems had begun again.

As they left the Federal Building and stepped out on the sidewalk, he said to her, "Anything you want to tell your old man, honey?" The sun was out, and the temperature was in the fifties. The breeze was a bare, featherlike touch. Women were coatless; men strolled by with their jackets slung over their shoulders.

"No, I . . . ," Ann said, then licked her lips, her gaze on the sidewalk. "I'm fine, Daddy, it's you we have to worry about."

"Bull, daughter."

They stepped to the curb and waited for the light to change so they could cross Commerce Street to the parking lot. "You need your strength," she said. "Don't worry about me."

She was too distant, too formal. Too hell-bent on keeping his attention on his own problems. Whatever it was, she was in a world of trouble. "There's nothing too bad to come to me with, Ann," he said.

She didn't answer. As the light changed and they started across the intersection amid a crowd of pedestrians, she took a handkerchief from her purse and blew her nose.

Bino wondered how Ronald Reagan and Bill Clements, guys like that, handled their press conferences. Every time he saw the president or the governor on TV, the reporters would ask their questions one at a time and wait respectfully while the prez or guv smoothly gave a long and detailed answer, usually closing with a little joke that put the reporters into giggling stitches.

But Bino's own press conference wasn't working out that way. As Bino walked into the big conference room down the hall from the courtroom and took a seat at the table beside a guy who identified himself as the public relations specialist from the United States Attorney's Office, Susie Sin said, "Here's the lawyer. Where's the client? What about the judge, Mr. Phillips? Are you hiding him?"

Bino clasped his hands on the table before him and leaned over toward the microphone. "Well to tell you the truth, it's been a trying time for my client. He needs some rest. But I've discussed things with him at length and I'm prepared to—"

"Did you tell Emmett Burns not to talk to the newspapers?" The interruption came from the back of the room, to Bino's right, and the speaker was a young guy, middle twenties, wearing gold-rimmed glasses and a plaid sport coat. His question had been asked in an accusatory tone, and he followed the question by regarding Bino through narrowed eyes.

Bino said, "Why, no, he—"

"Well, then, why isn't he here?" A girl, about the same age as the guy and also wearing gold-rimmed glasses, narrowed *her* eyes at Bino from his left. A brother and sister kamikaze team.

Bino's neck was getting warm. "Now look, I'll be happy to answer your questions one at a time, but I—"

"Are you going to work out a deal with the prosecution?" said a chubby guy whose tie extended sideways from its Windsor knot and was draped over his shoulder like a suspender. "Or do you plan to try the case?"

Bino tried to cover his frustration by turning aside and faking a cough into his cupped hand. Susie Sin, standing out among the crowd in a sweater-and-skirt combination that hugged her curves in all the right places, was watching him with the beginnings of a smile on her face. Was she being encouraging, or was she just getting a kick out of seeing him make an ass of himself? Bino adjusted the mike and leaned toward it. Beside him, the guy from the U.S. Attorney's Office expelled a sigh.

Bino said, "Well to begin with, my client isn't guilty. And as for strategy, plea bargains and whatnot, we haven't gotten that far into the case yet."

"Then you *might* work out a deal?" Susie Sin said. "For a guilty plea?" Visible beyond her, a sandy-haired, slender guy braced a video camera on his shoulder and pointed it in Bino's direction. Bino moved his chin slightly to his left. Annabelle had always said that his right was his stronger profile.

"No," Bino said. "Not for a guilty plea. But there are a lot of different kinds of plea bargains. You, sir. You with your hand up." Bino was pointing at a balding man who was probably about to scratch his head. Anything to get the floor away from Susie Sin.

The balding guy paused, his face turning crimson, his fingers just inches from his scalp. "Huh?" he said.

"Let me ask a direct, to-the-point question, Mr. Phillips," Susie Sin said. "Do you deny that your client has ever accepted any bribes, gratuities, whatever, from an attorney by the name of Frank Bleeder?"

Bino opened his mouth to deny everything, then paused. Evidently Goldman had given Susie Sin one helluva lot more information than he'd put in the indictment. Bino said, "That's a good question, Miss Sin. Exactly what bribes does the prosecution say that my client accepted from Mr. Bleeder? Or anybody else, for that matter?"

Her plucked eyebrow arched. "Don't you know?"

"Well, not really," Bino said. "I've read the indictment over a couple of times, but I—"

"I'm afraid our time is up, folks." The publicity man from the U.S. Attorney's Office was on his feet. He was around forty, with a full head of wavy, black hair and a thin, neat Clark Gable mustache. His teeth looked as though he'd won them in an Ultra Brite contest. "You've been more than kind, and we thank you for your patience. Always glad to cooperate with representatives from the media."

Bino's mouth was agape. He'd wondered when he'd come into the room what *this* guy was doing here and had even glanced around to see if Goldman was making an appearance. Whose fucking press conference was this, anyway? The reporters and photographers were rattling briefcases, folding papers, putting cameras away.

The U.S. Attorney's man leaned over, holding his palm firmly over the mike as he said to Bino, "They do get out of hand sometimes. I thought you were holding up pretty well under the circumstances, but enough is enough."

"Enough is . . . ?" Bino stood. "Yeah, I was holding up pretty well. God-*damned* well, if you ask me. In fact I was just getting warmed up." He faced the reporters and raised his voice. "Hey, anybody got any more questions? I don't have to be anywhere."

The newspeople didn't seem to hear, just kept moving single file out the door into the corridor, spiral notebooks under their arms and cameras suspended from shoulders by straps. Only Susie Sin hadn't moved. She was sitting in a folding chair with her hands resting loosely in her lap and an expectant look on her face. Bino realized that his voice wasn't carrying over the speaker. He glanced down. The U.S. Attorney's man had his thumb on the black button at the base of the mike. The fucking guy had turned it off.

The public relations man's smile now appeared painted on his face, as in a cartoon. "I'm really doing you a favor, Phillips. Don't you know they were ready to barbecue you?"

"Don't you know I was about to find out what this case is all about?" Bino said. The guy's look said that, yeah, he knew it damn well. Bino started to really lay into the guy, really give him a tongue-lashing, when Susie Sin caught his eye.

She was sitting straight as a ramrod, her elbow bent and her hand on a level with her ear, making little circles in the air with her palm facing Bino. She winked at him, then cut her eyes in the direction of the exit. She got up and went into the corridor, high heels moving in graceful rhythm, toes pointed straight ahead.

Bino started to follow her. The public relations guy put a hand on Bino's arm and said, "I'd be careful, pal. What you say to her might not come out the same, when she repeats it."

Bino paused. "Well it may not, but at least I'll get to talk to her. Which is more than I've done so far. Don't try to get in the way, huh? They might have to hire a new press relations man. Or bankroll you a new set of pearly white teeth, one of the two."

Susie Sin said, "Well, we might have some information to trade, you and I." She checked her slim gold wristwatch. "I'm running late. Rehearsal. They call it preparation, but we do a lot of one-liners and practice grinning at each other quite a bit. I'm on at six and ten, but I've got a couple of hours in between. I can't divulge any of my sources, of course. To you *or* the other side." The last part sounded like something that she said to everybody.

"Have you ever been to Joe Miller's Bar?" Bino said. He was leaning against the corridor wall. Beyond Susie, the elevator doors were open and men and women were climbing aboard.

"On Lemmon Avenue? Once or twice. A lot of writers hang out there. Boy, and some really *weird people*." Her pretty Oriental face tilted quizzically. Bino made her out to be around thirty, but she could have been older.

"Yeah, well . . . I go there occasionally myself," Bino said. "You know, for something different. To get a gander at the weirdos." He grinned. "How about seven-thirty? Hey, I appreciate this. I know you want to be objective in your coverage, Miss Sin."

"I'll be there." She threw him another wink, one that was beginning to grow on him, then left him leaning there and took a few clickety-clack steps toward the elevator. She stopped and turned back to him. "Oh, and Mr. Phillips," she said. "That stuff about newspeople wanting to be objective and unbiased is just like the story about networks giving equal time. They're both a lot of bullshit."

13

"Yeah," Barney Dalton said. "The Oriental lovely, on television. Jesus, she's coming here?" He was wearing a dark windbreaker with the Crooked River Golf Club logo on its breast. In the dim light inside Joe Miller's Bar, Bino couldn't tell whether the jacket was navy or dark green. Barney had one shin propped against the foam padding on the bar. He was drinking something that was colored amber—unless he'd switched since last night it was a J. & B. and water—and beside his tall glass lay a stack of hundred-dollar bills with a few loose twenties and fives spread out on the bar next to the pile of C-notes. Three women were strung out on barstools to Barney's right. Dolly, the cute pixie of a brunette whom Bino had met the other night after he'd left Emmett Burns's house, was closest to Barney. The other two gals were blonds, and

Bino didn't know them. Just moments ago the bartender had poured fresh drinks for the girls and taken the money for the drinks out of one of Barney's hundreds. Barney had tossed out a ten-dollar tip with a flourish, and the bartender had gobbled it up.

"She'll be here in about fifteen minutes," Bino said. "And listen, Barn, I got a favor to ask."

"Say no more." Barney glanced at Dolly and the blonds. They didn't seem to be listening. Barney said, a little louder than before, "*Saa*-ay no more, buddyroll. What're friends for? Hey, it was you that put me onto that big easy score last night. A hundred enough?" He held one of the C-notes, folded in half, between his first and middle fingers and dropped it on the bar in front of Bino.

"Hey," Bino said. "You're a prince of a guy, but that wasn't exactly what I meant." He replaced the bill atop Barney's pile of hundreds, then said, "What I was going to ask is . . . Well, you know she's a celebrity, and people like that get really self-conscious. So what I was going to ask is if you could, like, cool it while she's here."

"No problem," Barney said. "Hell, I'll treat her just like one of the girls." Visible beyond him, Dolly leaned over and whispered something to one of the blonds. They both looked at Barney, cupped their hands over their mouths, and giggled.

"Well that isn't exactly it either, Barn. Could you just sort of, like, ignore us? Like we weren't even here?"

"*Ignore* you? Say, you wouldn't be going big-time on me. Hey, buddy, a lot of the guys we hung out with in school don't know us no more, but I never thought I'd be hearing that kind of shit from you." Barney folded his arms.

"Are you, are you fucking kidding me? That's not it at all, Barn. Look, I've got business with the lady, and I sort of promised her there wouldn't be a lot of people crowding around. Makes her uncomfortable. You remember how it was, guys coming up to you when you were in the drugstore buying toothpaste or rubbers or something and saying, 'Hey, aren't you Barney Dalton, the shifty little point guard?' "

"Well I wasn't never *rude* to anybody," Barney said. He looked at Dolly and the blonds. "Hey, girls. When Mr. Big here, formerly known as Bino, has a few drinks in a little while with Susie Sin, pretend you don't know him, huh? Mr. Big don't want to have to give out no autygraphs or nothing." Then he said to Bino, "That okay?"

Dolly leaned over. "Susie Sin? The *newswoman*? She's coming here, to Joe Miller's?"

Bino thought, Why didn't I just meet her someplace else? At that instant the front door swung wide, a slash of light from the streetlamp appeared on the red carpet, and Susie entered the bar. She raised herself on the balls of her feet, swaying slightly as she looked around.

"She's here, Barn," Bino said. "Excuse me. Just this once, huh, buddy?"

"Well, hey, sure," Barney said. "I wouldn't want nobody thinking you and me were *friends* or anything." He drew air in through his nose and turned his back.

Bino started to put his hand on Barney's shoulder, started to try to explain some more, then changed his mind. What the hell, Barney would live. Unconsciously straightening the knot in his tie, Bino went up near the entrance and said hi to Susie Sin.

"Where are you?" she said. "Jeez, it's like a cave in here." A looseleaf hardcover notebook was under her arm, a pen clipped to its cover.

"I guess you need some light," Bino said. "To make notes or something."

"It would help," Susie said. "You don't want me to misquote you, do you? Heaven forbid."

"There's a table over there with a candle," Bino said, indicating a setting for two with flickering light inside a red glass holder on top. "It's not much, but at least you can see to write." He took her elbow and steered her alongside the bar. Barney said in a stage whisper as they passed, "Play like you don't notice 'em." One of the blonds glanced at them over her shoulder, then quickly turned back around.

"Oh, I'll *see*," Susie said. "My handwriting may be sort of wavy, I hope I can read it. It's really *brrrr* outside. I'm going to have to remember to start wearing a coat."

As he held her chair, then sat down across from her, Bino said, "I thought it had warmed up some, since the snow."

"Well it might be warm to you," Susie said, opening her notebook. "But for a Southern Californian any temperature below fifty-five is like fireplaceville."

"Southern California? L.A.?"

"Mission Viejo, Orange County. The only time I lived in L.A. was when I went to Southern Cal."

"What brought you to Dallas?" Bino said.

She offered him the notebook. "You want to interview *me*?"

"Not . . . hey, not really. I'm just making some small talk. Breaking the ice."

"It's already broken. I don't really have time for small talk." She looked around. "But I am sort of thirsty."

Bino motioned to Melinda, the chunky, pretty-faced bartender, who came over to the table and said, "I'm not sure if I'm supposed to do this or not, Bino. Barney said to ignore you."

"What?" Susie said. Over at the bar, Barney swiveled on his stool and locked gazes with Bino for an instant, then turned his back and glugged some Scotch.

Bino said quickly, "I'll have a Michelob. And you?"

"Perrier and lime," Susie said, raising out of her chair and smoothing her skirt. "I've got another set to do at the station. Who's Barney?"

"Oh, one of the regulars, I guess," Bino said. Melinda slapped a napkin down and stalked back to the bar. Bino said to Susie, "You were saying?"

"Well," Susie said. "To begin with, just a couple of things about you. You've been a lawyer around here for a long time. From SMU." She bent over the notebook and prepared to write.

"SMU undergraduate, but my law degree's from South

Texas College of Law, in Houston. Eighteen years I've been practicing. I've been around the courthouse, yeah, you could say that."

She wrote what looked to be about half of a sentence, then said, "How about other cases of note? Who else have you represented? Besides the judge."

He wasn't ready for the question. Hell, he'd come here to talk about Emmett Burns. Mentally he sifted through a list of his clients, but all he could come up with was an image of Weedy Clements. He said, "Oh, a few guys, I guess. I've even won a case or two."

She said coolly, "So I've heard. Would it be fair to say that you've made your reputation defending some unsavory characters?"

Melinda appeared at Susie's elbow. She set down a stubby glass of Perrier with a lime slice impaled on its edge, then bent over the table and presented Bino with a foamy glass of Michelob. He gave her a ten. She counted out the change and offered it to him on a small plastic tray. He scooped up the money, leaving three quarters as a tip. Melinda pointedly dropped the quarters on the table and retreated, her generous fanny twitching from side to side. She stopped beside the bar and said something to Barney. Barney nodded and stared straight ahead.

"Well, have you?" Susie said.

"Have I . . . ? I'm sorry," Bino said.

"Have you built your practice by defending a lot of pimps and whores and pushers?" She smiled. "Maybe you can understand the question better that way."

"Well, I'm . . . Gee, I'm a criminal lawyer. Hey, you know the Constitution guarantees everybody a proper defense." He tried to hold back, then couldn't resist saying, "Even newspeople, if one of them ever gets in trouble."

"Touché," she said, writing something down. She laid her pen on the table. "Do you resent being interviewed by a woman?"

"Do I . . . ? Jesus Christ, what does that have to do with anything?"

"Just an observation. You strike me as one of those wild west, grab-'em-by-the-hair types. Divorced, aren't you?"

"Yeah," he said. "Hell, fifteen years ago. So what?"

"So nothing, I suppose." She picked up her ballpoint. "And you have won a lot of cases. But, well, I'm curious about something. Don't you, don't you find it a little odd that Emmett Burns would pick someone of your background to represent him? Rather than one of the white-collar firms."

Bino thought, What the hell am I doing here? He said, "You'd have to ask somebody else that question. I'll 'fess up, Miss Sin, that all of my clients aren't members of the Lions Club. But I've got a pretty good record, and I do know a thing or two about trying a case."

"I'm coming to that," she said. "Haven't you tried a few cases in Emmett Burns's court? With him on the bench?"

"Sure. A few, the luck of the draw has put me in front of just about every judge around here at one time or the other."

"One in particular," she said. "An acquittal, two years ago. It was a pretty large cocaine conspiracy, wasn't it?"

As big as they come, thought Bino. Only most of the cocaine came from the DEA or FBI, and all of the conspirators except for my client were wired-up federal snitches. "That's right," he said.

She was scribbling furiously now. "Let's talk about that. I know it's been two years and your memory might not be really fresh, but wasn't a lot of the government's evidence in the case excluded from the jury? By Judge Burns?"

A warning bell went off in Bino's head. "Did Goldman tell you that?" Bino let his gaze wander, following Dolly as she left her stool beside Barney and paraded off in the direction of the ladies' room. She glanced at Susie Sin as she went by.

Susie blinked innocently. "Did *who* tell me that? My sources, I told you earlier."

"Well," Bino said, "did your sources happen to mention that Goldman was trying to play the jury some wiretapped evidence, and that during the course of the trial we found out that the court order authorizing the taps had been altered? And that on the date the magistrate was supposed to have signed the orders he was in New Orleans at some kind of seminar that the Fifth Circuit Court of Appeals was having? Did Mr. Marvin 'Source' Goldman happen to mention that?"

"No, my source didn't." She sipped some Perrier, made a face, squeezed some lime juice into the glass, and laid the spent rind on her napkin. "Did you have any conferences with Judge Burns either before, during, or after the trial, outside the courtroom and without the federal prosecutor being privy to the conversation?"

Bino filled his cheeks with air, then expelled the air slowly through pursed lips. The sound was like that of a slowly deflating tire. He said, "I don't play those kind of games, Miss Sin. I leave that up to guys like Marvin Goldman. I don't play those games and neither does—*did*—Emmett Burns. The only time the judge and I were alone during the trial was on the elevator. We happened to catch it at the same time. I faced the front and so did he, like a couple of wooden soldiers."

She wrote something down. "Then you admit to meeting with Judge Burns on an elevator. In secret."

"In *secret*? What is it with you people?"

"Did the meeting occur before the judge ruled on the admissibility of the government's evidence?" she asked. "Or after?"

Bino's upper lip curled. "Before. Judge Burns wouldn't give his ruling until after he counted the wad of money I slipped him on the elevator. Is that what Goldman—?"

"Do you want me to broadcast that?" She smiled.

His chin moved to one side. "Broadcast what?"

"The part about you slipping the judge the wad of money."

"Jesus Christ, I was *joking*."

"It didn't sound like a joke to me," she said.

"Yeah, well, let me tell you something." Bino wagged his finger.

"Please do." She laid her pen down and folded her arms.

"Boy. Boy, you people don't give a flying hoot in hell about the truth, do you? Like if Emmett Burns is pure as all get-out and is just getting screwed, that doesn't make near the story as if he's a crooked judge on the take. As long as everybody will tune in to Susie Sin instead of the football player turned newsman on the other channel, well, that's all that matters. Just who gets the biggest audience."

"It's called ratings," she said. Her tone was defensive. She'd gotten Bino all worked up, just as she'd obviously planned, but, swinging wildly, he'd struck a nerve.

"Well, hey, I've got a good idea," Bino said. "Why don't you start doing your broadcasts in the nude, Susie? Like buck nekkid or something. That'll really knock 'em dead in the old ratings."

She bowed her head. "That's a low blow."

"You think so? Well how about this? You say"—he raised the pitch of his voice and spoke in a high, mimicking falsetto—" 'Well maybe we do have some information to trade, Mr. Phillips.' " His tone returned to normal. "Then you come running out here acting like this is a fact-finding mission when it's really nothing but a hatchet job on me *and* my client. Who're you working for? *Goldman?* Hell's bells."

She twisted her fingers in her lap, then slowly lifted her chin. "It's called keeping your sources happy."

All the foam had disappeared from the surface of his beer. He sipped some. It was warm, and he wondered briefly whether Melinda had brought him a glass of Michelob that had been sitting around for a couple of hours. He said to Susie, "A minute ago you said, 'It's called ratings.' Now it's called 'keeping your sources happy.' Well I don't care what it's *called*. I'm just wanting a fair shake in the media, that's all. Hell, I've *never* had one, not when I've been in federal court, not in eighteen years. I don't even know why you people bother interviewing anybody. Why don't you just let *Goldman* write your script for you? Him or that publicity guy, the one with the phony grin. Then you can just go on the air and read what they write. Spend your free time playing golf or fishing or something."

"Or making egg roll in Wing Woo's," she said, suddenly feisty again. Then her features softened, the shadows inside the lounge deepening the creases that ran from the corners of her mouth to the sides of her nose. "Look . . . it's like this. Our information on federal criminal cases comes from the U.S. prosecutor. If we don't give the story the right slant, well, the information stops flowing. I've got a career to think about. If I become some sort of crusader for the defense, well, end of career. That's the way the game is played."

"Hell, I know that," Bino said. "I don't know of anything you can do, including being a lawyer, where everybody *isn't* playing a game. Life's a bitch. I'm sitting here with a case where I think my client's innocent, and I can't . . . Hell, I don't even know for sure what Emmett Burns is charged with."

"Fraud. Being a crooked judge, whatever. Isn't that it?" Susie said.

"There's no such charge as being a crooked judge. Jesus, that's always bugged me. They've got a bunch of crime reporters running around who don't even know what is and what isn't a crime. Look, in order to make a case they've got to pick out a guy who's paid him a bribe, somebody he's let off the hook in exchange for money, something like that. You know, some specific act that's a crime. But the way that Goldman's got the indictment worded, I can't even figure out what crimes they're saying he committed. And it sure isn't an accident; they don't *want* me to know. They want me to have to pull it out of them. That way I won't have as much time to put together a defense. How'd you like to defend somebody when you don't even know what his crime is supposed to be? But I'll bet Goldman told *you* what the crimes are. Bet you a dollar."

She closed her eyes tightly and shook her head. Her long, dark hair moved from side to side. "I can't. I just . . . Look, whatever else you may think of me I do protect my sources. It's the code, or whatever."

He looked her over, studied the tilt of her pointed chin, the occasional stray beam of light that illuminated her dark, almond-shaped eyes. "Well, then," he said. "What in hell do you have to trade, Susie?"

She picked up her pen, cool and professional now. "Just answer the questions, please, Mr. Phillips."

"Bino. Why would I want to answer any of your questions at all, when you're just going to run to Goldman and—?"

"Just listen to the *questions*, Mr. Bino. Do you happen to know a Mr. Louis P. Thorndon?"

He looked beyond her, read the lighted Budweiser sign over the cash register three times, then gazed at her as he said, "Oh. I get it. I'm going to learn something from the questions you're going to ask."

She tilted her head to look at the ceiling. "Yankee white man so *velly, velly intellihent*." She bent forward in a writing pose. "Did Mr. Frank Bleeder ever act as a go-between to carry some money from Louis Thorndon to Judge Burns in return for a dismissal of some charges?"

Bino reached for his beer, almost toppling it over, then steadied the glass with his hands. He took a long swallow. "Hell, not even Goldman can get away with that one. That just isn't the way things are done in federal court. The charges against Thorndon . . . well, the government itself dropped them. The judge doesn't have anything to do with that."

"Oh? Well what if the judge were to call up the prosecution and say that if they didn't dismiss he was going to throw the case out? Like that their evidence wasn't strong enough to go forward."

The light flashed on in Bino's head. It was lucky for Goldman that he wasn't within reach right now, sitting here in this bar. Come to think about it, it was probably lucky for Bino too. Bino said, "Wait a minute. Is that the kind of crap that Goldman's putting out? Look, even if my client was on the take he wouldn't be *that* dumb. Tell you what. I'll bet you a pizza at Tirelli's Italian when we leave here that I can finish the questioning for you."

She lifted, then dropped, her shoulders. "Are you asking me for a date, Bino?"

He hadn't really considered it, but maybe he was. He sat there with his mouth open and didn't say anything.

She checked her watch. "Rain check on the pizza if you are. But I'm fascinated. What questions do you think I'm going to ask?"

"For one, you're going to ask if my client called up a worm over at the U.S. Attorney's office named Buford Jernigan and put the heat on him to drop Thorndon's charges."

She giggled. It sounded a little strange coming from Susie Sin, as though she was a little girl for an instant, then a big, grown-up superstar newslady once again. "Well I wouldn't say *worm*," she said. "That's *your* word."

"Jesus Christ, Susie, it was the other way around. Jernigan called up the judge and tried to talk him into doing something out of line to help the government get a conviction. Emmett Burns told Jernigan to take a walk. He told me all about it, the first time he talked to me about representing him."

Her eyebrows lifted. "Can I quote you on that?"

"You rootin'-tootin' you can, girl," Bino said.

The tip of her nose cast a shadow over her upper lip as she wrote that one down. She said, "It'll make news. It won't make you really popular down at the Federal Building."

"I'm *already* unpopular down at the Federal Building. Is that going to be Goldman's whole case? The Thorndon thing?"

She looked thoughtful. "Be patient. I've got some more questions. There are several counts in the indictment, aren't there? Doesn't that mean that there are several crimes involved?"

"That's a laugh," Bino said. "It makes it *look* like there are several different crimes to somebody that doesn't know what's going on. That's why the Feds like mail-fraud prosecutions. Every time a letter gets mailed—it doesn't matter whether there's one plot or fifty plots—but every time a letter gets mailed it's another count. I've already figured out that one count in the indictment is when the court secretary mailed Thorndon's dismissal order over to the district clerk. Another count is when the district clerk made a Xerox of the order, file-stamped it, and sent it back to the court. That's two counts right there, and my client didn't mail either one of the envelopes himself. Hell, the Feds can turn one crime into five in nothing flat, it's what they're experts at doing."

"I don't know anything about all that legal stuff," she said, "but I do have a bonus question for you."

"Shoot."

"Do you—and you've really never answered my question about Mr. Bleeder carrying some money to the judge—but do you deny that the judge's own daughter was involved?"

That one really threw him. Not that Bino believed for a minute—not yet, anyway, even in spite of what Half had heard—that Emmett Burns had taken any bribes, but Goldman trying to rope Burns's daughter in on it, well, that just took the cake. "Involved in what?" Bino said.

"Let me ask the question another way," Susie said. "Did Judge Burns's daughter Ann collect some money from Mr. Bleeder, who was acting as Thorndon's attorney, take a cut for herself to cover her gambling losses, and give the rest of the money to her father?"

Now she'd said a mouthful. Bino tried hard but couldn't think of a real cute answer. He said simply, "I don't know, Susie. I wouldn't tell you if I *did* know, but I really don't. Is Goldman about to bring Ann Burns into this? It might kill her dad, you know."

"I don't have anything to do with bringing anybody into anything," Susie said. "I'm just a newsperson, remember? But I'm going to give you a break and let you reanswer that question. If I report it the way you said, it's going to sound like the judge's own lawyer thinks it's possible that his daughter *did* pay him a bribe." She smiled, candlelight dancing on olive-complexioned cheeks. "Maybe I'm getting soft. Got a thing for big whitehaired guys. My grandmother didn't see too many cotton-tops back in Tokyo, maybe I inherited a fetish."

Or maybe you're just trying to get my guard down, Bino thought. He said, "Well let's change my answer to just plain old 'ridiculous.' It really is pretty ridiculous. Emmett Burns wouldn't let his little girl get mixed up in that, not even if he was taking payoffs right and left. One meeting with the guy, you can tell. His little girl's his whole life. Hell, he'd beg, borrow, or whatever to pay her gambling debts before he'd let her chance going to jail. Where's Goldman coming up with all of this? From Bleeder?"

"I haven't seen his witness list," she said, raising a hand as though someone was swearing her in. "Honest. But you already know Mr. Bleeder's going to be the star. I'll have to be going now, Mr. Bino. Duty calls. But catch me on the air, I may not carve you up as much as you think." She closed her notebook.

"Tonight?" Bino said. "Are you going to report on our interview tonight?"

"No. I'll need a day or two to edit this stuff. Just the bond hearing is all we'll have tonight; that's old hat to you. If you think of anything else, give me a call at the station." She stood, holding the binder in the crook of her arm like a coed in the student union. "Besides," she said. "You haven't finished asking me for a date. It'll give us both something to think about."

After Susie had left, Bino went over to the bar and said, "Hey, Barn. No hard feelings, huh? Lemme buy you a drink."

Barney kept his back turned and said to Dolly and the two blonds, "There's a guy down here wanting to buy me a drink. You don't figure him for a *homo*, do you? There's all kinds of characters running around these bars."

Bino ordered another beer for himself and tried for a second time to give Melinda a tip. "Keep it," she said. "Call it my contribution for when you pass me again on the way down." Bino took a couple of sips, then stalked out of Joe Miller's into the parking lot.

Susie had called the weather right; since sundown the thermometer had nosedived. Bino's trench coat was in the Linc's backseat, and the cold air made him shiver. He jammed his hands into his pants pockets and hurried across the asphalt toward the Linc. Across Lemmon Avenue, cars waited in line at the drive-in window to the Burger King. Bino decided that a double-meat Whopper with cheese might just hit the spot and made up his mind to get one as he inserted his key in the Linc's door. Behind him, a horn beeped. Still shivering, his breath coming out in wisps of fog, Bino turned.

Not ten feet away sat a dark-colored Cadillac stretch limo, smoke rising from its exhaust. The car had one-way black windows. An electric motor hummed as the back window slid down. A gloved hand appeared and beckoned.

Well, last night it had been Annabelle. Tonight . . . who knew? He dropped his keys into his pocket and went over to the limo.

A man wearing an overcoat with padded shoulders was sitting in the backseat. Bino made out tinted wire-frame glasses, a slim nose, and a wide, expressionless mouth. The man said, "It's cold outside, friend. Come in and warm up, have a little talk." He wore a dark snap-brim hat and spoke with a fast northern accent.

Bino glanced through the window toward the front seat. The driver wasn't wearing a chauffeur's uniform, was bare-headed with thinning hair and jug-handle ears. He didn't turn around, just kept his hands, motionless, on the steering wheel.

To the guy in back, Bino said, "Have a little talk with who?"

The expressionless mouth curved into a smile. It was a pleasant enough smile, but Bino couldn't help thinking of the grinning Cheshire cat in *Alice in Wonderland*. He briefly wondered if this was Bainbridge, the office leasing guy.

The guy said, "Come on, now. We been sitting here two,

three hours, don't play 'who-you' games. I saw the Chinese broad go in and come out, so you been talking to the television. I'm not muscling you, Phillips; this here is a friendly visit. I don't think you want to change that."

"She's Japanese," Bino said. "I'm like you, though, it's hard to tell the difference. And I still don't have little chats with people unless I know who I'm talking to."

The driver stretched his arm out over the seatback and turned around. The man in the backseat said, "Just keep driving, Matthew. This guy's not giving us any shit, he's just curious is all." The driver faced the front and put both hands back on the wheel. The guy in back extended a gloved hand through the window. "Lou Thorndon. I'm the guy your bookmaker's been asking around about. Half-ass, ain't it?"

Bino hesitated, then shook the hand. "His name's Half-a-Point. If you're saying his investigating is half-assed, well, I won't comment on that. Glad to know you, Mr. Thorndon. At least so far I am."

A latch clicked, and the door swung outward. As Thorndon slid over to make room, warm air from the car's interior flowed on Bino's cheeks. Thorndon said, "Well you may be even gladder once our little visit is over. Come on in. Maybe we'll get along better than you think."

Bino climbed aboard, feeling soft, cushiony leather give under his thighs and buttocks, and closed the door. The limo moved forward. The stereo was playing music from *South Pacific*. "Bali Ha'i." Bino said, "I don't have long, I got to get home."

"This ain't going to *take* long," Thorndon said. "Just long enough for me to tell you some things that'll help you with this case you got. Then you're going to think Lou Thorndon's a pretty good guy." He belched. "I hate doing that, excuse the shit out of me. Fucking pastrami gives me gas. Hot mustard, I got to lay off that shit."

They turned east on Lemmon. Visible through the limo's front windshield, rows of headlights overhead on the North Central Expressway bridge over Lemmon Avenue passed one another going in opposite directions. The limo crossed underneath the freeway and headed out Washington Street, moving along between rows of houses with weather-beaten, chipped paint, standing behind postage stamp–sized, weed-infested, and rock-strewn yards. The neighborhood had seen better days.

"You got good press on the street, Phillips," Thorndon said. "Good for a lawyer, anyway. Must be different, having one of those judges for a client. I'd trust a stickup man 'fore I would a judge."

Bino crossed his legs and didn't say anything.

"Listen," Thorndon said, "you already heard some stuff about me. And I tell you, I'm tired of moving the fuck around. Three big towns—L.A., Chicago, St. Louis—all three of those places I had to move from. Not 'cause I don't like them places, not at all. Just because some people with big mouths go spreading a bunch of shit about me around. So here in Texas I make up my mind to stay, no matter what. You understand what I mean?"

"I've seen it happen before like that," Bino said. "When a guy decides to make the right connections and settle down, well, he makes them. Shows up in all the right places." He paused and scratched his cheek. "Sports the right women around, hey?"

There was a rustling sound as Thorndon sat up straighter. "Who you been talking to?"

"What difference does it make?" Bino said. "So I know a few people. Listen, I'm not your lawyer, and from what I hear your lawyer's done you a pretty good job. You're what, a three-time loser running around on probation? Jesus, I've got clients with better records than you got that're in the basement of the jail, underneath it, you know, just trying to get some bunk space on the ground floor. So you're connected. Big deal. What do you want with me?"

"So how come you're getting on my case?" Thorndon asked. "I haven't done nothing to you; hell, I'm trying to help you out."

"Call it this mood I'm in. You want to help me out? Tell Bleeder to quit lying his ass off about my client taking bribes. The only thing I can't figure out, what's Bleeder getting out of this? Or you either, for that matter, you've already got your state probation and walked on your federal beef."

Thorndon was silent, leaning forward, watching the Mexican men and women going in and out of the string of cheap beer joints along Bryan Street: the Rocket Lounge, the Astro Club, the Moon Landing with a sign out front showing a spaceship descending onto a cratered surface. Finally, Thorndon said, "We better take Mr. Phillips home, Matthew." Then, as the limo made a wide-swinging left onto Fitzhugh Avenue, he said, "What makes you think the guy's lying? Bleeder."

"Come off it," Bino said. "I don't know who set it up or why, but Emmett Burns didn't take any bribe. And especially he didn't take any bribe with his daughter mixed up in it."

"That all sounds real stand-up," Thorndon said, "you being his lawyer and all. And you can think what you want. But they're going to convict him, bet your ass. I'm not even a lawyer and I can tell you that. So make it easy on the old guy. Shit, he's not up to what they'll put him through. You know how the Feds operate, better'n I do." Huddled in the corner in his overcoat, Thorndon might have been fat, might have been skinny. He had a slender man's voice, and Bino hoped that he was slender. He didn't like to picture Ann Burns going around with a big fat guy.

"Make it easy on him how?" Bino asked.

"Shit, you know the answer to that. Tell him to cop out. Take a little time, hell, it won't kill him. They'll put him in one of those cushy prison camps. I was in one, Allenwood, Pennsylvania. He can walk, play some tennis, shit, he might live longer. It'll be a helluva lot easier on him than dragging his little girl through it. Her little ass is muddy enough, in case you don't know it." The limo was passing beneath the North Central Expressway again, now on Lemmon Avenue, on the way back to Joe Miller's.

"You might have the right idea," Bino said.

"Sure I do. And listen, I figure a high-dollar lawyer like you is costing him pretty good. He can save some money, use it in his old age. Tell you what, I'd like to help him out on that." Thorndon reached inside his coat, withdrew a fat, sealed envelope, and dropped it on the seat. The envelope made a soft, weighted, thumping sound. "Fifteen thousand worth," Thorndon said.

Bino rubbed his palm over the papery softness of the envelope. It was bulging at the seams. "That's a lot of money, Mr. Thorndon. And what'll it do? Keep your name out of the trial, I guess, if I can talk my client into copping a plea."

"Now you're getting my point," Thorndon said. The red and yellow lights of the Burger King were visible up ahead, directly across the street from Joe Miller's. Visible through the Caddy's dark windows, the approaching headlights on the other side of the median were a sluggish parade of dull white orbs. The limo slowed, its turn signal bonking monotonously.

"Well it's not a bad idea," Bino said. "I get a fat fee and you can stop worrying."

"And don't forget the judge," Thorndon said. "Hell, things'll go easier all the way around. You're a pretty smart guy for a lawyer, Phillips, and believe me I've had some dumb ones. Maybe I can steer a little business your way."

The Caddy stopped beside the Linc in the parking lot. A light drizzle had begun to fall, spotting the Caddy's windshield. The driver turned a knob, and the wipers thunked slowly back and forth. Bino opened the door and stood up on the asphalt. Icy moisture stung his cheeks and nose.

Thorndon leaned over and offered the envelope. "Hey. Don't forget this."

"Oh, I'm not forgetting it," Bino said. He bent and looked Thorndon over, then said, "And I'm not taking it. You can shove it up your ass if you want to, Mr. Thorndon. Or better yet, save it. You might need it in case you have to leave town again, get a fresh start someplace else. You ever been to Boston?"

14

Bino had set his digital clock radio to turn on at six-thirty in the morning, and he awoke in darkness to the jumping sounds of Michael Jackson doing "Billie Jean" over KVIL-FM. He groped his way over to the window, blinked dully in the yellow glow from the porch light across the way, and called Dodie's apartment. She answered after the third ring. Her voice was crackly and sleepy.

"I'll be out of touch today," he said.

"With reality? What time is it?"

He hadn't called her home number since he'd spent the night with her only weeks (it seemed longer) ago, and he felt a pang of guilt that quickly subsided. Tough guys don't get involved. He said, "I'll be working on the judge's case. Look, Dode, I want you to do something for me. Get with Half, and between the two of you I want a written statement, synopsis or whatever you call it, of everything he's found out so far in his investigation."

"In English?" she said. "Or bookie talk? Like, 'Stanley the Stiff told me this broad might not be on the square.' That's what he told me yesterday, word for word."

"*Translate*, Dodie. That's what you went to college for. I want notes I can carry into the courtroom. This stuff is all coming together, and I think I can solve the judge's problem without any trial. And pretty damn soon."

"For real?" she said. Muffled in the background, a male voice said something that Bino couldn't quite understand. Dodie giggled.

Dammit, thought Bino, she's just your *secretary*, for Christ's . . . What if you *did* . . . ? And besides, what Dodie does on her own time is none of your business. You're trying to keep an arm's-length relationship, right?

"Who's over there?" he said.

After a few long and drawn-out seconds of silence, she said, "Why?"

He felt as though he should be tugging on his ankle, trying to pull his foot out of his mouth. "Oh, no reason. Forget I asked."

"Well I'll tell you one thing," she said. "It's not—"

"Hold on, Dode, I *said*—"

"—somebody from the FBI or somebody I—"

"—to forget it. It's none of my business what you do."

"—picked up over at Joe Miller's Bar. It's my brother, in fact. He's eighteen, and he spent the night on my couch. And what he said was that somebody who goes around calling people before daybreak must be some kind of nut."

His neck flushed. "Oh."

"Anything else you want me to do? Before you hear a loud bang when I slam the phone down in your ear?"

His shoulders drooped. "Nothing I can think of offhand. I'll be in touch, if anything should come up."

There was a sharp click as she disconnected. He listened to the hum of the dial tone for a moment, then gently put the receiver back into its cradle.

He padded rather sheepishly into the bathroom, showered and shaved—cutting himself twice and dabbing on small pads of toilet paper to soak up the blood—then blew his snow white hair dry in front of the mirror. One cut was on his cheek, the other on his square chin. His blue eyes were clear this morning, and he thought that if he could get into the habit of rising this early every day he'd be healthier for it.

He dressed in jeans, gray, bulky pullover sweater, and tan Dingo boots, then put on an emerald green Duckster windbreaker and billed cap to match. The windbreaker had the Crooked River Gold Club logo on its breast; the hat a picture of an oil derrick over the words "Rocky Ford Drilling Co." on its crown. He poured steaming black coffee into a Styrofoam cup and took it out with him. Cecil goggle-eyed Bino suspiciously as he left.

Tilly Madden's apartment adjoined the building manager's office. He rang the doorbell and waited with his free hand jammed into his pocket and his shoulders hunched against the cold. Tilly opened the door the length of the chain lock. She was wearing a pink housecoat and no makeup. Her bleached hair was up in curlers and covered by a blue scarf.

"I've already told you," Tilly said. "I'm going to see that your ceiling gets painted. We've been busy. Strong-arm bill-collector tactics will get you nowhere."

Bino extracted his car keys from his pocket, spilling a few drops of coffee as he did. "That's not— Hell, I wouldn't do that. I'm getting used to the ceiling. It looks like a map of Utah, you know, the Great Salt Lake? Listen, Tilly, I need a favor. To borrow your pickup for the day. I'll leave you my car. How 'bout it?"

Her scarf was tied underneath her chin. She tilted her head to one side. "The Lincoln?"

"Well, yeah, it's the only car I got."

"What's going to . . . ? Let me guess. Somebody else is after you with a shotgun. I'm not falling for that one. What happens when you bring the truck back with the window shattered?"

"No way," he said. "I just, well, need a vehicle that nobody's going to recognize."

Tilly scratched her cheek. Minus scarlet lipstick and rouge, and in the dawn's early light, Tilly wasn't as dominating as usual. But almost. Bino had wondered for years whether Tilly's husband, a skinny, timid little guy, ever got to be on top in the sack. He doubted it. Tilly said, "Until tomorrow morning and we might have a deal."

"I don't have that long, Tilly. What I've got to do has to be today."

"I don't mean *wait* till tomorrow. That's how long I want to trade for. You can have your Lincoln back in the morning, if you don't come banging on my door at the crack of dawn, for Christ's sake."

A shiver ran through him, partly from the cold and partly from the fact that he knew it was coming. He didn't know what *it* was, but it was damn sure coming. He thoughtfully sipped some coffee. It had already cooled to lukewarm. He smacked his lips. "What's the deal?" he said.

"It's Buddy. He's got a date tonight; I'd like to surprise him."

"Buddy?"

"You know, Bino. Buddy. My middle boy."

Bino winced. He knew Buddy, all right, blocky little towhead, Tilly's spitting image. The last time that Bino'd seen the kid, Buddy had bombarded the Linc with mud balls and had shot Bino the finger. He grinned weakly. "Has he got a driver's license?"

"He's six*teen*. Sure he has, since last month. Passed his test on the second try." Tilly favored Bino with an indignant blink.

Bino pictured the Linc parked on a deserted country road.

In his mental image, two teenagers writhed and squirmed in the backseat, tearing at each other's clothes while a second group of teenagers sneaked up and relieved the Linc of its wire-spoke wheel covers. Bino swallowed hard. "Buddy's already dating, huh? Boy, don't they grow up in a hurry?" He shrugged. "Sure, Tilly, I guess it'll be okay."

"Sure it will," she said, then quickly snatched the keys from Bino's hand. "Buddy's a good boy, and he'll appreciate it," she said. "Tell you what, he'll even buy you some gas. Couple of dollars' worth be enough?"

Tilly's pickup was a gray, ten-year-old, half-ton Ford, and it took four tries for Bino to get the truck running. Oh, the engine started easily—the truck had a strong chugging starter hooked up to a red-hot battery, and every time Bino turned the key the motor caught in seconds—but each time he'd drop the lever into the Drive position, the Ford would lurch forward a couple of feet and die. Finally he started the motor and left the lever in the Park position. Then he leaned back resolutely with his arms folded, waiting for the engine to warm while he listened to the radio.

The radio—AM only, no FM dial—was tuned in to a country and western station that was playing oldies. After he'd listened to Tammy Wynette sing "Stand by Your Man," and had heard George Jones gallop through "The Race Is On," he turned the knob and tried to locate a different station. From one end of the dial to the other he found only crackling static. He finally gave up, retuned the knob to the country station, and hummed a few bars of "Funny How Time Slips Away" along with Willie Nelson.

Suddenly the morning sun popped its edge into view over the roof of the apartment complex. Its rays glinted from the beads of frost on the truck's windshield; Bino squinted against the brilliance and looked away. He dropped the shift lever into Drive again. The truck bucked forward, coughed, then kept on going as its engine smoothed out. The sudden forward surge caught Bino napping; he jammed on the brakes and barely avoided plowing into the side of a Dodge Caravan. He sighed, backed up, and steered the truck forward between rows of cars until he finally stopped behind the Linc. The pickup's door squealed in protest as he opened it and stepped down on the asphalt.

Bino went over to the Lincoln, his breath turning to wisps of fog. He groped under the right front fender and located the magnetized box that contained his spare key, then unlocked the door and sat in the passenger seat. He opened the glove compartment; the barrel of the Mauser pistol was pointed directly at him from within the compartment, and he jumped slightly. He hefted the gun and checked its clip. Only one round remained. His spare shells were also in the glove box, in a metal can marked "Red Man Chewing Tobacco." He loaded the clip and, with the pistol heavy in his jacket pocket, got out and locked the door. He replaced the spare key underneath the fender, trudged back over to the pickup, and climbed aboard. The truck chugged out of the parking lot, nearly stalling at the gate, then bounced and creaked its way into streaming traffic along the Dallas Parkway.

It was ten minutes until eight—actually, the guy on the radio said that Slakey Mitchell would be along in a sixth of an hour with the 8:00 A.M. Farm and Weather Report, and it took a few mental gymnastics for Bino to figure out what time it was—when the truck rattled to the curb a couple of houses down the street from 478 Crystal Hills Drive. It was windless. The pruned fir trees in the judge's front yard stood like pointed sculptures. Santa and the reindeer, still perched on the roof, looked in the sunlight like just what they were, painted plastic and papier-mâché. Bino's view of the front door and its Christmas wreath was blocked by the two cars sitting in the judge's drive. The judge's four-door green Buick was parked nose-on to the garage; the yellow Pontiac Tempest behind the Buick was probably Ann's car. Bino wondered briefly whether Ann had stayed home last night and played dutiful daughter or had taken to the streets to feed her gambling habit. Either way he wouldn't have been surprised.

He dropped the Mauser into the truck's glove box and slammed it closed. As he did, a brown cocker spaniel with floppy ears and a lolling pink tongue came trotting down the street in his direction. The dog paused, sniffed, pissed against the curb, and sat on its haunches. Panting, it cocked its head to one side and regarded Bino as if it wondered what the hell he was doing here. As Bino leaned on the armrest and waited, he began to wonder the same thing.

An hour later Bino was still sitting there in Tilly Madden's pickup, parked two doors down the street from Emmett Burns's house. His left elbow was stiff, and so was his right knee. His bum ankle was beginning to throb. During the time he'd been sitting there, the judge's next-door neighbor—a younger guy, around thirty-five, wearing thick glasses that lent a bookish look—had eyed the pickup suspiciously as he'd backed out of his driveway and motored off in the direction of the golf course, and an ancient woman moving with the aid of a walker had come out of the house across the street, stood on the front porch for a few moments, and then gone back inside. The cocker spaniel had gotten tired of trying to figure Bino out, had sniffed his zigzagging way into Emmett Burns's yard, then had stopped and looked around before squatting and taking a monstrous dump. Aside from marveling over the size of the pile of dog shit that now festered on the judge's lawn, the most interesting thing that Bino had found to do was watch the fir trees' shadows as they shortened under the rising sun.

The temperature was still in the thirties, but as the morning had worn on the interior of the truck had taken on a greenhouse effect. Sweat was pouring down Bino's cheeks and sticking his gray pullover sweater to his skin. He'd just opened both windows, and was making up his mind to drive to the nearest phone booth to call the judge's number under an assumed name, when Ann Burns came out the front door and down the walk, with her red hair shining and her high heels clicking.

She paused beside the dog shit and pursed her lips in disgust. Bino didn't blame her; the pile was pretty disgusting even from *his* distance. Her gaze now averted from the dog droppings, Ann continued down the sidewalk and opened the bricked mailbox at the curb. She was dressed to go somewhere, wearing her mink jacket and a purple, straight skirt. There was a matching purple scarf knotted at her throat. When she reached into the mailbox and withdrew a folded slip of paper, Bino sat up straighter in the truck and frowned.

He'd been here since before eight, and no postal truck had come by. So, unless the folded paper was left over from yesterday's delivery, someone besides the postman had put it there. As Bino watched, Ann unfolded the slip and read it. The same look crossed her face as had been there when she'd looked at the dog shit. She stood for a moment with the paper dangling from one hand and her purse from the opposite arm, then walked purposefully over to the yellow Tempest, got in, and started the engine. She backed out of the drive and headed straight for where the pickup was sitting.

Bino jammed his golf cap tighter on his head and turned up his windbreaker's collar. He needn't have bothered. Ann went past with her gaze straight ahead; she didn't even glance his way. By the time he could start the truck, pull into a vacant driveway across the street, and turn around, she was two blocks away and turning left toward Stevens Park Golf Course. Bino floored the accelerator, herded the pickup up to fifty miles an hour, and careened down Crystal Hills Drive and around the corner in hot pursuit. The yellow Tempest was still in sight, cruising around the gentle curves up ahead. A foursome was on the golf course to Ann's right, two men in an electric cart and two more walking along carrying their clubs suspended by shoulder straps. Bino slowed and kept pace with the Tempest. He was grimly clutching the steering wheel with both hands.

It wasn't until Ann Burns had skirted the western edge of downtown Dallas on Stemmons Freeway, the Ozlike ball atop Reunion Tower on her right, and had taken the interchange that crossed over to Dallas North Tollway, that Bino snapped that she was headed directly toward his apartment. Jesus, he could have stayed right at home and waited for her. He was just crossing under the Royal Lane overpass for the second time that morning, and trying to remember whether or not the carpets were vacuumed and Cecil's tank was clear of fish crap, when Ann's right-hand turn signal blinked and she took the exit that led onto the LBJ Freeway eastbound. Bino veered across two lanes of traffic to follow, nearly sideswiping a Volks-wagen van and feeling his neck flush as the van's horn beeped angrily.

Ten minutes later he was in crawling traffic, waiting to turn left from Preston Road into the parking lot that sur-rounded Valley View Mall. The lot was a jam-packed, hundred-acre mass of cars. The Christmas shopping mob was out early; according to the clock atop Valley View Bank, it was still five minutes until the mall's ten o'clock opening time. Two cars— a Buick Park Avenue and some kind of little silver foreign make—waited between the nose of the pickup and Ann's yel-low Tempest. Bino stretched high in the seat to keep from losing sight of her. She'd taken off her mink and draped it over the seatback; her red-nailed fingers drummed a rhythm on the steering wheel.

The green left-turn arrow flashed on, and Ann turned into the parking lot. Bino crept along behind her up and down three rows of parked cars until she finally located an angled head-in space midway between the freeway and the mall's main entrance. She shrugged into her mink, opened the door, and alighted on the asphalt. Bino ducked his head slightly and moved on. By the time he'd found his own empty parking space, two rows over and about a hundred yards closer to the freeway than Ann's Tempest, she was nowhere in sight. He stood for an instant with the truck's door ajar, hesitated, then dug into the glove box and dropped the Mauser into his jacket pocket. What if she was only going shopping, for Christ's . . . ? He pictured a security guard approaching him in the crowded mall. *Hey, Bud, whatcha hanging around here for, and whatcha got inya fucking pocket?* If something like that happened, Bino was going to feel pretty stupid. He locked the pickup and went through yawning glass doors into the mall.

He passed a lit-up Jas K Wilson's men's store and a Waldenbooks—featuring, equally, *Kaleidoscope* by Danielle Steel and *Texas* by James Michener in its display window—on his way to the walkway that ran the perimeter of the mall's second level. The mall corridors were a madhouse, women hustling along holding kids by their hands, men in suits and guys in slacks and sport shirts and jogging clothes. A piped-in orchestra was playing "Deck the Halls" as Bino reached the walkway, went over to the rail, and looked down on the lower level.

The second-level walkway on which Bino stood was wide enough to accommodate the Texas Aggie Marching Band, a dozen abreast, with room left over for the Ags to go through a few snappy maneuvers. On Bino's left a second, slanted walkway, equally wide, descended at a thirty-degree angle to the mall's lower level. Around the lower level were more shops—Mostly Chic, a high-dollar women's wear outfit, the Footlocker, featuring Nike, Reebok, and L.A. Gear, a Zale Jewelry, and the entrance to the monstrous I. Magnin's that occupied three levels at one end of the mall—with a cluster of fast-food counters—Chick Fil-A, Mr. Potato, The Grand and Glorious Chocolate Chip Cookie, and even a McDonald's takeout—in the yawning open area between the shops. Sitting on the floor of the lower level, and extending clear to the mall's domed interior roof, was the biggest Christmas tree Bino had ever seen. Jesus, the thing must have been seventy-five feet high, decorated with at least a thousand yards of glittering tinsel and what must have been two thousand red and green and clear glass balls. Near the tree's base sat a Santa on a wooden throne, holding out his arms in greeting to a seemingly endless line of giggling little boys and girls who were holding their mothers' hands. Behind the snow white mass of whiskers the guy probably had an expression of pure terror on his face. Bino gave the entire area a quick once-over and was just about to retrace his steps toward the mall entrance when he spotted Ann.

Her wealth of red hair caught his attention. She was seated far below, at a small, round table in the dining area between the fast-food counters. There was a pay phone just feet from her, mounted on a pole. Her mink was draped over her chair-back; in addition to her purple skirt and scarf she wore a purple vest over a white blouse with puffed sleeves. As Bino watched, she got up and went over to the cookie counter. She returned in a moment, carrying a chocolate-chip cookie that was around a foot in diameter, wrapped in a big wax-paper napkin. She sat, crossed her legs, took two small bites from the cookie, then crumpled the napkin around it and threw the whole conglomeration into a nearby trash can. She fooled with her wristwatch. She played with her gold earrings. She undid her purple scarf and retied it. Bino moved over to the descending walkway, dodged women and children and men in suits on his way to the lower level, and approached Ann from the rear.

When he was standing a couple of feet away from her, he said, "When you tell a guy you want to talk to him, you sure do make it tough for him to follow up."

For just a second he thought she was going to bolt from the table and run. She turned wide blue eyes in his direction, and one corner of her mouth was twitching. Then she recognized him, and her features relaxed. She expelled a deep breath. "How did you find me?" she said.

"I didn't find you. Not exactly. I've been following you."

As he sat across from her, a furrow of anxiety creased her forehead. He said, "I didn't want to call you because—"

"I don't know if you should be sitting here," she said. "Someone might be watching."

He glanced around him. "So they might. Hell, a lot of people are watching. Thousands of 'em. Like I was saying, I didn't call you because I don't want your dad to know I'm talking to you. So it's okay if anybody sees us; it won't do much damage to your reputation. I waited down the street from your house. If your dad had left before you did, I was going to ring your doorbell. I figured one of the two of you had to go somewhere, some time or the other."

She looked beyond him, first to her left and then, fleetingly, to her right. "No, you don't— Look, somebody *told* me to wait here."

His chin moved slightly. "Was that the note in your mailbox?"

"You saw that? Yes. They've been watching; they had to know that Daddy never checks the mail."

"*Who's* been watching? Look, Ann, pretty as you are I think you should know I don't give a damn about your private life. But when what you do starts affecting my client it gets to be my business in a hurry. So I don't like playing Philip Marlowe. What the hell is going on with you? Thorndon? Is that who you're supposed to be meeting here? Bleeder maybe? Jesus Christ, a lot of people accuse *me* of picking my dates up over at the dog pound. But you take the cake, lady, far as I can see."

She arched an eyebrow. "I don't need that and I'm not going to sit here and take it. Lou and Frank aren't—I don't *have* any dates. I have . . . acquaintances. And you're wrong; it's not either one of them. I don't *know* who's meeting me. Look, when I said I wanted to talk to you I needed your help. I still need your help. But reaming me out isn't very helpful, thank you. What I found in the mailbox was a typewritten note telling me to come here and wait for that phone over there to ring. So that's what I'm doing."

"Great," Bino said. "So you find notes in your mailbox and go trotting off all over hell-and-gone on the instructions of people you don't even know. That's a lot to swallow."

She clasped her hands on the table and studied them. "My whole life's a lot to swallow," she said. She raised her gaze to meet his. "To tell you the whole thing would take a million years or so. Which we don't happen to have right now. Listen, somebody's blackmailing me, and I don't know for sure what they want. I'm afraid it isn't money. I suppose I'm going to find out what they want when that phone rings. If seeing you sitting here doesn't scare them away."

Bino leaned closer. "And I guess you're going to tell me that you don't even know what they have on you. To blackmail you with."

Her gaze remained steady as a rock. "Oh, I know that, all right. You want to hear a dirty story? It's what most men seem to want to hear."

Judy Roo reached up underneath her pink sweater, adjusted her bra, and scratched her armpit. "Holy shit. That dude's tall as a tree. Reckon he's somebody she knows? Or just some guy trying to hit on her."

Daryl was leaning on the mall's second-level rail. He was wondering about the tall guy as well, big, rangy drink of water who was wearing a green windbreaker and matching golf cap, and who was walking up to the table where the redhead sat and pulling up a chair. From this distance Daryl couldn't see the guy's face, but he was pretty sure that the treetop wasn't anybody he knew. On the opposite second-level walkway, nearly hidden from view behind the giant Christmas tree, people were going in and out of the Waldenbooks. Visible through the window of the Jas K Wilson's store, a man was trying on a sport coat with a salesman at his elbow, chattering a mile a minute. Daryl had been in the Jas K Wilson's a few moments ago, and he hadn't liked the clothes he'd seen. Give him his own Harbor Lights jacket from Marshall Field's, molded around his shoulders and belted at the waist.

"Doesn't really matter who the guy is," Daryl said, "long as he's not a cop, FBI or somebody. Which he's not. A cop would be hiding out in the shithouse keeping an eye on her. Hell, he wouldn't fucking *sit* with her, not out in the open." A female voice was crooning over the loudspeaker, "Oh, by gosh by golly, it's time for mistletoe and holly." Daryl wondered who the singer was. Joni James? No, hell, the number wasn't that old. Might be a reworked song by Linda Ronstadt or somebody. Who gave a shit?

"I got the phone booth number wrote down like you told me," Judy said. "You want me to stand here while you go make the call?"

He smiled at her, really turned on the charm. "No hurry, doll. She'll sit there till hell freezes, that's how bad she wants to know what we got to say. You know, the tall guy could be some kind of adviser or something. You know, some guy that's screwing her and thinks she needs some advice in this big fucking crisis she's going through. Going to tell her, stand firm, or, don't let them think they're scaring you. Let's just watch the sights awhile. It's an advantage, knowing where she is and she don't know about us."

"That's an awful purty tree, Daryl." Judy was looking out over the rail, her eyes big and round. Sally from the sticks, looking up at the tall buildings.

"And you're a pretty girl," Daryl said. "Too pretty to be holding out on me."

She turned and leaned her elbows against the rail. Her hair was in a ponytail that hung between her shoulder blades. "Whatcha saying?" she said. She looked uncertain, as though she didn't really think he was going to slap her or anything but wasn't quite sure. She wore a beige waist-length cloth jacket over her fuzzy pink sweater.

"What am I saying? Well let's see." He looked away from her toward the table where Red (Mama Longlegs? He wasn't sure which name he liked the best) sat with the tall man. Daryl said, "You know I'm not a nosy person, Judy. Really I'm not. So I take people at face value, at least until they show me I got something to worry about." He slowly cracked his knuckles, one at a time, still smiling, a guy out shopping with his best girl.

She shrugged and put her hands in her jacket pockets. "Well you ain't got nothing to worry about with me. I done what you said."

"Sure. That's right, you did. But you know how you looked around in my gear while I was asleep and found those pictures? Well this morning while you were taking a shower I did the same thing. I went through your pockets."

"I ain't got nothing in my pockets. Not that I'm scared for you to see."

He threw her a sidelong glance. "You know, I believe you? Anybody else, no. But you sweet little dummy, I don't even think you realize. What's that ID card with your picture you're carrying around?"

Her lips parted. She licked them. "Well it ain't nothing. Just my identification."

"Hey, I been to prison, Judy. It's your halfway house ID. You're still a prisoner."

"So?" she said. "It ain't no big deal."

"Jesus Christ. It's not a big deal except that you're not where you're supposed to be. Come *on*, Judy. How long since you called in?"

"Holy shit," she said. "Called in where?"

"Called in to the fucking studio to see if you got a rehearsal coming up. Jesus, the halfway house. Don't you know they got warrants out for people disappear from halfway houses? No, I guess you might not even know that."

"Oh, I *know* it. I done told you I ain't stupid, Daryl. But how they going to find me?"

"I'm not believing this," Daryl said, looking once more toward the giant Christmas tree. "You're on the computer; all you got to do is stub your toe. Get a traffic ticket, anything. Plus we're out walking around, what if you run into somebody that knows you?"

"Anybody that knows me would be somebody that's been

in trouble theirselves," she said. "They wouldn't turn me in or nothing."

"Fifty-fifty," Daryl said. "That's all the odds you're going to get from me. About half of them that's . . . got some experience, you know, about half of them are running around just looking for somebody to drop a dime on. Makes them look good to their parole officer, at least they think it does."

"Well what you want me to do, Daryl? Holy shit, I can't just *disappear*. Don't seem to matter what I do, it ain't right according to you. Mr. Big Shot." She sniffed.

Daryl looked her over, studied the big doe eyes, the pretty, vacant expression on her face. Like a little puppy dog, wanting somebody to take her in. Daryl wasn't *mad*. Jesus, how could he get mad at somebody who didn't have enough sense to . . . shit, do *anything*? It wasn't Judy's fault, but that didn't make her any less dangerous to hang around with. Daryl had enough problems.

He showed her one of his best slowly spreading smiles and patted her behind. "Say, now, Judy. Hey, I'm sorry. I didn't mean for it to sound like I was getting on you. Tell you what, you give me that number you wrote down and I'm going down the hall to the phone. You keep an eye on her and that tall guy. Don't let 'em out of your sight." He took a slip of paper from her and unfolded it. "That's my girl," he said. "Just stay right here and keep a lookout, Judy. I won't be long. This'll all be over before you know it."

"Didn't you ever try Gamblers Anonymous?" Bino asked. "What'd your husband have to say about it? Looks like he would have tried to help, if nobody else would."

Absently, Ann moved the napkin holder across the table about a foot and set it down. Visible behind her, a little blond girl was sitting in Santa's lap and tugging on his whiskers. "Eddie?" Ann said. "Oh, he helped. Only it wasn't me that he was trying to help. It was them, people like Lou Thorndon. Eddie used to drop by Lou's crap game in Chicago, sit around and have a few drinks while I lost my money. The pictures were Eddie's idea. Thinking back on it, I guess maybe Lou Thorndon thought it up to begin with, but it was Eddie that pushed and pushed and finally pushed me into it. My own husband."

"Sounds like a first-rate guy," Bino said.

"It's funny, but you know how I felt the first time he brought it up? You've got to realize that up to that time I'd never even *seen* any . . . pictures like that. Miss Finishing School and all. You'd think I would have been, at least offended or something. But by that time I was so sick and desperate with all the gambling that nothing mattered. Even when it was time to perform for the camera, for God's sake. I wasn't sick. I wasn't disgusted. I wasn't anything. It was just a way for me to get some money to gamble on, and if I could have that money, that was all . . ." She hugged herself and trembled. "Did Eddie *help* me? In a way he did. He watched the door to make sure that nobody walked in on us, and once he even offered to work the camera. My darling hubby, not wanting to stand in the way of my career."

"Where'd you meet this guy to begin with?" Bino asked.

"At school," she said. "Vassar, can you believe it? He was a tennis bum, hanging around the country clubs. He gave me a few tennis lessons and I married him. Even in college I had to bet on everything, including tennis. Eddie liked to gamble, and I guess that's what I saw in him. Mother and Daddy nearly died when we got married, but I wasn't going to let anything stop me. And we got married and moved to Chicago—that's where he was from—and then he introduced me around to all of his friends. I met Lou Thorndon through Eddie. The bastard."

Bino wasn't sure what to say to that. She might be inviting him to join her in cussing old Eddie Satterwhite from here to hell and back, but then again she might not. There were women, a lot of them around, who'd rake their husbands—or ex-husbands—over the coals to anybody who'd lend them an ear, but woe to the unsuspecting somebody who had the nerve to agree with them. And, for the moment at least, Bino needed Ann Burns on his side. He finally opted to say, "Well how long did it go on? The pictures."

She lowered long red lashes. "Three times. God, I'd never even seen the guys before. They were porno actors. I guess I'm really lucky I didn't come up with AIDS. They even used fluffs, that's what they call the girls who sit off camera and get the males ready to perform. I don't understand myself. All that happening, and I don't feel any shame, no remorse. I don't feel *good* about it, don't get me wrong. I just don't feel anything, can you understand that?"

"Well how are you going to feel," Bino said, "if those pictures wind up sending your dad to prison?"

"If they . . . ?" She touched her hair at the nape of her neck. "How?"

"I don't know how," Bino said. "But it's all tied in. I met your friend Thorndon last night and he wanted me to— Hell, I'm getting ahead of myself. First I've got to ask you some things, and, hey, Ann, I don't have any attorney-client relationship with you. Not like with your dad. What I'm saying is that what you tell me isn't privileged, and if anybody were to put me on the stand and ask me I'd probably have to testify to it."

Ann blinked. "I can live with that. At least I hope I can."

"That makes two of us who are hoping," Bino said. "Three, counting your dad. You know he'd rather go to jail himself than have anything bad happen to you, don't you?"

"Yes. I'm not worth it, but, yes, I know. I'm crazy about Daddy, have been since I was a little girl. But this mink I'm wearing? He gave it to me as a homecoming present when Eddie and I split up. And the other night at the tennis club, the night I saw you and that girl showed me the pictures? Well I was going to hock it for gambling money, that's how much I care. The only reason I didn't was that the girl got to me first, with the pictures. By the time I got back to the club

□ 204 □

the gambling was over, so I had to take my coat and go home. That's too bad for me, isn't it?" She gave a short, bitter laugh.

Bino scratched his white eyebrow. "You've gotten money from Frank Bleeder in the past. Quite a few times."

"Not that many," she said. "That Mr. Goldman, Daddy's prosecutor. He asked me about that."

Bino's jaw dropped. "You've been talking to Goldman?"

"Once. He called and asked me a lot of questions. Said he wanted me to testify against Daddy, isn't that weird? I hung up on him, but one thing I remember is that he did ask me about getting money from Frank. He told me that if he wanted to he could make me testify. I don't know to what. I don't like Mr. Goldman very much. He got really nasty over the phone."

Bino decided that, whatever else, she was telling it straight about Goldman. If she'd been playing footsie with the prosecution, she would never have brought Goldman's name up. Bino said, "Did Bleeder give you some money around the time Lou Thorndon was up on his federal charges?"

"I suppose. Right around then. It was twenty thousand dollars."

"Ann, didn't you ever wonder why it was that Bleeder was so generous about giving you money?"

She sort of smiled. "I thought it was because he wanted to get laid; that's what all men expect. More bounce for the buck. I was gambling and I didn't care. I met Frank when I was gambling; he took me around to a few things—dinners, basketball games, and whatnot. But he never even tried to get me to bed; that was strange."

"He's got the same problem you do," Bino said. "Or about the same; he goes about his betting in a little different way."

"I know that now," she said. "He even guaranteed my credit at the crap games, and I thought that was a pretty big deal."

Bino glanced toward the mall's upper level, at the sign on the Jas K Wilson store that was visible above the second-level railing. He said to Ann, "It wasn't as big as you think. Frank was hooked into the gamblers and was giving them legal work in trade. I'll bet you never had to pay your tab either."

"Frank paid it, until just recently. They've cut my credit off."

"Ann. Bleeder wasn't *paying* anything. He was just getting you hooked like he was. They were all in on it—Thorndon, Tirelli."

"Who's Tirelli?" she said. "I met him once, at a basketball game."

"This guy. Bad guy. They knew whose daughter you were, and they wanted you hooked in case they needed you."

"And that's what Frank was getting at," she said. "I met him for lunch one day, and he told me I was going to have to . . . do something."

"Yeah," Bino said. "At Bek's Hamburgers."

Her head tilted. Her lips parted.

"I saw you," Bino said. "Only I didn't know who you were at the time. You made sort of a scene."

"I know," Ann said.

"What did he want you to do?"

"He wanted me to say about the, twenty thousand dollars, the money he gave me that you asked about. He wanted me to say that I gave that money to Daddy." Her eyes misted. "And that's what I'm hiding. From Daddy and everybody else. He told me that if I didn't do what he said he was going to Daddy for the money I owed him. *Owed* him; before he'd always said he was giving me the money. That's when I threw his lunch all over him. God, I can't say I gave *Daddy* the money, but I can't have Daddy knowing that I've been . . . And now there's the pictures."

"They play rough, Ann. But then the very next night, that's when I saw you get some more money from Bleeder."

She wrung her hands. "That's how sick I am. The next night there we were and I wanted to gamble. I told Frank I'd think about doing what he wanted."

"*Think* about it?" Bino said.

Her expression tightened; she'd been going to fudge just a little. No big deal, thought Bino, people who'd been through it like *this* girl always had trouble leveling. Finally she said, "No, that's not exactly right. I told him I'd do it. I'd have done anything to get some money. But I didn't intend to. I wouldn't, not if it came down to it."

Bino was finally putting it together. Everybody was bullshitting everybody else. Thorndon had given Bleeder the money and thought Bleeder had used it to bribe Emmett Burns. Only the money hadn't gone to Burns, had it? Thorndon to Bleeder to Ann Burns to the crap tables. Thorndon had made the mistake of trusting a gambler, Bleeder, to get some bribe money to a judge through another gambler, Ann Burns. Any money given to a gambler was money pissed off in the wind. Half-a-Point Harrison, 101. For the first time Bino was sure, really certain, that Emmett Burns was pure as rainwater. That didn't necessarily mean that Goldman wouldn't convict Burns anyway, but it was nice to know. Bino opened his mouth to ask Ann to pinpoint the date when she'd gotten the twenty grand, but before he could say anything the pay phone rang.

Amid the noise and hubbub in the mall, the ringing of the phone sounded faint and far away. Ann tensed, showed Bino a wide-eyed, frightened glance, then put her hands on the edge of the table and started to rise.

Bino reached over and gripped her forearm. "I'm not sure this is the right thing to do, but let me answer it. The worst thing that can happen is that they'll hang up on me. I don't think you're in any shape to talk to these people."

Her forehead creased, then her features relaxed. She nodded. Still wondering whether or not he was screwing up, and thinking that representing Weedy Clements had been a whole lot simpler than representing Emmett Burns, Bino went over and picked up the phone.

"If you're calling Ann Burns you're going to figure out real quick that I'm not her," Bino said. "But she's with me. What do you want?"

A man on the line said, "What I want's got nothing to do

with you, bud. So why don't you take a fucking hike and put Red on? Disappear, you know?" The voice was tenor and had a fast midwestern accent, which fit right in with Thorndon and everybody else from Chicago who seemed to be be mixed up in this thing.

"There's nothing you could say to her that you can't say to me," Bino said. "Plus, if you're looking to get some money or something, I'm the one to talk to about that."

"What're you taking me for?" the voice asked. "You think I'm going to stand here and tell your fucking tape recorder anything? Give me a little credit, you know?"

"I'm going to give you a *lot* of credit." Bino glanced at Ann. She was sitting up straight, her back rigid, watching him. Bino said into the phone, "I'm going to give you credit for figuring out that if somebody was taping you, you'd be talking to the girl instead of me. How's that for some credit, huh?"

"Well if you're not taping me," the voice said, "you're going to one hell of a lot of trouble to help a broad. You must be getting some of that. Her pussy that good?"

Bino shrugged. There had to be some reason, something this creep would believe, for Bino to be running interference. "Come to think about it, it isn't bad," Bino said.

"I got to admit, bud, it don't *look* bad, you know? Well that's okay, I don't mind dealing with you. But I'm going to know whether or not you're giving her my messages by what she does, and you can bet your ass she's not getting what she wants until I get what I want. Tit for tat, you know? So you better not be bullshitting me any."

"I won't be," Bino said.

"So about three miles west of here this freeway crosses over another one, I-35. You following me?" the voice said.

"Yeah. Yeah, I know it, I've lived around here all my life."

"A real hometown shitkicker, hey? Well that's nice. That's not me, pal. I don't know my way around, how you fuckers say it? My way around these parts. I needed a road map to set this up, you know? A real homeboy like you's got to know where Valley View Lane crosses Highway 114, right? Like it's way out in the boonies?''

"Right," Bino said.

"Okay. Around a mile, give or take, south of the highway on Valley View Lane there's a turnoff. Gravel road, a sign says 'Private Drive, No Thruway.' Only you're a real outlaw, bud; you're not paying any attention to the sign. You're going on down the road like you owned the place. No sweat, there's nobody home out there. I've checked it out, you know?''

"I've got you," Bino said. "So far."

"That's good, cowboy. That's very good. Now we're going to get into some real serious stuff. Some breaking and entering, you know? Only, don't flake out, you're not going to have to break anything. There's this little building on your right, and I can't really tell you what the turdkicker owns the place uses it for 'cause I don't know. Only it's red brick, and there's a picture of a cowboy roping a longhorn over the front door. Real Saturday matinee shit. You go right on through that front door, cowboy. You'll find some sofas and chairs and shit; you sit down. You going to bring your girlfriend with you?''

"Do I have to?" Bino asked. "And what's all this cloak and dagger, why don't you just tell me what you want over the phone?'' At the table Ann had picked up a napkin and was twisting it between her fingers.

"I don't like talking on the phone, cowboy. It's up to you about bringing her, I don't give a shit. Not that I object to a little beaver shot, you know? But as long as she's getting the message I don't care if she comes or not.''

"I don't guess I'll bring her, then. She's pretty shook up." Bino scratched his chin. This boy on the phone really liked to hear himself talk. That was okay. Bino was going to re- member the voice.

"Okay by me," the voice said. "Maybe even better, 'cause I'm going to have a broad with me. She gets real jealous, you know? Maybe if you're real good I'll have a bonus for you. With my broad. I believe in sharing, cowboy. Oh, and hey. I can see you coming from a long way off, so I wouldn't try to fuck me around. If you're pulling any shit I'm going to know about it."

"Don't worry about that," Bino said. "All you got to worry about is satisfying me that if she does what she says, you'll do what you say. That's all. You sure don't have to worry about me trying to fuck you around. I'm too scared of you for that. You're going to get a pretty good head start on me, I got to stop off in the men's room on my way out of here. You got me about to piss in my pants, you know?"

15

Daryl leaned on the windowsill and rested his chin on his crossed forearms. Beyond about twenty yards of scrubby brown grass and rocks surrounding the building, a one-lane gravel road stretched into the distance between twin rows of stately elms. Red and brown and orange leaves dotted the ground outside. "Not long now, Judy girl," Daryl said. "I can see him coming. Would you believe this dude is driving an old pickup? Well he is. Jesus Christ, you'd think anybody that was dicking something which looks like old Red, well, he'd be tooling around in a Caddy or Mercedes or something." He glanced back over his shoulder, looking away from the window. "I got to hand it to you, Judy, this is a good spot you found for us. Who said you were dumb? Me, did I say that? What is this little building for, anyway? You and your boyfriend, did you use it for a little spot to get away? Not too likely, it's too close to his house over there. How long did you live here, Judy? Shit, you had it made, then you had to go and rob this place and get sent off to the joint. Come to think about it, I guess you are pretty fucking dumb."

Judy Roo didn't answer. She was sitting in a straight-backed chair near the window, facing Daryl. Her wide, unseeing eyes stared straight ahead. Her hands were tied behind her back. Her tongue protruded from between bluish lips. From the waist up she was naked except for a wispy white bra. Her pink sweater, the one Daryl had bought for her in Foley's, was knotted around her neck. The flesh on both sides of the knot was swollen and bulging. Her face was the color of ripe plums, the color slowly fading as the blood drained into her legs.

Daryl stepped back from the window. He took Judy's cloth coat from the top bunk bed and draped it around her shoulders. "There, that better?" he said. "I don't get you, Judy. You told me about prison, all about this guy you lived with, everything else about you. How come you didn't tell me about you and the halfway house? Don't matter anymore, I guess." He returned to the window. "A pickup's damn sure what he's driving, believe it or not. Next couple of minutes we're going to have us some company, you and me. You think you can handle that? Now you mind what I say and keep quiet, we don't want him hearing us. Let's be like a couple of mice, you know?"

Bino turned left off two-lane, blacktop Valley View Lane and onto the gravel road, rattling along between silent, stately elms whose leafless branches reached skyward like skeleton fingers. It was spooky as a ghost story. One minute he'd been cruising along in bright winter sunshine with the hillbilly station blaring over the radio; the next minute he was in the deep shadow cast by the elm trees. Interference from the trees changed the radio noise instantly into crackling static. Bino switched the radio off. It was windless, the trees like statues, a row of scrubby bushes beneath the elms like short, fat men with hands on hips.

□ 212 □

He'd driven onto somebody's ranch or farm; the rolling land before him was grazing land, divided here and there by marked fences. Far in the distance there was a huge red cattle barn, standing beside a two-story brick home with neat white trim. In the house's front yard stood a stock-still windmill.

He was approaching a low-slung brick building with a gray-shingled roof, sitting on the right-hand side of the road. A dark blue two-door Ford was parked nose-on to the building. Bino felt a tingle where his neck joined his spinal cord. The tingle grew into a full-blown shiver that ran upward through his scalp. Goose bumps the size of spider eggs rose on his forearms. The heft of the Mauser in his jacket pocket helped some, but not much. The pickup bounced and rattled, and loose gravel pinged against its underbody.

He stopped, motor idling, alongside the Ford. Its passenger door was ajar. Bino parked. He checked the Mauser for maybe the twentieth time and found its clip still loaded. Then he alighted, warily approached the Ford, and looked its passenger door over.

The door's inside handle was twisted and bent at a strange angle, as though somebody inside the car had tried like hell to keep somebody outside from getting in. Bino didn't know what to make of that. As he bent for a closer look, he caught a flash of yellow in the corner of his eye.

The keys were in the ignition, and the flash of yellow was a plastic tag that dangled from the key chain. The tag swung in decreasing arcs just below the level of the steering column.

This wasn't making any goddamn sense. The guy, the spooky voice on the phone, sure wasn't being very careful. The guy was supposed to be on his toes—at least you'd *expect* him to be on his toes, a pro going around blackmailing people—yet here he was parking his car out in plain sight of God and everybody, and leaving its door open with the keys in the ignition. Slowly, carefully, Bino eased into the passenger seat and slid over behind the wheel.

He touched the key and nudged it further into the ignition switch. Immediately the warning buzzer, the same safety apparatus that drove Bino nuts when he tried to leave the Linc's motor running outside a convenience store while he dashed in after a six-pack, began to whine. Bino loosened the key. The whine stopped abruptly. He leaned around the steering wheel and inspected the yellow tag on the key chain. It was an Avis Rent a Car tag showing Avis's Love Field address.

So our boy's from out of town, Bino thought. Or he'd rented the car to make himself *look* like an import, take your pick. The goose bumps on his forearms growing like inflating balloons, the shivers running up and down his spine like waves at high tide, he got out of the Ford and inched his way across a rock-strewn yard of sparse brown grass to the front porch of the building.

The picture over the door wasn't quite what the guy on the phone had said it was. It was a cowboy, all right, reared back in the saddle atop a charging roan with flared nostrils and waving a lariat in a circle over his head. Only what he was roping wasn't a longhorn; it was a wide-eyed, half-grown Brahma calf. So okay, the guy hadn't known the difference between a Brahma and a longhorn. The building's front door was made of thick lacquered planks bound together by three bands of steel. Bino turned the handle, then stepped back as the door swung inward with a protesting squeak.

He was looking into some sort of sitting room. There was a long, low cloth divan against the far wall; at right angles to the divan sat two green, stuffed armchairs. A genuine-looking print of a western painting hung on the wall over the couch. Somebody around here was a Jasper Roberts freak; the original of the picture hung in the State Capitol in Austin. Bino had seen it before, a gang of cowpokes sprawled out around a glowing campfire.

The floor inside the room was polished hardwood, and Bino went in as though he was stepping on eggs. His boots creaked. He didn't wear the Dingos very often (they raised him an additional couple of inches over his six-foot-six and made him feel like sort of a freak), and they weren't broken in too well. He thought about taking the boots off, then forgot about it. Whoever was here was expecting him anyway.

There was one closed door in the room, directly behind and to the right of the divan. On Bino's left was a mock fireplace (there hadn't been any chimney on the roof, Bino recalled). Another Jasper Roberts print hung over the mantel, this one masked rustlers in hot pursuit of a herd of bug-eyed cattle. Bino went over and sat in one of the easy chairs. His elbow pressed against his side; the Mauser's handle prodded his arm through his windbreaker. He riveted his gaze on the picture of the rustlers and waited.

In a few minutes a cold draft blew on his neck, and the same voice he'd heard earlier on the phone said from behind him, "That's good, cowboy. Don't, don't turn around and don't look at me. I mean it, you turn around and you're going to make us both unhappy, you know?"

Bino hadn't heard the closed door open, but it was the only way that the guy could have entered the room. The draft on his neck told Bino that somewhere in the house a window was open. There weren't any windows in the room where he was sitting. Bino's neck muscles bunched as he said, "You're the one putting on the show. So I won't look at you, okay? But don't spend a lot of time telling me how tough you are. Like I told you on the phone, you got me scared shitless already."

"You're a real funnyfuck, sport, you know? I see you up close now you got white hair underneath that silly hat. Maybe you should start a nightclub routine. Only I'm not laughing. I don't have the time or I'd find out just how funny you can get. But I'm getting down to business. That's what we both want, right? So look these over, sport. No fair getting a hard-on, now."

Bino sensed, rather than felt or saw, the hand that moved near his head. The hand tossed a brown, legal-size envelope, which landed heavily in Bino's lap.

"Hurry now, cowboy," the guy said. "Remember, these

are strictly business. If you want to later on you can jerk off while you take a closer look. I don't give a shit what you do on your own time."

The envelope wasn't sealed. Bino reached inside, pulled out a stack of six-by-eight glossy photos, and leafed through them. Ann hadn't been kidding; if anything she'd been soft-pedaling the truth. The pictures were real hard-core jobs; they'd bring a lot of money individually, even more if somebody wanted to sell them to a porno mag. Which meant that if they were for sale they were going to cost quite a bit of something; Bino was pretty sure that money wasn't what the guy was going to ask for. Even through the sleaze, even through the queasy feeling in the pit of his stomach (Jesus Christ, but she must have been desperate; one of the pictures showed her with two white guys and a black guy), Bino couldn't help marveling over the wanton beauty, the sheer, knocked-out, bring-it-on, earthy sexiness of Ann Burns. He blinked as he pictured the look that would cross Emmett Burns's face if the judge ever saw these. Bino shoved the pictures back inside the envelope. "So? What're we talking about?"

"We're talking about what your girlfriend's going to do to keep out of the public eye. They're pretty good, sport. You think maybe I should get myself an agent? Shop them around, you know?"

Bino was conscious of the odor of . . . spearmint? A Cert, maybe, that the guy was sucking on, and the fainter pungent smell of either onion or garlic. Bino said, "Now who's being a funnyfuck? So I already knew about the pictures. Ann told me. You're wasting my time with all this crap. What do you want?" Bino hoped that he sounded a whole lot tougher than he felt. He wanted to keep the guy talking, get a real solid feel for the voice.

The guy snickered. "Well I've decided to give her a choice. Underneath all the bullshit I'm a pretty nice guy, you know? The first choice is for her old man to cop a plea and go away quietly. He'll do easy time; it won't be so tough."

"That's what all you convict assholes tell me," Bino said. "But what you're saying, that's not even her choice. It's for him to make. Her dad."

"Come on, sport. You know better than that, or if you don't he does. She's his little girl. Light of his eye, all that shit."

"Yeah, but . . . look," Bino said, "nobody's going to talk him into pleading guilty, not without showing him these"— he tapped the envelope in his lap—"and telling him what's going to happen if he doesn't cooperate. And that's the whole point as far as Ann's concerned, keeping her daddy from seeing these. If somebody's already shown them to him, what's in it for her to tell anything to anybody?"

"I'm not teaching a strategy course." The guy expelled a breath from somewhere near Bino's right ear, and this time the garlic odor wasn't diluted by spearmint. "She can talk him into copping, I don't care how she does that, or she can testify. Be a nice little federal witness, don't you just love 'em?"

Bino shifted his gaze. He'd been staring so hard at the western picture that an outline of the rustlers and cattle seemed to float before him on the wall. "Testify to what?" Bino asked.

"To whatever, sport. Whatever comes into her head, so long as what she says don't have anything to do with a guy named Lou Thorndon."

Now wait a fucking minute, Bino thought. Hearing Thorndon's name didn't surprise him, but this guy was getting it all wrong. Hell, the stuff about the bribe flowing from Thorndon to Bleeder to Ann (Tinker to Evers to Chance?) was what Goldman *wanted* Ann to testify to. If she didn't testify to that, then she wouldn't be helping the government any. Maybe this guy was just a fuckup, getting the message from Thorndon crossways. If the guy *was* working for Thorndon. Bino was beginning to wonder.

"So you're giving her a choice," Bino said. "She can show the pictures to her daddy and maybe give him a stroke, or she can testify against her daddy and maybe send him to prison.

Jesus Christ, Thorndon's the guy they want her to testify about. Are you sure you don't mean for her *not* to testify? It'd make more sense that way."

"I'm not sure about you, sport. How come you know so much about all this? So maybe you're not just some guy that's dicking the broad and trying to help her out. What are you, Whitey?"

Now Bino'd really blown it. He'd been worrying so about what the guy was telling him that he'd forgotten that he was just supposed to be a bystander. Change the subject, he thought. This boy's attention span probably isn't too long. Bino said, "I'm what I told you, her bosom buddy. How long is Thorndon giving her to answer?"

"Thorndon? *You* said Thorndon was doing it, sport. I didn't. But I tell you, she can take all the time she wants, so long as I know by day after tomorrow."

That wasn't much time, but it was better than nothing. Bino said, "How'm I going to get the answer to you?"

"You're going to, you're not going to get anything to *me*. You talk things over with Red. That's my pet name for her, sport. No offense, you know? You just tell her, what we talked about. I'll be in touch. Don't worry, you're going to hear from me. Or she is."

Boy, did this guy ever like to hear himself talk. Talk without saying anything—his instructions weren't making any sense. Almost as though he was making everything up as he went along. Bino thought, Maybe he's not wrapped real tight. Now *that's* a comfort, sitting here way out in the country in a strange room, looking at a western picture while a lunatic rants and raves in your ear. Bino shifted in his chair. He put his elbow on the armrest and his fingertips near the handle of the Mauser as he said, "Everything you're saying sounds like a lot of bullshit to me, tell you the truth."

A fist suddenly bunched the rear of Bino's collar together in a vise grip. The guy said, "What it sounds like to you's not important, Whitey. What's important is that you fucking do it, or you're not going to like what happens next. Or your girlfriend's not going to like it, and that'll be bad for you, sport. She might cut you off from her poontang, you know?" The fist released its hold. A board creaked. The garlic odor diminished, then faded completely. The guy said, from farther away, "I got no more time for you, cowboy. Consider me gone, only don't you move from that chair until you hear me drive away. I'll be watching the doors and windows, cowboy. Don't make me have to shoot you. And hey. After I go you ought to look around this place. Never know what you might find. Adios, motherfucker, I'm going now."

It was all Bino could do to keep from turning around and having a look as footsteps retreated. The draft on his neck increased as the outside door opened, then eased off as the latch clicked. Bino counted to twenty-seven, stuffing the envelope with the pictures inside his windbreaker, before he heard the Ford's engine kick over. By the time he'd counted to thirty-five he was peeking through the front window at the Ford as it bounced over the gravel road toward Valley View Lane. Bino memorized the license plate, ten to one a waste of time. It was a rental car, and maybe a stolen rental car. As the Ford disappeared around a curve in the road, Bino took one long stride in the direction of the exit. Then he halted in his tracks.

Look around, the guy had said. Look around for what?

Or for who?

Bino grabbed the Mauser, checked its clip once more—Jesus Christ, he thought, how many times are you going to check the fucking thing?—then moved over to the door behind the couch. It was partway open. Being careful not to touch the handle (there wasn't a chance in a thousand that the guy had left any fingerprints, but you never knew), Bino put stiff fingers against the wood and pushed. The door swung wide. Bile rushed up into his throat, and he gagged.

There wasn't any point in feeling for a pulse. The girl who was sitting in the chair was dead, okay, staring right at him with unseeing eyes, her swollen tongue between her lips, her neck purple and bulging over the folds of the cloth coat that was draped around her shoulders. Dead as a fucking . . . What kind of nut would . . . ?

There was a wadded wrapper on the floor, plain white, treated paper with an outer layer of tinfoil. There was fancy red lettering on the foil; Bino made out *l-a-z-a*. Taco Plaza. He bent from the waist, gingerly picked up the wrapper, and sniffed it. It smelled of onion and garlic. So the guy had stood there after doing this to the girl and had himself a taco. Bino shuddered. As he replaced the wrapper on the floor, the girl moved her head.

Bino jumped back a foot, his boots thudding on hardwood, aired the Mauser's hammer back, and froze. For a long instant he stood like a stone, then uttered a silly, nervous giggle. Shit, he was standing here pointing a gun at a *corpse*. The head movement had been some kind of postmortem reaction; the girl's cheek now rested on her shoulder. The sideways lurch had pulled one corner of her mouth up in a crooked grin, like that of a Raggedy Ann doll.

Bino had seen plenty. More than plenty. He made tracks, jogging through the front room, out across the porch, and over the rock-strewn yard toward the pickup. His chest heaved. He was gasping for breath. He swallowed bile. He dove behind the truck's steering wheel, dropped the Mauser on the seat, then started the engine. Gravel spun from under his tires as he backed out and headed for the farmhouse.

Jesus, he had to find a telephone.

16

Bino held the Styrofoam coffee cup in shaky hands. He watched the waves roll across the steaming black surface of the liquid. No way. No way could he drink from the cup without pouring half the coffee down the front of his shirt. He bent his head, affixed his lips to the cup's rim, and slurped. The coffee was too hot, burning his lips and tongue, but it seemed to help. He set the cup on the desk. Hot coffee sloshed over the rim and onto the back of his hand. He dug a handkerchief from his back pocket and dabbed at the sticky stuff.

From across the desk, Assistant Dallas County District Attorney Mac Strange said, "You want me to get you a straw?"

Strange's desk was government-gray metal, its top surface a thin coating of hard gray rubber. His nameplate was plastic, black letters on a white background reading simply "McIver Strange." Mac wore a light blue broadcloth shirt and solid navy tie. He was cleaning his fingernails. Visible behind him through his office window, seven floors below, traffic whizzed back and forth on Stemmons Freeway. On the other side of Stemmons, the parking lot surrounding the mammoth Loew's Anatole Hotel looked to be about half full.

"It's not funny, Mac," Bino said.

Strange had a chubby face and a thin, sharp nose. His throat puffed out over his collar, and his thinning brown hair was combed straight back away from his forehead. He held up his nail clippers and inspected a tiny ball of dirt that was impaled on the point of the swiveling file. The clippers disappeared beneath the level of the desk as he wiped the file on his pants leg.

"Why ain't it funny?" Strange said. "Shit, people discover bodies all the time. Paperboys, maids, you name it. I don't know any of 'em that get as jumpy about it as you, though. What do you think, Hardy? Check his underwear, maybe?"

County Detective Hardy Cole sat in a folding metal chair by one end of Strange's desk. He was lean and angular and, Bino suspected, just about as tough as he looked. He favored Bino with a shit-eating grin and didn't say anything.

"Well I made it through the first body okay," Bino said. "It was the second body that got to me."

"Well you're a big criminal lawyer," Strange said. "You ought to be three times as tough as a paperboy. And, what the hell, it ain't like you found the Chicago student nurses or anything. I doubt if anybody's going to miss those folks out there. As long as you're going to find a couple of stiffs, they might as well be dead horse's asses, right?" Strange and Cole broke up, guffawing and holding their sides, and Bino wondered if the both of them might not have been just as crazy as the guy he'd talked to out at the farm.

"You didn't see it," Bino said. "The guy hanging over the bathtub with a fork sticking in his ass."

Cole was suddenly serious. "He was pretty carved up. But what do these people expect? A guy, rich guy like that, hanging around some honky-tonk and taking home the first bimbo looks like she's going to fuck. The amazing thing is we don't find more of 'em cut to pieces. You know the broad used to live out there with him? Hey, we'd have been out there in the next couple of hours even if you hadn't called. That make you feel any better about it?"

Bino paused, about to try another sip of coffee. "How's that you would have?"

Strange and Cole exchanged looks, then Strange said, "The guy that owns the Velvet Swing, the kinko joint where Mr. Stiff and your friends got together night before last. Donny Something-or-Other. The joint's in Irving, near Texas Stadium; couple or three times a month the Irving cops get disturbance calls. Last week it was a woman didn't take to a guy giving her husband a blow job in a back booth, you know what kind of joint we're talking about.

"Anyway," Strange said, "the guy that owns the joint's been trying to call the dead guy ever since he left with the crazies the other night. Probably's got the hots for the guy; lot of AC/DC characters hanging around the Velvet Swing. He dropped a dime, finally, told the law to go out to that farmhouse and check on the guy. Just about the time you called."

Bino pictured the spots of dried blood on the farmhouse carpet, floors, and wall, the spots of blood that had formed a trail into the bathroom; the man he'd found, nude, hanging by his ankles from a cord that was tied around the shower nozzle. There'd been a trickle of dried blood running from the fork that had protruded from one of his buttocks, down between his cheeks and along the ridges of his spine. Finally Bino pictured his own panic-rigid fingers as he'd tried to punch the police emergency number into the phone. "I wish he'd called a couple of hours earlier," Bino said.

"Me, too," Strange said. "Then we'd only have a couple of stiffs to worry about. Now we got two stiffs plus a quivering jellyfish for a witness."

Through his jitters, Bino was getting mad. He'd heard Mac Strange go on this way quite a few times when the two of them had been tipping a few over at Joe Miller's, and there were times when Bino thought that Mac was a pretty funny guy. This wasn't one of the times, though. Bino cleared his throat. "Well I don't know about being a jellyfish, but I do know something about being a witness. Shit, Mac, the guy was standing behind me. I couldn't identify him if he walked in here and shot us the finger."

Hardy Cole's chair squeaked metallically as he tilted it back and intertwined his fingers behind his head. "We know who the guy is. We just don't know *where* he is."

Bino raised his eyebrows, his gaze shifting from Strange to Cole and back again. Strange nodded. With a wry grin, he fished into his top drawer and produced a stiff brown file folder. He opened the file. There was a stack of papers inside, and what looked to be a fingerprint card stapled to one cover along with some mug shots.

"Daryl Ralph Siminian," Strange said. "Have a look, in case you see him again." He offered Bino the file.

Bino looked at a front and a side view of a guy who didn't quite go with the voice out at the farm. The guy in the pictures was a pretty boy, curly hair over a handsome, square-jawed, olive-complexioned face. The cruel downward curves at the corners of the mouth were the only hint; otherwise the guy might have been a Latin screen idol. "How do you know this is the guy?" Bino asked. He tossed the file, still open, onto the desk. It landed with a flat slap.

Strange put his nail clippers away and folded his hands. "Deduction. Two and two, you know. And we could be wrong; there's a five percent chance. He's on the FBI's top-ten list as it is, and I figure next week he'll be Public Enemy Number One. Started out as a two-bit bank robber. Worked alone, handed the teller a note and hauled ass with whatever she happened to have in the drawer. A few thousand dollars at a whack, no more. They gave him a dime to do in the federal joint up at Oxford, Wisconsin, and, I don't know, something snapped in the guy. He got into a beef and busted up four guards pretty good, spent two years in the psycho ward up at Springfield, Illinois. Now I'm a prosecutor and not a doctor or a penologist, but, well, the Feds like to keep everybody up at Springfield shot up with Thorazine. I hear a lot of doctors say that stuff keeps 'em quiet, but it sure fucks up their minds over the long haul. Seemed to with this cat. They were trying to load him onto a bus to take him back to Oxford when Mr. Siminian got his hands on a shank someplace. He killed one hack and got ahold of a riot gun, then made another hack drive him the hell out of there in the warden's car. Shit, these Feds are a real piece of work. If a state prisoner escaped like that it'd be all over the papers. Page one. Until we started checking on Mr. Siminian nobody ever even heard of the guy."

"I don't need to hear all of this," Bino said.

"Well it ain't no bedtime story," Strange said.

"How's this guy tied in to somebody named Lou Thorn-don?" Bino asked.

Now it was Strange's turn to look surprised. He and Cole exchanged glances and shrugs, then Strange said, "What do you know about Thorndon?"

"Well for one thing, I know he's a three-time loser running around on probation," Bino said. "The newspapers say you guys are getting tough on crime. Giving out probations to guys like Thorndon doesn't sound too fucking tough to me."

Strange swiveled in his chair and faced the window. "Don't be getting on my case, Bino."

"I'm not getting on *your* case. I'm trying to get on my client's case. Judge Emmett Burns."

"I know who your client is," Strange said. "You're a big teevee star and all. Which makes using you as a witness on this . . . these killings just a little bit touchy."

Bino drank some more coffee, his hand now steady as a rock. "Well, Jesus Christ, let's don't be getting on any touchy subjects. I mean, don't worry about any little shit like double homicides, or the fact that Goldman's trying to put a judge in the penitentiary on a phony mail-fraud beef. Let's just don't get touchy, okay?"

Still gazing out the window, his round head unmoving, Strange said, "Fuck you, Bino."

"Fuck you, too, Mac," Bino said.

Cole gave a nervous snicker. Strange put one foot on the windowsill and shoved off, spinning his chair around to face Bino across the desk. "No," Strange said. "Fuck *you*. We got nothing to do with your federal case and you damn well know it. So don't ask me anything about Thorndon's state criminal case, it's got nothing to do with you. Besides which I'm sick of hearing about it. As for what we're talking about here, the murders, I'll tell you we've had two complaints that put Mr. Siminian right here in the Dallas area. The first one came from Mr. Lou Thorndon."

"Jesus Christ," Bino said. "*Thorndon* filed a complaint against somebody? I bet that was an experience for him."

"Maybe it was, I don't know. Thorndon did time with Siminian up at Oxford. So about, about a month ago, Thorndon said this Daryl Siminian called him up, talking crazy. He . . . you tell it, Hardy."

Cole rested one ankle on his knee and propped his shin against the edge of the desk. "Siminian called Thorndon up and told him he was in town to help him out. According to Thorndon he told Siminian, 'Help me with what?' Siminian said a lot of incoherent stuff about how old Lou was really going to like it, what Siminian was going to do, and then Thorndon says he hung up on the guy. Between you and me I think the call scared the shit out of Thorndon, and if *Thorndon's* afraid of him, Mr. Siminian must be a real badass." Cole pinched his own cheek.

"I guess that goes without saying, after today," Bino said. "I'll tell you, though, the part about Thorndon not knowing what the guy was going to help him with, well, that sounds like a lot of bullshit to me. Like Thorndon was trying to make everybody think he didn't know what was going on."

"We thought about that already," Cole said. "And I ain't saying you're wrong. But, well, shit like that happens quite a bit in the pen. Thorndon's a big shot, all the cons think so anyway, and when a guy like that goes to the joint he has to beat them off like flies. Punks like Siminian follow them around—'Can I get you anything, Mr. Thorndon? Wipe your ass,' things like that. A lot of times they keep right on tagging after the guy once the both of them hit the street. The punk thinks maybe if he can find something to do for the guy, then maybe the guy will give him some money. Or maybe just a pat on the head; these convict assholes are funny that way. And when you're talking a wacko like Siminian, well, it's just possible it happened just the way Thorndon says it did."

"Plus," Strange said, "even if Thorndon was going to hire something done, he wouldn't use a crazy motherfucker like Siminian. Shit, he'd be *asking* for heat."

Bino's green golf cap lay on an empty chair to his left. He picked it up, poked his index finger inside the crown, and twirled the cap around as he said, "Plus, you guys are going to do everything you can to make Thorndon look good. I mean, if a guy you let out on probation was to get mixed up in something like this, it'd kind of put egg on your faces."

Strange picked up the file, turned it around so that it was right side up to him, and put it away. "Fuck you double, buddy. Look, Thorndon's got no reason to do any of this. He's already got his probation, he's got no profit motive. And as for the dirty pictures of the girl . . . hell, Thorndon just doesn't have any reason to."

Bino put on his cap, tilted it back on his head, and flashed his best you're-a-great-guy smile, directed at Strange. "Look, Mac, I know you got a job to do, and I wouldn't do anything in the world to put your tit in a wringer. But I've really got my hands full on the Emmett Burns thing and I need to know. How come you guys agreed to give Thorndon probation? I mean, probation's not Dallas County's usual style for a kid gets caught with *one joint*, for Christ's sake. Much less a guy like Thorndon."

Strange blinked dully. "I told you not to be asking about that shit."

"I know you did. But hell, it's not like it was a case that you're working on now. The Thorndon deal is water under the bridge; what difference does it make if you just tell me how come you made the deal?"

Strange glanced toward Cole, then lowered his eyes. "It'll make a difference if it gets out that I told you. To the wrong people."

"Well who's the wrong people?" Bino said. "Make a difference to who?"

Strange propped one foot against the edge of his desk and rested a forearm on his knee. "You don't know? I got to spell it out for you? Shit, Hardy, the man's got a reputation like F. Lee himself and a brain like Dumbo."

Bino let that one pass. This was like having sex with a sadist; if he was going to get anything at all out of Mac Strange, he was going to have to let Strange get in a few licks first. Bino said, "From the way you're acting, I guess it's Goldman you're worried about."

"Well maybe you're a little smarter'n Dumbo," Strange said. "Not much, but a little."

"So Goldman, or at least somebody from the Feds, told you to give Thorndon probation. Is that it?"

Strange rubbed a front tooth with his index finger. "I didn't say that. Hardy, you hear me say anything like that?"

Cole folded his arms and grinned. "Naw. Didn't nobody say anything like that except Bino."

Bino leaned back and crossed his ankles. "For them to do that, well, Thorndon would have to be snitching on somebody, right? Who's the snitchee? Not my client; Thorndon's not testifying against the judge."

"Well I thought for a minute he was getting somewhere, Hardy," Strange said. "Now he's gone from Dumbo to Einstein and back to Dumbo. Quick as a flash."

Einstein to Dumbo to . . . ? Jesus Christ, what *had* the

Feds wanted Thorndon to do? Bino started as the answer flooded over him. Mac Strange had been right. Bino *had* been thinking like Dumbo.

He snapped his fingers and pointed at Strange. "Bleeder," Bino said.

Mac yawned and cupped a hand over his mouth. "Bleed who?"

"Well, fuck a duck," Bino said. "Thorndon got off the hook with the Feds by snitching on his own lawyer. How 'bout *that* for a new angle, huh?"

"Yeah. It'd be novel, okay," Strange said.

"But, let's see, Thorndon told Goldman—or, what's the other asshole's name? Buford Jernigan, yeah, Goldman's stooge—that his lawyer was going to pay a bribe to get him off. So now the Feds jump up and dismiss the case against Thorndon and tell you guys to— Yeah, now they *really* got Bleeder by the nuts. Only Bleeder doesn't like being the snitchee, so he's got to have somebody to snitch on himself. So what if he's lying his ass off, he can give Goldman somebody that'll make old Marv's mouth water. Like my client, f'r instance."

"Now I ain't saying you're doing bad," Strange said. "And I ain't saying you're doing good. But I am saying that if it gets around that me and *Hardy* told you any of this shit, you can kiss your ass good-bye."

"Don't be ridiculous, Mac." Bino got up and paced back and forth, his hands clasped behind his back. "Now Thorndon's problem is—and that's why he's trying so hard to get my client to cop a plea—Thorndon's problem is that he doesn't want a snitch jacket. Which is what he'll be wearing if all this goes public in a trial. These boys got a funny code; being a snitch is about the worst thing that you can be called."

"Which makes it more likely that this Siminian might be working for Thorndon," Cole said, straightening up in his chair.

Bino halted and raised an index finger. "So Bleeder's got

it coming and going now. He was one up on everybody at the U.S. Attorney's office, 'cause he knew something that they didn't know. That Ann Burns had a gambling problem. Jesus, I bet Goldman about had an ejaculation when he found *that* out. Not only does Goldman have Bleeder going for him, he finds out that the judge's own daughter has a weak spot that makes her vulnerable to some heat. Now they think they can make Ann corroborate whatever Bleeder's telling them. One minute they're ready to give Bleeder a little trip up the river for trying to bribe the judge, the next minute they're applying old Frank's makeup so he can be their star witness."

Strange got his clippers out and resumed cleaning his nails. Cole unwrapped a stick of Doublemint gum and popped it into his mouth. Neither one of them said anything. Bino resumed his Sherlock Holmes–style pacing, hands clasped behind his back.

"But there's something they weren't figuring on," Bino said. "Emmett Burns is one of those rare birds that wouldn't steal if you gave him the key to the vault and six months' head start. Plus his daughter, through all that's wrong about her, is crazy about him, and they can't roll her over no matter *what* they threaten her with. Goldman did call her up and try to put some heat on, Mac."

"Do tell," Strange said.

"Let's see," Bino said. "This is Thursday. It's what, two-thirty? I got to hustle down to the Federal Building before the clerks all go home. If I can set up a hearing tomorrow, on a dismissal motion, then maybe the judge's case will be history by tomorrow night."

"You sure do make it sound easy," Strange said.

Bino was really fired up now, jabbing the air with his index finger to drive his points home as he continued to pace back and forth. "I'll put Ann Burns on the stand, and she'll testify to what kind of pressure Goldman tried to put on her on the phone, plus what Bleeder tried to talk her into saying while they were eating lunch. Tell you the truth, I don't even think it'll come down to a hearing. I'll tell Goldman beforehand what I'm going to do, and I think he'll drop the charges before he'll let me catch him with his pants down in open court. If that doesn't get 'em, then I'll put Emmett Burns himself on the stand and have him testify about what Goldman—not directly, but through Buford Jernigan—tried to get him to do in connection with Thorndon's federal case. Now that's something that'll cook old Marv's goose for sure, Mac, whatcha think?" A triumphant grin on his face, Bino stopped his pacing and stood with his hands outstretched, palms up.

Strange produced a fat Hav-a-Tampa cigar from his drawer, stripped the wrapper, and licked the cigar from end to end. He poked it into his mouth and applied flame from a Bic disposable lighter. "I think," he said, puffing, "that you're talking like a forty-foot trailer rig ran over you."

Bino's grin faded. "Huh?"

Strange extinguished the flame, fished in his drawer, and placed a glass Caesars Palace ashtray on his desk. He blew a plume of bluish smoke at the ceiling. Bino closed his nasal passages; it was a cheap cigar and smelled the part. Strange said, "I think that you're ranting and raving. Maybe some of Siminian rubbed off on you, out there at that farm. Now Hardy Cole is sitting here"—he waved the cigar in Cole's direction—"and whatever comes down in this room is your word against ours. But if you think for a minute after all this spouting off in the newspapers and on TV that you're going to get Marvin Goldman to drop any charges, well, I got a Trinity River bridge for sale."

"Oh, I don't think he's gonna *want* to," Bino said. "He's going to have a choice between dismissing the indictment and having a lot of crap on the record that ain't going to sit well with a lot of folks."

Strange rolled his eyes. "Bino . . . shit. Look, you and me have been down the pike a long way, and you know there's some stuff we got to do sometimes to get a conviction that I ain't real crazy about. But these Feds make us look like Ned's

First Reader. Jesus Christ, you think Goldman goes around indicting federal judges under his own steam? You got to go to DC to get a decision like that. You want to find out what's really going on, go take a look at the records."

Bino sank slowly back down into the chair, briefly glancing out Strange's window. Traffic on Stemmons Freeway was building to a midafternoon peak, and if Bino was going to get to the Federal Building in time to set up a hearing for the next day, he was going to have to get on the stick.

"What records?" Bino said.

"Goddamnit, the court records. The . . . district clerk's records. Federal criminal cases. Emmett Burns has been on the bench for a coon's age, so forget going all the way back. Try the past five years. Check out how the Feds have done in Burns's court, conviction versus acquittal, then do the same for all the other courts. I've never seen any figures on what I'm talking about, but I'll lay you a twenty-five-dollar bill to a Titleist there've been ten times the acquittals in your client's courtroom than all the other federal judges in the district put together."

Bino's eyes narrowed. "Now hold on, Mac. I don't think I like what you're getting at. Even if that's so, it doesn't mean my client's on the *take* or anything. If it means anything at all, it means he's running a tight ship. Giving everybody a fair trial, which is what a judge is supposed to do. In theory, anyway."

Strange held the cigar clenched between his teeth, only his lips moving as he said, "Buy the man dark glasses, a cup, and a cane, Hardy. Jesus, I should have gone to work for the Feds; I'd never lose a case. I don't know why I'm opening up to you, Bino; tell you the truth, I might be putting my own balls in a vise. But our state judges have got to be elected ever so often, not that that makes 'em any pillars of honesty. But what it does do is make 'em bend over backward to give the defense a break, 'cause that defense lawyer over there might be a guy that gave heavy to the judge's campaign fund. But with the Feds, forget it. The president appoints federal judges, at least that's officially the way it's done. But everybody that knows shit about it knows that the president appoints whoever the local U.S. Attorney recommends. And who do you think that's going to be? Somebody like you? Shit, no, the U.S. Attorney is going to recommend one of his own assistants, somebody that'll make every ruling for the Feds in the courtroom. What you have in federal court is the judge wanting a conviction as bad as the prosecutor. Hell, they're both on the same payroll.

"But Emmett Burns is a horse of a different color," Strange said. "He's a Johnson appointee, a leftover. Since Nixon came along every federal judge that's been appointed has been some kind of wild-eyed conservative, hang-'em-high prick. Burns calls 'em the way he sees 'em no matter who gets hurt. Which don't make him popular up at the attorney general's office. So what you got here ain't really no big mystery. A. The Feds want Burns off the bench. B. Along comes Bleeder like Shoeless Joe from Hannibal, MO. Burns has a lifetime appointment, and the only way the Feds can get him off the bench is to send him to jail."

Bino put his elbows on the armrests of his chair and intertwined his fingers. "Yeah, I guess they'd do that. Press a case against a judge just to get rid of him."

"Goldman damn sure would," Strange said. "All he needs is the green light from upstairs. DC."

"I owe you one, Mac, leveling with me. I'm still going to set the hearing up."

"I don't blame you for that," Strange said. "Just don't expect Goldman to give you a medal for it. Your income taxes paid? Next Goldman will be indicting *you*, if you ain't careful."

Bino grinned. "What the hell, I got nothing to lose. I don't even know where I'll be officing next year. They're blowing my fucking building up."

Cole stood. "Just be careful that Goldman don't have you locked up in there when they push the plunger."

Bino started to leave, then paused. There was a question

he'd been wanting to ask earlier, but it had slipped his mind. "Mac," he said. "Those pictures. Let's say I buy the fact that the crazy guy, Siminian, isn't working for Lou Thorndon after all. If he's not, then where the hell did Siminian get the pictures of Ann? According to her it was Thorndon that set up the photo sessions, up in Chicago."

"I can answer that one," Cole said. "Ann Burns's ex-husband."

Bino's forehead wrinkled. "Eddie Satterwhite? How's he get in on this?"

"Well only after a fashion," Cole said. "His body's in on it, but his soul ain't. His body they found six weeks ago in his fuckhole of an apartment, in Cicero. That's right by Chicago, in case you ain't a geography expert. Somebody'd ransacked the joint, and it looked to the Cook County cops like somebody'd beaten the living shit out of Satterwhite before they offed him. Two plus two tells us that Siminian went up there, made Satterwhite cough up the photos, and then you know what. Had to be Siminian, the way all this is coming down. That Siminian. I'd look out for the crazy sonofabitch if I was you, Bino."

17

Bino decided that he'd better not go down to the Federal Building dressed as though he was going on a duck hunt, so he stopped off at Vapors North to change into a suit. The thermometer had climbed to near seventy degrees, and as Bino strode through the breezeway on the way to his apartment he stripped off his windbreaker and folded it over his arm. He ducked underneath a low-hanging limb, climbed the steps to his porch, jiggled the key into his front doorlock, and turned it. The door made a feathery, sliding noise over lush carpet as he pushed it open. He took one step inside his apartment and halted.

It was silent as a tomb. There was no sound anywhere in the apartment, not even the distant hum of the refrigerator. Visible in the small bachelor kitchen, through the opening over the bar, were the twelve-speed blender on the counter and the pale green, upright Amana fridge. Cecil was floating motionless with his tail pointed in Bino's direction, like a drifting black parabola. Nothing was out of place as far as Bino could tell. The red sofa and matching easy chairs stood in their proper alignment, facing the fifty-one-inch Mitsubishi TV and the fireplace of rough white brick.

So it wasn't that anything *looked* out of order that had him buffaloed, not at all. It was just too damn quiet. Bino had a sudden mental image of the nude man hanging over the farmhouse tub. The hairs at the base of his neck stood on end. He dug the Mauser out of his jacket pocket and held the pistol ready.

There wasn't anybody hiding behind the TV, or crouched behind the bar, or waiting in the kitchen. The hall closet was empty save for the overcoat and leather jacket—he'd bought the jacket four years ago, worn it once, found out what it was going to cost to have the damn thing cleaned, and as far as he could remember the jacket had been there ever since—that were on hangers over the canister vacuum cleaner and hose attachments. He didn't find anybody in his bedroom either, and upon entering his bathroom he came within an eyelash of shooting his own image in the mirror. Pistol held ready, he yanked the shower curtain aside. Rows of green tile dully reflected light from the open doorway.

Feeling sort of dumb, but still a little bit jumpy, Bino went back into the bedroom and put the pistol away in his nightstand. He rummaged around in his closet, then changed into a charcoal gray suit, white, patterned Christian Dior shirt, and solid red Countess Mara tie. When he left the apartment and hustled toward the parking lot, it was a quarter past three.

Midway between the building and the pickup, he threw a longing glance in the direction of his own numbered parking space. The Linc was still there, its hood and fenders gleaming white in the afternoon sun. Bino had just made up his mind to retrace his steps, go to Tilly Madden's apartment and ask to borrow—*borrow*? Hell, it was his car—the Linc for the rest of the day, when the Linc began to move.

It wheeled backward out of the parking space. Its tires screeched. A blond towhead—Bino had thought Buddy Madden a little taller than he actually was, the kid could barely see over the steering wheel—was visible through the rear window. The Linc reversed its direction and surged forward. More rubber burned as it careened out of the parking lot and, fishtailing, barely avoided a collision with an East Texas Motor Freight bobtail as the Linc turned south on Dallas Parkway.

Bino gritted his teeth and trudged over to the pickup. As he climbed aboard, he said a little prayer for the Linc and crossed his fingers.

The lady behind the counter in the U.S. district clerk's office, a fortyish woman in a shapeless gray dress, who had dull brown hair tied into a bun and who was wearing thick, round bifocals, glanced irritably at the clock on the wall. "What kind of motion? We go home in a half hour, you know."

Bino forced himself to smile and assume a humble attitude. "It's . . . gosh, it's really important or I wouldn't be imposing on you. It's a motion to dismiss the case, and, well, my client's been through a lot. I'd like for him to look forward to the weekend with a load off his mind."

Emmett Burns's case file lay open on the counter. Behind the counter were rows and rows of big wooden drawers containing hanging folders; the far left wall was solid four-drawer, metal filing cabinets. In the center of the work area, two young girls were typing away while a third woman sat behind her desk with her legs crossed, buffing her nails. There was an open doorway at the back of the room that led to an inner, private office. To the right of the doorway hung a huge photo of the U.S. district clerk herself, Nancy Hall Doherty, shaking hands with then-President Gerald Ford. Bino thought the president looked a little bit pained, as though he'd just barked his shin or something.

The woman with the thick bifocals sniffed. She said to Bino, "Well, have you talked to Mr. Goldman about this?"

"No, I haven't," Bino said. "If you'll put us on the docket,

I'll sure get in touch with old Marv. All parties to the case will be here, I guarantee it."

She leafed through the file, papers rustling. There was a faint sweet scent about her that reminded Bino of his grandmother's sitting room, when he'd been a little kid out in Mesquite. She said, "There isn't even a judge assigned to this case. This is the one where they're calling in a visiting judge, from out of town. A judge to judge a judge, so to speak." Bino assumed that he was required to chuckle at that one, so he did. She went on. "You're really making it hard on us, Mr. Phillips. Who's going to hear your motion? I suppose you'd like for your client to hear it himself." She gave a short, smug laugh.

Bino wondered who was running things in federal court, the judges or the clerks. He said evenly, "Oh, any judge will do. Just put us on anybody's docket, I'm not particular." Jesus, he thought, any district judge can give a ruling. What's the big deal?

She regarded him through narrowed eyes behind her bifocals, then said, "If I *must* help you with this on such short notice, you'll have to wait here a moment." She picked up the file and held it in the crook of her arm, schoolmarm fashion. Then she marched primly into the private office with her high heels clicking angrily on the tile. She closed the door behind her.

Bino expelled a long breath, put his hands in his pockets, crossed his ankles, and leaned against the counter. There was a cork bulletin board on the wall to the left of the counter. Civil Service Employment Opportunity notices were hung from side to side and top to bottom on the board, impaled there by silver-headed thumbtacks. Bino read a few of them over. The Civil Service Commission was looking for GS-7 Classifier Trainees in Ogden, Utah. If somebody was willing to move to some place called Three Rivers, Texas, they could hire on with the Bureau of Prisons as a nifty GS-5 Correctional Officer. Bino yawned, rubbed his eyes, and then one particular notice really caught his attention.

The notice, hanging in the lower-left-hand corner of the bulletin board, announced, in bold black print, four GS-14 openings for attorneys with the Department of Justice in Seattle, Washington. *Jesus*, Bino thought, *has Goldman seen that?* He was edging toward the bulletin board, fully intending to swipe the notice and show it to Goldman at tomorrow's hearing, when one of the women behind the counter cleared her throat.

It was the gal who was buffing her nails. She had short brown hair, big brown eyes, and big bosoms jutting out against a red sweater. She smiled at him. Bino leaned back against the counter, watched the ceiling, and whistled a few bars of "Take It to the Limit," an old Eagles tune.

This was taking one hell of a long time. Bino had been around the courthouse for enough years to know that all it took to set up a hearing was for the clerk to make an entry on the docket. What was that woman doing back there in that office? Bino's gaze swept the big area on the other side of the counter and came to rest on a four-line rotary telephone that sat on top of a file cabinet. One of the buttons on the phone was lit. Two of the clerks were still typing and the third was still buffing her nails and giving him the eye, so that left only the woman back there in the private office to be talking on that phone. Bino went through the swinging gate beside the counter and picked up the receiver. He pressed the lighted button. Miss Nail Buffer put her emery board down. Her red lips parted. Bino held up a silencing hand in her direction.

Over the phone, Marvin Goldman's voice was saying, "And I don't care what you have to tell him. If we can't get on her docket, put the thing off somehow."

"I can't just make up a story, Mr. Goldman," the woman clerk said. "I suppose I'll have to jam the hearing in somewhere on Judge Sanderson's docket for tomorrow. She's got a pretrial on a civil suit at one. I'll just have to put the civil matter off; the lawyers will probably have something else to do on Friday afternoon, anyway. Like playing golf."

Bino said, "Hi, Marv."

There was stony silence. The woman clerk opened the private office and stuck her head around the doorjamb. The receiver was still flattening her ear. Bino guessed that she was staring daggers at him, but he couldn't tell for sure. Her thick bifocals distorted her eyes.

Finally Goldman said, "How you doing, buddy?"

"I'm doing a lot better, buddy," Bino said. "Oh. Judge Sanderson will be fine, if we can't get into Hitler's court. I don't care who the judge is, Marv. Just be here. And why don't you bring Buford Jernigan along, okay? You might need somebody you can send out for coffee or something."

18

Lou Thorndon didn't get where he was in life by flying off the handle when he was talking to the cops. That was just what they wanted you to do, get all shook up and start cussing them and telling them off. Made you a sitting duck for the bastards.

And this particular cop didn't just climb down off a load of hay from out in the sticks. Short, sallow-complexioned, wiry bozo with thin lips that stayed pursed in a doubting expression, as though he thought that everything you had to say was a lot of bullshit. Probably a pretty tough little weasel, the kind of guy which could take a lot of punishment. Dish out a lot of punishment, too, if he got the idea that somebody was fucking with him. County cop. County cops as a rule were easier to buy off than the federals were, mainly because the county guys worked for less money and generally had a few more smarts about them. County detective name of Hardy

Cole, according to the oblong printed business card that now lay faceup on Thorndon's desk.

Thorndon used his middle finger to push his tinted wireframe glasses up on his nose. He gestured toward the asphalt car lot outside his office window. His face expressionless, he said, "What do you see out there? That look like a pile of turds or something?"

"No," Cole said. "It looks like a pile of junk cars." He leaned forward in the metal folding chair and rested his forearms on his thighs. His coat lapels parted with the movement, revealing the leather holster strap that ran across his chest.

"You think they're junk," Thorndon said. "I ask you. All them keys over there hanging on that board? Those hooks they're hanging on are numbered. The numbers go with the numbers on them parking spaces out there. You find one"— he raised an index finger—"car on my lot that won't start up and purr like a kitten, I'll take a nap in the middle lane out on the freeway. Just one. Your pick, try me out. I got one sixty-seven out there, the bullet-looking Malibu, third row. If that jewel got, say, more than seventy thousand real on the clock, well, I'll bugger the exhaust pipe is all I can tell you. Look, these people, they got some kind of job down at the car wash, filling station, Taco Pronto or some shit, they get a hundred a week, so what? So I let them come in here and give me a hand job about how they can fade sixty a week, just as car payments—they got three, four kids running around in dirty underwear with snot on their faces. Sure they can't make the payments. Can I help it? I ain't fucking the guy, I'm somebody's Dutch uncle or something? First thing you know they're a couple weeks behind, we send the wrecker out. If my man don't get an assful of buckshot, Jesus, they can't make their car payments but every one of 'em's got a Remington twelve-gauge runs three hundred and fifty dollars, that or a Doberman could whip Rin-Tin-Tin, then we get the car back and spend all the payments the asshole made us fixing it up to sell again. So then the guy wants to file a complaint with the county saying we hosed him good when we sold him the car. So what do you get? Man's down here trying to make a living, I got the county on my ass once a month. Listen, you want a coffee? Pop or something, I got a machine out back makes change." Thorndon's own reflection was visible in the glass partition behind the county man. With his hands folded on his desk, in his beige shirt and brown tie, Thorndon figured that somebody could take him for Honest Lou, the Thinking Man's Candidate. He thought that his snap-brim hat gave him just the right sharp-guy look. Might do better with clear instead of tinted glasses, but there was too much glare down here in Texas, even in winter.

Cole brushed off his lapel. "Nothing for me. Mr. Thorndon, I ain't investigating any complaint. Far as I know your probation officer's got no complaint, either. Says you're being a square guy."

Thorndon half-rose. "Now look—"

"And I ain't here to hassle you 'cause you're on probation, ex-con or any of that shit. Let's understand one another. For right now I don't care if every one of them junkers out there is on some police force's hot sheet, so don't give me no sales pitch."

"About time," Thorndon said, sinking back down, "somebody from the county or city come out here that's not trying to make a phony case on me. Now we're talking. So what? You collecting for something?"

Cole was fishing inside his coat, withdrawing a small spiral pad and a ballpoint, steadying the pad on his knee, and getting ready to write. His eyes narrowed slightly. So maybe he didn't like the question about whether he was collecting for something. First Bino Phillips, now this fucking guy. Acted like Lou Thorndon's money was counterfeit.

"So it's good you're not collecting," Thorndon said quickly. "For right now I got no spare change, tell you the truth. Trying to make a go of this little lot here and being the new boy on the block. Right up the street I got this guy Goss on Ross Avenue, been here since Teddy Roosevelt or some fucking president, coupla blocks on over this W. O. Bankston's got himself a used-car lot where he gets rid of the trade-ins on those new cars he sells out on LBJ Freeway. Shit, I got more competition than a candy-bar company."

"I'm trying to find a guy," Cole said.

"So? What guy?"

"A guy you phoned in a complaint on here while back. A Daryl Ralph Siminian."

Thorndon waved a hand in a shoofly motion. "Don't talk to me about that fucking guy. What's he into?"

Cole held the ballpoint between his index and middle fingers and tapped its point against the edge of his notepad. "I'm not at liberty to say; there's an investigation going on. The last make we have he's driving a current-year-model Ford two-door, midnight blue. It's an Avis Rent a Car, reported missing from Avis's Love Field location. The guy that rented it is an IBM man out of Buffalo, here on a sales meeting. The guy is missing, too, along with the car."

"Jesus, Daryl's going around stealing cars and offing guys?"

"I can't say that," Cole said. "But yeah, I'd like to visit with him about the car. A couple of other things, maybe. 'Course the Feds would, too, they'd like to get him back in the joint and maybe talk about a couple of problems he's got."

Thorndon smelled motor oil. A stained, pale-red shop rag lay on a file cabinet by the back door. He wrinkled his nose. Greasy-assed mechanics weren't worth shooting. Thorndon went over and picked up the rag, tossed it out the door onto the asphalt, closed the door. The glass pane in the door was streaked with dirt. "Look," Thorndon said. "I . . . hey, I told what I knew about a month ago, when I heard from the guy. He, he called my sister in Chicago since then, but she don't know nothing about where he is. I doubt he's going to call me no more; he knows I don't want nothing to do with no ex-capees. Hell, I can't afford to. Guys like that don't contact anybody they know, not if they got any sense at all." He went back over to his desk and sat down.

Cole chewed thoughtfully on his thumbnail, then said, "I got to level with you, Mr. Thorndon. I mean, it's really important we get a line of communication going here. There's some people think maybe you and Mr. Siminian got some things going together."

"I thought you said you weren't giving me any of that ex-con shit," Thorndon said. "Which is all me and that Daryl boy got in common. A guy like that I got enough trouble without. I got enough crazies running in and out of here buying cars without I got to hunt up more crazies to pal around with."

"That's really a funny coincidence," Cole said. "You come in town, new guy, used to be Siminian's buddy up at Oxford—"

"*Buddy?* Shit, I know the guy is all."

"Siminian escapes from the federal joint and, what do you know? He shows up in town and gives you a ring. Right down here in Dallas, Texas, of all places, and right after that, you know what? Well, an old girlfriend of yours starts hearing from him."

Thorndon unwrapped a stick of Doublemint and popped it into his mouth. "You ever try to quit smoking? It's a bitch; half the time this gum just makes you want one more. I don't have no old girlfriends, Detective Cole. They get over thirty I put them out to pasture."

"Now that's a good one. Over thirty, hey, that's pretty good. Well maybe the one I'm talking about you might make an exception; she ain't lost none of her looks even if she's maybe got a few miles. Thirty years old on the nose, matter of fact. Ann Burns. Who just happens to be a federal judge's little girl. Emmett Burns, you ever heard of him? He was the judge on your federal case, wasn't he? Another funny coincidence."

Thorndon moved the wad of gum with his tongue, moved it from one cheek to the other. He was really dying for a cigarette, and the way this little talk with this cop was going made him want one even more. Thorndon said, "I know, yeah, I know Ann Burns. She was married to a guy I used to know up in Chicago. So I know what you're coming to and, look, so help me God I didn't have no idea about that, that she's that judge's girl when that little case of mine comes up in his court. Those kind of games I do not play, my friend. You learn. You learn the hard way that when some kind of beef comes down you're better off going ahead and taking your medicine. You start, say, trying to take out some insurance by getting next to a judge or prosecutor or something, you're just asking somebody, 'Please, go ahead and bite my head off, will you?' " Thorndon thought that he sounded pretty convincing. Hell, he might even have believed himself.

"That's not what they're saying around," Cole said. "That's not what they say at all about you; at least the Feds don't say that in this case they got right now against their own judge. Just so you'll know, Mr. Thorndon, that I'm being on the up-and-up and not trying to let you talk yourself into a corner, I'll tell you I already got you taking Miss Ann Burns around to a couple of functions. Just about the time, maybe a little bit before, she started hearing from this Siminian."

"Yeah, well, I'm a single man coming to town, I don't know any girls. I needed somebody to, you know, take around to some get-acquainted parties. She was around, and she's not a bad-looking lady in case you ain't checked her out."

"I can't argue with you about that," Cole said. "She's really photogenic."

Thorndon paused, letting the cop know he was thinking about his answer. Didn't want to sound too natural. What you had to do to fish in a cop was make him think he was really putting you through the wringer. Finally, letting just the right amount of nervous quiver into his tone of voice, Thorndon said, "I guess you could say she takes a pretty good picture. I give a guy twenty bucks for a shot of the two of us, me and her, at dinner down at the Fairmont Hotel. She looks good in that one, okay."

Cole put the end of the ballpoint between his teeth and lightly bit down on it. "You know what, Mr. Thorndon? You're fucking with me. The pictures you had taken of her up in Chicago, three on one, one on one, daisy chain, whatever. Hell, I got copies of them. And I ain't here to bust anybody's porno ring; I told you I ain't here to find out anything about what you're doing. What I want is this Daryl, nothing more. But if you keep on fucking with me I'm going to cause a lot of heat to come down on you. Not 'cause I don't like you, but I got to get some answers." He steadied the notepad on his thigh and crossed his legs. "Think of it this way, I might be helping you. Might even be saving your ass. How long since you heard from Eddie Satterwhite?"

Poor old Eddie, Thorndon thought. Dumb and dead. He said, "Eddie? Two, three months maybe. Listen, nobody can make nothing out of that, me going out with Ann. She and him are divorced a long time."

"I ain't *making* anything of it," Cole said. "I'm just wanting to know when you last heard from the guy. See, unless Eddie's got one helluva long cord on his phone, you ain't going to hear from him anymore. Somebody didn't like Eddie much, and they went to killing him. Just before this Siminian shows up down here in Texas."

Thorndon was doing such a good job with this playacting that beads of sweat were actually forming on his upper lip. He said, "I, I don't like to hear about nobody dying. Eddie Satterwhite wasn't no bad guy, and there's a shortage of them around. What, you're making Daryl for killing Eddie Satterwhite?"

"I don't say what we're making Daryl for and what we ain't making Daryl for," Cole said. "That's you that's saying that."

Thorndon's chin lifted slightly. "Well, that's good. That's very good that you don't make Daryl for that killing and that you ain't really trying to find out what I'm doing. I don't believe a fucking word you're saying, you know that?"

"Well you're a pretty sharp guy if you don't," Cole said.

" 'Cause I don't believe you either. I don't believe you when you say you don't know where Siminian is at. I ain't sure I don't think you got something going with him. You need to get down with me, Mr. Thorndon, in case you really *don't* have nothing going with him. Our boy Daryl's been acting pretty spacey lately. You might not be safe."

Bingo, Thorndon thought. Perfect. Perfect lead-in for telling this cop how to find old Daryl without making it look as though Lou Thorndon was wanting to turn anybody in. Got to string this cop a little bit longer, really convince him Lou Thorndon ain't wanting to talk about anybody. Thorndon said, "Well since we both know we don't believe each other, I guess we got nothing more to say. I mean, why would anybody want to talk to anybody they think's pumping them full of bullshit."

Cole got up and went over to the back door, looking through the dirty plate glass at the rows of old Chevys and Fords mostly, a couple of Plymouth Valiants and even one Buick Roadmaster, a fifty-five model. To the rear of the lot was a big wooden shed with an overhead sliding door. Thorndon didn't want this sharp-nosed county cop poking around that shed. There were two almost-new Mercedeses hidden in there, along with one two-year-old Eldorado that one silly bastard out of San Antonio was supposed to have picked up this morning but hadn't showed up as yet. Probably had gotten a skinful someplace.

The open blinds that hung on the door cast straight-line shadows across Cole's cheeks and nose. He said, "I'm a cop, Mr. Thorndon, conducting what some people might laughingly call an investigation. *Everybody* tries to pump me full of bullshit, but you know what? The square johns lie more than the in-guys do. The in-guys, the ones that've been through it before, got no reason to bullshit me except where they got something to hide. The square johns, though, they're pansies. They get scared shitless when somebody hollers cop, and then they lie their asses off about everything, including even where they live. So you're an in-guy. With you I think I can flip a coin. There's a fifty-fifty shot you got something going with this Siminian, maybe you're wanting him to scare somebody out of bringing your name up in connection with certain things, and if you got something going with him you'll bullshit me. Only I tend to not think so. Siminian is off his nut; I mean, we think the man is doing some things that nobody does but a pure psycho. So either you're not in with him, in which case I'll get straight stuff from you, or you do have him doing something but you don't know about this crazy wild shit that's happening. We're talking some serious homicides here, not even like shooting somebody after you rob them, which makes some kind of half-assed sense. We're talking Manson-type shit, no sense to it. I'll tell you something else. If it ever comes down that I know you been hiding this Siminian, I'll see you get charged along with him if I have to build some kind of frame around you. With your record that wouldn't be so hard to do, you know what I mean?''

Thorndon pictured the look on another cop's face, the detective out in Los Angeles who'd told Thorndon he could lease out his Eighth Street car lot and hit the road, or come in one morning and find a bunch of DEA's running around, who in turn were going to find a few bags of cocaine hidden inside some inflated tires on cars. Thorndon knew what this Hardy Cole meant, all right, about building a frame. Building a frame around a guy was the best way in the world for a cop to get a guy to talking. Which, in this situation, made things even better for Louis P. Thorndon, Esq.

Thorndon said, "So you're going to come down on me. You checked me out before you come over and you know you ain't getting no cherry. I been through it, my friend. But, look, you got to understand about this Daryl guy. Up, up at Oxford I made a big mistake with the boy. Fourteen months I bunked in with him, same two-man cell; I ain't talking any homosexual shit, but a peaceful man like me in the joint needs somebody like Daryl. I don't want nobody fucking with me, you know? So I had a little money up there, not what everybody seems to think; Jesus, I had that kind of money I'd be in Palm Springs next door to Frankie and Dino and them guys. But I took care of Daryl, made sure he had plenty commissary all the time, and he was a little bit crazy even back then. Nobody screwed around with me 'cause they weren't quite sure what he'd do about it. Come to think about it, I didn't know for sure either, not till he got into it and busted up them four hacks so bad. You know about that, huh?"

"It's in my file," Cole said.

"Okay. I figured you did. Daryl used to lay around talking about what me and him were going to do when we got out, that we'd do this and that, hide out in the mountains, real crazy shit. Tell you the truth I mighta led him on some; I was in this situation where I didn't want to piss the guy off. Say, Detective, they showed this old movie up at Oxford one time, on Wednesday night. Classic night, they called it, showed a lotta Bogart stuff. One Wednesday they showed this movie called *Of Mice and Men*, had this guy in it, same guy that played Stallone's manager in the *Rocky* pictures, only he was a lot younger when he made this picture. Yeah, and this other guy in it was the same one played Lyle Talbot, you know, the wolf man in the old Frankenstein shows."

"Lon Chaney, Jr.," Cole said. "Burgess Meredith, he was the little skinny guy."

"That's them. Chaney was this big dumb bastard that was dangerous as shit, 'cause he was so stupid he didn't know how strong he was. Wound up killing this girl out in a barn, just grabbing her by the hair and holding her off the ground, something about one of these kittens he had that died."

"Lennie was the guy's name," Cole said. "Chaney. Burgess Meredith was George. I musta seen it a hundred times."

"You seen it, huh? Well you remember how the big dumb guy used to sit around and tell the other guy, George, he'd say, 'Hey, George, tell me about the rabbits.' And George would say, 'I told you about the rabbits three, four times already,' then the big guy would go, 'Please, George, tell me again.' And George would tell him, bullshitting the guy, about how someday they was going to have this house with a white picket fence and all these rabbits they was going to raise, and the big dumb bastard was going to get to feed all these fucking rabbits. Real weird, that George guy, and I'll tell you something, Detective. I didn't sleep too good that night after we seen that picture, 'cause the big dumb guy talked just like Daryl had been talking to me, laying around in the cell. Tell you the truth I got to thinking that Daryl boy might be just as spacey as the guy in the movie.''

"He's a helluva lot spacier," Cole said. "It looks like he is."

"Yeah, I'm not— Well, listen, I'd as soon you didn't tell me whatall you think Daryl's been into, but I can imagine," Thorndon said. "All my life I been stand-up—you guys call it uncooperative—and I never once called a police number in my life till I made that complaint on Daryl you was talking about. But I was scared, tell you the truth. I got this call from Daryl one day, zap, out of the blue, like he was my long lost kid brother or something. He says he's got these pictures—he was talking about the ones with Ann Burns in them—and he knows all about this problem I got with the law down here in Texas. He says he's going to use them pictures to help me out. I go, 'Daryl, what the hell you doing with them pictures?' I knew all along he was excaped, but I didn't let on to him. He said Eddie Satterwhite give him the pictures.

"You know I told you I know Eddie Satterwhite from Chicago?" Thorndon said. "Well Eddie come to visit me coupla times at Oxford, that's where Daryl knew him from, so I guess when Daryl busted out he went to Chicago and looked Eddie up. 'Course I was the one Daryl was really looking for, but I was long gone down to Dallas by that time, so I'm guessing Daryl got Eddie's number from somebody. If somebody done Eddie I can only figure, probably, Daryl knocked him off for the pictures."

"That," Cole said, "or he just went out there to rob the

guy and the pictures come as a bonus. Either way you got one dead guy." He left the door and went back to his chair. He sat down.

"Yeah," Thorndon said. "I can't remember exactly what I said to Daryl on the phone, some shit to cool him off, but soon as I hung up I called the law."

"Before or after," Cole said, "you had your lawyer try to pay somebody off? You don't go for blackmailing nobody's daughter, huh? Just a little bribe or two."

Thorndon jabbed the air with an index finger. "Now that's something you are not going to get me to talk about. The Feds told me not to say nothing about that to nobody."

"Sure," Cole said. "I know, they're the ones talked us into giving you probation, which I got to tell you I think is absolute bullshit, you not doing no time. But I got no control over that, that's up to the prosecutors. Pretty slick. You're getting off 'cause your lawyer's going to help the Feds build a case against their own judge. And while all you assholes—you, Bleeder, and Goldman—are playing ring around the rosy, I'm sitting here with people hacked and beat and stabbed to death. Nothing important I'm fucking with, it's a helluva lot bigger deal to make sure you don't tell me nothing that might screw up a federal prosecution."

Thorndon took his gum wrapper from his desk, spat his gum into it, rolled the paper, gum inside, up into a ball. He tossed the wad into the trash can, running his tongue over his front teeth, behind his upper lip. "I don't make none of these rules, Detective. I just go to the library and check out a rule book, like everybody else."

"Jesus Christ," Cole said. "That's supposed to be the cop's line."

"Why's it supposed to?" Thorndon asked. "I can play the game, same as you. Shit, we're all playing it. 'Cept Daryl. Daryl's playing his own game. Look, suppose I can tell you where Daryl's at. Just suppose. If I did I'd be due pertection; you know what that boy's liable to do to me."

"How can you get more protection than you already got?" Cole said. "Palling around with the FBI. But, yeah, I can guarantee you that. We get our hands on that boy, he's never gonna see any daylight to be doing anything to anybody."

"Well just suppose," Thorndon said. "See, Daryl used to talk about Texas Stadium all the time. Seen it on TV, when the Cowboys was playing somebody. Daryl used to say he ever came to Dallas, he was gonna check into that Holiday Inn, right across the freeway from the stadium. I was going to look for him, I think I'd try out there. Listen, you sure you don't want a pop or something?"

Cole fished in his pocket and found a couple of quarters. "Tell you what, I'll match you. Odd or even? I don't want nobody saying I paid you a bribe."

Lou Thorndon watched Hardy Cole leave, watched the county detective walk over to the curb, stand beside the unmarked county Plymouth, and look around—taking everything in, his gaze darting at the front of Lou's building, once again sweeping the rows of cars on the lot, then lingering for a moment on the broken-down Windjammer Inn motel across the street, at the big-breasted black girl, probably a hooker, who was silhouetted in one of the upstairs windows—before poking a toothpick into one corner of his mouth, climbing into the county vehicle, and driving away. This was one cop that would take care of business, would go out to that Holiday Inn and ride Mr. Daryl Siminian straight on downtown. Mr. Hardy Cole was one pretty smart cop, but hadn't no cop ever been born could outsmart Mr. Louis P. Thorndon. Lou Thorndon knew something about insurance policies.

The phone call to the police department, right after he'd sent Daryl to Chicago after those pictures (how the hell could Thorndon have known that the crazy bastard was going to off old Eddie? That was something Siminian had done on his own), that was a little insurance policy that Thorndon had figured out. Slick as a whistle. Advance warning to the law that just in case old Daryl was to go nuts or something (hell, the crazy asshole had escaped from the joint; never could tell with that Daryl boy), Louis P. Thorndon didn't have anything to do with the guy. And the policy was paying off in spades. Daryl was about to get himself back in the joint (in a hole where you'll never see the sun, kid), and he could holler till hell froze over that Lou Thorndon put him up to all of it and nobody was going to believe him. Louis P. Thorndon was smelling like a rose once again.

And it was good that the detective had come along when he did, was going to take the worry of Daryl off Thorndon's mind, because Lou Thorndon had plenty of other things to worry about right now. Like what had happened to this fucking asshole who was supposed to have shown up hours ago to haul the Mercedeses and Caddy down to San Antonio. Forty, count 'em, forty thousand dollars pure profit in the cars, ID numbers all filed down smooth and restamped, paint job would fool the manufacturer, license plates clean as Snow White's under- wear; only thing standing between Thorndon and his forty grand was for this wino burnout to show up and take the heaps on a five-hour ride. It wasn't like there was any time to waste; the San Antonio dentist who was buying the Mercedeses, one for him and one for his wife, and the C & W Disco owner who wanted the Eldo (Thorndon had made the nightclub man come up-front with the money a hundred percent, a lot of these disco guys were shaky propositions when it came to paying) were going to get antsy if Thorndon didn't meet the Friday delivery. The county cop had been right about one thing, these square johns were a nervous bunch of assholes. First thing you knew the disco owner was going to start hollering fraud. All Thorndon needed, another fire to put out.

But at least he didn't have Daryl to worry about anymore. Just the thought of that psycho bastard made Thorndon grind his teeth. Instead of Daryl, why couldn't Thorndon have had a homo or something for a cellie up at Oxford? Would have worked out better in the long run. Thorndon needed a ciga- rette. He patted his empty shirt pocket as he went out the back door and crossed the lot to the shed. Force of habit; Jesus, he was never going to shake it.

Daryl coming along when he had, that was another lousy break. Just a phone call—*Hi, Lou, I'm out of the joint, you got anything I can do for you to maybe make some bread?* Just so happened at the time that Thorndon had been in a crack; he'd needed a lot done, anything to put a little heat on that judge to get a deal made. And Daryl, how was anybody to know the guy was on the run? Thorndon hadn't known it, not until Daryl had already gone up to Chicago and offed Eddie Satterwhite (another silly bastard, nobody was going to miss *that* guy) and Thorndon was already in too deep. That's when Thorndon had used his head and made the phone call. Now let old Daryl try and tell the law that Lou Thorndon had anything to do with what had been going on. Just let the bastard try; they'd laugh at him.

And Thorndon thought that now he had the problem over the judge's case worked out by handling things himself, just like he should have done to begin with. Jesus, what a fuckup, huh? Bleeder had told Thorndon he could fix things for forty grand. Thorndon hadn't had much cash at the time, but he'd raised the money. And Bleeder? Why *that* dishonest sonofabitch, not only had he not paid over the money to the judge, he and Ann Burns had used the forty grand to settle up their gambling debts. Served Bleeder right for Thorndon to stool him off to the Feds, and served the crazy broad right to have those pictures flashed around. The only thing was that Thorndon couldn't afford, no way could he afford, for that case to come to trial in public.

Thorndon couldn't let the case be tried because he himself had gone to Dante Tirelli for the money. Tirelli and some other guys who didn't take too kindly to getting fucked around. Only what Bleeder didn't know, what nobody but Lou Thorndon knew, was that at the time Thorndon had needed some money for himself. So he'd storied a little bit. He'd told Tirelli he needed eighty grand, not forty, to handle the judge, and that's how much Tirelli had given him. The extra forty, in fact, was what Thorndon had used to open this car lot he was now standing on. Now then, if Bleeder got on the stand and went to saying how much Thorndon had really given him, then Louis P. Thorndon was going to be in deep shit. No way could he afford for that to happen.

But that was okay, too; Thorndon had it handled. Just yesterday he'd taken a set of the pictures down to a messenger service and had them delivered to the judge. If Bino Phillips didn't want to cooperate, and if Daryl Siminian was going to get crazy on him, then Thorndon had to take things over himself. Right at the moment, in fact, Judge Emmett Burns was probably reading the note that had gone along with the pictures, the note telling the judge what was what, and that if Emmett Burns didn't want to see those pictures all over town he'd better make sure nothing was said about Louis P. Thorndon. That ought to handle things, but good.

Thorndon was now approaching the shed's overhead door. It was fifty degrees, but Thorndon was in shirtsleeves. The county cop had put on his overcoat when he'd left, as though it was cold or something. These Texans didn't know what real cold was. Let 'em try Rush Street this time of year; let the wind off the lake whistle up their asses for a coupla blocks.

Thorndon grabbed the pull rope on the overhead door, grunted as he yanked on it. The door creaked and groaned as it slid open. Some way, he wasn't sure how, Thorndon had to get those cars delivered. Plus he had to get the wino which hadn't shown up, had to get the guy taken care of. Thorndon could have kicked himself for letting the wino have the hundred bucks the other day. No way could he let the wino be going up and down the street telling that you could stiff Lou Thorndon and get away with it. Have 'em lined up around the block looking for a handout, he let the wino get away with that.

Inside the shed the odor of musty wood mixed with the stench of oil-soaked rags. His feet made muffled slapping sounds as he moved across the concrete floor. The walls were lumber; against one wall sat a scarred wooden desk. The desk was cluttered with Autolite spark plugs, a cigar box overflowing with assorted nuts, bolts, and screws, an uneven pile of wrinkled yellow invoices. There was a calendar advertising Big State mufflers hanging on the wall above the desk. The calendar pictured a car raised on a mechanic's lift, a chimpanzee standing underneath the car holding a new muffler aloft. The chimp was showing a monkey's version of a happy grin. So easy to use that an ape could install the fucking thing, huh? Well if it was that easy, how come Thorndon's mechanics couldn't put one on without it rattling like a bastard? Thorndon had given both mechanics the afternoon off; he hadn't wanted them hanging around when the wino showed up to haul his cargo away. Now he wished the mechanics were still here; he could use one of them to deliver the cars. The Mercedeses and the Eldo stood side by side in the shed, their fenders gleaming in the light from the single overhead bulb.

There was a grime-smeared window overlooking the alley, which exited, a half block away, onto Carroll Street. That was the direction from which the wino should have come with the truck and trailer. Groping once more at his shirt pocket, Thorndon peered out the window. Where the hell *was* that silly . . . ?

His chin lifted in surprise.

The truck was out there, parked right beside the shed, the long flatbed trailer dusty and empty. Nose-on to the truck was a midnight blue, two-door Ford. Jesus, wasn't that the kind of car the cop had said . . . ?

On Thorndon's left, partially hidden in the shadow cast by an overhead rack loaded down with thin-treaded, worn-out tires, Daryl Siminian said, "The guy's over here, Lou. Jesus, I guess I killed him. The guy starts giving me a bunch of shit about what I'm doing here, what am I supposed to do? I can't have him calling anybody."

Blood pounded in Thorndon's temples and in his carotid artery. His fingertips trembled as he turned toward the sound of the voice—it was that loony Siminian, okay, although the voice was a little higher pitched than Thorndon remembered it being—and watched Daryl step out from the shadow and extend his hands, palms up, in greeting, like one of the apostles. Thorndon had to admit, shocked as he was, that Siminian was a dresser. Daryl was wearing a tan, wide-shouldered corduroy jacket that had set somebody back a dollar or two and a spotless white turtleneck sweater. With his handsome, square-jawed, Sicilian features and his full head of dark, curly hair, Daryl sure didn't fit with the image of a nut. He looked more like an international jet-setter, really a good-looking boy. Didn't take long to wipe out the first impression, once you got to know the fucker.

"What a trip, huh?" Daryl said. "It makes me feel better seeing you. You looking good, Lou. How you doing?"

Got to stay cool with this wacko, Thorndon said to himself. To Daryl he said, "Can't complain, I, no I can't. What guy you're talking about? Giving you shit about being in here." In the corner of his eye, Thorndon caught a glimpse of scruffy shoes, dirty khaki pants, and argyle socks, the pair of legs sticking out from underneath the Eldo's front bumper.

"I don't know who the fuck," Daryl said. "It's not like I didn't reason with the guy." He stepped closer. His smile was different than it had been in the joint, a prettier smile, the work on his teeth down at Springfield. One thing about Daryl hadn't changed, though. His mouth was the only part of his face that smiled. His eyes were deep-set, empty holes. "I been waiting for you, Lou," Daryl said. "We got to talk. The guy comes driving up in that truck out there, accuses me of breaking the fuck in here. I told him I was waiting for you. What can I do, you know?"

That would shake up the wino, Thorndon thought, coming in here with a hangover and finding *this* guy standing around. The wino probably had figured Daryl for a cop. Thorndon's nerves were quieting. He thought about the Smith & Wesson .38 Police Special revolver that was in the desk drawer, over there underneath the picture of the grinning monkey and the muffler. "Well I guess we do need a little chat," Thorndon said. "I got to say you been really surprising me, Daryl, this stuff you been doing."

Daryl grasped his own jacket's lapels, one in each hand, adjusting the coat and at the same time rolling his head around and flexing his neck muscles. "Yeah, well, I always told you. At least I *tried* to always tell you, you're my best buddy, Lou, anybody starts fucking with you they're fucking with me. But there's some things that, well, some things kind of got out of hand here lately. There was this broad that . . . You and me have talked about that before, that women can make you do these things. I took care of that, I'm not seeing this broad anymore. Tell you the truth she won't be seeing anybody, not anymore. So now I can really make things right for you. Not much longer, you know?"

Slowly, carefully, his head cocked in a listening attitude, the wino's shoes, one with a hole worn in its bottom, still visible in the corner of his eye, Thorndon edged nearer to the desk. Jesus, the cop didn't know the half of it; this bastard was crazy as a bedbug. Daryl was following, ranting on and on, talking like a lunatic, waving his arms around.

Thorndon said, "You forgot to tell me when you brought them pictures back from Chicago. You and Eddie Satterwhite have a beef or something?" Anything, just say anything to the guy, Thorndon thought. Keep him talking.

Daryl paused, looking confused for an instant, then the painted-on smile returned. "Eddie? Hey I got to explain about that, Lou. Eddie, Eddie, see, he wasn't really your friend like you thought. He wasn't going to cooperate. Those pictures, he didn't want to give them up, not even after I explained real careful what we needed them for. He wanted some money, can you believe it? It's really a break, you know? Now nobody knows but you and me."

"Yeah, it's . . . yeah, a break," Thorndon said. "You're doing good, Daryl, but we still got this little problem. You have really got these cops shook up. They've really got a hard-on for you, son. So how are we going to take care of that? I'm thinking maybe you should go on a trip somewhere." Thorndon took a short step backward. The corner of the desk was now in reach, behind him and slightly to his left.

Daryl scratched his forehead. "A trip? Lou, I can't be taking any trip. We got things to do, you and me. We got to take care of things so we don't have any more problems, you know? Hey, there's this guy I talked to, man, you ought to see this big white-haired dude. Seven foot, damn near. He's got something to do with Red, Mama Longlegs, you know? Maybe he's only dicking her, but I ain't sure. I'm getting in touch with him tomorrow about them pictures. And man, I give him the message, see, I let him see what I did to the broad just so he'd know I'm business. You'll see. Just about this time tomorrow you won't have anything to worry about, not about that judge's trial."

Big white-haired . . . ? Jesus, Thorndon thought, now he's been talking to Bino Phillips. Somebody else to make the connection, the connection between Daryl the crazy and Louis P. Thorndon. Thorndon forced a smile. "Big white-haired guy, huh? Man, you're doing good, kid, you got a reward coming. Just a second, lemme get this cashbox out."

Thorndon kept on smiling, raised one finger in a just-a-minute sign, watched the goofy smile fade from Daryl's face. Thorndon turned his back, sat down in the swivel chair in front of the desk, and opened the middle drawer. There it was, right there, the cigar box that held the Smith & Wesson. It was a decades-old Muriel box, showing a cheesecake pose of Edie Adams over the slogan "Why don't you pick me up and smoke me sometime?" Thorndon picked up the box with both hands. It was empty, weightless. Behind him, Daryl uttered a strange, faraway sigh.

"There's not any money, Lou," Daryl said. "No gun anymore either. I been looking around, you know?"

Panic welled in Thorndon's gullet as he spun the chair slowly around. Daryl hadn't moved; his face was expressionless, almost puzzled. One big fucking pistol was in Daryl's hand, some kind of Magnum it looked to be, steady and leveled at Thorndon's chest. The Smith & Wesson .38 was dangling loosely from his other hand.

Thorndon swallowed hard. Jesus, he had to reason with this lunatic; he'd always been able to talk to Daryl. Thorndon spread his hands, palms down. He said, "Now look."

The Magnum blasted, deafening. It bucked in Daryl's hand and pointed toward the ceiling. Something heavy, something numbing, slammed into Thorndon's chest. His chair tilted violently backward. His head banged against the corner of the desk. His eyes staring in disbelief, a final shock wave passing fleetingly through his brain, Lou Thorndon gasped, and then died.

Daryl's head ached. His ears rang with the Magnum's blast. The odor of burnt gunpowder singed his nostrils. There was a pain in his chest and a lump the size of a basketball in his throat.

What happened, Lou? he thought. Was it Red? She get to you? Jesus, we talked about women, over and over. How you let a broad do this to you?

I can't wait around, Lou, all that fucking noise is going to bring somebody. But don't worry, buddy, she's going to pay, Red is. Like I promised you, I'm going to take care of things.

He jammed the Magnum underneath his belt, dropped the Smith & Wesson into his side coat pocket, and shuffled awkwardly over to stand beside the Eldorado. Daryl wasn't aware of the change in his walk, but it was the same shuffle he'd moved with for two years up at Springfield, when the Feds had kept him shot full of Thorazine. His head hurt him most of the time now, and he was having a hard time remembering things. He wasn't sure why, but bad things were happening, and they all had to do with Red. He was going to have to take care of Red; then he could . . . what? He wasn't sure. The Eldo's keys were in the ignition. Daryl smiled mirthlessly, patted the Eldo's fender. Then he opened the door and climbed into the driver's seat.

19

Bino was going out for the evening, but first he had a couple of things to do at home. It was five-thirty, already getting dark, as Tilly Madden's pickup took him bouncing into the parking lot at Vapors North. He parked and cut the engine, waited while the truck shuddered through some postignition vibrations, then got out and started across the asphalt toward the building. Darkness was bringing the cold back in a hurry. Bino shivered. He really felt the chill as he entered the shadow of the apartment house; it was ten degrees, minimum, colder in the shade. With a final longing glance at the Linc's vacant parking space, he ducked under the archway and made his way down the corridor into the courtyard. The clipped grass and pruned shrubs were winter-dead brown. Steam rose like trails of ascending ghosts from the heated blue water in the pool.

Inside his apartment, Bino dropped an unlucky minnow

into the fish tank, watched Cecil run the darting little fella down and swallow him whole. Bino really wasn't a violent guy; he hated bullfights, cockfights, and dogfights, all three with a purple passion. But for some reason, watching Cecil commit murder in his fish tank gave Bino a big charge. He couldn't have explained it if he'd tried.

He stood in the living room for a moment and let his gaze linger on the pale green Princess phone that sat on the coffee table. He had a call to make. A big, *big* call, but he didn't want to make it until he got his thoughts organized. A change of clothes might get his think tank into gear, so he went into his bedroom and took his suit off. He tossed the suit on the floor of the walk-in closet, then put on a gray basketball warm-up suit with "SMU" stitched across the front in big red and blue letters. The warm-up was the sole survivor left out of a dozen or so that Bino and Barney had pilfered from the SMU locker room late one night nearly twenty years ago, as they'd swigged Lone Star beer from squatty brown throwaway bottles. The cuffs were frayed, and there was a pretty good-sized hole worn in one knee, but Bino liked the warm-up because it was comfortable as hell and made him feel as though he might have a fadeaway jumper or two left in him.

He went into the kitchen, clinked two ice cubes into a tumbler, and added three fingers of Johnnie Walker Red. Back in the living room, he fumbled through his tape cassettes. Finally he plugged in a Whitney Houston tape and had a couple of belts of the Scotch as he listened to her sing "The Greatest Love of All." The phone hadn't moved; it still sat innocently on the coffee table. Bino plopped down on the couch, cradled the receiver between his shoulder and jaw, and punched in Emmett Burns's number. The judge answered in person.

"It's Bino, Emmett. Listen, I may have some good news. Now I don't want us getting our hopes up, but we do have a hearing tomorrow on a motion to dismiss."

Without a second's hesitation, Burns said, "On what grounds?"

Did *that* one ever throw Bino for a loop. Jesus, he'd expected Burns to say, "Great news," or, "Go get 'em, big albino," something like that. He kept forgetting that his client knew as much about the law as a herd of circuit court justices. And Burns had asked one helluva question. Bino had been so busy running around finding bodies and charging down to the courthouse to set the hearing up that he didn't know for sure *what* his legal grounds for the motion were going to be. Sure, he had a lot to jump around and holler about, but if he didn't have solid grounds for the motion, Goldman and Judge Hazel Burke Sanderson were going to laugh him out of the courtroom.

Bino said, rather lamely, "Well that's what I want to talk to you about, Emmett. Insufficient evidence?"

The sound over the phone was like paper being wadded, but the noise was probably Emmett Burns giving a derisive snort. Burns said, "Where did you go to law school, son? Insufficient evidence is only a ground for appeal, after you've already lost the case. Hell, they haven't put on any evidence yet, how can their evidence be insufficient? You're going to have to come up with something better than that. And by the way, did you send a package down to my office?"

Bino raised an eyebrow. "Nope. Not me. Unless Dodie did it, I've been gone all day."

"Well somebody did. I haven't been going in; hell, I don't see much point in working on anything until I see whether I'm still going to be a judge or not. Until this case is over. But one of the secretaries called, and a guy from a messenger service delivered a package down there for me. Sort of mysterious; there's no return address on it."

"I wouldn't worry about it right now," Bino said. "Probably something that doesn't have anything to do with this case."

"Maybe, but it's strange. What time is your hearing? I can probably run by my office and pick up the package afterward; it's in the same building."

"One o'clock. I tried to make it a morning deal, but I'm afraid I couldn't do any better."

"God amighty," Burns said. "Well you'd better get to cooking on some legal grounds; they'll kick us out on our butts if your p's and q's aren't up to snuff."

Bino's ears reddened. Not only was Burns right on the money, but a second-year law student knew better than to run around setting up hearings without the right legal grounds. Right now Emmett Burns was probably thinking that his lawyer was sort of stupid. Bino straightened his posture on the couch, lowered the pitch of his voice an octave, and said, "Well you sure passed the test, Emmett. I was just keeping you on your toes, talking about insufficient evidence. The legal grounds for the motion are going to be that"—his mind raced—"the indictment is insufficient because it doesn't tell us exactly what you did that was against the law."

"Now that's more like it," Burns said. "What judge is going to hear the motion?"

It was on the tip of Bino's tongue to tell Burns exactly what had happened down at the clerk's office, and exactly what Bino thought about the selection of judges for the motion, but he changed his mind. Putting down Hazel Sanderson to another judge—even one whose nuts were going to be on the line in her courtroom tomorrow—wasn't such a good idea. Bino said merely, "Judge Sanderson has agreed to hear us."

"Damn," Burns said. "*That* old battle-ax. You'd better not let *her* get her panties in a knot. So now you've got legal grounds for your motion, what are you *really* going to try to get across?"

Which pretty well sums up the system, Bino thought. The *legal* grounds for having a hearing are never the *real* reason for going to court. The whole frigging system is a bunch of hot air. Bino said, "Somebody's framing you, Emmett."

"You don't have to tell *me*, son," Burns said.

"I know I don't. And we may never know who the somebody is. But I've come up with just enough, at least I think I have, so we can show Goldman he's wasting his time going ahead with the prosecution. I think that, after the hearing, Goldman might drop the charges to save face. Or even if he

□   265   □

won't, the judge may grant our motion. She won't want the government trying a loser any more than Goldman will."

"Well it may be the hope that springs eternal and all that," Burns said, "but this is sounding better and better. You got any witnesses to call?"

Bino examined a hanging thread on the cuff of his warm-up suit, then raised his wrist and bit the thread in two. Choosing his words like a man looking for ripe fruit, Bino said, "Oh, I think so. Listen, Emmett, is your daughter home?"

"Ann?" Burns's voice was suddenly weaker and there was a defensive tone to his speech.

The lie that Bino had thought up while he was changing clothes raced quickly through his mind. "I just want to ask her a couple of questions. I think we should cover all bases; that's what you're paying me for. If it should ever come down, God forbid, to a conviction, we're going to need some daughterly testimony at a sentencing hearing." And maybe at the same hearing, Bino thought, Goldman will have a few porno pics to show around. The idea made him shudder.

Burns uttered a wounded sigh. "I can't argue with that. And, yeah, she's here. Hold on."

While the judge went off to get Ann, Bino studied his knees. Emmett Burns was doing his best to act tough, but the poor guy was sinking in a hurry. When he'd been discussing the law, Burns had sounded like his old self. But when Bino had asked for the judge's daughter, Burns's tone had changed in a flash to that of a frightened old man. And when you boiled it all down, that was exactly what Emmett Burns was. The thought that he might actually end the nightmare for Burns once and for all made Bino cross his fingers and hope like hell. Ann Burns's soft voice said, "Hello?"

"I told him I wanted to talk to you about, well, maybe testifying as his daughter. Like a character witness. So he doesn't know anything about what's . . . the pictures and all. So if he's sitting there listening to you, you need to watch what you say. *Capisce?* So, is he listening?"

"Yes." Her voice was faint, like a little girl's voice.

"Okay," Bino said. "First of all I know who's trying to
. . . who it was on the phone, out in the shopping mall. He's
a real crazy, Ann, and he's subject to kill you. You don't know
me that well, but I don't exaggerate when I'm talking about
stuff like that. The guy's as dangerous as they come. He's done
some things that I won't . . . well, let's say there are enough
cops hunting for him that he probably won't come out in the
open. But you watch yourself, you hear? Now you pretend
that I just asked you if you'd be willing to testify for your dad
and say something. For *his* benefit."

After a moment's hesitation, she said, "Well of course I
would. If it will help."

Bino drank more Scotch, swirling the liquid around in his
mouth and swallowing it leisurely. With the voice of Whitney
Houston still warbling faintly in the background, he said,
"Good girl. That's the scary part; here's the plan. It's a good
news–bad news deal. The good news is that I'm going to see
somebody tonight, to try and get them to testify tomorrow.
At a hearing. Your dad will fill you in on that if he hasn't
already. If I can get this person to testify, your dad's troubles
may be over."

"Who's going to do that?" she asked.

Her question didn't make any sense until Bino pictured
Emmett Burns, probably doing his best to look unworried,
sitting there in the room with her. Whatever Ann Burns had
or hadn't done, she sure wasn't dumb. And she might make
a pretty good actress to boot. "You mean, who am I going to
see?" Bino said.

"That's right," said Ann.

"I'm not going to tell you just yet. The witness I'm talking
about probably isn't going to want to show up, and that gets
us to the bad-news part. If I can't produce the witness, well,
I'm going to have to put you on the stand. And I won't kid
you, it's going to be rough as a cob."

"God, I—" There was a catch in her voice that was close
to a sob.

"You're going to have to tell the whole enchilada, Ann.

All about your gambling, your past in Chicago. Maybe we can get around the pictures, I'm not sure about that. But you're going to have to tell about Goldman calling you, and what Bleeder wanted you to say when he talked to you in the restaurant. Goldman will get to cross-examine you. That won't be much fun, but that isn't the worst part. You're going to be telling some things that your dad doesn't know about, and he's going to be right there in the courtroom."

"That's what— I don't know if I can do that to . . . anybody," she said. Bino pictured her casting a furtive glance at her father, maybe turning away from him and speaking more softly into the phone.

"There isn't any way around it," Bino said. " 'Course, I'm still pulling for myself to come up with the witness, but I've got to say the odds of that happening aren't too good. But here's what we can do to soften the pain some, if it comes down to it. My office is in the Davis Building, in the thirteen hundred block of Main Street. Old red-brick job, stands out like a sore thumb. You know where it is?"

"I think so. I can find it," she said.

"Okay. I'm on the sixth floor. Be down there at twelve-thirty tomorrow. I'll be gone already, down to federal court for the hearing. But you check in with my secretary. Her name is Dodie, and you'll like her. She's . . . I don't want to get into your personal problems, Ann, but you and Dodie have a lot in common. She used to have a dope habit, which is at least as bad as what's wrong with you. She came through it like Lady of the Decade, and, take it from me, you can pour your heart out to her. You with me so far?"

"I hope I am," Ann said.

"Great. The hearing's not going to take over an hour, and half of that time will be Goldman jumping up and down objecting to everything I try to get into evidence. So if you and Dodie start hoofing it over to the Federal Building at one, then you'll show up just about the time I need to put you on the stand. Which I won't, if I have this other witness I'm talking about. But if it comes down to your having to testify, I'm going to call time-out. Ask for a recess. Old Hazel, that's the judge, she'll do a lot of glaring and looking prune-faced, but she'll have to give us one. Then . . . well, you and your dad and I, we'll have to have a little talk. And you'll have to bring him up to date on what you're going to say on the stand. Think you can get up for it?"

The sound of Ann taking a deep breath came over the line. She expelled the breath, then said, "I'll have to be. If it'll help, anything."

Bino liked the way she'd said that. "It'll make things better in the long run," he said. "Now I'm off after the witness. You stay at home tonight, and do whatever it is that you and your dad like to do together. Play a game of chess. Or maybe just sit and talk. I'll bet it's been a long time since you did that."

"It has," she said.

"All right. Keep your fingers crossed for me."

"I will," she said. She hung up.

Bino replaced the receiver in its cradle, then checked the digital clock on his VCR. It was six-fifteen. He needed to wait a few minutes before he made another call, and something about the time jingled a bell inside his head. Jesus, wasn't it time for . . . ?

He hustled back into the kitchen, freshened his Johnnie Walker, returned to the living room, and disconnected Whitney Houston with a faint pop from the speakers. Then he flipped the switch on the Mitsubishi TV, pushed the channel selector, and carried the remote in one hand and his Scotch in the other as he went over and sank down on the couch. He stretched his legs out and crossed his ankles on the coffee table.

Bigger than life and in living color on the fifty-one-inch screen, two newspeople faced the camera. They grinned in turn at each other and then at the viewing audience as they rustled through papers before them that Bino suspected were blank. The newsperson on Bino's right was the broad-shouldered, pearly-toothed sports announcer, whom Bino remembered to be an ex–Baylor Bear tackle. On Bino's left, Susie Sin's on-camera face appeared slightly fuller than the real-life version had inside Joe Miller's Bar. Bino wasn't sure whether he liked her looks more in person or on the screen. Either way she was a knockout.

The sports guy was saying in a rich baritone, ". . . and one way or the other, the answer seems not too far in the future. Will Bum Bright keep the Cowboys, or if he doesn't who will the new owner be? And if there *is* a new owner, what does the future hold for Schramm? Or for Landry, the only coach the Cowboys have ever had? It's a continuing saga, folks, and you can follow it all right here. Susie?" He showed his pearly whites, half for Susie's benefit, half for the audience's.

"I'm pulling for Landry to stay," Susie said.

"A lot of people are," the sports guy said.

"Well what about you?" Susie said.

The sports announcer deadpanned. "No comment," he said.

The camera zoomed in on Susie, and the sports guy disappeared from view. "The news tonight from federal court," she said, "is all about the government's case against U.S. District Judge Emmett Burns. Burns, the longest-sitting judge in the Northern District of Texas, was indicted this week on multiple counts of mail fraud and conspiracy. I took a few minutes to chat with Burns's attorney."

Bino sat forward, elbows on knees, his drink held in both hands.

Susie tilted her chin slightly to one side, and, with a pleasant but professional expression on her Oriental face, said, "The attorney, W. A. (Bino) Phillips, said in no uncertain terms in our exclusive interview that not only is his client innocent of the charges but the government is relying on trumped-up and, on at least one occasion, totally falsified evidence to convict the judge."

□ 270 □

at Thorndon's chest. The Smith & Wesson .38 was dangling loosely from his other hand.

Thorndon swallowed hard. Jesus, he had to reason with this lunatic; he'd always been able to talk to Daryl. Thorndon spread his hands, palms down. He said, "Now look."

The Magnum blasted, deafening. It bucked in Daryl's hand and pointed toward the ceiling. Something heavy, something numbing, slammed into Thorndon's chest. His chair tilted violently backward. His head banged against the corner of the desk. His eyes staring in disbelief, a final shock wave passing fleetingly through his brain, Lou Thorndon gasped, and then died.

Daryl's head ached. His ears rang with the Magnum's blast. The odor of burnt gunpowder singed his nostrils. There was a pain in his chest and a lump the size of a basketball in his throat.

What happened, Lou? he thought. Was it Red? She get to you? Jesus, we talked about women, over and over. How you let a broad do this to you?

I can't wait around, Lou, all that fucking noise is going to bring somebody. But don't worry, buddy, she's going to pay, Red is. Like I promised you, I'm going to take care of things.

He jammed the Magnum underneath his belt, dropped the Smith & Wesson into his side coat pocket, and shuffled awkwardly over to stand beside the Eldorado. Daryl wasn't aware of the change in his walk, but it was the same shuffle he'd moved with for two years up at Springfield, when the Feds had kept him shot full of Thorazine. His head hurt him most of the time now, and he was having a hard time remembering things. He wasn't sure why, but bad things were happening, and they all had to do with Red. He was going to have to take care of Red; then he could . . . what? He wasn't sure. The Eldo's keys were in the ignition. Daryl smiled mirthlessly, patted the Eldo's fender. Then he opened the door and climbed into the driver's seat.

19

Bino was going out for the evening, but first he had a couple of things to do at home. It was five-thirty, already getting dark, as Tilly Madden's pickup took him bouncing into the parking lot at Vapors North. He parked and cut the engine, waited while the truck shuddered through some postignition vibrations, then got out and started across the asphalt toward the building. Darkness was bringing the cold back in a hurry. Bino shivered. He really felt the chill as he entered the shadow of the apartment house; it was ten degrees, minimum, colder in the shade. With a final longing glance at the Linc's vacant parking space, he ducked under the archway and made his way down the corridor into the courtyard. The clipped grass and pruned shrubs were winter-dead brown. Steam rose like trails of ascending ghosts from the heated blue water in the pool.

Inside his apartment, Bino dropped an unlucky minnow

Go, Susie, Bino thought.

"Phillips said that the key incident under investigation, an alleged bribe in exchange for dismissal of some charges, actually happened in the opposite manner to what the government contends. In court documents and interviews, Assistant U.S. Attorney Marvin Goldman has stated that Burns put pressure on prosecutors to drop charges in a criminal case, and that the government expects to prove that Burns was in fact illegally compensated for his actions."

But that ain't so, is it? Tell 'em, girl. Bino crossed his fingers.

Susie's expression was suddenly serious. Her mouth set itself in a point-making line, and anybody who thought Susie Sin wasn't a first-rate pro just needed to watch her get ready to deliver her knockout punch. She said, "Phillips, however, tells an entirely different story. According to him, prosecutors in the government's case against Louis Thorndon, a car dealer, contacted the judge outside chambers and asked that he make some rulings to further the government's case against Thorndon. Phillips says that when Burns declined and cited judicial ethics as his reason for doing so, the government decided to prosecute the judge. When asked to elaborate, Phillips declined, saying that the facts would all come out at trial.

"The trial itself," Susie said, "is set for early next year and should prove to be one of the focal news stories of the season. If the government can put its case over, then one of the outstanding jurists of the past two decades is going to exhibit feet of clay. But on the other hand, if Bino Phillips has his way, then the local U.S. Attorney's office is going to look at the world through a very large, very swollen, black eye. Either way it should prove interesting."

Bino came within an inch of standing up in his own living room and leading Cecil in a cheer. If Goldman was watching—and odds were that he was, Bino'd never known the U.S. prosecutor to miss a newscast when he had a case on the front burner—then smoke was curling out of old Marv's ears. How's it feel, Marv? Bino thought. How's it feel for once, just once, to have the other side get some coverage, huh?

Fired up now, Bino went over and switched the TV off, actually considering for an instant giving Susie's image on the screen a big, wet, passionate kiss. He went into the bedroom and rummaged through his dresser until he found a dog-eared business card with a phone number written on the back in pencil. As he flopped down on the king-size and picked up the bedside phone, he whistled a few bars of the SMU fight song. Hell, Emmett Burns might have a chance after all.

20

Hardy Cole thought that his cover car, a cream-colored four-door Olds with *Countdown Messenger Service* painted in script on each front door, was a whole lot nicer transportation than Dallas County had ever provided him. Matter of fact, he knew it was. The Olds had a padded dash, AM-FM stereo, plush velour seats, and big, powerful shocks that rode like a dream over every expansion joint and asphalt-filled crack in the Airport Freeway. In contrast, being in the county heap that Cole had been driving was like riding around in a hollow metal locker. So even messenger boys drove better cars than the county cops. So what else was new?

And the clothes that the manager of the *Countdown* office had furnished, well, they weren't too bad either. A little bit loud for Cole's taste—a pale green blazer with a black plastic name tag over the pocket (*Countdown*, Fred at Your Service), worn with dark green slacks, a white broadcloth shirt, and green-and-white striped tie—and the fit wasn't perfect (what did he expect from a messenger boy's hand-me-down?), but basically real nice stuff. And it was all right with Cole for the coat to be loose, the extra room provided cover for the compact Bersa Model 85 .38 thirteen-shot automatic holstered underneath his armpit. Cole kept one hand on the wheel, reached underneath his coat, and adjusted his shoulder holster, then picked up the off-white business envelope from the seat and looked it over.

The envelope was addressed simply to "Mr. Harriman—Holiday Inn Airport Freeway." Harriman had been the first name that had popped into Cole's mind when he'd made up the envelope, and it wasn't exactly a coincidence. Mr. Harriman from Buffalo, New York, was the guy who'd rented the Avis car, the one that had been parked behind the mechanic's shed where they'd found Thorndon. Cole wondered briefly where they'd find Harriman's—the *real* Harriman's, not this phony Siminian guy's—body. In the neighborhood around Love Field would be a good place to start looking. Cole flipped the Olds's signal switch, listened to the monotonous bonk of the turn indicator, eased over one lane to his right. He followed a yellow Mustang onto the exit ramp beside semidomed Texas Stadium. Dark was coming on, and it was getting colder. The forecast for tonight included a possibility of some freezing rain.

Cole stopped for a red light, waiting to turn left across the freeway. The green and white and yellow Holiday Inn sign was visible beside the access road on the other side of the interstate. The glass-fronted office was beyond the sign, sitting before the horseshoe-shaped, two-story motel building. The motel parking lot appeared to be about half full, mostly pickups with camper covers over their beds and late-model passenger cars, many with U-Haul trailers attached to their bumpers. Cole tucked his chin and spoke to the left lapel of his blazer. "Goose One here. Gimme a sign."

In the lane behind the Olds was a dark blue Plymouth

sedan. A broad-shouldered, sandy-haired man was driving the Plymouth, with a gray-haired man who sported a thick mustache and wore a Texas Ranger batting helmet riding shotgun. Cole looked in his rearview mirror. The younger guy inside the Plymouth shot him the bird.

"Cute," Cole said. "Your age or your fucking IQ? So I'm going in the office and set things up with the motel people. Goose Two, you park to the right of the office. Goose Three to the left. I got to get the room number from the clerk; when I come out of the office, you guys follow me. Be cool about it, okay? No grab-ass. And don't be waving a bunch of guns around until we get set up and I'm knocking on the door. That ain't no Iwo Jima out there, and you're liable to give some poor old broad a heart attack."

Now the sandy-haired young cop showed Cole a circle with his thumb and forefinger over the top of the Plymouth's steering wheel. As Cole turned left across the bridge, he raised his right arm and showed the Plymouth his own version of the finger, a real down-to-business finger, middle digit stiff with both adjacent fingers bent, showing pointed middle knuckles. South Dallas shaft.

Cole parked the Olds underneath the motel canopy, watched the Plymouth creep on past and find a parking space between a red Toyota and a white Volkswagen van. The tan Ford that had been following the Plymouth was already nose-on to the curb around a hundred yards to Cole's rear. The occupants of the Ford were a beefy detective named Bennett, on loan from Narcotics, and a tall, skinny cop, Edelman by name, who claimed not to be Jewish but looked and talked like a Hebe and who still owed Cole twenty bucks from the Cowboys-Giants game. Cole didn't particularly like the guy. Edelman was dressed in jeans and a denim jacket along with brown western boots. Bennett had an unkempt beard and wore beads around his neck, like a ten-year-out-of-date dope peddler. Cole was going to have to teach the boy how to dress. He got out of the Olds and entered the motel lobby.

The desk clerk, a round-faced guy of around thirty wearing

thick, rimless glasses, turned a registration card topside up on the counter in Cole's direction. The clerk said, "How many nights—?" Then he stared bug-eyed at Hardy's badge.

"This is serious police business," Cole said. "I may not *look* very serious, running around in this parrot costume, but take my word for it. You've got, at least you're supposed to have, according to what we hear, a guy staying here. This guy." He snapped his wallet closed and showed the clerk Daryl Siminian's mug shot, front and side view.

At Cole's mention of the parrot costume, the clerk's gaze had flicked downward. Cole noted that the clerk's blazer was lemon yellow, his plastic name tag green. Otherwise the clerk's uniform was almost identical to the one Cole was wearing. The clerk said, "We've got him. His name is Harriman."

"You're shitting me," Cole said.

"Nope, that's the way he's registered. Been here four or five days. Room Number— Just a minute." He turned, pulled out a metal sliding tray, and flipped through the cards. Cole retreated a step and glanced around the lobby. One man in a business suit sat on a couch reading a newspaper. Visible through the open entrance to the coffee shop, two women sat at the counter and munched on sweet rolls. The clerk said, "Two twenty-seven. It's an outside room, about midway down"—he gestured to his left, Cole's right—"facing the freeway. There going to be trouble?" The clerk's name tag identified him as Charles. The message slots were behind him; the slot for Room 227 was empty.

Cole folded his arms and put one foot slightly in front of the other. "Charles, I'd be lying if I told you. Probably not, but let's be on the safe side, okay? Make a few calls, let's say two rooms on either side of 227, the room below it and the one directly behind it. Empty 'em out; get the people down here to the coffee shop. Dinner on the county, okay? Like I say, ninety-nine percent chance there's nothing to worry about. Just following procedure, is what we're doing."

Hardy Cole had an uncle who'd been a marine second looie in the Pacific, during World War II, and who didn't like to tell old war stories. He'd once confided in Cole that just thinking about leading a platoon of jarheads onto one of those sniper-infested islands made him break out in a shivering sweat. Times like this, Hardy Cole could really relate to his uncle.

He stood on the landing outside Room 227, held the dummy envelope in both hands, and looked around to check his backup. Edelman was crouched on the motel's red-slate roof, directly above the room. Thirty feet to the left of where Cole stood, Bennett was flattened against the wall on the landing, his service revolver held near his ear. A story below in the parking lot, the sandy-haired cop who'd given Cole the finger earlier and the older guy in the Ranger batting helmet lounged against the sides of two different cars and pretended not to be concerned. In fact they probably *are* pretty uncon-cerned, Cole thought; if anybody gets his ass shot off, it sure won't be them. Beyond the parking lot, rush-hour traffic on the Airport Freeway was bumper to bumper. Cole adjusted his shoulder holster, stepped forward, and banged his knuckles against the door. "Countdown. Message for Mr. Harriman." He hoped that his voice wasn't as hoarse as it sounded to him. Beads of perspiration popped out on his forehead.

Seconds dragged by, probably thirty of them. Overhead on the roof, Edelman shifted his position and gave a muffled cough.

Cole put his ear to the door and knocked again. *Christ, is somebody moving around in there?* He wasn't sure. He grabbed the knob. It turned easily, and the door opened a foot. Cole shut his eyes and winced.

He was suddenly conscious of rapid breathing beside him and the odor of cigarette smoke. He spun, dropping the en-velope and digging underneath his coat. It was Bennett, his revolver at waist level, a filtered cigarette dangling from the corner of his mouth. Cole sighed in relief. He nodded, yanked his Bersa from its holster, put one shoulder to the door, and shoved. Then he was down on the carpet inside the room, rolling, then coming up slowly, right hand extended, holding the gun, left hand steadying his wrist.

There was nobody in the room. Cole followed the noise of a dripping faucet into the bathroom. Nobody in there either. He lowered the Bersa to dangle by his hip and returned to the bedroom. The bed was made. There was nothing in the dresser drawers. On the nightstand beside the bed was a stack of the same photos, featuring Ann Burns, that were in Cole's desk downtown. He picked up the top picture and looked at it. There was a thick mucous substance adhering to the print, on the graceful curve of Ann Burns's thigh.

Bennett stood in the doorway. He said, "What's the deal?"

Cole's throat was dry. He swallowed. "It's jism," he said. "Fucking guy's been jerking off in here."

21

Wimpy Madrick, his wizened head cocked to one side in the moonlight, surveyed the situation with one eye closed. A filterless Lucky dangled from his lips. He adjusted the collar of his jumpsuit—it was a tan jumpsuit, exactly like the ones issued to prisoners at the Dallas County Jail, and Bino suspected that it was one Wimpy had lifted during one of his sentences—then used one finger to close a nostril on his enormous nose. Wimpy blew a wad of snot onto the pavement. Bino's stomach churned.

"Getting cold as a bitch," Wimpy said.

"How come you don't wear a coat?" Bino asked. In spite of the windbreaker and bulky pullover sweater he'd put on over his SMU warm-ups, Bino was freezing to death. His knee was cold where the wind whistled through the hole in his pants leg. He wore low-quarter Reebok basketball shoes.

"Guy calls and says for me to meet him," Wimpy said. "I'm way to fuck out in South Dallas County checking on some things, I got no time to stop by for a coat. You're lucky you got me at all."

Bino folded his arms and regarded his toes. Tilly Madden's pickup idled by the curb with its lights on; Wimpy's ancient Dodge three-quarter ton was parked behind it. The Dodge's bed contained a pile of lumber with a few nails poking out here and there, a couple of tin five-gallon gas cans, and a gray-steel, two-compartment toolbox. Up and down the tree-lined street, Christmas lights twinkled in windows and from the roofs of houses. A plastic Santa held a bell in a ringing posture on a clipped lawn a half block away. Visible over the single-story rooftops was the brick wall surrounding the parking lot at Preston Center and the pointed spire atop Park Cities Baptist Church.

"So how come I'm lucky?" Bino asked. "The Red Dragon Lounge, it's the same place where I've left your messages for years. What, did you change beer joints or something?"

"Naw, but I been feeling some heat. A guy's been hanging around the Dragon that don't look right, you know, sits around and nurses his beer and looks at everybody. Dresses in sport coats and ties and shit. Either he's some uptown dude hanging around looking to buy some pussy or he's a cop, one of the two. I'm having the guy checked out; till I do I'm steering clear of the Dragon. Only reason I got your message is I called in to see if the guy's still hanging around. Look, Bino, you ain't in some kind of trouble, are you?"

"Me?" Bino said.

"I seen funnier things. One time my own sister tried to set me up; they told her if she'd come with some evidence on me they might forget about this little dab of heroin they found over at her place. Cost me . . . fuck, I can't remember if that was when I done the three years on Darrington Farm or the two years on Beto I. Now you're wanting me to do this for you. How I know you ain't wearing a wire? I'm a habitual,

Bino, I ain't catching no life sentence for nobody. Damn near gives me the drizzlies just standing around in this high-dollar neighborhood. University Park cops are liable to stop you just 'cause you don't look rich enough to be fucking around out here."

Bino shrugged. He reached over and got a pack of Luckies from Wimpy's breast pocket, tamped a cigarette out of the pack, and poked it into his mouth with one hand while sticking the smokes back into Wimpy's pocket with the other. "Gimme a light, Wimp," Bino said. Wimpy lit a butane disposable and cupped his hands over the flame while Bino lit up. Then, puffing, Bino said, "I'm going to tell you once. I shouldn't even *have* to tell you once. You don't do life for anybody, I don't snitch on anybody. Look, who's kept you out of the joint for the past couple of years? Who put his nuts on the line for you the last time the county wanted to send you away?"

"That time you had me be my own lawyer?" Wimpy grinned. "Say, that worked pretty good. I told a coupla guys about it."

Bino pictured a herd of Wimpy's buddies, all down at the jail and clamoring to represent themselves. Might start an epidemic. "That's what I'm talking about," Bino said. "Now I don't want to hear any more about wires or your sister or how you're a habitual. What I want is, I want you to do what comes natural." He flipped glowing ash on the pavement. "That house there," Bino said. "I want to get inside. Nobody's home; I checked that out before you got here."

They were standing beside the curb in front of a brick-veneer, one-story house. The house was on a deep lot, far back from the street. In its front yard were two forty-foot oak trees. Wimpy squinted and peered. "How they get these prices for these houses out here? What, coupla hundred grand for *that* dump, just 'cause it sits in Park Cities? They spend more on the burglar protection shit than the whole house ought to be worth. Goddamn burglar bars around every door and window, to top it off"—he pointed at a small sign by the curb that read "Protected by Jones Detective Agency"—"they got an alarm system where if you open one fucking window you're going to think Scotland Yard's running around the neighborhood from the racket that siren in the attic's gonna kick up. Makes a working man earn his keep. Come on." He went to his truck and hoisted his toolbox out of the bed.

Bino followed a few paces behind Wimpy, keeping him downwind. If the breeze had been coming from the opposite direction, Bino would've led the way. Wimpy didn't bathe too often. When he was spending time in jail, Wimpy *really* got ripe.

"Hell, if it's that tough maybe we better forget it," Bino said. "I don't want us setting off any burglar alarms."

Wimpy stopped and looked over his shoulder. His cigarette had burned down to within a fraction of an inch of his lips. "You shitting me?" Wimpy said. "The only people that burglar crap keeps away is somebody that ain't going to break in anyhow. They look up there and say, 'Old Joe ain't home, we better not go fucking around up there 'cause the siren might go off.' Anybody knows what they're doing, this is a piece of cake. That's what I'm trying to say. All these security services is bigger crooks than I ever thought about being. Waste of people's money, is all it is."

Wimpy's metal cutters made a thick clunking sound, like a depth charge banging a hull in a WW II submarine movie. He lifted a section of burglar bar out and laid it on the ground beside two more identical chunks. There was now a gaping three-by-five hole opening up outside a large bay window at the side of the house, alongside the double ribbon of concrete that formed the driveway. It was getting colder. Visible past the corner of the house, Wimpy's Dodge pickup was about a hundred yards away beside the curb. The moon was glowing through a wispy cloud.

"Now that's the easy part," Wimpy said. "Shit, burglar

bars wouldn't keep my mother-in-law away. This next part is tricky, so pay attention. You're going to have to help me." He fumbled in his toolbox, came up with four metal clips held together by two crossed wires, then reached back into the box and hefted a claw hammer. "Listen careful, Bino. If there's a fuckup, this is where it's going to be."

Bino took his hands out of his pockets, accepted the wires and the hammer, and stepped forward. "I'm all ears," he said.

There was a tiny flashlight in Wimpy's breast pocket, wedged in between his cigarettes and his chest. He flipped the switch and pinpointed the beam on the glass at the base of the window. "You see that tape along there?" he asked.

Bino bent closer. A silver metallic strip, about an inch wide, ran along the bottom, up both sides, and across the top of the pane. There was, maybe, two inches of glass between the tape and the windowsill. Bino nodded.

"That shit's conductive," Wimpy said. "It makes a circuit, and what sets the alarm off is if the circuit gets broke. Now when you hear me holler, you smash this fucking window. You're going to have, well, fifteen seconds to clip those wires onto the busted tape ends. That'll keep the circuit going and be one helluva lot easier on your eardrums than that fucking siren will, in case you don't do it right."

"Why're you going to yell?" Bino asked. "We're standing five feet apart."

"We ain't going to be," Wimpy said. "I'm going way the hell in back of the house. See, once the alarm's disengaged there's a power-pack battery someplace inside the house that kicks in and runs the circuit. That's the fifteen seconds, the time it takes for the battery to start cooking." Wimpy was beginning to sound less like a burglar and more like an engineer from MIT.

"How do you disengage the alarm?" Bino said. "You got an electronic something-or-other that fools the circuits?"

Wimpy had taken four or five steps toward the rear of the house. He stopped and turned. "Naw. I'm going to find the breaker box and shut off the electricity. That's all. You been watching too many 'Mission Impossibles' or something."

From far, far away in the backyard, Wimpy's voice carried to Bino over the frigid night air. "Go!"

Bino flinched, turned his face away and shut his eyes, and swung the hammer. The impact shuddered its way through the handle and up his forearm. There was the tinkling sound of shattering glass. Bino stepped away from the window and looked.

The jagged hole was about a foot in diameter. The metallic tape was severed in two places, where the hammer had sliced through it in breaking the window, and, to Bino's left, where a spiderweb crack in the glass ran from the edge of the hole to the sill.

Fifteen seconds.

Bino counted under his breath—*thousand one, thousand two, thousand three*—as he fumbled with the clips. The wires were tangled. *Jesus, the fucking wires were tangled.* His fingers like pieces of wood, he untwisted the wires and straightened them.

—thousand four, thousand five, thousand six—

He clipped onto the tape on both sides of the hole, first on his right, then on his left. One connection made. He grasped the remaining two clips and stretched the wire across the pane toward the bottom of the crack. It wouldn't reach. *God Almighty. Jesus H. Christ on a crutch, the wire's too fucking short.*

—thousand nine, thousand ten, thousand eleven—

There was a hitch in the wire, a tiny loop around one of the clips at the edge of the hole. He carefully undid the loop and stretched the wire some more. He clipped onto the tape on one side of the crack.

—thousand thirteen, thousand fourteen, thousand—

His breath rushed between his teeth as he clipped the final wire into place, stepped away, and stood for an instant with his arms upraised like a rodeo calf-roping contestant, then put his fingers firmly into his ears and closed his eyes.

Nothing happened. There was no sound, nothing.

Bino relaxed and expelled the air from his lungs.

Footsteps dragged on concrete as Wimpy came around the corner of the garage, whistling a decades-old hillbilly tune. "Honky-tonk Angels." He came down the length of the driveway, grunted slightly as he set the toolbox underneath the window on the ground.

"Good job," Wimpy said. "Now you reach in and unlock the window, then I'll shut off the power again while you raise it. You'll have another fifteen seconds to climb inside and close the window behind you, but that's a helluva lot easier'n clipping the wires. Piece of fucking cake, just like I said."

"One thing's bothering me, Wimp," Bino said. "How come *you* didn't clip all this together while I shut the power off. Clipping the wires takes a little know-how."

Wimpy scratched his nose. "Whatcha take me for? Look, if that alarm goes off I'm hauling ass over the back fence. That way, if the law drives up I ain't the one fucking with the window. Like I told you, Bino, I ain't doing no life sentence for nobody."

Bino stood on lush and springy bedroom carpet, bent from the waist, and looked out through the hole in the window. Outside, Wimpy was hugging himself and shivering. Moonlight shone on Wimpy's bald spot.

"So far so good," Wimpy said. "Now you stay put and I'll go get the bags."

"What bags?" Bino said.

"The bag bags. Gunnysacks. They're in the cab of my pickup. For the silverware and jewelry and shit."

"Jesus Christ, Wimpy. We're not *stealing* anything."

Wimpy thoughtfully scratched his cheek. "Then what the fuck you doing in there?"

"Wimpy," Bino said, "how much you figure to make on a burglary like this?"

"In *this* neighborhood? Seven, eight hundred bucks, minimum. More, if they got any good gold jewelry. Big hot diamonds're hard to move."

"So you get your half," Bino said. "Drop by the office next week, Dodie'll have an envelope for you. I won't need you anymore, not tonight."

Still looking puzzled, Wimpy turned to go. Then he stopped and returned to the window. He peered in. "I don't know what's going on," he said. "But I shoulda known better than to think you'd be heisting anything. You being a lawyer, you don't have to."

Bino could have easily told that Frank Bleeder had been married more than once even if he hadn't known Bleeder's history. There were two different china patterns in the breakfront cabinet in the dining room, and the small bookcase in the master bedroom held hardbound editions of Jackie Collins novels alongside Joyce Carol Oates short story collections, with one end of a shelf taken up by thick copies of *The Clan of the Cave Bear*, *The Valley of Horses*, and *The Mammoth Hunters*, all by Jean Auel. Strictly women's reading, by Bino's way of thinking, and there wasn't any way the same gal would go for all three authors' work. The red-jacketed copy of *It*, by Stephen King, which featured a picture of a monster's tentacle poking out of a sewer, and which lay at an angle across the top of the bookcase (Jesus, *It* was thick enough for *three* books), was probably Bleeder's.

The layer of dust on the den furniture—a Sony big-screen TV, a glass-topped coffee table with wooden legs carved into the shape of animal paws, the wooden portions of the Early American sofa and easy chairs—along with the loaded dishwasher in the kitchen, the dirty plates in the sink, and the half-eaten pizza in the cardboard box on the counter said that old Frank was a bachelor at the moment. A green parakeet was perched inside a cage by the kitchen window. The folded newspaper in the cage's bottom was covered with greenish-yellow mounds of bird crap and empty seed shells. Bino told the parakeet hello. It growled at him. He picked up a folded sheet that was draped over a chair and covered the cage. The bird cussed him through the cloth. Bino thought, Ungrateful little shit, and turned his attention elsewhere.

There was a built-in desk in the wall behind the TV. On the desk were a stack of bills and a pad of checks. The checks were imprinted "J. Frank Bleeder, Attorney," with Bleeder's office address underneath. A drawer was on the bottom right-hand front of the desk; it slid open easily; inside was a letter-size cardboard file with alphabetical dividers. Each lettered compartment was bulging with papers.

Bino wasn't sure exactly what he was looking for, nor did he have the slightest idea how much time he had in which to rummage around. But the file looked as good a place as any to start. He sat down in a straight-backed cushioned chair in front of the desk and went to work.

Bino's eyelids felt as though he needed a couple of toothpicks to prop them open. He leaned forward in the recliner and peered around behind him at the digital clock on Bleeder's den wall. A quarter till two. He yawned, glanced at the stack of papers he'd transferred from the file drawer to the coffee table, stretched out on the recliner, and returned his attention to the book in his lap.

He'd decided that he had Stephen King's act figured out, and he had to admit that King was pretty smart. Hell, King was the Master of the Macabre. How could anybody knock a guy who sold around 40 million copies of everything that he wrote, and who'd had more movies made out of his stuff than most *screenwriters*, for Christ's sake? Old King had the answer, okay, and during the past three hours while he'd been sitting there reading *It*, Bino was pretty sure he'd discovered the secret.

It's as plain as the nose on your face, Bino thought. People buy books by the *pound*, the same way they buy oranges and potatoes. I mean, Jesus Christ, nobody in this world in their right mind would pay sixteen ninety-five for a skinny little novel by Elmore Leonard or George V. Higgins or somebody, when for only five bucks more they could have a book that not only was written by *Stephen King* but would build up their forearms while they were reading it as well. And reading it and reading it, on and on and on, going over each chapter four or five times until they figured out what the fuck the story was all about.

Bino had just flipped from page 283 back to page 276, trying to decipher whether the passage he was now into was going on in the present or was a flashback thirty years into the past, when a series of beeps sounded over the intercom speakers. Somebody was punching a code into the keyboard panel on the front porch to disarm the burglar alarm. The front door opened. Bino laid the book aside—or *tried* to lay it aside; halfway to the floor the monstrous volume slipped from his fingers and thudded to the carpet—and straightened up in the recliner.

The front door closed with a bang that shook the house. More electronic beeps put the burglar alarm back in business. Footsteps sounded in the entry hall, then stopped abruptly. Frank Bleeder's voice, hoarse and fearful, called out, "Who's there?"

Bino leaned back and intertwined his fingers behind his head. "It's me, Frank. Bino Phillips. Come on in, hell, I'm not going to hurt you."

Bleeder came into the den. He blinked in surprise. He was wearing a dark, iridescent suit with a vest that was a shade too tight for him. His shirt collar was unbuttoned, and his tie was loosened. A tan overcoat was folded over his arm. His complexion was beet-red, and he needed a shave. He showed the beginnings of a nasty scowl.

"How'd you come out tonight?" Bino asked. "You win or lose?"

Bleeder tossed his coat onto one of the easy chairs, stalked over to the counter that separated the den from the kitchen, and picked up the phone. "I'm calling the police."

Still in the same relaxed position on the recliner, Bino said, "Okay, you just fucking call 'em. You won't get any trouble out of me; I'll just take these notes of yours along with me when they take me downtown." He waved a hand at the papers on the coffee table.

Bleeder hung the phone up. "How'd you get in here?"

"I broke in. Nothing to it for an old second-story man. I cut a hole in your burglar bars and busted your bedroom window. Might cost you a few bucks. Just send a bill to my office, if Goldman can't get you a government check to pay for the damages."

His gaze flicking toward the coffee table, then back at Bino, Bleeder said, "I've already told you, I've got nothing to say to you."

"Sure you did," Bino said. "And you told your client Thorndon that you used his money to bribe the judge, when really you fucked it off at the crap table. And you acted like you were helping Ann Burns by giving her money to gamble on, when really you were just trying to get her hooked to where she'd have to testify against her own father. And not just *testify*, she'd have to lie her ass off to back up the bullshit story *you're* going to tell. You've turned into a real prick over the years, Frank. What in hell happened to you?"

Bleeder's shoulders sagged. He fumbled as he unbuttoned his vest, then he walked hesitantly over to the vacant easy chair and sat down. He folded his hands in his lap. "I don't owe anybody any explanations," Bleeder said. "Especially not you."

"Naw, I don't guess you do. But in the future I'm damn sure not letting anybody know I went to the same law school as such an asshole. You know, you've done a pretty good job of spreading the dirt around. Half-a-Point heard on the street that the judge really *did* take the bribe, and I'll admit that threw me for a loop for a while. Until I got to thinking. Birds of a feather. Shit, Frank, you represent the same kind of sorry bastards as I do, only I will say that with me they get a better shake for their dough. You just put the word out that you gave the judge the money, and your clients spread the story like wildfire. What I'm not sure of is whether that was your idea or Goldman's."

Bleeder straightened his posture, and his nostrils flared. "Where do you— Where do you get off pointing the finger at *me*? I'm just a witness, like any other citizen."

"Like any . . . ?" Bino stood, picked up the papers from the coffee table, and leafed through them. "Question," he read. " 'How many times did you talk to him?' Answer. 'Once in chambers and once in a restaurant.' Question. 'Was there any doubt in your mind that he knew what the money was for?' Answer. 'No.' These are just the *lines* that you and Goldman are rehearsing, Frank. What about the background music? Who's the director? Capra? Spielberg, maybe? He's pretty good at fantasy." He tossed the stack of papers at Bleeder. Some landed on Bleeder's chest, some in his lap, while others slid off and rustled to the carpet.

Bleeder didn't move, but his eyes misted. "Man's got a right to get by. What does everybody want from me?"

"I don't want anything from you. Somebody *needs* something from you, but I'll get to that. You know, Frank, I've been giving you too much credit. I thought Goldman was holding something over your head, but he wasn't. Shit, you went to *Goldman* with the deal. After you'd lost Thorndon's money gambling, you were scared shitless, 'cause you knew Thorndon wouldn't fuck around with you for a second. He'd kill you, Frank. So you came up with the idea to go to Goldman, tell him you'd cooperate on prosecuting the judge if the Feds would get your client off. I hate to admit it, but I owe Goldman an apology. Not much of one, but I do. I thought Goldman probably knew that this was all a frame-up from the word *go*. And that he was in on it all along. But he wasn't. Hell, not even Goldman is *that* much of a fuckhead."

Bino paused, waited for Bleeder to say something, to try to deny everything. But Bleeder didn't waste his breath, just sat there with his round belly rising and falling under his open vest and buttoned shirt. Bino went on. "And Thorndon trying to bribe *me*, that was a tough one to figure. But, shit, you had Thorndon in the dark, too. Old Lou was scared to death that the judge was going to tell all. He didn't know Emmett Burns didn't have anything *to* tell. Things that bad, Frank? Hell, you can't even level with the bad guys."

Bleeder folded his arms and stared straight ahead. His eyes didn't seem to be focusing on anything in particular. Some of the papers still lay in his lap; a few others, upright, leaned against his belly. "So who's going to tell all that?" Bleeder asked. "Lou's dead."

Bino had opened his mouth to say more, but now he closed it. He'd been toying with the idea of using Thorndon as a witness, if he could come up with the right incentive for Thorndon to testify, and it took a few seconds for what Bleeder had just told him to sink in. Finally, Bino said, "What happened to him?"

"Shot," said Bleeder. "They found him in the mechanic's shed behind his car lot. And another guy, too. Two dead guys, and nobody seems to know what's going on."

"Going on? Hell, I do. There's this crazy fucker running around town that's— The guy knew Thorndon in the joint. Up north, somewhere."

"I've heard about that," Bleeder said. "The nut, or whatever he is, is somebody I never heard of. The county cops already asked me."

"That doesn't bother you?" Bino sat back down in the recliner, propped his elbow on the armrest, and rested his chin on his lightly clenched fist. "That there's a crazy running around?"

"Yeah. Yeah, sure. It bothers me along with a lot of things. Like you being here bothers me. Life's a bother, so what?" Bleeder continued to stare off into space, speaking in a listless monotone as though he'd sunk so low that he plain didn't give a damn.

Bino softened the tone of his voice, saying, "There's a hearing tomorrow, Frank."

"Great," Bleeder said. "So there's always a hearing, that's

what the courts are for. Keeps the judges and clerks in business."

"It's at one o'clock in Judge Sanderson's court. I want you to testify for me."

"That's a laugh," Bleeder said.

"Emmett Burns wouldn't think it was a laugh. He's a fine man. None finer, you know that. And you can save him a lot of grief."

Bleeder looked at Bino. Bleeder's cheeks were puffy, and his irises appeared painted on his eyes, like a store-window dummy's. "And cause a lot of grief for myself," Bleeder said. "What do you think Goldman's going to do if I fuck his case up for him? Everything I told him about . . . the bribes and all, I did it without immunity. If I fall down on the stand Goldman can prosecute me. I don't think I'd like the federal joint, do you?"

Especially, Bino thought, with the number of sold-out clients of yours that're running around in there. "It wouldn't be easy," Bino said. "But if you can, you know, say the right things on the stand, we can tie Goldman's hands. He wouldn't touch a case against you with a ten-foot pole if he thought you might air out some dirty laundry from the U.S. Attorney's office."

"Maybe he would and maybe he wouldn't," Bleeder said. "But the way things are now, I don't have to worry about it. And I'd rather not have to. You know the code as well as I do, pardner. The Feds don't prosecute their own witnesses. I think I'm better off being one."

Jesus, trying to reason with this guy was like banging your head against a cement wall. Bino decided to try a different angle. "Wash Patman wouldn't like to hear you talking this way, Frank."

A look of guilt? (Bino wasn't sure) crossed Bleeder's face for an instant; then all expression left him as he said, "You going to bring up *that* old shit. That was fifteen years ago." In the kitchen, the sheet covering the birdcage was twitching. The sound of their voices was bugging the parakeet.

"Yeah," Bino said. "Fifteen years. I was in the courtroom that day; hell, every lawyer in town wanted to see you in action. Didn't anybody give Wash the chance of a snowball in hell of ducking the electric chair. That was the best closing argument I ever heard, Frank. Henry Wade's been retired as D.A. for what, a year or two? I dropped by his retirement party for a coupla belts, and you know what? He was still talking about that Patman case. *Henry Wade*, Frank, the man himself. I heard him tell a couple of his old assistants—Doug Mulder, I think, and, yeah, Bill Alexander—that he'd never forgotten the way you snatched Wash Patman out of Old Sparky's clutches. That was a great job, man, and there's a lot of ghetto kids that owe you one. Whaddya say? Can we go back to those days tomorrow, you and me? Give 'em a kick in the ass, a good one?" He gave Bleeder a hopeful smile, at the same time mentally crossing his fingers.

Bleeder took a deep breath. He lowered his head and scratched alongside his nose. "You're on the wrong road, Bino," he said. "Get off of it."

Bino was suddenly mad as hell. Blood pounded in his temples. He stood, fists balled, and advanced a step. Then he relaxed, his shoulders sagging. "What the hell," Bino said. "Beating the shit out of you's not going to help my client. I'm going to win the case, Frank, no matter what you do. You could make it a lot easier for me, but fuck it. I'll use Ann Burns. I think she's going to be enough." He skirted the chair where Bleeder sat and strode firmly for the entry hall, the torn fabric of his warm-up suit flapping around his bare knee. Halfway to the front door he stopped and turned. "You should get yourself a Christmas tree, Frank. Buy yourself a present. It's a cinch nobody else is going to." He continued on his way.

Bleeder lurched to his feet and followed into the entry hall. "You think you're any better than me? Well, you're not."

Bino didn't answer, just kept on marching.

"We're all in the same pile of shit," Bleeder said.

Bino yanked on the handle and threw open the door. Frigid

air rushed in on his cheeks. "Fuck you, Frank," he said. He went out on the porch and down the steps.

"Wait a minute," Bleeder said. "The alarm."

"Fuck the alarm," Bino said from the side of his mouth, over his shoulder.

The siren went off. The high-pitched "*Gong*-gong-*gong*-gong-*gong*-gong" pealed through the neighborhood. Up and down the block, porch and window lights came on. At the house with the lighted Santa in the yard, a guy came out in his robe.

Bino reached the pickup, climbed in, and started the engine. As he peeled away from the curb, Bleeder stood on his front porch and jabbed in frustration at the security panel.

22

Marvin Goldman, clad in black, his starched white cuffs glistening, his goatee combed into a near-perfect triangle, paced back and forth in the hallway in front of the majestic, dark-stained oak entrance to the United States District Court. Goldman's hands were behind his back. His jaw was working nonstop. The red-faced FBI agent who'd brought Emmett Burns's indictment over to Bino's office, who was also wearing a black suit, stood just outside Goldman's path with his hands at his sides. The agent didn't look happy. Susie Sin, the apparent target of Goldman's dressing-down, stood her ground in a light blue, short-skirted business dress. Her elegant Oriental head was tilted in an attentive attitude, and she looked sort of amused. Goldman waved his arms and then jabbed the air with a forefinger. Susie shifted her weight from one high-heeled foot to the other. The FBI agent continued to stand at attention.

Bino halted in his tracks, ten feet after leaving the elevator, and placed a restraining hand on Emmett Burns's arm. "I think there's a revolution in progress," Bino said. "Trouble in Paradise or something."

The judge seemed in a whole lot better frame of mind today; there was a sheen in his auburn hair and a spring in his step. Probably a pleasant evening at home with his daughter had a lot to do with it. Burns said, "Far be it from me to interfere."

"Tell you what, Emmett," Bino said. "You go on in the courtroom and have a seat. Maybe I'll visit with old Marv for a second and get some groundwork out of the way." His gaze swept the hallway end to end. Buford Jernigan was nowhere in sight. Not surprising. Goldman wasn't going to allow Jernigan within a country mile of the hearing, not when somebody might put Jernigan up on the witness stand.

His shoulders square, his back straight as a ramrod, Burns strode purposefully toward the big oak door. Five yards from the entrance he encountered Goldman, face to face. The two locked stony gazes for an instant. Goldman surrendered first, his head bowed. Burns shouldered around the prosecutor and entered the district court.

Bino leaned his shoulder against the corridor wall and watched Goldman take up where he'd left off, giving Susie Sin hell. Goldman paced one way, then the other. He stopped, opened his mouth to say something. His gaze froze on Bino from across the corridor. Goldman dismissed Susie with a wave of his hand, then barked some orders to the FBI agent out of the corner of his mouth. The agent went sheepishly into the courtroom. Susie gave Goldman a final haughty toss of her head, then left in the opposite direction from the agent. Goldman faced Bino. The prosecutor folded his arms and stood in a waiting attitude.

Bino left his place against the wall and approached Goldman. He passed Susie halfway across the hallway. Her cheeks were flushed. Her heels were clicking angrily. She threw Bino a guarded wink, then rolled her eyes as she went by.

"Fuck 'im," Susie murmured.

"Second the motion," Bino whispered.

As Ann Burns pulled into a vacant space in the Park 'n' Lock across Main Street from the Davis Building, she brushed a tear from the corner of her eye. She was smearing her makeup, but it didn't matter. All that mattered right now was Daddy.

Last night she'd sat in his lap, cried on his shoulder, told him she loved him. Daddy's little girl once more for a while, and what a wonderful, top-of-the-world feeling it had been. Now if she could just bring herself to . . . Well, according to Bino Phillips, odds were high that before this day was over she was going to have to tell Daddy some things that would hurt him. If they only didn't make him stop loving her, she could get through it.

She alighted from her yellow Tempest, paid the attendant, and crossed the street with the light amid the horn honks and exhaust fumes of downtown Dallas, a lovely redhead in a navy business dress with a white starched collar, wearing a simple cloth, cream-colored coat. At the entrance to the Davis Building she paused for an instant with her head bowed. Then she squared her shoulders, lifted her chin, and went through the revolving doors into the lobby with her hips swaying modestly.

Missed you, Mama Longlegs, Daryl Siminian thought. Not for long, though.

He'd missed her by no more than thirty seconds, and this goddamn *limp* he'd developed (what in hell was wrong? Could he maybe have Lou Gehrig's disease?) was all to blame. Just an absolute perfect job of casing her house, pulling his gleaming white Eldo (Lou Thorndon's Eldo. But Lou wasn't around anymore. What in hell had happened to Lou?) into the alley at the back, crouching behind the shrubs in her backyard until the old judge had driven away. Forty fucking feet, no more, was all that had separated him from her back screen door, and he'd been covering the distance lickety-split when the limp had set in.

It hadn't even hurt; that was the really scary part. One second he'd been loping along as smooth as you please, and then, *bam!* No pain at all, nothing, just all of a sudden his right leg was dragging the ground and he was practically bent over double, like one of the old farts he'd seen up at Springfield. Struggling, gasping for breath, he'd made it the final twenty feet or so, had actually grabbed the door handle, ready to pull, when the front door to the house had opened and then slammed. He'd scrambled, Quasimodo fashion, to the side of the house and watched her go, his fists pounding his thighs in frustration as she'd clicked her way down the driveway, swung her long, elegant legs onto the floorboard of her Tempest, and driven away. She hadn't been wearing her mink. Mama Longlegs belonged in mink.

As soon as she'd gone the stumbling paralysis had left him. Just like that, *bam!* again. One instant he'd been some kind of spastic, the next old smooth-running Daryl once more. Christ, he was going to have to see a doctor as soon as he'd done . . . what? He was having a hard time remembering things.

He'd jogged back to the Eldorado and backed it out of the alley just as she'd turned left in front of the golf course. It hadn't been easy keeping her in sight on the ride downtown along the freeway, but he'd done it. Now he sat in the Eldo near the curb, motor idling, downtown traffic creeping by on his left, and watched Ann Burns enter the Davis Building. Where you going, Red? he thought.

The parking lot where she'd left her car was a half block ahead on his left. He pulled in and drove around until he located her Tempest, then parked directly across the lot from it. Perfect spot; he could watch her car and the entrance to the Davis Building at the same time. He cut the engine, threw his arm across the seatback, and relaxed.

You got to come out sooner or later, Mama Longlegs. Doesn't matter how long, I can wait. I got the time. For you, Red, I got all the time in the world.

Dodie Peterson thought, Wow, talk about *beautiful* . . . She backed up a step, holding the cup in one hand and pouring coffee with the other, and peeked around the doorjamb. She was standing inside the storage closet in Bino's office. Ann Burns was sitting on the pale red sofa in the reception area, her long, milk white legs crossed, her hands primly in her lap, her long red lashes lowered. Her coat was spread out behind her on the back of the sofa.

"How many sugars?" Dodie asked.

"Just one, please." Ann showed a dazzling, magazine-cover smile. "I'm a little speechless, frankly. When Bino told me to see his secretary, I expected someone older. Not anyone so *pretty*, God."

And flattery will get you everywhere, Dodie thought. To have *this* luscious creature sitting here telling her she was *pretty* . . . well, talk about the pot and the kettle, whatever, wow. She plunked a sugar cube into one Styrofoam cup, dumped a spoonful of powdered cream into the other, carried both cups into the reception area. She gave Ann the one with the sugar and retreated to sit behind her desk. "It knocks me over that you should say that," Dodie said, sipping. "From you that's like, maybe, Mark Aguirre telling me I was a good basketball player or something." Her forehead puckered. "Just what *did* Bino say I looked like? He can be pretty much of a clod when he wants to be."

Ann laughed. "Well he didn't say you looked like anything. It's just that, my God, here he went on and on about how efficient you were and all, I didn't expect you to be a beauty queen as well. You don't look like anybody that's ever had a problem in their lives."

"Well I have," Dodie said. She propped her elbow on her desk and rested her chin on her small fist. "Trust me, I have. Five years ago . . . that's where Bino found me. I was one of his dope clients." She giggled. "Not a big pusher or any-thing; I was one of the people that the pusher, well, pushes stuff to."

Ann sipped some coffee and a strange, sad look crossed her face. "You'd never know it. Listen, doesn't it bother you at all to talk about it? Especially to a stranger."

"It used to," Dodie said. "It really used to, but I've gotten to where, so what? I was a teenage dope fiend; there, it's not very hard to say. Now it's like saying I used to have the measles or mumps or something. If anybody's got a hang-up with it, it's *their* old problem." She blinked round blue eyes.

Ann's round blue eyes widened. "God, you're so natural about it. Are you in a group?"

Dodie was puzzled at first, then she got it. "Oh, you mean like AA. I've gone, but it's not really my bag anymore. I'm not knocking it; the group therapy's terrific for a lot of people. But if *I* want to tell old druggie stories, I tell them to Half and Bino. Half, he's the investigator but he's really a bookmaker, if you can figure that one. They're a pretty good sounding board, even if they do make me repeat the drugs-and-sex sto-ries over and over. The drugs-without-sex stories they only have to hear once."

"Could you . . . ?" Ann leaned forward and brushed her fingertips across her forehead. "If somebody had a problem, do you think you could . . . ?"

"Listen, Ann," Dodie said. "Bino means well. *Everybody* means well. It's easy as pie for them to go around telling you to pour out your heart to this person and that person, partic-ularly when they've never been through it themselves. They don't have any idea how much it hurts. Wow, I'd been away from drugs for two years before I could really open up about it. So what I'm saying is, I'm here. Anytime. But don't push it, okay? Take your time. Today we're going to court; that's what we have to do. Think about that. Tonight find something else to do. 'One day at a time' is a pretty worn-out saying, but it works."

☐ 300 ☐

"I'm hoping it does," Ann said. She set down her coffee cup. "God, but I'm hoping. Well. Are we ready to go?"

"I'll get my coat," Dodie said. "Just remember to cool it. Nobody can do it but you, no matter what they say."

Bino had gotten just about as far with Marvin Goldman as he'd expected to. He told Emmett Burns as much as the two of them sat with their heads together at the defense table in the courtroom. "The guy's on an ego trip," Bino said. "He's done all this spouting off around town, and now Susie Sin's gone on TV and said there's a chance that the government's whole case is fabricated. Goldman wouldn't drop the charges now if you showed him a video of somebody offering you a bribe and then you personally handcuffing the guy and leading him off to jail."

Burns gazed toward the bench. Judge Hazel Burke Sanderson, her lips pursed as though she'd warmed up for the hearing by sucking on a lemon, shuffled through papers at her elevated station. Burns said, "It's a sad comment on what we've come to."

"We're going to have some long evenings by the fire to kick that one around," Bino said. "Emmett, I've come up a little short on this hearing. Hey, my motion's on file with the clerk; Dodie typed it up and brought it over this morning, so that's not the problem. I'm one witness short. I thought I could talk some sense into a guy, but I couldn't. So what I'm saying is, well, I'm going to have to put your daughter on. She's on her way down here. Dodie's bringing her."

Burns's features sagged. "Ann? She didn't say anything about . . ." He trailed off.

Bino studied his hands for a moment, then raised his head. He tried to look Burns square in the face but couldn't quite manage it. He was looking more *past* Burns than *at* him, more at the row of wooden pillars that decorated the far wall of the courtroom. Bino said, "I'm just the lawyer in this. It's my job to try and win the case the best way I know how. So, well, what's between you and your daughter is between you and your daughter; I've got nothing to do with it. I'm going to ask for a half-hour delay in the hearing. Ann has some things she wants to tell you about."

Burns's neck stiffened, and his jaw thrust determinedly forward. "Well I think you'd *better* ask for a delay. Yeah, I guess you had. You're not exposing my little girl to . . . anything. I'll go to prison before I'll let you do that."

Burns was as serious as a heart attack; Bino didn't have one single doubt about that. He expelled a long, deep breath. "That's your choice to make, Emmett. I can't make it for you." He stood and glanced quickly around the courtroom. Susie Sin, her cameraman, and a group of reporters, some of whom Bino recognized, sat at the far rear of the spectators' section. Besides the media there were about twenty people seated; most of them would be lawyers with cases on the docket. The FBI agent was whispering something to Goldman at the prosecution's table. Goldman was laughing. The agent was probably telling Goldman a good one, maybe the one about the guy in prison who didn't have any teeth. The other cons had knocked them out to keep the guy from biting them while they were making him give them blowjobs. Old Marv would like that one. Bino squared his shoulders and faced Hazel Sanderson. "Your Honor, may counsel approach the bench?"

Judge Sanderson looked up from her reading, glanced toward Goldman, then at Bino. Bino thought her hair was a little stiffer than usual this afternoon; maybe she was trying out a new spray. "Make it quick, sir," she said.

Bino walked over to stand in front of the judge. Goldman joined him at the bench. The federal prosecutor was practically swaggering in place. Judge Sanderson lifted her eyebrows expectantly. Bino leaned closer to her and said, "I need a half hour, Judge. Can we have a delay?"

"A delay?" Hazel Sanderson put down the file folder that was in her hand with an emphatic slap. "You've charged down here demanding a hearing, got my whole calendar in an uproar, now you're wanting a *delay*?"

Goldman scratched his goateed chin. "Judge, as you know I make it a practice never to snipe at opposing counsel. But this is ridiculous. I mean, I really had to juggle things around to come down here this afternoon at all."

"What'd you juggle, Marv?" Bino asked. "Your coffee break?" He could have bitten his tongue in two, and he mentally winced as he got ready for the tirade that was sure to come from the judge. He looked at her.

Her gaze was to the rear of the courtroom. "What does *he* want?" she said.

Bino and Goldman turned as one. Frank Bleeder stood just beyond the railing, his hand on the top edge of the gate. Bleeder looked fresh. He was clean shaven, wore a modest gray suit and conservative pale blue tie, and had a steadiness in his bearing that Bino hadn't seen in Bleeder in years.

His gaze on Bino, Bleeder lifted his free hand to shoulder level and waggled his fingers. "Put me on," he mouthed silently.

Bino whirled, his mind racing, and faced the bench. "About the delay, Judge. I withdraw my request."

"Objection," Goldman said.

"And it's a lot to lug around," Dodie said, hustling along down Main Street in step with Ann Burns. She was talking about the big leather carrying case that she was clutching by its handle and that was bumping against her thigh as she walked. "But it comes in handy. Besides all these legal papers and whatnot there's an extra compartment where I can carry my keys, compact, whatever, you know, the same stuff as I'd carry in a purse. Might even be a Ding Dong or a cupcake or two in there, I can't remember. Brrr, it's getting colder." They were abreast of and across Main Street from the entrance to One Main Place, the forty-story, gray-rock skyscraper that housed a branch of First Texas Bank. The cloud cover had thickened as the day had worn on, and the wind had picked up. Dodie was wearing a dark brown, imitation leather overcoat with an imitation fox collar. As she and Ann passed One Main Place, a man with gray sideburns, wearing an army green London Fog topcoat, came outside among a mob of people. He spotted Dodie and Ann. His jaw dropped. A short dishwater blond beside him yanked on his arm and gave him hell.

"One more block straight ahead and then one to the left," Dodie said. "I'll say this for the weather, it makes you move faster. You going to hold up okay?"

Ann's hands were deep in her pockets, and her collar was turned up. She shrugged. "I'll have to. It's the first step, at least I'm hoping that's what it is. I'll have Daddy to lean on. I'll make it."

On their right, amid the thickening traffic on Main, a horn honked.

"That's the spirit," Dodie said. She shifted the satchel across her body, from one hand to the other. "And just remember, the more time that passes the easier it's going to get."

The horn honked again, two short toots this time.

"I swear, these *guys*," Dodie said. "Downtown they'll drive you crazy. Honk, honk, hey, mama, like you were a piece of meat or something. Wow, this guy's driving an Eldorado; I bet he *really* thinks he's a stud."

The white Eldorado pulled to the curb beside them and stopped. Its door swung open.

About time, Daryl thought. It's finally here, Red, and you can bet it's going to be worth waiting for, you know? He left the engine running, gripped his Magnum, climbed out on the sidewalk. Got a blond girlfriend now, Red? I might have time for her and might not, you know? But I'll have plenty of time for you, Mama Longlegs. You can count on it.

He approached the two women, his Magnum level and steady, saw them turn to look at him, saw the blond's leather coat blowing around her legs, her fine, silken hair moving in the wind. Red's lips parted in—fear, maybe? She might be afraid for now, but Daryl was going to make her smile before it was all over.

He'd covered a dozen feet of sidewalk, was just a couple of steps from his goal, when the limp set in. Just like before, his right leg dragging behind, his body bent, his smooth athletic walk turning into a crablike scramble. He lurched the final step, and she was there, her red hair soft on his cheek, the sweet scent of her in his nostrils. He encircled her throat with his arm and pulled her to him, placing the barrel of the Magnum against her temple.

He was hoarse. "Been waiting for you, mama." Limping, dragging his right leg, he backed toward the curb where the Eldo sat waiting. Gasping for breath, sobbing, she followed him, one halting step at a time.

Suddenly the blond threw back her head and screamed at the top of her lungs.

A block away, a beefy young Dallas policeman stood in the center of the intersection of Main and Akard streets, directing traffic. He wore a heavy navy jacket over his uniform and thick cotton gloves. One of his arms was straight, the other windmilling. He was tooting a silver whistle that he held lightly clenched between his teeth. At the sound of Dodie's scream, his head snapped around.

There were two women over there on the sidewalk, one a redhead, the other a blond. A man with a strange, scuttling walk was forcing the redhead toward a white Cadillac that was parked at the curb. The man was holding a gun to the red-haired woman's head.

The cop ran over to the curb, dodging traffic, his ample flesh bouncing up and down. He drew his service revolver and steadied it. "Hold it right there. Police. Stand away from that woman."

This goofy cop didn't have any idea who he was fucking with, throwing down on Daryl Ralph Siminian. Silly asshole was going to find out in a hurry, though. Daryl released his choke hold on Red (Be back in a minute, Mama Longlegs, don't worry about me), spun, dropped awkwardly to one knee, and aimed the Magnum.

Bino hadn't counted on having to battle *two* lawyers. Goldman wasn't a problem any longer; Bleeder's unexpected appearance on the witness stand had reduced the federal prosecutor to smoldering rubble. Goldman did manage to offer a few halfhearted objections, but each time Marv would object, Bino would merely face the bench and say, "For the record, Your Honor, on what ground does the government's objection stand?" At which point Goldman would mumble under his breath and withdraw his objection.

No, Goldman was all but finished. But with the prosecutor in effect out of the way, *Judge Sanderson* was taking up the government's cause.

Bino had just asked Bleeder, who was being a perfect witness, sitting erect and answering questions in a straightforward, level manner, whether Lou Thorndon had ever given him money for the purpose of bribing Emmett Burns. Hazel Sanderson cleared her throat. "The question is out of order, counsel."

Bino half-turned in his position in front of the witness and faced the bench. "Huh? I mean, excuse me, Your Honor?"

"It's out of order." She rustled papers, picked one typewritten page out of the bunch, adjusted her Martha Washington glasses to the end of her nose, lowered her head, and read silently. Then she looked up and said, "The motion before the court has to do with the clarity of the government's indictment. What you're going over is evidence, which should be contested at trial." She laid the paper down and glared triumphantly. "Your question's out of order, Mr. Phillips."

Bino licked his lips, vaguely conscious of movement in the corner of his eye as Bleeder shifted his position in the witness chair. There was a big American flag hanging from a gilt pole to one side of the bench. The flag was limp, its end practically touching the carpet. Bino licked his lips again. Hazel Sanderson had just tossed him a hot potato, and if he didn't come up with an answer pronto, the hearing was going to be over. She'd dismiss the fucking witness and call it a day.

Bino licked his lips a third time. "If the court will bear with me," he began, then paused. A light bulb switched on in his brain. He said quickly, "We're getting to the point. The government's charged that certain events occurred. If we can establish—establish through the government's own trial witness, which Mr. Bleeder is—that the witness has no recollection of said events, then we can show that the indictment's insufficient. We can't prepare to defend against something that never happened, Your Honor." He held his breath and stood silent.

It was a half-assed stab in the dark, and Bino knew it, and so did Hazel Sanderson. If they'd been in private, back in her chambers, she'd have hooted him the hell out of her office. But out here under the spotlight, everything was going on the record. The court reporter, a plumpish woman in her forties, sat waiting with her fingers poised over the keyboard. If old Hazel terminated the hearing right now, the Fifth Circuit Court of Appeals might, just might, turn a conviction around. Let the old heifer take *that* one and try to twist it to suit her purposes.

Judge Sanderson shuffled more papers. She cleared her throat once more. She took her glasses off and rubbed her eyes. "Oh," she said. "Proceed, sir."

Bino nearly gave himself a whiplash as he turned back to the witness. "Do I need to repeat the question?" He hoped he didn't sound as though he was gloating *too* much. Maybe just a little.

"No," Bleeder said evenly, his face open and honest. "You asked if Lou Thorndon ever gave me any money which I was to use to influence Emmett Burns."

Bino walked to a point halfway between the witness box and the defense table. "And did he?"

"Yes," Bleeder said.

"How *much* money?"

"Forty thousand dollars."

Bino looked to the defense table and threw Emmett Burns a guarded wink. "And did you ever give the money to Judge Burns?" Bino asked.

"No, sir." There was just the slightest catch in Bleeder's voice.

"Oh?" Bino said. "What *happened* to the money?"

Bleeder folded his hands in his lap and bowed his head. "I lost the money gambling. I've . . . got a problem."

Bino went over and leaned an elbow on the witness box railing. At the defense table, Emmett Burns was brightening up. Bino said, "And at any time whatsoever, did you discuss the offering of a bribe with Emmett Burns?"

Bleeder didn't hesitate. "No, sir."

Bino raised a hand. "A moment, Your Honor." Then, before Hazel Sanderson had a chance to blister his ears, he walked quickly to the prosecution's table, leaned over, and whispered to Marvin Goldman, "You going to drop the charges?"

Goldman looked as though he was watching a horror movie. "You must be out of your mind," he hissed. "You go to hell."

Bino tilted his head and grinned. "You asked for it, Marv," he said.

He returned to the witness. "Mr. Bleeder," Bino said. "Did you and I have a conversation last night?"

"Yes," Bleeder said.

"And did the subject come up of some papers you had in your possession?"

"Yes."

Bino folded his arms and crossed his ankles. "Oh? And what were those papers?"

"My notes," Bleeder said.

"Your . . . notes. Notes you'd made during meetings with Mr. Goldman, the prosecutor?"

"Yes, sir," Bleeder said, looking straight at Goldman.

"In fact, weren't they a list of questions Mr. Goldman was going to ask you on the stand, along with the answers you were going to give?" Bino asked.

The blur that Bino caught in the periphery of his vision was Goldman, bouncing to his feet like a fourth-stringer that the coach had just called into action from the bench. *"Objection.* Your Honor, that's privileged."

Judge Sanderson looked a little bit confused. *"What's* privileged, Mr. Goldman?"

Goldman came around and stood beside the defense table. "What he's asking. That's attorney-client privilege."

Bino snorted, bowing, then slowly lifting, his head. "Now wait, wait just a minute, Marv. Your Honor, attorney-client privilege is just what it says it is. Mr. *Bleeder's* not the lawyer for the government. Mr. *Goldman* is. And Mr. Bleeder's not Mr. Goldman's client, either, the government is. I couldn't ask Mr. *Goldman* that question, if he was on the stand, but Mr. Bleeder's just a witness in this case. At least that's what they taught where *I* went to law school. Maybe they taught Marv something different, whatever school he went to."

There was a ripple of laughter among the spectators. Most of the lawyers in the courtroom had big grins on their faces. Most of the nonlawyers wouldn't have gotten the joke. The broadest grin Bino could see belonged to Emmett Burns.

Hazel Sanderson banged her gavel and pointed her finger. "Enough of that. Mr. Phillips, any more levity in this courtroom will buy you some contempt time in the county jail, sleeping next to some of your illustrious clients. Is that clear, sir?"

Any more . . . ? Hell, that's just what this system needs, is a few laughs, Bino thought. The whole rigmarole is a joke, anyway. He forced himself to look serious and, he hoped, humble. "I apologize to the court, Your Honor." But if the old bat expected any more ass kissing from Bino Phillips, he was apt to tell her where to get off. He briefly wondered which of

Wimpy's buddies were in the hoosegow right now, and which of them liked to play a little gin. "The government has raised an objection, Your Honor," Bino said.

Hazel Sanderson fiddled. She fidgeted. She frowned. Finally she said, "Overruled," as though she'd rather take a beating than let the word come out of her mouth.

Bino turned to Bleeder. "Mr. Bleeder, I've asked if your notes were actually a question-and-answer list furnished you by Mr. Goldman over there. The government objected and the court has overruled the objection. Will you now answer?"

Bleeder sat up straighter and opened his mouth.

"Your . . . Honor," Goldman said, coming forward. "I think we've had—I think we've *heard* enough. The government . . . We're going to dismiss the indictment, so I guess there's no point in going on with this."

Emmett Burns stood up—almost leaped—from his chair. Bino *did* jump, about six inches into the air, his heels thumping on the carpet as he came down. Hell, he couldn't help it. Let her hold him in contempt if she wanted to.

Judge Sanderson snapped furiously, "Is that final, Mr. Goldman?"

Goldman locked his hands together behind his back. "I believe it is, Your Honor," he said.

Bino fully expected Emmett Burns to hug his neck. Instead, Burns shook hands, firmly and warmly, and said, "Great job." Then he turned, went through the gate, and headed for the exit.

"Emmett," Bino called from the rail. "Where you going?"

"My office," said Burns over his shoulder. "I've got work piled up." He took one more step, then turned around and said, "And it's *Judge* Burns to you, Counsel. I don't believe in fraternization." He grinned and winked. "But if you ever want to have coffee and talk some law, come by."

Just like that.

Burns paused at the door in response to a question from

Susie Sin. He shook his head, said something to her, then pointed in Bino's direction. Burns left. Bino looked around for Bleeder.

Bleeder was standing by the government's table, looking downcast. Goldman was wagging a finger in his face. The federal prosecutor was talking a mile a minute.

Bino went over and said, "Indict him if you want to, Marv. For what? *Not* bribing Judge Burns? Defrauding Thorndon out of his bribe money? Hell, Thorndon's dead, he can't even testify for you."

"Butt out," Goldman said.

"Hell, no, I'm butting *in*," Bino said. "What are you going to do about it?" He looked first at Goldman's shoes then raised his gaze to look the prosecutor straight in the eye.

Bleeder put a hand on Bino's arm. "Cool it, Bino. Hell, he *ought* to indict me. I should go to jail. Now excuse me, fellas, I'm going to my office. I got a lot of thinking to do. Thanks, Bino. You know where to find me, Marv. I'm not running anywhere." With that, Frank Bleeder went through the gate to the back of the courtroom and exited by the same door through which Emmett Burns had gone.

Bino thought, Jesus Christ. Sidney fucking Carton.

Ever since the guy had gotten out of the Cadillac and approached her and Ann Burns with that big, ugly pistol in his hand, Dodie had been operating on pure instinct, fueled by her own adrenaline. When he'd grabbed Ann and begun to drag her back toward his car, Dodie's instinct had told her to scream. Now, as the lunatic knelt just feet from her and aimed his pistol at the policeman who was maybe two hundred feet down the block with his own gun drawn, Dodie acted on instinct once more.

She swung the big leather satchel that she was carrying high overhead and, with her eyes squinched tightly closed, brought it crashing down on the crazy man's outstretched arm. The satchel landed with a loud thud. The pistol clattered to the pavement and—*bam!*—went off. Something whined scant inches from Dodie's face. The gold-plated clasp on the satchel popped open, and typewritten pages fluttered and flew. Wow, Dodie thought, there goes Bino's case down the tubes. The crazy man grunted, then scrabbled crab fashion along the sidewalk, reaching for the gun.

Instinct reached out once again and grabbed Dodie. She knew one thing: If the lunatic got his hands on the gun, Dodie was going to be in big trouble. She swung her leg over and straddled him, piggyback style. Her skirt rode up to expose her thighs. With a startled *oof!* the lunatic sprawled flat on his belly. Mesh fabric gave as Dodie's panty hose ripped; there was a stinging sensation in her knee as it scraped pavement. She'd kept her grip somehow on the leather handle; she now raised the satchel and smashed it down on the back of the crazy's head. At the same instant she caught a flash of milk white calf and navy spike-heeled pump as Ann Burns kicked the lunatic in the rib cage, just below his armpit.

Dodie swung the satchel again.

Ann kicked again.

As Dodie prepared to strike once more, an arm extended itself between her body and the crazy's head. The arm was encased in a heavy jacket sleeve. Its hand was covered by a cotton glove, and the glove was wrapped around the butt of a pistol—some kind of revolver; Dodie didn't know squat about guns. The pistol's barrel steadied against the back of the lunatic's head.

Dodie froze, still straddling the crazy man's back, the satchel poised over her head. The arm belonged to the cop. He was beefy, broad shouldered, and, Dodie couldn't help noticing, not bad looking at all. He grinned at her. "I'll take over, miss. He's pretty well finished."

Dodie scrambled to her feet and, panting, looked around. Ann stood with hands on hips a couple of feet away. Her chest was rapidly rising and falling. A knot of passersby had gathered; more people were running to join the group.

A man who was wearing a brown overcoat said to the cop, "What took you so long? He could have killed them."

"Hell, man," the cop said, still grinning at Dodie, "the two tomatoes were kicking the crap out of the guy. I was a little bit scared to get in their way, tell you the truth."

Bino was beginning to feel like pretty much of a superstar. He was standing in the Federal Building lobby with autos and pedestrians streaming back and forth on Commerce Street outside the floor-to-ceiling windows, giving Susie Sin an interview. He was grinning into the camera. Every time Susie asked a question and then held the mike for him to answer, she regarded him with a saucy gleam in her eye, and Bino was doing some serious picturing of how Susie would look curled into one corner of the sofa in his apartment with a glass of wine in her hand.

He'd just turned what he believed to be his better side—his right—to the camera while saying, "That's a good question, Susie, and I'll say it *did* take some intensive research on our part to find the chink in the government's armor," when Dodie burst into the lobby with Ann Burns close on her heels.

Both women were disheveled, hair out of place, and they were breathing hard, as though they'd been running. They stood off to one side while Bino quickly terminated the interview—after whispering to Susie that he'd be in touch in a few days—and went over to them.

"I'm going to put a smile on your face, Ann," he said. "The government's dropped the charges. Nothing more to worry about; it's over."

Her red lips had been parted, and she'd drawn in her breath to say something, but now she closed her mouth, exhaled, and said merely, "Where's Daddy?"

"Well you may not believe this," Bino said, "but he's working. In his office. Upstairs, he . . . took off lickety-split as soon as the hearing was over. He's quite a man. I don't see how he does it."

"Oh," Ann said. "I've got to . . ." She went past Bino and headed for the elevators, looking back over her shoulder and saying, "Thank you. I'm just so . . ." A tear was rolling down her cheek.

After Ann had gone, Bino said to Dodie, "We did it, Dode."

She looked up at him, her feet slightly apart, one hand clasping her opposite forearm, the other hand gripping her satchel's handle. She didn't say anything.

He brushed a white lock of hair back from his forehead and leaned closer to her. He lowered his voice and said, "Look, this might not be a good time to bring this up. But, well, I know you're busy and all, but hey. Maybe you should, sort of, check yourself over in the mirror before you come down to the courthouse. Your hair's sort of . . . well, needs some attention, maybe, and . . . well, did you know you've got a run in your hose? It's pretty noticeable, Dode, on your knee and shin. You know, we *do* need to keep up our image down here." He flashed her a patronizing smile.

Her eyes narrowed, and her cheeks flushed. "You shut *up*, Bino Phillips. Unless you want me to whomp you with this satchel, you shut your mouth right this instant."

23

Ann Burns hesitated outside her father's office. There was no secretary seated at the desk, and Daddy's door was partway open. A slash of light from inside the office reflected on the beige carpet of his reception room. He was there, so why didn't she just walk right in? What was stopping her?

She smiled to herself. It was habit, nothing more. Habit formed in childhood, almost as hard to break as the habit of breathing itself. When Daddy was at work, the child didn't bother him. She composed herself and went on in.

Emmett Burns was behind his desk. He was holding a large brown envelope in one hand and a letter opener in the other. The envelope was hand addressed; the cursive writing on its front was facing Ann. There was a printed logo on one end of the envelope, a picture of a messenger with wings on his feet. One end of the envelope was slit open.

"I don't think I've ever been this happy," Ann said. "How can you work?"

Burns gave her a look that said he was as happy as she was, then covered it up with his stern I'm-a-judge expression. He'd never been able to fool her, but she'd always let him think he did. "How can I *not* work?" he asked. "With people delivering strange packages that nobody seems to know anything about. With my luck, it's probably a bomb."

"Daddy."

"Or some kind of hate letter. I probably shouldn't open it."

"Daddy, I've got some things to tell you."

He laid the envelope aside and placed the letter opener on top of it. "And I've got some things to tell *you*, daughter. That young man Bino Phillips is one helluva lawyer. I owe my hide to him. Not that I'd ever tell him that, and don't you be repeating it either."

"These things can't wait, Daddy. I'll never have my nerve up again."

Burns put his fingertips together. "That bad, huh?" He swiveled his chair and looked at the large photo of himself shaking hands with LBJ that hung on his office wall. "Well, me first. I'm the judge, you're the daughter, it's my right. I had a pretty good practice going when I took this job. Not a bang-up, high-dollar deal, but a good practice. And it stood to get better. You know why I took this appointment?"

"I think I do," she said. "Mom and me?"

"Righto. One wife, one child. Security. Being a judge is probably the lousiest job in the legal profession, princess. Nobody likes you. You don't have any friends, and you make less than the junior partner in a pint-size law firm. But the federal bench does have security." He turned to look at her. "At least I thought it did, until this cyclone blew through my life. But that's over, and you know what? I'm going to keep right on doing it the same way I always have."

"That's what I'd expect you to do, Daddy. Is that what you were going to tell me?"

"I'm not through." He picked up the envelope, blew a puff of air into the slit, and peeked inside. "Take this, for instance. Here's something from somebody who doesn't even want to identify themselves. There's no return address. I can't stand people who don't even have the guts to let people know who they are. That tells me there's something in this envelope that I'm not going to like. Something else neat about being a judge. If I was somebody else, some private lawyer, I'd throw the damn thing away without opening it."

She studied him. He was putting up a front, not cutting her off but not wanting to hear what she had to tell him. She took a determined breath. "What I have to say's important, Daddy."

Burns's stern exterior shell was suddenly gone. In its place was a man who was actually about to cry. Tears were welling in his eyes. "Don't you . . . ?" He coughed into a cupped hand, took out his handkerchief, and blew his nose. "You're not even hearing me, daughter. What you have to tell me is just like what's in this envelope. Bad news, and I don't want any of that. I know something's been troubling you. Hell, I used to change your diapers. My little girl grew up and went away from me. Then she came back, and she had troubles. That's what daddies are for, to make troubles go away. So now you're going to tell me about more troubles, and, Ann, I don't want to hear about them. All I want is for you to be my little girl. Can't you give me that?"

There was a tugging at the corner of her mouth. So he didn't want to know. And why should he? He had a *right* not to know. He had a right for her to be just what he wanted her to be, from this day forward. Her lashes lowered. "I can, Daddy. That much I can do. Depend on it." She looked up. "Take me out to dinner?"

He wiped his eyes with his handkerchief. "Sorry to be such a . . . Sure, dinner. Starting now. Right this minute, I'll get my coat." He looked the envelope over again. "And I'm not hearing *this* guy's troubles either. If he wants something he can see me in person." He wadded the whole package into a big lump and dropped it in his wastebasket. He stood. "You remember where your favorite eating place was? When you were little?"

A warmth she hadn't felt in years flooded over her. "My *very* favorite? I had several."

"Not as favorite as this one. Come on, I'll let you guess. On the way, I'll even give you some clues."

Emmett Burns took his daughter by the arm and ushered her out the door. His eyes were shining. They went down the hallway, the sounds of their laughter drifting along behind them.

24

Three days before Christmas, TexasBanc folded. The business section of the *Dallas Morning News* carried a banner headline about the FDIC takeover and the removal (and possible FBI investigation) of key directors. The story's text said that TexasBanc stock was to be sold overnight by the Fed (for peanuts) to a New York group. The New York folks were announcing their new board of directors, which included, among other prominents, Mrs. Dante (Annabelle) Tirelli. A slightly less gaudy article in the same section of the paper announced record-breaking losses predicted in the final quarter for MCorp, the parent company of MBank. Buried low on page 4, still in the business section, was a third story: the declaration from Citibank that due to unrest in the Texas real-estate market, the megabank was withdrawing all financing commitments for developments in the Dallas area until further notice.

On the morning these stories appeared, H. Taylor Anspacher went in to take a shower. Anspacher, the just-removed chairman of TexasBanc, was scheduled for an 11:00 A.M. meeting. The meeting was to be held in the offices of the attorneys for the estate of his cousin, Winston Bennett Anspacher III. The cousin's death two months earlier had been ruled a suicide. H. Taylor Anspacher had been named executor, and the purpose of the conference was to discuss certain discrepancies in his first accounting to the heirs.

H. Taylor Anspacher never showed up for the meeting. Instead he half-filled his bathtub, stripped the insulation from the cord on his Pro-Styler hair dryer, then stood in the water, held the bare wire in his mouth, and inserted the plug. Found among his belongings was the grand jury subpoena that had been served on him the previous afternoon.

On that same December morning, Westy Sullivan was opening up the bar in the Oilman's Club atop InterFirst Tower. Westy was wiping down the counter (and idly wondering if business that day was going to be brisk enough that he could siphon some of the till money to settle up with Half-a-Point Harrison) when J. J. Donaghey came in. Donaghey, whose fourteen office complexes were built with MBank financing, and who made it a policy never to drink before five, sat at the end of the bar and ordered a martini up, with a twist.

"Early for you, ain't it?" Westy said, pouring. "I never seen you saucin' it in the mornin'."

"You've never seen me broke before," Donaghey said. "Run me a tab on credit, my boy. I own this fucking bar, remember? Hell, I'll never be able to pay myself anyway."

As H. Taylor Anspacher forlornly shoved in the plug, and as J. J. Donaghey dejectedly gulped his gin, Bino Phillips sat in his office on the sixth floor of the Davis Building. He tossed the business section of the *Dallas Morning News* high in the air. The pages separated and rustled to the carpet. Bino threw his head back. "Go, Ponies. Hook 'em, Horns. Pig Sooey, and all that shit."

Dodie stuck her head around the doorjamb. "Whatever . . . ?"

"They're broke, Dode. Busto. The deal's off. Call Bainbridge and tell him if he doesn't get his bleeping old sign down off the sidewalk, I'm gonna chop it down myself."

"I've *already* called him. I couldn't make heads or tails out of your new lease."

"And?"

"His phone's disconnected."

"Whoopee," Bino said. "Where's Half?"

Dodie came inside his office, backed up to lean against the wall, folded her arms, and crossed her ankles. She wore a white blouse with puffed sleeves, a maroon skirt with matching high-heeled pumps, and her long blond hair was tied back into a ponytail. "It's sort of hard to explain," she said. "Barney was Santa Claus last night, over at Stanley the Stiff's."

"For all the little stiffs," Bino said.

"Right. Anyway, according to Half, after the kids went to bed Stanley and Barney decided to play some poker. But, wow, there was only two of them."

Bino leaned back in his swivel chair. "They didn't."

Dodie moved away from the wall and stood in front of the old SMU team picture. Bino's hands in the picture, holding the giant conference trophy aloft, were visible over her shoulder. "I'm afraid they did," she said. "They called Half."

"Barney and Stanley the Stiff played poker with *Half*? How much did Half win?"

"Playing," Dodie said. "Win-*ning*. Present tense. Half called about fifteen minutes ago, and he wanted to know if you owed Barney any money. I told him I didn't think so, but I got the idea maybe . . . you know."

"That Half wants me to pay *him* any money that I owe Barney. Well he's out of luck there. I don't owe Barney anything." Bino stood. "So we're alone. Switch the phone over to the answering service, Dode. We're going out."

She looked hesitant. She was still being pretty cool toward

him around the office, and he'd made up his mind to do whatever he had to in order to clear the air. "Out where?" Dodie asked.

"Oysters on the half shell. Crab legs. Trout, smothered in lemon-butter sauce. Vincent's, Dode, it's your Christmas lunch. And then I'm giving you the afternoon off."

She arched an eyebrow. "What's the catch?"

"No catch. It's on the square; it's high time I started showing you some appreciation."

"Well I'll tell you right now," she said, "we're not winding up in your apartment. I don't need for you to be *that* appreciative."

"Hey, would I . . . ? Nothing like that, honest. Get your coat."

She nodded, still looking pretty skeptical, then went into the outer office and covered her typewriter. As she moved over to the coat rack, the phone rang. She turned around.

Bino was standing in his doorway. He raised his hand. "I'll get it, Dode. I told you, you're off for the day." He went over and sat on the corner of her desk, pressed the flashing button, and picked up the receiver. "Lawyer's office."

"Sleigh bells ring for newshounds, too," Susie Sin said. "I thought you were going to call."

He bent his head and lowered his voice. "I've been meaning to."

"Well I'm not waiting any longer," Susie said. "I'm off tonight, and I thought we could go out to Arthur's, they've got an afternoon combo today—"

"Susie," he said.

"Then maybe a couple of steaks and, well, you never know. Do you?"

Bino expelled a long sigh. Dodie was now standing beside him, wearing a fuzzy pink coat with a white furry collar. He said, "Great you should call, but I've . . . got some business today."

Susie's voice rose an octave. "You're turning me *down*?"

He chuckled weakly. "Well, not really, it's just that . . . I can't, is all."

Anger crept into her tone. "Do you have any idea how many men I've ever had to throw myself at? In my life?"

"Not many, I'll bet," he said. Dodie went to the exit door and stood waiting expectantly.

"Bingo, buster," Susie said. "Zero, that I can remember. And with me you've got one toss. One pitch. You've had yours, Charley. Tune me in sometime." She hung up.

Bino wistfully eyed the receiver, then disconnected and called the answering service. When he'd arranged for his calls to be switched over, he went to the rack for his overcoat. It was a new one, a thick, off-white job that looked to him like something Al Capone would wear. He put it on and followed Dodie out into the hall.

They stood across the street from the Davis Building for a moment, their breaths turning into fog on this clear, cold day, and watched pedestrians jostling one another as they moved along on the sidewalks laden down with Christmas packages and listened to the echo of honking horns from the downtown canyon walls. Each sidewalk sign pole had a green foam-plastic Christmas tree attached near its top, and as they looked west on Main Street toward the Ozlike ball atop Reunion Tower on the skyline, the staggered row of trees on poles marched into the distance in an endless parade. Up the street in a Neiman-Marcus display window, jolly mechanical elves hammered on shoes, stacked huge ABC Playskool blocks, and stuffed and wrapped gay packages amid mounds of artificial snow. Somewhere high-pitched chimes were playing "Silent Night."

The stone lions over the Davis Building's entrance seemed more majestic than usual as they gazed down on the pageant below, and even the brick and mortar on the old building's face seemed to glow with an eternal sheen. On the sidewalk beneath the lions, a crew of workmen was dismantling the developers' sign. With a final satisfied glance upward at the stoic lords of the jungle, Bino tightened the belt on his overcoat and took Dodie by the elbow. He steered her up the block toward the parking lot that housed the Linc. He lit a filtered Camel, inhaled, and blew out a plume of smoke to mix and mingle in the light Texas air.

As she swung gracefully along beside him with the top of her blond head on a level with the point of his shoulder, Dodie said, "We got a pretty Christmas card today. From Ann Burns."

"Oh?" Bino said. "It wasn't in with my mail."

"Well I sort of held it out," Dodie said. "It wasn't addressed to you, exactly. The envelope said, 'Offices of W. A. Phillips,' and I guess I'm a part of that. And there was a note on the card that I'm pretty sure was meant for me."

"I guess that's okay, Dode. A *personal* note?"

"It didn't *say* it was personal. But I took it personally. It said, 'You're right. Groups are fine, but Daddy helps even more.' Wow, what a neat thing to say. I think she's going to make it. I'm crossing my fingers for her, *and* my toes, and if I had anything else to cross I'd cross that too." Her nose wrinkled in a Tinker Bell grin.

"Some make it and some don't," Bino said. "Word is that Frank Bleeder's right back at his old haunts, gambling high. He was damn sure king for a day, though. Took a lot of guts to get up on the stand and do what he did."

They'd come abreast of the parking lot now, and as they turned to go in and pick up the Linc, Dodie paused. Her long-lashed eyes looked down, then back up. "Look, Bino," she said. "I don't mind. Really I don't, but you're the one that's always talking about images we're keeping up. Don't you think this looks sort of, well, high-schooley?"

He looked down as well, and his cheeks reddened. He hadn't realized it, but for the last half block or so he'd been holding her hand.